COUNTRY BOY

HOT OFF THE ICE BOOK 2

A.E. WASP

Country Boy
HOT OFF THE ICE
BOOK 2

COUNRY BOY: HOT OFF THE ICE #2

Cover Art by Ana J. Phoenix

First Edition: June 2017

AUTHOR'S NOTES

The Beavers did play two games against Huntsville on Dec 30, and Dec 31 in 2016.

The Key Arena is real but hasn't been renovated for NHL play yet. Estimated 2021. I hope there is a bar like the Pucker Up that gets a boost when that happens.

The Thunder are not a real team. Other teams mentioned are, though some players may be fictional if I need them. Any mistakes in how things work in the world of hockey are completely my doing. Any mistakes in general are my fault.

I apologize in advance.

I'm very excited that hockey season is once again upon us!

ACKNOWLEDGMENTS

More so than others, this book required a lot of long conversations with many people.

Sharon Simpson spent hours on the phone with me, working out Paul's complexities. I needed to make sure I was writing him authentically and respectfully. And she had faith in me when I promised her everything would work out, just keep reading.

I think I talked everyone's ear off on this book. So a big thank you to everyone who heard me rant.

Thank you to Liza and Elan for letting me crash for a week so I could write. They even supplied a cat for petting and binged the entire season of Yuri on Ice. Really, what more could you want?

My team of volunteer proofers and beta reader were, as always, invaluable. These books would very literally not be as good without them. I can never repay them for the hours they spend going over the ever changing documents cleaning up my errors and fixing my sometimes strange syntax.

And a special thanks to every person who ever made a video about hockey and put it on YouTube. I've watched more locker room tours, top 10 moments, and interviews than you can imagine. It's a tough job, but someone's got to do it.

My roommate, Travis, deserves kudos for putting up with me listening to the same ten songs over and over for months as I write in the dining area of the house we share. I have completely taken over the kitchen table.

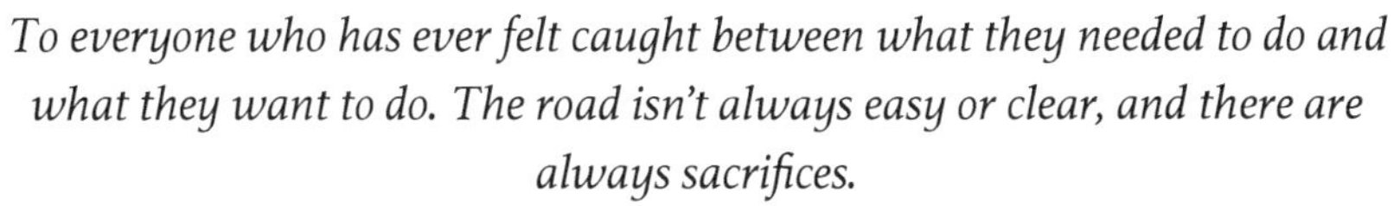

To everyone who has ever felt caught between what they needed to do and what they want to do. The road isn't always easy or clear, and there are always sacrifices.

May we all find the strength to live our authentic lives, and may we find people to support us along the way.

To our families, the ones we've found and the ones we were born into. Thank you for being there.

1

ROBBIE—IT'S BEEN A LONG TIME COMING

The last time Thunder defenseman Robbie Rhodes met Paul Dyson off the ice, they ended up naked in Robbie's bed. The last time they met on the ice – which had been the night after - Paul punched Robbie in the face and called him a faggot.

Third time's a charm, Robbie thought as he slammed Dyson into the boards with a vicious and highly illegal check.

Luckily, this wasn't a game so Robbie wouldn't get penalized.

Unfortunately, it was a team practice, so Robbie was definitely going to get yelled at by anywhere from three to five people, depending on who noticed the hit. If he were really unlucky, he'd get pulled from the game tomorrow.

Totally worth it.

Robbie's blood had been boiling since his first glimpse of Dyson on the ice that morning.

Not that it was a surprise. After all, he'd found out at Thanksgiving at Bryce's new house that Dyson had been brought up to fill in the slot left open when Rasmussen broke his leg in two places during a snowmobiling accident. He wouldn't be back this season.

But apparently knowing Paul Dyson was going to be there was different from actually seeing it.

Robbie tried not to let Dyson get to him. He ignored his stupid southern drawl and avoided looking directly at his sky blue eyes with their frankly embarrassingly girly fan of sandy brown eyelashes.

The rebel yell Dyson had given after nailing an admittedly difficult passing drill had been the straw that broke the proverbial camel's back.

"Rhodes! What the fuck was that?" Assistant coach O'Reilly yelled from across the ice. The tall redhead looked pissed off. That was a look Robbie tried really hard not to have directed at him. A third-generation Irishman from South Boston, Liam O'Reilly had the stereotypical Irish temper and a way with words Robbie envied unless he was on the wrong end of a tongue-lashing.

Robbie reached quickly for a believable lie, but, as usual, his brain failed him, providing him with a jumble of words in no particular order.

Before he could panic, Paul hopped up from the ice and skated up behind Robbie. He put a heavy hand on Robbie's shoulder. "It's okay, Coach. I deserved it. Last time we met, I was a dick to him."

He turned to Robbie. "We even now? You feel better?" His blinding grin didn't reach his eyes and showed teeth instead of the dimples Robbie knew popped out when Paul was actually smiling.

Robbie stared at him, looking for something that would let him know what Paul's angle was here.

Paul brought his closed fist up and without losing his smile rotated it across his chest in the ASL sign for *sorry*.

At least that's what it looked like. But it couldn't be. It had to be a mistake.

Dropping his smile, Paul looked him in the eye and mouthed the word as he repeated the action.

"Are you fucking kidding me?" Robbie asked.

"Nope. I'm just trying to apologize." He reached out a hand. "Truce?"

Robbie ignored the outstretched hand. He slid his stick between Paul's skates and twisted.

Paul crashed to the ice.

Robbie's gloves hit the ice before the other man could get his breath back. "Get the fuck up, Dyson," Robbie snarled, hands curling into fists.

The startled yells of his teammates echoed in the empty stadium. "Rhodes!" barked Jake Donovan, the captain of the Seattle Thunder.

Paul stared up at Robbie as if he had never seen him before. Red flared up behind Robbie's eyes, and he threw himself onto Paul. Paul took the first few hits without defending himself.

Robbie vaguely registered hands grabbing his shoulder as Paul finally started to fight back. Fists flying, Paul landed a solid hit on the side of Robbie's head.

With a roar, Robbie rained hits down onto the other man, unleashing two years of rage he hadn't known he'd been carrying around.

"Rhodes! Stop it! Get the fuck off the new kid." Jake hauled Robbie off Paul, flinging him backward.

Like the backstabbing son of a bitch he was, Paul took the opportunity to nail Robbie in the stomach with a knee.

Sergei Progav, the starting goalie, shot out of the net and grabbed Paul, manhandling him up and pinning his arms behind his back. Paul struggled, but the veteran goalie had arms of steel. Paul wasn't going anywhere.

From the look in Dyson's eyes, Robbie wasn't sure if the guy wanted to fuck him up or just fuck him.

Robbie knew the feeling.

Head coach Williams was on them in a heartbeat, skidding to a stop in front of them with a fan of ice crystals. "What the hell is going on?"

Robbie wrenched his arm out of Jake's grip. Yanking off his helmet and shoving his sweaty hair out of his eyes, he jerked his chin in Paul's direction and struggled to find the words. "Him. He's in the way. The whole freaking practice."

"Maybe you just need to learn how to skate better, then you can stay the heck out of my way," he drawled in that Bubba Gump Alabama accent Robbie knew he could turn on and off at will.

"Bite me, Dyson."

"Hey," the coach shouted. "Rhodes, you've had a chip on your shoulder since Dyson showed up. I don't know what the hell your issue is, but you had better work it out before the game tomorrow."

Paul snorted, and the coach wheeled on him. "Cut the shit, Dyson. I've got my eye on you, too."

"Yes, sir," Paul said, looking down at the ice. "I mean, I will, sir."

The coach looked at Jake. "Get everyone into the room. I want to watch some video. Whatever is going on with these two clowns, make them work it out. If they can't keep it together on the ice, they'd better be fucking satisfied with sitting on the goddamn bench for the rest of the season." He skated away.

Jake shook his head at Robbie, disappointment clear on his face, then skated towards the gate.

Paul followed him, then turned back to Robbie and signed *I'm sorry* again before heading down the tunnel.

What the absolute fuck?

Sergei put an arm around Robbie's shoulder. "You really hate that guy, eh?" he asked in his heavily accented English.

Sergei had been twenty-two when he'd been drafted to the NHL. He'd spent a few years with the Habs up in Montreal before getting traded to the Thunder. As a result, he spoke a weird mixture of Russian, Quebecois, and English. English was his third language. Most of his televised interviews aired with captions.

He didn't mind that Robbie didn't talk much. Sergei talked enough for both of them.

Robbie sighed and took a long pull from his water bottle. "I don't hate him." It wasn't quite a lie. He searched for a quick way to explain his feelings for Paul Dyson that Sergei would buy.

If only he knew how he felt.

He didn't think he would have been so pissed at Dyson's presence if the timing hadn't been such shit. Paul may have been an asshole, but it wasn't the first hard hit Robbie had taken, and it wouldn't be the last. Robbie came out of every game feeling like he'd been a bar fight.

But it really sucked having to see Paul so soon after he'd been dumped by Drew, and right after watching his hockey idol and former teammate Bryce Lowery fall in love and come out. The last thing Robbie needed was a reminder of another guy that had loved him and left him.

Not that it had been love. But he'd liked the guy well enough that he'd been considering hooking up again next time they were in the same town.

Sergei watched Robbie's face as he thought. He was very good at giving Robbie as much time as he needed to get his thoughts out. He never jumped in and tried to finish Robbie's sentences for him.

"He's from Huntsville. University of Alabama in Huntsville." Robbie forced a smile. "I went to Bemidji State in Minnesota. College rivalries, you know? It's hard to let go."

Sergei gave Robbie a loving smack on the shoulder that almost knocked him down again, and shook his head. "You have to let that go, *bratishka*. In this profession, you may oftentimes find yourself playing with one set of teammates and then, poof, two days later, you are on another team, facing your former brothers across the ice."

He stepped onto the rubber walkway, graceful despite the pounds of padding he wore. "You have to put it all aside. Leave the animosity behind and start every day like it is a new slate."

"How?" Robbie asked. "What if someone was, had been, well, mean?" God, he sounded like an idiot.

Sergei turned and tapped Robbie on the chest with the blade of his stick. "You be the bigger man. You talk it out. Maybe the meanness is not directed at you, in particular. Maybe they are fighting battles inside that you cannot see."

Robbie quirked his lips. "Maybe," he said doubtfully. "Doesn't make it hurt me less."

"Only you can do that, my friend."

"How?"

"You forgive them," he explained as if it were that easy. "If this Paul was mean to you in the past, leave it in the past. Or talk to him and ask him why. Or forgive him without asking. It's up to you."

Robbie sighed and followed Sergei to the locker room. He knew Sergei was probably right; he was going to have to have it out with Paul. But he wanted to hold on to his righteous anger a little while longer, was that so wrong?

With a sigh, he headed off to the locker room for a nice post-practice soak in the hot tub and a massage. Both of those things would make him feel better.

~

Robbie managed to avoid fighting with or talking to Paul for the rest of the morning. He kept people between them in the locker room, rushed through his work out, and waited until Paul was done to hit the shower room.

His luck ran out after practice. Dyson lurked against a pillar of the parking garage as if he'd been waiting for Robbie to come out. Great.

"Rhodes," he called out as Robbie passed him on the way to his car. Robbie ignored him, but Paul followed him as he walked to the brand new Prius that was the first, and so far only, thing he'd splurged on with his hockey money.

"This your car?" Paul asked in disbelief, leaning close to look inside. "Or did you borrow it from your meemaw?"

Robbie was used to being teased about his Prius. Most of the other guys drove sports cars or SUVs more suited for the Serengeti than the streets of Seattle. Maybe he should have gotten something cooler, more fun. He could admit to a little envy when Jake roared by in his Porsche.

But it seemed so wasteful, so needlessly showy. Sure, Jake must be making a ton of money, but it seemed tacky to flaunt it. It didn't seem fair to spend eighty thousand dollars on a car when there were children starving right here in America. His parents used to have that conversation at least once a week.

"It gets good gas mileage," Robbie muttered, trying his best to ignore how good Paul smelled as he leaned close. His blond hair was still damp at the ends from his post-workout shower.

"You're a wild man, Rhodes," Paul said.

"Still driving a pickup truck? Some other kind of penis-mobile? Oh, wait." He held up his hand to forestall Paul's objections. "You're not gay, so no penis metaphors. Sorry."

"Screw you," Paul said.

"That's a pretty gay thing to say." Robbie's smirk slid off his face at Paul's pained expression.

Paul groaned and ran both hands through his hair. "Why are you bein' such an asshole?"

Robbie whirled on him, getting right up into his personal space. They were pretty much eye to eye. "I don't know. Maybe because the last time we met, you called me a faggot and then slammed me into the boards so hard I broke my nose. Maybe that. What do you think?"

2

PAUL—DON'T LET SOMEONE TELL YOU YOU'RE NO ONE

Fuck. Hearing Rhodes repeat his words back to him flat out like that brought rushing back all the shame Paul had thought he'd buried.

When he'd found out he would be playing on the same team as Rhodes, he'd felt a surge of hope that he could somehow rekindle the tentative friendship between them that he had killed.

He had hoped Robbie would have either forgotten all about that night or at the very least would pretend it had never happened, and they could start fresh.

No such luck. Rhodes had been giving him the stink-eye since minute one. He'd snubbed Paul in the locker room, and had been selfish with the puck during their scrimmage, not passing to Paul until the coach called him on it.

"You know, I wasn't angry with you that day."

"No shit, Sherlock," Robbie answered with an eye roll.

Paul's jaw dropped. "You knew?"

"You think you're the first closet-case I've ever met?" He put a hand to his chest and mocked Paul. "'Oh, I'm a closeted jock with internalized homophobia. If only some guy would fuck me and help me deal with these scary feelings.' Real original. I could see it a mile away," he said scornfully.

Paul took a step back. Hearing the issues that had been tearing him apart for years being dismissed so flippantly hurt worse than the punch. He covered his mouth with a hand and looked away.

When their eyes met again, Robbie looked remorseful. *Sorry*, he signed with a hand to his chest.

Seemed like they were destined to hurt each other. "If I was so pathetic," Paul forced out, "why did you...?"

Robbie held his gaze. "Have sex with you?"

Paul flushed remembering all the things they had done and the feel of another man's body under and on top of his. They hadn't done everything, though. There were still boundaries left uncrossed. "It wasn't really sex," he insisted.

Robbie was unimpressed. "Whatever you have to tell yourself to get through the day. Are we done here now? I promise not to hit you any more or out you to the team. Your secret gay urges are safe with me."

Suddenly Paul wanted to punch him again. Punch him or push him back against the door of his stupid ass yuppie mobile and grind against him until they both came in their pants.

In other words, exactly how he felt every time he saw Robbie.

~

Even angry, Robbie was gorgeous with his chocolate brown eyes and hair somewhere between red and brown. He'd grown in the last two years and broadened out across the shoulders.

"So, why did you fool around with me if I'm such a cliché?" Paul asked again. "Because, not to sound like a twelve-year old, but you started it."

"Aside from the fact that you were smoking hot and gagging for it?" Robbie asked crudely. "What other reason would I need?"

Both of those things were true, but still, Paul didn't buy the explanation. From the little he knew of the guy, Rhodes seemed like a pretty intense person. He doubted Robbie had ever done anything casually in his life. "Yeah, besides that."

Robbie threw up his hands. "Don't you think I've asked myself that? I don't know. What was I supposed to do with you laughing and looking up at me like that with those stupid blue eyes and those kiss-me lips?"

Was that how Robbie saw him? Paul's fingers drifted to his lips. Robbie's eyes flicked down to his mouth, and Paul remembered how it had felt when Robbie kissed him — better than anyone else's had before or since.

Kissing Robbie would never be something Paul regretted. "So, if I'm a self-hating closet case, what does that make you?"

"I'm nobody," Robbie said, the answer too quick and too practiced for Paul's liking.

Paul scoffed. "Right. You won the Hobey Award and Defensive Player of the Year last year because you're nobody."

Robbie grimaced. "Yeah, I'm real good at hitting things with a stick. I should be getting my Nobel Peace Prize any day now."

Paul shook his head. He wasn't letting Robbie get away with that. "The Hobey is also for demonstrating 'strength of character on and off the ice' remember?"

"Oh, yay. So I didn't smoke cigarettes or, I don't know, curse around nuns." Robbie waved away the suggestion that he'd done anything remarkable.

"Day-um," Paul said, stretching the word out to two syllables. "Talk about self-hating. And I thought I had issues."

"Oh, you do," Robbie said quickly but with a small smile.

Paul crossed his arms over his chest and examined Robbie. "So why do you do it? Why play hockey if it's just 'hitting things with sticks'? What's the point?"

Robbie looked down at the floor. A car slid quietly out of a spot from down the row. Another Prius, Paul noted. Damn things were too quiet; Paul didn't trust them. The driver looked at them curiously as he drove slowly past.

The guy looked vaguely familiar. He'd been introduced to so

many people that morning; it was going to take a while for him to remember who was who.

Paul thought it was one of the guys from the equipment rooms, probably wondering why he and Robbie were talking and not fighting.

Finally, Robbie looked up. “Hockey is the only thing I’m good at. And I love doing it. When I’m on the ice, when the crowd is cheering…” He trailed off, shaking his head.

“You feel like somebody,” Paul finished for him.

“Yeah,” Robbie said, “I feel like somebody. Pathetic, isn’t it?”

Jeez, between them they had enough baggage for a month-long holiday. Paul grabbed Robbie’s shoulders and shook him. “You are somebody,” he said forcefully. “‘*You are a child of the universe, no less than the trees and the stars.*’”

Robbie looked at him wide-eyed. “What is that from?”

“It’s from my mom’s favorite poem-thing. She was always quoting it to me.” He let his hands fall from Robbie’s shoulders instead of pulling Robbie in for a hug the way he wanted to.

“Wow. Is there more?”

“Yeah, it’s kind of long. I’ll find it and email it you.”

“Okay.”

The silence stretched awkwardly. Paul wasn’t sure where to go from here. They weren’t really exes, no matter how it almost felt like that. They weren’t college rivals anymore, but although they were teammates now, they weren’t quite friends.

Robbie jangled his keys, the electronic beep of the unlocking doors echoed sharply in the underground garage. “I guess I’d better get going,” he said.

Paul grabbed his arm. “Wait. I really am sorry about what I did.”

“Which part?”

“All of it?”

“Really?” Robbie raised one eyebrow. “You regret *all* of it?”

Paul shook his head quickly. “No. Never. Not that night. But the next day.” He sighed remembering. His fear always had come out as anger. It was something he was working on. "I shouldn't have hit you, and I shouldn't have called you that."

"Faggot," Robbie said with no inflection.

"What?"

"Say it. Say the word." Robbie stepped closer, almost chest to chest with Paul.

"I don't want to." He glanced down at the dirty parking lot floor, suddenly fascinated with the rainbow sheen of an oily puddle. "I really am sorry. I was," he shook his head, and kicked the puddle, disrupting the colors. "It was a really, really bad day." He looked right into Robbie's eyes. "Right after the best night of my life."

Robbie sighed, pinching the bridge of his nose. "What do you want from me?"

Absolution. Reassurance. Things he couldn't have, that was for sure. God, if they couldn't work this out, it was going to be a crappy three years. "I thought that maybe...I don't know. Maybe we could be friends?"

"Sure. Because what we have is a solid foundation for friendship." Robbie ran his hands through his thick auburn hair, pulling it back from his face then letting it drop again. "Don't worry, Paulie, I'm sure the other kids will like you. Just share your candy with them. You don't need me."

"I do need you. You're the only one." Paul blushed scarlet. "You're the only one who knows about me."

"Knows what, Dyson? Just spit it out." Robbie pressed the car key fob again. The locks thudded into place, the car beeped, and the lights flashed. Robbie cursed under his breath and unlocked the car.

Paul had to say something quick or Robbie was going to leave. "Knows that I'm gay." He whispered it, then looked over his shoulder to make sure they were still alone. A few cars were pulling in. They were full of parents with kids.

"Are you?" There was a challenge in the look he gave Paul.

"You know I am," Paul whispered. "You of all people."

Robbie shook his head. "I don't, actually. All I know is that we fooled around two years ago, you seemed like you enjoyed it a lot, and then the next day you turned on me. That doesn't scream out and proud."

"Yeah, well, just because I don't, can't, do anything about it doesn't mean it isn't true."

Robbie scoffed at him. "You mean won't do anything about it."

"I mean I can't. Not everyone is like you, Rhodes. Not everyone believes the same things." Robbie just didn't get it. Everything came so easily for him. His parents loved him just as he was. As a non-believer, he didn't have the threat of eternal damnation hanging over his head. "My father saw you dropping me off that morning."

"So, your dad saw you? So what?" Robbie shrugged. "Did he say something to you?"

"Oh, he said a lot of things."

All these years later, and Paul still felt trapped between the carrot of paternal love, conditional though it might be, and the stick of excommunication. Thanks to his new hockey contract, his father couldn't use withholding financial support as a threat anymore.

"He said a lot of things," Paul repeated. "All variations on the same theme. If I keep choosing to be a deviant, then I'm out."

"Out of what?"

"Everything. The family, the Church, the whole circle of our friends."

Robbie scowled. "If the people who are supposed to love you kick you out because you're gay, how can they pretend to love you? What kind of religion does that? Tell them to shove it."

"They do love me. They're trying to save me." Paul knew that was true for his father, at least. However, he was starting to have some doubts about the motives of some of the other members of the congregation. More often than not he'd felt disgust and smug superiority more than love coming from some of the more vocal opponents of gay rights.

Robbie's face went through several expressions as he obviously stopped himself from saying a few different things. "I want to understand," he finally said. "I do. But I just don't."

Paul rolled his eyes. He was seriously tired of having to justify the way he lived his life to everyone. As if he needed their seal of approval on his choices. "Really? You don't understand why someone might not be ready to walk around waving a rainbow flag? That's why I saw pictures of you and your boyfriend on the cover of Sports Illustrated? Because you're so out and proud?"

"You sound like Drew," Robbie frowned. "Just because I don't want my relationships dissected by the fans and the media, doesn't mean I'm in the closet. If I were dating a woman, I'd feel the same way. Probably. Besides, everyone who needs to know knows," he said defensively.

Paul shoved him back with a finger to the chest. "That's bullshit. You don't know who needs to know. Some kid down in the bible belt might need to know he's not the only one, so he doesn't go trying anything stupid."

Robbie pushed Paul's finger away. "Like what?"

"Like trying to freeze himself to death in the middle of fucking nowhere Minnesota," Paul spit out. "You're a fucking condescending ass, but you saved my life that night."

Robbie's jaw dropped. "You were trying to kill yourself?"

Paul crossed his arms and looked away. "No. Not directly. Kind of. I don't know. Suicide is a sin, too." Paul's laugh held no humor. "A literal 'damned if I do, damned if I don't' situation."

Robbie grabbed Paul by the arm. "What? But you were so - "

"So what?" Paul asked.

Robbie frowned. He signed words and phrases with his arms too quickly for Paul to follow.

"Too fast," Paul said and signed simultaneously.

Robbie signed, hand hovering near his chest, palm down, fingers wiggling. "So present. So there, I guess."

Paul wrapped his arms around himself. "I'm good at faking things."

"I guess you'd have to be."

"I remember the first second I saw you, you know," Robbie said. "I didn't recognize you right away. I just thought you were a random idiot."

3

ROBBIE—LONELY BOY FAR FROM HOME

Two years earlier. Bemidji, Minnesota

The headlights of Robbie's car slid across the face of the man standing in the one shadowy space of the Holiday Stationstore in time for Robbie to avoid hitting him.

Robbie cursed and yanked the wheel to the right. The whole damn gas station was lit up like Vegas, and this guy has to find the one dark corner to hide in? Robbie glanced over as he stomped past the guy. He wore a Huntsville Chargers sweatshirt and a haunted expression.

The look in the guy's eyes followed him into the store, plucking at his memories as he debated between the brats rolling around under the heat lamp or a pre-made sandwich. He settled on a brat and a Gatorade and tried to figure out why the guy felt familiar.

Outside, it felt like the temperature had dropped even further. The idiot was still standing there, and he was going to freeze to death. That gray hoodie he wore might have been fine in Huntsville, but it was no match for the weather on December 30th in Bemidji, Minnesota.

The guy stood with his elbows braced on the short brick wall separating the parking lot from the small pond on the other side. He swayed slightly. Robbie couldn't tell if it was from the cold, exhaustion, or if it had something to do with the crumpled brown paper bag at his side.

Either way, he couldn't in good conscience pass by without at least asking the guy if he was okay. Even if he was a Chargers' fan. The fact that he also had a great ass and broad shoulders, had nothing at all to do why Robbie was walking over to him.

Robbie walked up behind the guy, deliberately making noise. Why was he doing this? The guy was probably going to tell him to fuck off. But those southerners tended to underestimate the cold, and besides, no one stood in the parking lot of a gas station at eleven o'clock at night unless they had nowhere else to be. "Hey, are you okay?" Robbie asked.

The guy turned his head and looked blankly at Robbie.

Robbie frowned. The guy looked vaguely familiar. He had wavy blond hair, blue eyes, and an athletic build. If he was in Bemidji with Huntsville, maybe Robbie had seen him at the game earlier.

"It's too cold to be standing outside," Robbie continued. God, he sounded like his mother. But the wind was cutting through his heavy parka; it had to be passing through that hoodie like it wasn't even there.

The guy blinked. "I don't have anywhere else to go."

"You have nowhere to go? You here with Huntsville?" It was obvious from his accent that the guy was from somewhere in the South.

He nodded. Apparently, he was a man of few words. He clutched a bottle-shaped paper bag, but he didn't seem particularly drunk.

"Then don't you have a hotel?"

"I don't want to go back there."

"Well, you can't stand here all night, you'll freeze to death, and they'll have to unstick your body from the parking lot, and that's not fair to do to somebody." He smiled to show he was making a joke.

The guy looked down at the ground, and then back up at Robbie. "Where are you going?" he asked, with the beginning of a grin.

Suddenly Robbie recognized him. "You're Dyson, right? The D-man from the Chargers."

"Shit," the guy Robbie was ninety percent sure was Paul Dyson, muttered. The wind gusted across the open parking lot, and they both shivered. Paul's teeth chattered.

Dyson turned to leave, and Robbie grabbed his arm. "You are Dyson, right? I'm not taking some rando back home."

"Yeah," he answered. "Paul. Or some guys call me Chip."

Yeah, that wasn't going to happen. Chip was a stupid name. "Robbie," He said. "Rhodes," he clarified when Paul looked confused. "Beavers' defense."

Paul nodded. "Oh, yeah. Right. I remember you. You weren't bad tonight."

"Gee, thanks."

"No." For the first time, there was a little life in Paul's eyes. "I think if you changed it up, just a little, you'd be amazing."

"So, come with me, and you can tell me all about how I suck. You can get warm. And then if you want to leave again, I'll drive you somewhere, okay?"

Paul nodded. "Yeah. Okay." He followed Robbie.

"This your car?" he asked as Robbie opened the door to his fifteen-year-old Subaru Outback.

"It better be, or someone is going to be mighty pissed off when they come out and find it gone."

Paul got in and looked around the inside of the car as if were some strange machine he had never seen before. "Kind of girly, ain't it?"

"It's a car. There are no boy or girl cars." Robbie backed out carefully. "It gets great gas mileage."

Paul raised one eyebrow and turned the heater vent to blow directly on him.

Robbie broke his brat in half and handed one part to Paul. "Want it? It's probably ice cold by now, though."

Paul took it with a shrug. "Yeah. Thanks." He chewed thoughtfully, staring out the window as Robbie drove the dark streets back to his apartment.

Robbie's apartment was in the back of an old house. It was a little small and dark, and tended to be cold in the winter and hot in the summer, but it had a pond in the back that froze over every winter, and the owner kept it skating-ready. That made up for every defect the house might have.

"What about you missing curfew?" Robbie asked his silent guest.

"LaRoux took care of bed check for me," Paul said. "Guess I have to sneak in before breakfast. I reckon I didn't have much of a plan," he confessed.

Robbie flicked the lights on as he walked past the hockey sticks leaning against the wall, through the narrow kitchen, and into the living room-slash-bedroom. Two doors off the living room lead to the bathroom and a small closet. His futon/bed was pushed against one wall. The only other furniture was a bean bag chair and cheap wooden coffee table.

Hockey equipment filled up every nook and cranny.

Paul stopped in the doorway of the living room. He'd shoved his hands deep into the front pocket of his sweatshirt he looked oddly shy.

"Come on in," Robbie said. "I won't bite." Maybe Paul was rethinking his decision. "Unless you want me to take you back after all?"

"No. I want to stay," Paul said quickly and took the final step into the room. He paced around the small room, checking out the two tall bookcases lined with knickknacks, CDs, and DVDs.

Paul ran his fingers along the rows of CDs. "You have a lot of audiobooks." He pulled one with a plain white cover off the shelf. "Finance 101?"

"I learn better from audiobooks. My parents' friends were nice enough to record some of my text books for me." He tried to make it sound like no big deal, but it had been. It had taken them days of recording and editing.

Robbie had almost killed himself trying to get an A in that class. It was the least he could do. Too bad he'd only gotten a C+. As if the plus made a difference.

Paul put the CD back and continued his slow exploration of the small room. The next thing he pulled out was a collection of American Sign Language DVDs. "Can you speak sign language? Are you deaf?"

"No. Not deaf. Did I seem deaf while were talking?" He thought for a second. "Can you even play hockey if you're deaf?"

Paul shrugged. "I don't know. So why sign language then?"

Robbie had the feeling that if he moved too quickly, Paul would flee like a wild animal. He wasn't sure why, but he wanted the guy to stay for a while. Sure, he was good-looking; tall and with those All-American looks, blond hair and blue eyes. But it was more than that.

Robbie couldn't help but think of the sadness he remembered seeing in Paul's eyes during the game.

"I have a couple of learning disabilities," Robbie answered. "They make it hard for me to read and write. And talk sometimes. Some therapist suggested ASL as a way to maybe retrain my brain."

"Does it help?"

Robbie shrugged. "Yeah. Sometimes I can think better in it. Doesn't help me talk to most people."

"I think it would be mighty interesting." Paul pulled a DVD off the shelf, tilting it forward with one finger.

Even from across the room, Robbie could tell it was one of the seasons of Queer as Folk.

Paul let the DVD tip back into line, then turned back to the room.

Robbie followed his eyes to the rainbow flag stuck into the coffee mug that served as a pencil holder.

"I heard...well, some guys were saying that you're gay. Some guys from my team." Paul tried to sound casual.

"Yeah?" If Paul wanted to know something, Robbie was going to make him work for it.

Paul looked at him.

Robbie stared back, not giving anything away.

The longer he stared, the better-looking Paul got. With the first glimpse of his face, you got an overall impression of general attractiveness. But the more you looked, the more you noticed his perfect cheekbones, the cleft in his chin, and what an unusual shade of blue his eyes were. And how pretty his mouth was. The mouth that was moving as Paul said something to Robbie.

"What?" Robbie asked, snapping out of his lust-induced haze. Maybe he was too tired to be awake.

"I said, does your team know you're gay?"

Robbie shrugged. "I think so. Some of them. I'm not sure about the new kids. I don't hide it, but it's not like I say 'Hi, welcome to the team. I'm Robbie, I play defense, and I'm gay. Though maybe I'd get more dates that way."

Paul didn't laugh at his feeble attempt at a joke. "And they don't care?"

"If they do, no one's said anything to me about it."

"And your parents? Do they know?"

Robbie sat on the end of his futon bed. "Yeah, of course."

"Did they freak out?"

"Not even a little. I actually think they were glad. They think college sports are a waste of time and money. My dad's a writer, and my mom is a college professor. Gay they get. Athlete, not so much."

"Really?" Paul's eyebrows rose to his hairline.

"Really. But hockey is the only reason I got into college in the first place. They were thrilled when I got a scholarship to BSU, though I think they thought I'd stay in Ohio."

"Well, the Buckeyes at Ohio State are a Big Ten team."

"I know. But I kind of wanted to get a little further away from them. Know what I mean?"

Paul made a non-committal sound. "You're really lucky," he said. "You know your parents will always love you."

"Yeah. They love me." He lay back on the futon. "They just aren't very impressed by me."

"Maybe they know how much you suck," Paul said with a smile to show he was joking.

Robbie shook his head. "No. It's worse. Hockey is the only thing I'm good at, and they could care less."

Paul sat down next to him, not saying anything.

Robbie turned to him, and the guy flinched, his eyes dropping to Robbie's mouth. Robbie could feel the waves of nervous energy coming from him.

Paul wanted Robbie, whether he knew it or not.

Oh boy, Robbie thought. One of those. He sighed internally. Testing his theory, Robbie leaned forward. Paul swayed towards him like he was magnetic.

Tempting. But probably a terrible idea.

Robbie stood up. "I want hot chocolate. Want some?"

Paul nodded.

Robbie felt Paul's gaze on him the whole way into the kitchen.

4

PAUL—BOTH OF US LONELY, LONGING FOR SHELTER

Robbie's apartment may have been small, but the frozen pond behind it was sweet. Paul wasn't sure how he let the guy talk him back out into the cold, no matter how good-looking he was. Paul was a southern boy, born and bred. No matter how much time he spent in the Great White North, he never got used to the cold.

A few minutes ago, they'd been lying next to each other, short ways on the unfolded futon. Both feet on the floor, nothing improper. But a strange energy buzzing in Paul's head was making him dizzy. He was very aware of how close their bodies were to each other.

Still on their backs, they tossed a Nerf football back and forth, cups of hot chocolate cooling on the floor.

"I just don't get it, man," Robbie had said. "I know I'm good, but I feel like there's something holding me back."

Paul shook his head. "Nah. I was watching you; you're alright." He punched Robbie on the shoulder. "Have you ever tried holding your stick off-wing?"

Robbie waggled his eyebrows salaciously, "Well, sometimes I do like to switch it up for variety, but I'm much better with my right hand."

Paul turned his head and smirked. "Good to know." He looked at how they were positioned, with Robbie's left hand next to Paul's legs. "Should I switch sides?"

Robbie flushed red and didn't answer.

Paul returned his gaze to the ceiling, trying to hide his own blush, and tossed the football up, caught it, did it again. "If you can get used to it, it's a lot of help to be holding the stick with your dominant hand when you go one-handed."

"I've noticed a lot of Canadian guys do it."

"Yeah, that's why I started. Chargers are like fifty percent Canadian." He tossed the ball up and over for Robbie to catch. "I'm the only legit Southern boy on the team."

Robbie caught the soft football and trapped it against his chest. "I've tried. I suck at it."

Paul rolled onto his side. "Well, yeah, dude. It's hard. Takes practice. Don't go pussying out on me. You don't want hard; you can switch to badminton."

Robbie shoved him. "Then show me, big man. Give me some tips."

That was how Paul ended up bundled up in one of Robbie's parkas (the boy had more than one) over his sweatshirt and wearing his oldest skates in the middle of the night.

"I can barely move," Paul complained as he waddled to the frozen pond. "I feel like Ralphie in A Christmas Story."

"I love that movie." Robbie gave him a blinding smile.

It was freezing. Their breath left contrails in the still crisp air. But the moon lit up the surface of the snow and sparkled on the ice until Robbie flipped on a bare flood light stuck on a pole next to the pond.

The house Robbie's apartment was in backed up to a field that ended in a thick woods of fir and bare hardwood trees that looked like it stretched to Canada. "It's beautiful," Paul said.

Robbie leaned on his stick and looked around. "Yeah, it is."

He stepped out onto the ice and glided across the pond backward, motioning to Paul with his stick. "Come on. Teach me, Country Boy."

Paul followed more cautiously. Trying to get a feel for the

unfamiliar skates and the uneven ice. Growing up in Alabama, he hadn't had a lot of practice with pond hockey.

"I've never played on a pond," he admitted.

"It's not going to be the same without the boards blocking you. That's definitely going to take some getting used to." Robbie skated backward around the surprisingly smooth ice. "But we smooth it out as best we can. You probably won't hit too many bumps."

He hoped not. With a flick of his hand, he sent Robbie up the left side of the ice. "Grab your stick backward. You a righty?"

Robbie nodded.

"So keep your right hand on the top.

Robbie grimaced as he reached his left hand towards the bottom of the stick, wrapping his right hand around the top. "Ugh. It feels so weird."

"I know. And you're gonna have to get real good at catching a pass on the backside of the stick. My suggestion? Get a new one with less of a curve."

Paul stretched out his stick one-handed and tapped the puck over to Robbie. "Try this, reaching out with just the one hand."

Robbie did, batting the puck around with the stick held in his right hand. "I tried this before. I do like the control this way. But hitting off the boards, and catching a pass..." He shook his head. "I sucked at it last time I tried."

Paul skated backward in front of him. "Yeah, but how long ago was that?"

Robbie shrugged, grabbing the stick with both hands and pivoting around Paul, keeping the puck away from him, and skating leisurely down the ice. "Couple of years," he admitted. "My high school coach gave up trying to get me to switch."

"You're a better player now." Paul swept up from behind him and pickpocketed the puck with a lift of Robbie's stick. "Theoretically." Laughing, he sped off across the ice, twirling and deking the puck around imaginary players.

He took a slap shot at the empty net, raising his arms to an imaginary crowd and giving an almost silent cheer. Skating slowly to retrieve the puck, he said. "If we wanna make the show, we've got to be the best. We got to push harder and want it more." He tossed the puck on the ice in front of Robbie. "Do you want it more?"

"More than who?" Robbie stared into his eyes, hands resting on the top of his stick.

"More than anyone else does. More than you want anything else. Do you want it that much?"

Their eyes met, glittering in the harsh shadows of the bare lamp light. Finally, Robbie nodded. "Yeah. I do."

Paul tilted his head. "Then let's get to work."

They skated hard for some indeterminate length of time Paul knew he would never forget. The world had narrowed down to a frozen space of biting cold air, moon shadows, and the sounds of metal blades carving through the ice.

As they sped down the ice, Robbie right on Paul's tail, an owl broke out of the trees, swooping low over Paul's head with a swish of feathers and an eerie hooting. "Dang," Paul said, throwing up his arms and ducking.

"Oh, crap," Robbie yelped right before he crashed into Paul. Down they went in a tangle of arms and legs.

Robbie landed on top of Paul, knocking the air out of his lungs. Paul's first thought was that the parka did a great job of insulating him from the cold. The second was that having Robbie laying on top of him felt really good.

Robbie started to push away, and, Paul moved without thought, wrapping his arms around Robbie.

Robbie stopped, raising onto his elbows to stare Paul in the eyes. His eyes were such a warm brown. Paul's breathing grew heavy, and he felt Robbie's chest pressing against his with each exhalation.

He licked his dry lips, and Robbie's eyes dropped to his mouth, then back to his eyes. "Can I kiss you?" Robbie asked quietly.

Paul's muscles tightened, and his breath caught.

Mistaking his silence for a no, Robbie blushed and tried to pull away. Paul grabbed Robbie's coat awkwardly, fingers clumsy beneath the thick gloves, and pulled him back down.

Robbie's lips were cold, but his breath was warm as he kissed Paul gently. He lifted his head to check Paul's reaction.

Oh, Paul thought. *Oh*. He raised his head off the ice to reach Robbie's mouth.

Robbie kissed him again, harder this time, pushing him back down to the ice.

Paul whimpered at the feel of Robbie's lips on his. When Robbie's tongue flicked against the seam of his mouth, he opened willingly, letting the heat in. Robbie's thick gloves thumped to the ice as he pulled them off without breaking the kiss.

Robbie shifted on top of him as he explored Paul's mouth, aligning their bodies in a way that made Paul's eyes roll back in his head even as the ice numbed his ass through his jeans.

Skates scratching against the ice, Paul bent his knees, clamping his thighs against Robbie's sides.

Robbie took what he wanted from Paul, tilting his head to the side with a hand, and encouraging Paul to open up with sharp nips to his lips.

He pushed Paul's head back with pressure on his chin, his mouth moving down the column of Paul's neck as best as he could through the protective barrier of outerwear.

Paul panted through his open mouth as Robbie set his teeth on Paul's skin and sucked, tongue flicking against the pulse in Paul's neck. "Oh, fuck," he moaned, hips rising of their own accord as his body fought for some friction.

For most of a decade, he'd imagined what it would feel like to be held down by a man, to feel someone strong and hard pressing against him, matching their strength to his. His imagination had not come close to reality.

Robbie pushed up onto his arms, forcing his body down onto Paul's rapidly growing erection. The place where his mouth had been was suddenly freezing in the cold air. Paul's head to toe shudder threatened to throw Robbie off. "Oh, God, oh, God," Paul groaned. "Don't stop."

Robbie leaned down for a long hard kiss that stole the air from

Paul's lungs. He smiled as he looked at Paul. "If we don't go inside, we're going to freeze to death, stick to the ice, and Mrs. Pierson is going to find our bodies in the morning." He jumped up and held a hand out to Paul.

Paul couldn't process what was happening as he let himself be pulled up. Was that it? Was it over? Would the kissing stop when they got inside? Please don't let it stop. He needed it so badly. Needed to shut off his brain, just for tonight. Please.

Robbie skated off the rink and headed towards the door. Paul followed him.

5

PAUL—I KNOW I'LL KEEP SEARCHING

The warmth of the apartment was almost painful in contrast to the cold of the outside. Paul yanked off his parka before sitting on the small bench and taking off his borrowed skates.

"My jeans are frozen," Robbie said with a grimace. "Want to borrow some sweats?"

"Please," Paul answered. "And a shirt?" He stripped off his sweaty hoodie and T-shirt, trying to play it cool.

Robbie's eyes flicked to his naked chest, and he nodded, licking his lips.

Paul blushed, hesitating with a hand on the buttons of his jeans. You would think he hadn't undressed in front of countless guys before.

Of course, he hadn't kissed any of those other guys.

It felt weird to take them off right in the middle of the room, but the heat was starting to melt the stiff icy patches Few things were as uncomfortable as wet denim.

At least his erection had gone down.

Paul stepped out of the wet jeans, adding them to the pile of clothes on the bench.

Robbie grabbed up the sodden clothing. “I’m going to throw these in the dryer. Be right back.

Shivering, he went in the living room in his boxers. Robbie’s blankets looked warm, and Paul wondered if Robbie would mind if he wrapped one around himself to warm up. He sat tentatively on the edge of the folded down futon and ran his hands over the soft comforter, an oddly intimate gesture.

Robbie raised one eyebrow when he caught sight of Paul sitting nearly naked on his futon. “Mr. Dyson, I’m not that kind of a boy,” he said archly. He threw a pair of pants and a gray T-shirt at Paul.

Blushing, Paul shook out the clothes. The shirt was a Bemidji Chargers’ T-shirt with Robbie’s last name on the back. He held it up and made a face.

“Tough luck,” Robbie said with a laugh. “It was the only clean shirt I had left. Count your blessings.”

Paul tried to hide his trembling hands as he pulled on the shirt and sweatpants. All he could think of was how kissing Robbie had made him feel. His lips tingled, raw from the cold, the pressure, and the scrub of Robbie’s end of the day stubble.

He was twenty-two years old, had been with more than a few girls, but he felt like a fourteen-year-old virgin.

Sure, it wasn’t quite his first experience with a guy. He pushed that memory down deep. Six-feet-deep.

But even that time hadn’t been like this. Lending a friend a hand in the middle of the night was one thing. But kissing? Especially kissing like that? Soft and sweet? The kind Paul secretly ached for? That was gay.

And so, apparently, was Paul, despite how often he had prayed to God not to be. Evidence A? He wanted to kiss Robbie again, right now. So, how could he make that happen?

Suddenly Robbie was up in his space, a hand on his chest, pushing him down to the futon. “I lied. I am that kind of a boy.” He climbed onto the mattress, straddling Paul’s lap.

Oh. Okay. Paul’s heart jack-rabbited as he swung between terror and elation. He lay there, eyes wide and arms gripping the comforter that was as soft as he'd thought it would be.

Everything he was feeling must have shown in his eyes, because Robbie stopped, his palm flat against Paul's chest. The grin slipped from his face. "Are you okay?"

Paul nodded quickly.

Robbie didn't look convinced. "Are you sure? It's okay if you want to stop. I won't kick you out or anything."

Tentatively, Paul reached up and laid his hands on Robbie's thighs where they rested on either side of his body. His muscles were hard as rocks under the soft fabric of his sleep pants. Paul couldn't resist digging his fingers into them. "No," he croaked. "Don't stop."

Robbie curved down over Paul, his face inches from Paul. "Do you really want to kiss some guy from BSU?"

"Yeah, I really do," Paul said seriously. He might never get up the nerve up to do this again. If one night was going to have to last him a lifetime, he wanted to feel everything. "I want to do everything."

"That's a tall order," Robbie whispered, slipping his hands beneath the shirt Paul wore. "I'll see what I can do."

The kiss quickly turned hot and heavy. Robbie's tongue plundered Paul's mouth, filling it up and sliding heavy across his own. Without the impediment of parkas and the distraction of wet cold seeping through his clothes, Paul was almost painfully aware of every place Robbie's body touched his, especially how close his ass was to Paul's dick.

Robbie's fingers scratched over Paul's nipples, his hips rocked against Paul's erection, nothing between them but a little fabric, and his teeth nipped at Paul's lips. Paul could do nothing except shiver under the onslaught, his hands gripping Robbie's thighs.

Robbie sat up, breaking the kiss.

Dizzy with the lack of oxygen, Paul sucked in deep breaths. Why was Robbie stopping this time? Was Paul doing something wrong?

"You can touch me, you know," Robbie said with a twist of his lips.

Oh, God. It was his fault. He sucked at this. "I'm sorry."

Robbie rolled off him, landing on his side next to Paul. He propped his head up on his arm. "Maybe we should stop."

Paul pressed his hand against his embarrassingly prominent erection, threw his arm across his eyes, and groaned. "Oh, gosh darn it. Please don't stop. I'm sorry I'm so bad at this."

Robbie traced a finger across the waistband of the sweatpants. "Your accent is really cute."

Paul huffed an embarrassed laugh, and Robbie pulled his arm away from his face. "It's okay," he said kindly.

Paul rolled on his side to face Robbie. "I've never done this before," he confessed.

"Ever?"

"I mean, not nothing. But just, you know. Not with a guy." Not much with girls, either, but Paul wasn't about to tell him that.

"Never? Nothing?" Robbie raised one eyebrow and slipped a hand under the front of Paul's shirt. "Not even a brojob after practice? Never gave a friend a hand?"

Paul felt the heat coming off his face as he blushed to his hairline. He ducked his head, pressing it against Robbie's chest. "Just that second one. Once. At a church camp. I was fourteen."

"Church camp? Kinky." Robbie rubbed his thumb across the soft hairs below Paul's navel. Paul shivered at the intimate touch that felt more erotic than a hand directly on his dick.

"Then what happened? After camp?" Robbie asked gently.

Paul shook his head and risked putting a hand on Robbie's hip. The heat and energy coming from the other man's body felt incredible. He pressed his face against Robbie's chest and breathed deep. He smelled like clean sweat, cheap laundry detergent, and a scent Paul always thought of as simply male.

Robbie slid his hand across Paul's stomach, fingers curling around his hip bone. His thumb slipped under the waistband of the sweatpants, caressing the crease of his hip.

"Ain't nothing happened," Paul gasped. The crazier Robbie made him, the more he lost control of his accent.

"Me and him never talked about it." But Paul had thought about it every day.

Robbie's touches went directly to his cock. He needed Robbie's mouth on him, his hands everywhere, pressing hard, rubbing up and down. He would die if he didn't get it.

He rolled away just enough to lift his head and look Robbie in the eye. "Kiss me again? Please?"

"I can't resist that accent and those big blue eyes," Robbie said. He kissed Paul hard, pushing him back down to the mattress and rolling with him until he laid stretched out over Paul, their bodies pressed together head to toe.

Paul whimpered with the feel of it. He wrapped his arms around Robbie's back and twined their legs together needing to feel more. More weight, more heat.

He pushed his tongue into Robbie's mouth, desperate for a taste.

When Robbie sucked on it, one big hand on Paul's jaw, holding him in place, Paul's cock throbbed so hard he thought he would come just from that. With a groan, he let go of Robbie long enough to slip both his arms up the back of Robbie's shirt.

Pushing up onto one elbow, Robbie grabbed the collar of his shirt and ripped it off over his head, throwing it onto the floor. "Off," he growled, plucking at the T-shirt Paul wore.

Paul struggled out of his shirt much less gracefully. He pulled it over his head, arms still trapped in the material.

Robbie stretched forward and pinned his arms to the bed above his head. He rested his forehead against Paul's, his hair tickling Paul's temples. "Nice," he said, running a hand over Paul's chest.

When he pinched Paul's nipple, Paul gasped, so he did it again and again, hips grinding down against Paul's groin.

Panting for breath and close to exploding, Paul struggled against the cloth binding his arms. He needed to touch Robbie. He didn't want to come before he got the chance to get his hands all over Robbie. "Let me touch you, please. Please," he groaned. "I have to."

Robbie relented with one last pinch that had Paul gasping and writhing against the thin futon mattress.

"Fuck that's hot," Robbie said.

As Paul ripped his arms out the offending T-shirt, Robbie ran his fingers down the chain links of Paul's necklace to the pendant that had slipped over his shoulder.

Bracing himself up on one elbow, Robbie looked at the small medallion, flipping it over to see the back.

"Saint Sebastian," Paul explained, rubbing his palms over every inch of Robbie's skin he could reach. "Patron saint of athletes."

"Who's the other guy?" Robbie asked even as he dropped his head and mouthed along the line of Paul's jaw.

"Saint, uh, fuck yeah," he moaned when Robbie bit and sucked at the tendons of his neck.

Robbie raised his head, laughter in his eyes. "Saint Fuck Yeah? I don't remember hearing about that one."

"Shut up." Paul smacked him on the shoulder. "Saint Christopher. Travelers."

Robbie chuckled and started sliding down the bed, leaving a trail of kisses in his wake. "So are you Catholic?" he asked right before digging his tongue into Paul's navel.

"Oh, damn," Paul said with a shudder, legs clamping to Robbie's sides.

"Is that a yes?" Robbie asked with exaggerated interest as if Paul's erection wasn't pressing hard against his chest.

"No, you bastard. Baptist." Paul pushed his head back down. Robbie retaliated with a bite to the soft skin right below Paul's belly button. The sharp pain only made his cock harder.

With a chuckle Paul felt more than heard, Robbie worked his hand between them. Paul's eyes rolled back in his head when Robbie squeezed his cock, thumb running over the top through the thin material of the sweats. "So why the necklace?"

Clamping his hands on Robbie's shoulders, Paul shoved his hips hard into Robbie's grip, grinding his erection in his palm. "You want to keep talking?"

Robbie's fingers hooked over the edge of Paul's sweatpants. "Kinda," he said with a grin.

"My little sister gave me this when I went to Major Juniors after high school. To keep me safe. My father would flip out if he saw it. Happy now?"

"Ecstatic." He squeezed Paul's dick over the pants and looked up at him from between his legs. "So, can I blow you?"

Paul's breath caught in his throat. He'd never wanted anything so badly in his life, and he'd never been so terrified in his life. The competing sensations threatened to tear him apart.

If they stopped now, he would be in the clear. Technically, they hadn't had sex. Actually, according to some of his friends, there was some kind of sexual sin loophole. If they could get blowjobs from girls and still claim they weren't having sex; then he could get one from a guy without it counting.

Hell, some of his buddies tried to claim a girl was still a virgin if she 'only' had anal. Guys' virginity seemed a little less clear cut and a little less important.

So why was anal sex between men 'actual sex' but between men and women, it didn't count?

Images from the videos Paul sometimes watched when the urge got too strong to ignore played in his mind. That could be him. Paul's ass clenched at the thought, forcing his dick to slide across Robbie's palm.

Paul groaned. Fuck it. He wanted this more than air; he'd deal with the fallout later. "Please," he begged.

"Since you asked so nicely." Robbie eased the elastic waistband carefully over Paul's cock. Paul lifted his hips to help Robbie tug the pants and boxers down to the tops of his thighs.

Robbie hummed his approval as Paul's cock sprung free. His breath blew warm against his skin, and Paul shuddered. He felt so exposed, and he didn't know what to do with his hands.

"Nice," Robbie said, sliding his hand under Paul's balls.

Paul's head dropped down to the futon with a thud, and he gripped the comforter like it was the only thing keeping him tethered to the mattress.

Robbie ran a hand down Paul's trembling thighs, palm skimming over the light dusting of hair. His thumb brushed over the jut of Paul's hip bone and traced the outline of the muscle. "Your body is amazing," he said, dropping a kiss to Paul's inner thigh, then looked up at Paul. "You still okay? We can stop."

Paul lifted his head up and grabbed Robbie's shoulder. "Oh, please. No. Don't stop."

"Okay." He dipped his head back down and licked a slow stripe up Paul's cock.

"Oh, my God," Paul gasped, hand tightening on Robbie's shoulder. He felt Robbie smile against his skin. Then all he felt was Robbie's mouth everywhere.

He licked Paul's cock like an ice cream cone. Pushing up onto his knees, he pulled it away from Paul's body and swirled his tongue around the head before sliding his mouth down over the top.

Paul could only gasp for breath and take the Lord's name in vain like he never had before as Robbie slowly but steadily drove him right to the edge before backing off.

With a frustrated growl, Robbie pushed the sweatpants lower, finally ripping them off one of Paul's legs. With a hand on each knee, he spread Paul's legs, then bent back down between them.

His tongue dragged down the crease of Paul's thighs and over his balls. Every now and then he nipped at the skin or took Paul's cock as deep into his mouth as he could.

Paul trembled as his body tried to process the competing sensations of pain and pleasure, finally settling on translating whatever Robbie did to him into pleasure like he'd never felt before.

Three times he dragged Paul, trembling, to the brink of a world-class orgasm and then stopped.

"Fuck, fuck, fuck," Paul muttered as Robbie took his mouth off of the place Paul wanted it the most.

Robbie sat back on his heels between Paul's legs. Paul pushed up on his elbows in time to see Robbie wiping his mouth with the back of his hand. The sight made him shudder so hard it almost qualified as an orgasm.

"Damn," Robbie said. "I could do that all night. You're so fucking sensitive."

Paul groaned. "You're killing me. Why are you so mean?"

Robbie grinned and dropped down to his hands and knees over Paul. "Because it's so much fun to torture you." He lowered his head, forcing Paul back down with a deep kiss.

Paul moaned into Robbie's mouth even as he wrapped his arms around Robbie, pulling him closer. The friction of his clothed erection rubbing over Paul's wet bare skin made Paul's eyes roll back in his head.

Nothing he'd done before, no fumbling kisses with girls, or that one awkward rushed handjob as a kid, had prepared him for feeling like this. Like his heart would pound so painfully against his chest, or that he would sacrifice breathing in order to keep kissing someone, and that he would feel like he was burning up from the outside in.

Screw semantics. This was sex. This feeling was what the church fathers had been warning them about. If anything could turn your mind from the sacred to profane, it was the feel of the right person's body against yours.

Why did it matter that Paul's person was a man?

"Can I show you something else?" Robbie whispered in his ear. His cock was as hard as Paul's, and Paul's fingers slipped on the sweat of his back. "I promise you'll like it."

Paul nodded, afraid to speak.

In one swift move, Robbie lifted his hips up and pushed his pants down to his knees. He was pressed back up against Paul, trapping their cocks between their bodies, before Paul could get a look.

For a brief second Paul was disappointed, then Robbie shifted his hips, dragging his cock against Paul's.

"Holy fuck!" Paul yelled, hands closing spasmodically on Robbie's triceps.

"Good?" Robbie asked voice strained, as he kept driving his cock against Paul's.

"So good," Paul moaned. "So good." Without conscious thought, he reached down and grabbed Robbie's ass, urging him on with rough tugs.

His ass felt as good in Paul's hands as he had always imagined a man would feel. He loved the feel of the faint dusting of soft hair on smooth skin sliding over hard muscles.

Robbie stopped kissing him long enough to quickly lick his own palm. Lifting his hips slightly, he slipped his hand between them, wrapping it around both their cocks as best as he could.

Paul lost the ability to speak. With a garbled moan, he buried one hand in Robbie's hair, while the other dug into his muscled ass so hard Robbie would find bruises there later. All he could do was pant in time with Robbie's thrusts.

Gasping for breath, Robbie pulled his mouth away, rolling his forehead against Paul's head as he looked between their bodies. He rubbed his thumb around the tips of their cocks, spreading the wetness there across both of them.

Paul sucked in a deep breath, arched up off the thin mattress, and came harder than he ever had in his life.

Robbie's fingers clenched around Paul's arms, the muscles in his arms going rock hard, and he grunted as he came, as if each pulse was being punched out of him.

"Fuuuuck," he said, stretching the word out as he fell down onto the bed, twisting sideways as he did so he wouldn't land on top of Paul. Chuckling softly, he dragged his finger through the mess on Paul's stomach.

Paul almost swallowed his tongue as Robbie licked his finger clean. "Damn. We taste good."

Shit. Paul put a hand to his chest, feeling his heart pounding against his palm. Robbie lay next to him, their bodies pressed together, as they both came down from the high.

"Was that okay?" Robbie asked after the silence stretched beyond what felt comfortable. He hooked his leg over Paul's leg and rolled his head to place a kiss on Paul's shoulder.

Those light touches made Paul's heart ache in a way the more sexual contact hadn't. He'd imagined having sex with a man many times. But that kiss held a promise of something Paul hadn't even dared to dream of.

Could guys have this part of a relationship, too? The cuddling, the easy touches, the shared jokes? What if living as a gay man didn't condemn him to a lonely life of meaningless blowjobs with strangers in a grubby bathroom?

He wanted to ask Robbie about it, but he couldn't even begin to pick out a single question from the whirlwind of thoughts in his head.

"Paul?" Robbie asked again. "Was it okay? Did it suck? Did I turn you off men forever?"

Paul's laugh sounded strangled even to himself. If only. "God, no. Sadly, no."

"Oh, good. So, it was okay? It felt good?" He plucked awkwardly at the sleep pants still bunched around his upper thighs.

It finally penetrated Paul's orgasm-dumb brain that Robbie was concerned that Paul might not have liked what they just did.

He rolled onto his side to look Robbie directly in the eye. "It was the most incredible thing I've ever experienced."

Robbie's eyes widened. "Really?"

"Really." Paul looked down as his come-covered torso. "Even this is kinda hot."

Robbie wrinkled his forehead in a totally adorable way. "Kind of gross and sticky now." He ran his hand down Paul's side following the line of his body from shoulder to hip. "How about I get something to clean us up?"

Paul nodded.

Robbie smiled and then rolled Paul over onto his back, kissing him long and deep before continuing his roll right off the futon and onto the floor. He yanked his sleep pants off and hopped up to his feet.

Paul laughed. "Smooth."

While Robbie disappeared into the bathroom, Paul kicked his borrowed sweatpants the rest of the way off. Exhaustion was starting to settle over him like a heavy blanket. Between the travel and the game, and then the long walk in the freezing cold, skating with Robbie, and, well, the toe-curling orgasm, he felt like he could sleep for a week.

Then Robbie came out of the bathroom, gloriously naked, and Paul pushed up onto his elbows to take a nice long look.

Robbie was perfect. He had wavy auburn hair curling over his ears, a killer smile, broad shoulders, nice muscle definition, and a trail of brown hair from his navel to a nest of thick curls over his cock.

Suddenly, Paul felt a little less tired. He locked eyes with Robbie, tracking him as he closed the distance between them.

Robbie sat on the mattress next to Paul. Paul sucked in air between his teeth as Robbie wiped the wet washrag across his skin. "Sorry. Is it cold?"

Paul shook his head. They both watched as Robbie moved the washrag up and down Paul's body with more care than was necessary. When he reached Paul's cock, Paul held his breath, then let out a ragged exhale as Robbie dragged the rough cloth over it.

His thighs spread of their own accord as Robbie moved the rag lower. "I think that's good," Robbie said, tossing the rag over his shoulder to the floor. He massaged Paul's thighs, thumbs digging into the muscles sore from overuse.

Paul's head dropped back down to the futon. "God, that feels good. My legs are killing me. I can't wait until I go pro and there's someone to give a massage after every game."

Robbie's hands stilled. "You think you'll make it?"

"I have to. I have no plan B." That was just the reality of it. Hockey or bust. "What about you?"

Robbie ran his hands up and down Paul's legs, pushing the hair against the grain and making Paul shiver. "I think we should probably make out a little more, just to make sure it wasn't a fluke. That you really liked it. For science." He cupped his hand around Paul's junk, his palm resting against the balls and his fingers scratching through the hair at the base of Paul's dick.

Paul reached down, covering Robbie's hand with his own. "I think that is an excellent idea, professor."

Robbie crawled back over him, kissing him hard.

It felt even better than the first time.

They didn't get much sleep that night. Paul found out he came almost as hard from giving a blowjob as getting one, and that he really loved kissing.

He knew he would remember Robbie for the rest of his life. And to think he'd been considering killing himself earlier tonight.

It wasn't until he ran into his father the next morning that those thoughts returned.

6

PAUL—THESE DAYS I TEND TO LIE

It had still been dark when Robbie dropped Paul off at the back of the Country Inn & Suites attached to the Stanford Ice Center at the crack of dawn. They hadn't slept much the night before, and Paul was tired, wired, and possibly losing his mind. He leaned in the window at the last minute and made Robbie give him his number. Just in case.

He hesitated, a hand on the window frame. The car exhaust billowed about behind the old Outback in a white cloud. "You won't tell anyone, will you?" He hated to ask, hated how it sounded.

Robbie's face, which had been open and smiling even though he looked as tired as Paul felt, closed down. His smile dropped, and he sighed. "No. I won't tell anyone. Your secret is safe with me."

"I'm sorry," Paul said, fingers tightening around the door.

"For what?" Robbie asked, voice flat.

For not being brave, for using you, for wanting to hide. "I don't know." Paul shook his head.

"Well, if you figure it out, give me a call. See you tonight," he added, putting the car into gear.

Paul stood up, hands off the car. "Yeah. Tonight," he echoed.

Tonight at the second of their two games in a row. He was going to be useless if he didn't get some sleep.

With a sigh, he headed towards the motel, deliberately not watching Robbie drive away.

There had to be a way he could sneak in unnoticed. When he'd asked LaRue to cover for him last night, he hadn't cared about getting back in. His only thought had been to run. To get away. Breaking curfew had been the least of his worries.

Last night, before Robbie, he hadn't cared much about anything. Now he found he actually did care if he got kicked off the team.

Thank goodness his room key also unlocked the door off the parking lot. He could sneak down the unfortunately well-lit hallways and be in his room before anyone knew he'd been gone. Besides, he can always say he had gone for a walk.

He replayed the night's events in his head, trying to hold back a smile. Maybe he'd be able to see Robbie today before the game.

"Chip," a man's voice barked from behind him.

Paul felt his heart actually lurch, stop, and start again. Shit. Shit, shit, *shit*. No one outside of his family still called him that.

Shit. He stopped, forced his shoulders to relax, and plastered on a smile before he turned to face the last person he'd expected to see in Bemidji, Minnesota.

His father had driven him to meet the team for these road games right from Eubee's funeral. Paul couldn't remember if they'd said two words to each other either during the funeral or the drive, but he did remember his father's arm around him the entire time and the way he'd taken care of everything Paul had needed.

"Dad! What are you doing here? Is mom okay?"

He knew it was a stupid question but low-level concern for his mother was always there. She'd finished her chemo last month, but she hadn't bounced back from this round as well as she had from the previous ones. But if his mother had gotten worse, Stoney certainly wouldn't be flying to Minnesota to tell Paul.

Paul had volunteered to take a semester off and stay home to care for her, but she'd insisted he stay in school. They texted a lot,

FaceTimed when they could, and he sent her pictures of every game.

"Your mother is fine," his father said, dismissing his concern as usual. He refused to even contemplate the idea that his wife might finally succumb to the ovarian cancer that had plagued her for the last few years.

"So did you decided to come and see the game? Spend New Year's with the team?" He tried to make it sound like he thought it was a happy surprise as if his father would have taken a middle of the night flight from Alabama just to watch a non-championship hockey game.

"Who was that boy who dropped you off?" Paul Stonewall Dyson, Senior, or Stoney as he'd been called when he'd played football, did not sound even the least bit happy.

Fuck. Fuck. God-dang it. "Just a friend from Juniors. He's playing with the Chargers now. We went and got breakfast." Even he didn't believe his own excuse.

"You have a friend in Bemidji?" His father lifted a hand before Paul could even answer. "Whatever lie you're coming up with, I don't want to hear it." He held his cell phone up like it should mean something to Paul. "I want answers from you, and I want them now. Then we'll see if you'll even be playing hockey anymore."

Paul's stomach dropped. Good thing he hadn't eaten anything yet or it would be on the floor. He had no idea what his father had found, but there was no doubt it was incriminating. Paul wracked his brains. What had he done wrong recently that his father could have found out about?

He couldn't know about last night already, could he?

Stoney may have lost most of his peak football muscles, but he was still a big man. Paul looked a lot like his dad had at his age. Tall, blond, not bulky but strong.

"Find someplace private for us to talk, son. Unless you want to have this discussion in the hallway. Obviously, you have no qualms about displaying your...proclivities...in public." Disgust shone from his eyes.

Oh, holy fucking hell. Whatever this was about, it was serious.

Paul looked around for someplace private. His room was out, and the lobby was too public. He smelled chlorine.

"How about the indoor pool? It's early enough that no one should be there."

His father nodded curtly, and Paul led the way down the labyrinth of hallways. Dead man walking, he thought, as the waves of his father's anger beat against his back.

Humidity slapped him in the face as he pushed the door open. His father followed silently, leather dress shoes slapping against the tiled floor.

They sat at one of the small tables by the edge of the pool. Paul crossed his hands and waited for his father to speak.

Stoney stared at him across the table. It was one of his favorite tactics, letting the uncomfortable silence stretch while the object of his glare searched their mind for any wrongdoings and then finally bursting out with something self-incriminating.

It hadn't worked on Paul in years. He met his father's gaze calmly, holding on to the memory of last night like a talisman. Whatever the consequences of this conversation, no one could ever take that away from him.

Stoney broke first, sliding his cell phone across the table. "Would you like to explain these photos?"

Paul frowned and picked up the phone. The torso of a muscular man wearing nothing but a gold lame G-string stuffed with crumpled dollar bills stared up at him. The band around his chest loosened a little. He'd been expecting worse. Okay, he could do damage control for this easy enough.

He swiped through the rest of the photos, double-checking that there were no pictures of him with any of the strippers. So far, so good. It looked like these were pictures from his phone, so there were none of him.

He was usually so careful to not take any pictures that could be even remotely incriminating that he'd forgotten his father had all his texts and pictures automatically uploaded to the cloud.

"What about them?" he asked his dad. "Oh, that's a good one." He turned the phone to his father to show him an obviously drunk girl in a tiny dress and a pink sash reading 'bride to be' hanging over a different nearly naked guy.

His father grabbed the phone back. "What were you doing at a place like this?"

"It was Shelly's bachelorette party. The girls wanted someone to be the designated driver, so I volunteered. Figured I could keep them out of trouble." Paul threw the ball back into his father's court. "Should I have let them go alone and drive drunk?"

His father thumbed slowly through the pictures. "That still doesn't explain why you felt the need to take so many pictures of just the men." His eyebrows raised, and he lingered on one of the pictures.

Paul restrained himself from asking to see which picture.

Stoney laid the phone down on the table. He leaned forward, arms resting on the edge.

Paul forced himself not to lean back and show fear or lean forward and look like he was threatening his father.

"You know your mother and I have prayed for you for years," his father said sorrowfully.

Oh, Paul knew quite well.

He'd known there was something wrong with him since he was four years old and had begged and begged for the purple sneakers so hard that his mother had given in and bought them.

When his father came home and saw him wearing them, he'd lost his mind. Ranting about how no son of his was going to wear girls' clothes and in this house, they knew that men and women each had roles to play and a lot of other things little Paul hadn't understood for years.

By the time puberty hit and he could no longer deny that he didn't feel the way about girls he was supposed to, he understood all too well what his father had been worried about. What he had been right to worry about.

The door opened, and a woman in a one-piece bathing suit with a swim cap and goggles on her head entered the pool. They waited until she dove in, slicing cleanly through the water. They could hear the quiet slap of water against the sides of the pool.

Stoney dropped his voice. "If you can't control your behavior, we will have no choice but to pull you out of this school and send you someplace where they can," he swallowed like the word was stuck in his throat, "cure you."

Paul's blood froze. He'd been living under that threat all through his teens. He was twenty-two now. Too old to be threatened. Now he did lean forward, speaking forcefully but quietly. "You can't make me go anywhere anymore. I'm an adult."

His father sighed heavily and leaned back in his chair. He stared at Paul again, but there was no attempt to intimidate this time. Stoney looked thoughtful as if he were evaluating and assessing his son. He reached for Paul's hand.

Confused, Paul took it. Stoney wasn't usually a touchy person, especially with his son.

"I love you, son," he said much to Paul's surprise. "You know that, don't you?"

Paul hadn't, actually. Well, no, that was wrong. When he was little, even after the sneaker incident, he had been secure in the knowledge of two truths. His parents loved him, and Heavenly Father loved him.

Years of struggling with being gay had eroded both beliefs.

He had no idea how to answer his father, so he just sat there.

"Everything I do, I do because I love you. I'm just trying my best to keep you from a life of sin and sorrow and everlasting death. To live as a..." He turned away, rubbed his face and turned back. "To live in an unnatural way only ends in heartbreak. I know. Trust me."

He covered his mouth with his hand, resting an elbow on the table as if he were stopping himself from saying anything more.

Paul tilted his head back, trying not to let his father notice he was blinking back tears.

Stoney drew a ragged breath. "But, Paul," he continued, voice hard, "if you can't promise me that there'll be no more of this—" he waved the phone. Paul caught flashes of the incriminating photos.

"Then I will have no choice but to pull all financial support and cut you off from all contact with your mother and your sister."

"No!" The cry burst out of him against his will. He couldn't be cut off from his mother and his baby sister. They were his only family. Stoney never spoke to or about his family. Paul had gotten the feeling over the years that they had major disagreements over religion. His dad's parents definitely weren't saved. He thought they might be Catholic?

He vaguely remembered meeting his mother's parents and brothers when he was little. But they'd eventually stopped coming around, too.

All he had was his small family and his church family. They loved him, and he loved them.

So those were his choices: hide who he really was, deny his true desires, then fake interest in, date, and eventually marry some woman all to keep his family and his career; or give in to the demands of his body and lose everything.

No contest. His family meant everything to him, and he'd been working towards a career in hockey since he was six years old.

So why did he feel like the part of him that hadn't died with Eubee was dying? At this rate, there would be nothing left of Paul Stonewall Dyson, Junior.

The woman swimming in the pool flipped around and pushed off the edge. Two teenage girls came in, their voices echoing off the tiled walls.

Paul closed his eyes and pushed the memory of last night deep down. He could do this. It was for the best. Opening his eyes, he forced a smile. "There's nothing to worry about, Dad. Everything's going to be fine."

Stoney nodded once. "Good." Nodded again. "Glad to hear that." He reached across the table for Paul's hands. "Let's pray on it."

Paul dared a look around the room to see if they were being watched. His being Christian wasn't a secret he kept like his sexuality. Growing up, he'd assumed everyone in the world was.

There was a period during middle school where he'd bought into the whole 'Christians are persecuted' mindset. As he grew up and got more exposure he got to other cultures, he realized there was a large group of people who simply didn't care about religion. Who didn't take the Bible as the inviolate word of some god.

Despite the school being in the middle of the Bible belt, Paul was the only player on the team from south of the Mason-Dixon Line. Eleven of the 28 players were from Canada and one guy, Richard Buri, was from Slovakia. Paul had had to look the country up on a map.

No one went to church. Their reactions to the particularly Southern version of Christianity ranged from bemused indifference to outright hostility. So Paul had stopped going to church and kept his beliefs to himself.

He was fascinated by these people. They didn't spend their whole lives trying to be Christ-like and worrying about judgement either from the Church or God himself.

Of course, they also didn't feel the peace of knowing they were loved no matter what. But the more time he spent with them, the more he began to suspect that love, as defined by the people and Church in his world, was more conditional than he had been taught.

Slowly, he reached for his father's hands.

"You lead us," Stoney said.

Paul clenched his teeth on a sigh. This was his life now. Robbie's face flashed before his eyes. This was his fault. If he had just left Paul alone last night, Paul wouldn't have been forced into this choice. He'd made his choices before he'd left the hotel.

Paul wanted to be the son his father wanted and needed him to be. He wanted to believe completely and unquestioningly in a loving God the way he had when was a child.

But he'd prayed for years to feel differently, to feel for girls what he did for boys. His prayers had gone unanswered, and he didn't know what to make of that. It was easier not to think about it

His father squeezed his hands, and Paul bowed his head.

"Heavenly Father," he started, the familiar words coming effortlessly to his lips. "I come to You in prayer asking for the forgiveness of my sins. I confess with my mouth and believe in my heart that Jesus is your Son."

Stoney's voice joined his, and they finished the prayer together.

"Why don't you go up to your room and get some rest?" Stoney said.

Paul nodded. He gathered his stuff without making eye contact with his father, then left the room.

Halfway to the elevator, he realized he'd left his cell phone on the table with his father. Damn it. He really didn't want to see his dad again.

Maybe he would just leave it and get it later when he met back up with Stoney. They hadn't made any plans, but Paul had no doubt his dad would be his shadow all day.

Paul pressed the button for the elevator. But what if Robbie texted? He didn't want his dad to see that and start asking questions.

Feet dragging, he made his way slowly back to the pool.

The hallway smelled like chlorine as he peered through the door to see if his father was still inside. He was. Stoney sat at the table, his back to the door. Paul pushed the door open, and a blast of hot air hit his face.

The closer he got to his father, the more he got the feeling something was wrong. Stoney's shoulders shook.

Was he crying?

Paul froze. He heard his father's shaky inhale. Saw him smooth his hand over something on the table. Paul risked a few quiet steps closer. It looked like an old photo.

Forget the phone. There was no way he was getting involved in whatever was going on there. Keeping an eye on his dad, Paul backed out of the room as quickly and silently as he could.

He spent the rest of the day under the watchful eye of his father. Stoney even sat in the room while Paul napped fitfully. By game time, Paul was beyond exhausted. Rage filled him at the way his father and everyone he knew could take something as wonderful as he had with Robbie (and Eubee) and turn it into something hateful. Make it a sin.

It had only been one night, but Paul had been able to see the faintest outlines of a future that might just hold the promise of happiness. Then his father had come and dragged him back into the shadows where all his doubts and fears lived.

As he took the ice, all he could see was a dark, cold future, without his mother and without any hope of love.

He was ready to hit someone. Any one.

7

ROBBIE—BUT I SEE YOU

The day hadn't gone at all like Robbie had expected it to go. Not only did he not get to see Paul again, something he'd been hoping for in the back of his mind, but the headache he'd woken with only got worse as the day went on.

He spent most of the day in a dark room with a cold washrag over his eyes. By game time, the migraine medicine his doctor had prescribed had pushed the worst of the pain away, but his legs were weak and shaky. And not in a good way like they had been the night before.

During warm up, he scanned the Chargers' bench, hoping to catch Paul's eye and explain why he hadn't so much as texted all day. But Paul pointedly ignored him as he warmed up, keeping as much ice and as many people as he could between them.

Fine. Whatever. Robbie didn't have the energy to deal with his morning-after regrets. He wasn't the first bi-curious-at-night, freaked-out-in-the-morning jock Robbie had fooled around with.

He would, however, be the last. He had too much of his own shit to deal with to be able to baby anyone else through some kind of sexual crisis.

Skating back to the bench on trembling legs, the pain behind his eyes threatening to break free of its chemical chains, Robbie prayed for a quick, easy win.

Sadly, that wasn't meant to be.

As the final minutes of the grueling game dragged on with the Beavers down three goals, the coach pulled the goalie, leaving the net unprotected but giving the team an extra man in position to score.

At the line change, Robbie hurtled over the wall onto the ice, blood pounding at his temples in time with the seconds ticking down on the timer.

With the curses and labored breathing of his teammates in his ear, Robbie flew through the neutral zone towards the blue line.

A heated battle for possession of the puck surged in front of and then behind the net. When the Bemidji forward lifted his stick and sent the puck flying across the ice towards the boards, Robbie raced into position in the high slot to catch the rebound.

The puck slid towards Robbie like it was on a track. Winding back, he slammed the blade of his stick to the ice and then, a microsecond later, into the puck, sending it flying towards the net with the thwack of a perfect slap shot.

Robbie heard the roar of the crowd and caught a flash of white and blue out of the corner of his eye right as he was knocked off his skates and hurled into the boards so hard his helmet went flying across the ice.

"Faggot," a familiar rough voice spit out. He had just enough time to recognize Dyson's face before his head slammed down onto the ice.

By the time his concussion check was done, the game was over. Despite Robbie's highlight-reel worthy goal, the Chargers had lost, five to four.

"Happy New Year," Robbie called across the parking lot of the Stanford Center to a couple of his teammates.

He'd begged off any and all invitations to celebrate New Year's Eve. His head was killing him, everything ached, and he was exhausted. All he wanted was a horizontal surface in a dark room and ten hours of sleep.

His Outback sat alone under a parking lot light. As he got closer, a flash of light from something hanging from the door handle caught his eye.

"Shit," he said, reaching out to unwind Paul's Saint Sebastian necklace from the door. He looked around the parking lot for Paul, though he knew it was pointless. A cold breeze fluttered the edge of the napkin stuck under his windshield.

Paul had written I'm sorry and thanks in blue ink on the brown napkin. What the hell was Robbie supposed to make of that?

Sighing, he stuffed the napkin in his coat pocket. Inside the car, he started the engine and cursed his past self for leaving the radio up so loud.

He turned Paul's necklace over in his hands a few times as he waited for the engine to heat up, flipping from saint to saint. An amulet of protection for traveling athletes. Well, if things went the way they seemed to be, Robbie would certainly be traveling.

Shaking his head, he hung the necklace around the rearview mirror. "What do you think I should do, boys?" he asked the necklace. "Drop out of school and take the Thunder up on their offer, or turn down lots of money and finish my bachelor's degree and be one step further on the illustrious road to gym teacher?"

He flicked at the pendant, setting it swinging. "Yeah. That's what I thought." He put the car into gear and headed out of the parking lot. "Now, which one of you is going to tell my parents?"

Present Day

Two years later and there he was in a different parking lot, in a different state, with a brand new car and a different pendant hanging from the mirror. A tiny glass God's Eye his parents had bought him in Turkey took the place of the necklace, catching the light and banging against the glass when he stopped too short.

He listened to Paul's story about what his father had had to say to him after Robbie had dropped him off at the hotel. What a shock. A religious homophobe. Wasn't that new and special? It sucked for Paul though.

"So, your dad is some super homophobic religious fanatic?" Robbie should have realized there was something like that going on back then when Paul was being so weird about being gay. In his defense, he'd been exhausted and focused on other things.

"Yeah, exactly," Paul said, voice flat.

"What about your mother? Would she support you?"

"She died fourteen months ago."

Shit. Why did every conversation with Paul go this way? Not that there had been many of them. Three? Three conversations and three disasters. Robbie was suddenly exhausted. "I'm sorry. I didn't know."

"Why would you?" Paul shrugged. "It's not like I texted you about it."

"Yeah. Well, listen. You don't worry, I won't out you." He signed promise with a small smile. "Besides, you've had girlfriends. I've seen."

Paul smiled the first real smile Robbie had seen from him yet. "You been keeping tabs on me?"

Robbie had. But he wasn't going to give Paul the satisfaction of knowing it. "Not really. I just hear things. It's a small world."

The tension between them had lessened. Robbie was tempted to leave it, but there was something he had to say. Something that was at the heart of the anger he couldn't let go.

"Look, I don't want to keep beating a dead horse, but you really hurt me that night. And not just physically. That was the first and only time I've ever been gay bashed. You are the only person in the world who ever hurt me for being gay."

Paul looked away, sticking his hands deep in his pockets. "Well, like I've said before, you've been lucky."

Really? "That's it? That's all you have to say? That's your justification?" The urge to hit Paul grew stronger.

"No." Paul inhaled deeply, then exhaled slowly. "I hit you because I was angry and terrified of how I felt, how you made me feel." He looked at the pavement. "I can't be gay," he muttered to himself. Taking a deep breath, he looked Robbie square in the eye. "I'm not gay."

For Chrissake, Robbie thought. *Enough*.

He grabbed the front of Paul's shirt. "If you're not gay, then this shouldn't bother you." Not sure why he was doing it, beyond the fact that he hadn't stopped thinking about Paul in the last two years, he hauled Paul in for a kiss.

It was an angry kiss, a hard kiss.

Paul's whimper fueled the fire in Robbie's veins. His hands fluttered around Robbie's hips as if he wanted to touch Robbie but was afraid.

Robbie groaned at the thought and flipped them around, pressing Paul up against the side of the Prius.

Paul opened his mouth on a moan, and Robbie pushed his tongue between his lips. He slipped his thigh between Paul's legs.

"Oh, fuck," Paul gasped raggedly, thrusting against him. He latched onto Robbie's arms.

Robbie pulled away abruptly, leaving Paul gasping and hanging onto his arms with both hands.

"Fuck." Paul rubbed the back of his hand across his mouth. His eyes darted around the garage, checking to see if anyone might have seen them.

"Don't worry about it. No one saw, so it doesn't count. It's not gay if no one ever knows about it." Robbie's voice was hard.

Paul drew a ragged breath. Rubbing his hand across his mouth again, he took a few steps back from Robbie. He cleared his throat. "What do you want?" Paul asked. "From me. What do you want me to do?"

"Nothing. I don't want you to do anything. I'm sorry I kissed you. Forget it even happened."

“What if I don’t want to?” Paul whispered.

“Too bad. You can’t always get what you want.” Robbie turned away and got into his car. “See you tomorrow. It’s your first game. Don’t fuck it up.”

He couldn’t resist stealing a look in the rearview mirror as he drove up the ramp. Paul was watching him. Robbie resisted the urge to bang his head against the steering wheel. At the next stoplight, he gave in and dropped his head to the steering wheel, banging lightly until the car behind him honked to alert him to the green.

Why had he kissed Paul? Why?

8

PAUL—I SEARCH MYSELF, I WANT YOU TO FIND ME

What the hell was that about? Paul ran his hand through his hair and sighed. Robbie's kiss had stirred up the undercurrent of arousal Paul had been feeling since he laid eyes on the other man earlier that morning.

He wanted to forget that Robbie had ever kissed him. Or that he had kissed Robbie. Or done the other things they had done.

If only there were someone he could talk to about, well, about everything. Changes kept coming at Paul so fast and furious; he couldn't keep on top of them. He had a feeling his strategy of avoidance wasn't going to be viable in the long run.

He walked slowly over to his car. Trailing his fingers across the dark green metallic paint, Paul felt the mix of love and loss the 1976 Stingray always pulled out of him.

There was no way to avoid thinking about the past as long as he drove that car.

He'd lusted after the dark green 1976 Stingray his whole life. The car had belonged to his neighbor Pops Franklin for years.

The old man had been raising his only grandson, Eubee.

Back when everyone had called him Chip, Paul and Eubee had

been friends in the way only kids who grow up on the same block and ran around the fields together could be friends. Inseparable since they could toddle, people spoke of them in the same breath as if their lives were extensions of each other's. When he was very little, they'd spent a summer only answering to the name Chippeneubee.

Pop had let the boys sit in the Corvette, and help him wash it, though Paul had a feeling their help had been more of a hindrance than anything else. Still, the old man seemed to love having them around. He made sure they both knew everything about taking care of the car, inside and out. Paul could trace the wiring in this car with his eyes closed.

When he'd given the car to Eubee as a graduation present, they'd felt like the kings of the road. They'd driven miles and miles down the Alabama roads, including one unforgettable trip down to the Gulf. That summer before Eubee joined the Army was the best summer of Paul's life.

The day they got the news Eubee had been killed in a training accident was the worst.

Pops had covered the Stingray up that night. When Pops died two years later, Paul discovered he had left the car to him. Paul spent a lot of time not thinking about what, exactly, he and Eubee had been to each other.

Top panels off despite the chill of the early December day, Paul threaded the car through downtown Seattle traffic and tried not to think about Eubee or Robbie or anything but hockey.

Paul slid the Stingray into the private garage that came with his apartment. A safe covered space had been his main requirement for a place. He put the top panels back on and pulled a canvas cover over the car. The salt air wasn't the best for the finish, but Paul was willing to risk the car a tiny bit in exchange for the view.

He loved everything about this place, from the private elevator to the glassed-in room the realtor had called a solarium. But the best thing about it was the fact that it was 2,500 miles away from Huntsville.

He climbed the stairs to the solarium and dropped into the padded lounge chair that came with the place. His new pillow top mattress was all he owned outside of the random bits of furniture that the last owners had left behind. He'd ordered the mattress and set of sheets and pillows before he'd left Bakersfield, and they'd arrived the same day he had.

There hadn't been a lot of time to shop since he'd been called up from the Thunder's AHL affiliate team. They'd given him twenty-four hours to move. He'd only needed ten. He couldn't get out of Bakersfield fast enough.

He'd rented the place based on the pictures alone. Luckily, he'd been able to sign the lease yesterday. If it looked like he'd be staying, he would ask the realtor if he could buy it.

Of course, all he had with him was what could fit in a Stingray. So basically, not a lot.

As if to remind him how much better his life was now than it had been three days ago, the sun set over Elliot Bay in a riot of colors from palest rose to an almost blinding neon pink. Paul pulled out his phone and sent a picture to his sister with a message.

Sunset from my place. Beats the heck out of Bakersfield. When are you coming to visit?

The five years between Paul and his sister had felt like an unbreachable gulf when they were younger, but their mother's death had drawn them together. Now that Sissy was in college, and out from under their father's thumb a little bit, it was time to see if they could be friends.

On a whim, he looked up Robbie's contact information. What were the chances he still had the same number he'd had two years ago? What the heck? He had nothing to lose, and Robbie was the only person he knew in the entire state.

Before he could change his mind, he sent the picture to Robbie with a short message.

The next incoming text wasn't from his sister as he'd expected, but from Robbie.

Nice. Where are you living?

Alki Beach.

I have no idea where that is, but I'm going to assume on the waterfront.

Yeah, check this view out.

The solarium was basically a glassed-walled party room with an amazing view across Elliott Bay. It had a wet bar and everything. He couldn't wait until he made some friends and could have them over for dinner or something. He probably should get some furniture by then. He snapped a few shots of the view from different angles and sent them to Robbie.

Wow. That's gorgeous. I'm jealous.

Where are you living? Paul texted back.

I'm like one block down from the arena.

Convenient.

Yeah. But the view isn't nearly as nice. Mine looks like my apartment in Bemidji. He'd sent a picture along in illustration.

Sure enough, the only piece of furniture in his living room was that old futon. Paul would bet his last dollar that was the same comforter too. A shiver caught Paul by surprise as he imagined having a replay of their last encounter on that futon.

I think it's smaller than your old place, he replied steering his mind away from the past.

But that kiss Robbie had given him, that wasn't in the past. What was he supposed to do with that? Should he apologize again for hitting Robbie, or should he not mention it since they seemed to be having a less-than-hostile conversation at the moment?

How could he possibly explain everything he'd been feeling that night? Crushing grief over Eubee's death. Shame and guilt for what he'd done with Robbie, combined with a burning urge to do it again as soon as he could. Fear for himself.

It had taken him years to untangle all the emotions, and Paul kissing him today had kind of re-tangled some of those things, loosened the lids on some memories and emotions he'd worked so hard to repress.

Part of his anger had been over knowing that he wouldn't be able to keep in touch with Robbie, let alone see him again unless it was across the ice. His dad would be scrutinizing his interactions with guys even more than he normally did.

If his father had found out Robbie was gay? Well, it wasn't outside the realm of possibility that he'd try to make an issue of it, maybe even try to get Robbie kicked off the team. He wouldn't be able to do it, of course, but that didn't mean it wouldn't suck for Paul and Robbie if his dad made a stink about it. And who knows how it would have effected Robbie's professional career?

No, back then it had been better for both of them if Robbie thought Paul hated him.

That wouldn't be possible now, of course. Paul would have to find a way to earn Robbie's friendship while keeping him out from under Stoney's radar. If Stoney found out Robbie was gay, he would one hundred percent out him as publicly as he could. If he found out Paul was friends with a gay man, he would throw Paul under the same bus, get him kicked out of the church, and he could kiss goodbye his chances of ever seeing his little sister again.

Sighing, he checked his phone. Robbie hadn't responded to that last text, so Paul wandered back downstairs to flip through the menus the realtor had left him to find some kind delivery person to bring him food.

Paul looked around the mostly-empty apartment and contemplated going out into the world and getting something to eat. The night was gorgeous, and it would be nice to be able to go out with someone. Maybe take a walk along the waterfront and find a cool looking restaurant. Not like a date, obviously, just as friends.

Maybe he and Robbie would be able to be friends. One day. Though the fact that Robbie still hadn't responded to his text made that seem unlikely. He had probably just remembered he hated Paul.

Paul's phone vibrated on the kitchen counter.

Robbie had sent a photo of the view from the middle of a small, tree-lined street. The newly-renovated Key Arena was visible at the end of the street. *My view*, Robbie texted.

Oh crap. There it was. The place where Paul was going to be playing his first professional game in almost exactly twenty-four hours.

I can't believe I'm going to be playing there tomorrow, Paul texted back. *Why does it feel so weird to get something you've been working for your whole life*?

9

ROBBIE—TELL ME WHAT REALLY MATTERS

Laying on the futon and staring at the ceiling, Robbie tapped the phone against his teeth and considered Paul's question.

He was probably the worst person in the world to answer that particular question. He was living his dream, the same dream shared by thousands of kids playing hockey. Though it was early in his career and anything could happen, he could tell everyone had high expectations of him. There was a buzz in the air.

He loved it. So why did it still feel like he wasn't doing enough?

He'd spent years practicing and training, pushing his body to the limits for hockey, and his brain beyond what he'd thought possible. He'd struggled for years to keep his grades up so his parents wouldn't make him quit hockey.

After he'd been diagnosed with dysgraphia and dyslexia – he was a learning disabilities overachiever, alright – he'd agreed to all the tutors and special classes, and to writing aids and learning sign language, only to barely manage to keep his head above water academically.

He was never going to write a book or teach a class or even manage to speak more than a sentence in a row coherently. Hockey was the only thing he was good at. Promising himself and his parents that he would make something of himself, whatever that meant, he poured his heart and soul into it.

Unfortunately, according to his parents, making something of himself didn't mean 'playing games' for a living, as they referred to any level of sports. They didn't see much difference between the local bowling league and professional hockey.

"Well," his father, Grant, had said as he looked over the contract from the Thunder. "You'll be paid well for the next three years, at least." He put the paper down on the big table at which all business was discussed. "What happens after that?"

"I don't know," Robbie said. He looked down the table at Georgia for moral support.

"No one can say for sure, Grant," Georgia said to his father. "It's kind of like writing. You never know where or how that is going to work out either. Robbie is joining one of the most elite sports franchises in the country. They're spending millions on him, and they have a vested interest in seeing him succeed."

If anybody had asked him to describe his relationship to Georgia, Robbie would never be able to find the words. Thirty-five years older than Robbie, Georgia was somewhere between his best friend and his non-blood related aunt.

She was also a six-foot-tall fiery redhead whose fashion icon was Dorothy from The Golden Girls – a show Robbie had watched with her many, many times. He adored her.

Georgia, born George, had been a tight end for the Philadelphia Eagles. As an undergrad in Jenny's Gender Studies program, she'd come to live at the combination boarding house/writer's commune Robbie's parents ran. They usually only accepted grad students, but as a transitioning thirty-year-old freshman, she'd needed someplace better to live than a dorm.

Georgia had been sort of a nanny-slash-babysitter when Robbie was young, and she'd been the one to suggest a struggling Robbie try sports as an outlet for his frustration at school. She'd gone to every practice and every game and taught him more about how to live as an athlete than anyone ever had since.

Obliviously, she was the first one Robbie had called with the news. She'd cried. He'd cried. Through the power of the internet, she'd had a huge bouquet of flowers and congratulatory pizzas for him and his friends sent to his apartment.

"Isn't there any way you can put them off until you've finished your degree?" Jenny, his mother, had asked when he'd told them about the offer.

"No, Mom. I don't think so," he told her. He didn't add that the chances of him ever graduating hovered around zero.

Buoyed by Georgia's encouragement, Robbie signed the contract.

The funny thing was, his life hadn't changed much since joining the supposedly heady ranks of elite athletes. He still split his time between playing hockey, traveling somewhere to play hockey, working out, and occasionally, if he could squeeze it in, eating and sleeping. He just did it on much nicer buses and planes, he ate better road food, and stayed in fancier hotels.

The world hadn't changed because Robert Rhodes from Omaha was playing pro hockey. If he died today, the world wouldn't notice.

Not that he wanted to die. He just thought there should be more to life. Maybe. His parents made a difference. They created things. His father's books touched hearts and changed lives. His mother opened people's minds on a daily basis.

What could he do just by playing hockey?

He laid on the old futon and surveyed his kingdom. Paul was right. This place probably was the same size as his last place. But it came with a mortgage, something Robbie couldn't believe he now had. He didn't love it, but he didn't hate it.

He was hungry, but he knew there was nothing in the fridge but ingredients for meals. This cooking stuff was harder than it looked. He wondered if Paul would want to get something to eat.

No. That would be a terrible idea. They'd only talked for twenty minutes today, and Robbie had already kissed him. He was better off staying far, far away from Paul—call me Chip—Dyson.

Too bad they were going to see each other almost every day for the next few months.

He read Paul's message again. *I don't know*, he texted back. *But it does. You think it's weird now, wait until tomorrow. You'll be happy we have such nice bathrooms.*

He laughed when Paul sent back a text that was just a picture of a guy scratching his head.

You'll see.

10

PAUL—HOW TO MAKE BOYS NEXT DOOR OUT OF ASSHOLES

Robbie was right; this is a nice bathroom, Paul thought, even though he couldn't see much of it with his head hanging over the toilet bowl. But the fancy floor tiles were cool under his knees, and given his current circumstances, the room smelled surprisingly nice. Lemony.

At least his first game was a home game. How much more embarrassing would it be to throw up in someone else's bathroom?

Since he was already on his knees, Paul sent a short but heartfelt prayer of thanks along with a request for the strength to play his best tonight. And forgive me for praying against a toilet, he added at the end. It probably wasn't what Jesus meant when he said to go into your room and shut the door to pray, but he figured God wouldn't mind.

The outer door opened and closed, and someone walked over to the stall and knocked. The door swung open because Paul hadn't had time to throw the latch. "You okay, Dyson?" Robbie asked leaning against the door.

"Just peachy," Paul groaned, giving a shaky thumbs up. He leaned his head on his outstretched arm. "Is everyone laughing at me?"

Robbie chuckled. “Nah. Well, just a little. Mostly they’re taking bets on how many times you puked.”

“So far? Only two.” Paul pulled himself up to his knees. It was a start at least.

Robbie scoffed. “Not even close to the record. Lipe puked six times before his first game.” He reached a hand down. “Ready to go?”

Paul mentally checked in with his stomach. He pictured himself skating out in front of all the fans and facing the Penguins across the ice. His stomach clenched, but vomiting no longer felt imminent. “I think so. Ready as I’ll ever be.”

He took Robbie’s hand and let himself be pulled up. “How long did it take before you stopped being nervous?”

“I’ll let you know when it happens. Come on, let’s go get you suited up.”

Later in life, when Paul tried to remember his first professional hockey game, most of it would be a blur.

It had been minutes of tension interspersed with thirty or forty second bursts of heart-pounding action that left him bruised and dripping with sweat.

He’d thought he’d been ready after his years in the Major Juniors, then college hockey and then his months in the AHL. But this was a whole other level of play. Even the fourth stringers could skate circles around most of the guys he’d played with before.

Two things kept his head and heart firmly in the game. One, he was there, right? Nobody got a charity spot on a team. And it wasn’t a temporary call-up. The Thunder had wanted him. He had a three-year contract. Barring a last minute transfer, he was there for a while.

Two, Robbie. Somehow, through some miracle, they were paired up together for second string, and every time he felt like might be a little lost on the bench or on the ice, Robbie seemed to know. “You got this,” he said as they jumped over the wall for their first time skating together.

By the third period, he’d gone through two pairs of gloves and three jerseys. The last time he’d been this tired from a game was an OHL game that had gone into double OT. They were sixteen minutes twenty-seven seconds into the third period when the coach called for a line change. The Thunder were down two to one. Jake had scored their only goal in the first period with an assist from Anderson, the first line right winger.

Paul and Robbie leaped over the wall without looking at each other, racing into position while the puck was down at the Penguins' end of the ice.

An intercepted pass turned over possession of the puck, and the Penguins raced down the ice. As Paul blocked the Penguins' forward, Robbie got in position in front of the net. Robbie grabbed the puck on the rebound, and hugging the net, swung around for the breakout pass.

The Penguins winger caught his stick and Robbie went down. Paul was moving towards the middle of the ice before his body hit the ice.

The Thunder forward yelled 'change,' and Paul caught the Penguins' defense zipping towards the bench for a quick change. Jake sped up the middle of the ice, as Robbie quickly reached out, stick in his right hand, and batted the puck across the defensive zone right onto Paul's tape.

Paul scooped the puck up, sending a perfect saucer flying over the heads of the Penguins' offense and dropping flat on the ice in front of Jake.

The crowd roared as Jake barreled down the ice on a breakaway, nothing between him and the net but the goalie. He wound up, swung, and buried a slap shot right over the shoulder of the Penguins' goalie and deep into the back of the net, tying up the game with less than three minutes on the clock.

Paul registered the announcers saying something about him and Robbie being college rivals as they slammed into each other in a violent victory embrace.

The high from the play and the slaps on the back from his teammates carried Paul on a cloud through the last three minutes of play. He barely registered their second line center scoring the game-winning goal just two-minutes and ten seconds later.

The home crowd went insane. They may have been the franchise's newest fans, but they were also the most dedicated. Paul had been concerned that all white collar yuppies populating Seattle would be reluctant to let loose, but the fans screamed as loud as the best NASCAR fans, blowing horns, and ringing cowbells until the stadium rang.

The reporters were waiting for them as they made their way off the ice and back to the Thunder's fancy new locker room.

Paul leaped at Robbie's back with a whoop of joy. Robbie staggered under the weight, but grabbed his thighs and laughed.

"Robbie, Robbie," one of the reporters waiting in the hall called as they passed by. "Is it true you two were rivals in college?"

The team PR guy tried to hustle them into the press room so they'd have the nice Thunder Logo backdrop, but Paul yelled out anyway.

"Hell, yeah. Bemidji sucks." He slipped off of Robbie, standing in front of the reporter, sweat dripping down his neck and a smile he couldn't hold back stretching across his face.

"This guy, though, he ain't so bad. 'Course that move he did, I taught him that." Paul elbowed Robbie in the ribs.

Robbie rolled his eyes. "Yeah, yeah. Keep telling yourself that, Dyson."

"Is that true?" one of the reporters asked Robbie.

"Yeah, it's true," Paul answered for him. "Took him out on the pond and showed him a thing or two."

Robbie raised an eyebrow at Paul. "I seem to recall showing you a few moves back then, too."

Paul's jaw dropped. He didn't just...he wouldn't...?

Robbie gave him a challenging look confirming that he had, and he would. Lust mingled with the adrenaline pumping through his veins.

Robbie laughed at the look on his face.

"Okay," the PR guy said, "Can we move this out of the hallway?"

A young, handsome guy with dark brown skin and a neat Afro

turned to Robbie. “When Paul was on the Chargers, he got a hit on you that cost him two games, isn’t that right?”

“Yeah,” Paul jumped in. “I was totally a dick that night. I deserved it.”

“Is it hard playing on the same team now?” Tall, dark, and handsome asked Robbie, despite Paul having been the one speaking. He smiled more than Paul felt was strictly necessary.

Robbie pretended to think about it, then whacked Paul on the shoulder. “Nah, he’s a’ight for a country boy. We’re all dicks some days, right?”

Paul pushed between the two of them. “Rhodes is a great guy and a great player. I’m looking forward to playing with him and the rest of this amazing team. But now, I just want a shower.”

With a practiced smiled, the PR rep ushered the reporters into the press room where some other players and the coach were already waiting for them.

Paul and Robbie headed for the locker room.

11

ROBBIE—WE CAN MAKE THIS LEAP

The Thunder locker room might have been the nicest one Robbie had ever been in, but all the money in the world couldn't make a locker room smell any better.

He breathed in deeply as he walked carefully around the Thunder logo woven into the carpet in the middle of the room. The scent of sweaty men and damp pads might have been kind of gross, but it was more familiar to him than any other. It linked past and present and future in one unbroken smelly line.

The room was the normal end of game chaos as he clomped over to his changing stall. He stripped off his jersey, tossing it into the nearest laundry hamper.

Paul dropped down onto the bench next to him and pulled his jersey off with a sigh. Balling it up, he gave it an easy overhand toss into the hamper. "How awesome is it to have people to take care of this stuff now? And the equipment room," he went on before Robbie could answer. "Oh, my Lord, it's like I died and went to hockey heaven."

Since it had only been a few months earlier for him, Robbie remembered what it was like walking into the room and being told to take his pick of anything he wanted. He'd had time to break in new pads and figure out what sticks he wanted.

Paul was still using his equipment from before with some shells in the Thunder colors thrown over them. The jersey they had already. The team kept one with the names of all the players who might be called up from the A.

Robbie stripped down to his under layer before heading for the changing room. It was going to be a long night. They were flying out to Chicago for the start of five nights on the road. He hoped he'd remembered to take the milk out of the fridge.

Paul passed him on the way to the showers. Robbie deliberately didn't look at him as he peeled off his sweaty clothes and followed him into the room.

The shower room was full of steam, the splash of water on the floor, and the sound of laughter bouncing off the tiles. Robbie hesitated at the doorway. Paul had picked a spot two down from Robbie's usual shower head.

It shouldn't be a big deal; there was an empty spot between them. He contemplated using a different one this time, but he didn't feel like dealing with the inevitable questions about why he had moved.

No deviation from usual behavior went unremarked on in the locker room area. And nothing was off-limits in the shower.

"Jesus Christ, keep that monster leashed, Prog," Lipe said as Sergei turned around to rinse his hair off.

Case in point.

Sergei's laugh boomed through the room. He turned and waved his crotch at Lipe. "Aw *cher*, you love my *gos queue.* Don't be jealous."

Paul leaned over to look. Nothing wrong with that. It would be more obvious if he didn't. Robbie bit back a grin and watched Paul as he anticipated Paul's reaction.

Paul didn't disappoint. He flashed a wide-eyed look at Robbie before nodding appreciatively. "Damn, Serge. That is impressive. Tell your daddy he did good work."

"*Da*. The next time we speak, I will be sure to mention it." The big man shut off the shower and shook the water off his hairy body. The effect was mesmerizing.

Robbie choked on a laugh as Paul signed *Oh, shit* to him under the pretense of soaping up.

When Paul closed his eyes and rinsed the shampoo out of his hair, Robbie risked a quick look at his naked body. Paul was stronger and more muscled across the shoulders than he had been two years ago. His ass had gotten even more perfect, damn it, with a slight inward curve of muscle definition setting off the firm curve.

Paul cleared his throat, and Robbie looked up quickly, caught dead to rights. He shrugged at Paul's smirk. So sue him, he'd been ogling.

In return, Paul's eyes dropped with what Robbie was sure was supposed to be a covert checking out of his body. Let him look. Robbie knew he looked good. He fought the urge to turn the cold water higher at the feel of Paul's gaze on his body.

The smile slipped off Paul's face, and his eyebrows drew together as he stared at a spot near Robbie's collarbones. He leaned closer, soapy hands frozen on his body.

Concerned, Robbie looked down, reaching for his chest. *Oh crap,* he thought as his fingers touched the necklace he wore every day.

Paul's necklace.

Robbie had stopped noticing it against his skin ages ago, so he hadn't even thought about Paul seeing it.

The noise from his teammates seemed to fade away as he met Paul's eyes. The intensity there blew him away, and he remembered kissing Paul yesterday in the garage.

Feeling the blood rushing to his face and another place, he dropped his eyes to the floor and hurried through the rest of his shower.

It didn't mean anything. The necklace or the kiss or the way he responded to Paul. The guy just made him crazy, that's all. And so far his luck had been good, and he wasn't about to get rid of it and risk that changing.

Shutting off the water with a hard twist of the knob, he rushed out of the shower room.

With a little creative maneuvering and timing, he was able to avoid being alone with Paul for a while, but Paul caught up to him as he was changing back into his suit for the trip to the airport. Not caring about anything as abstract as personal space, Paul crowded right into Robbie as he buttoned up his suit pants.

Hooking a finger under the chain, he pulled the necklace out from beneath Robbie's T-shirt. He gently cradled the medallion as he bent down to examine it.

Robbie smelled Paul's shampoo and felt his breath on his neck. If he gloated, Robbie was going to punch him.

"I can't believe you kept this," Paul said quietly. "I thought for sure you were gonna throw it on the ground and then back up over it."

"I almost did," he admitted. His forehead brushed Paul's as he looked down at the necklace. They were almost exactly the same height.

Paul inhaled sharply through his nose at the touch, and he rocked his head briefly against Robbie's. Wrapping his fingers around Paul's, Robbie tilted Paul's hands so he could see the now-familiar image of Saint Sebastian.

"Why didn't you?" He sounded a little breathless.

The way Robbie was running his thumb across the pulse point on his wrist may have had something to do with Paul's breathing troubles as well as with the reason Robbie had kept the necklace.

Why? Who knew? Why did Robbie do any of what he did when he was around Paul? Like taking a near-stranger to his home, like kissing him last night, like the way he couldn't stop touching him.

The adrenaline from the beautiful play they had worked together on the ice simmered in his veins, urging him to fight or fuck. Again, the same way he always felt around Paul.

"I was going to give it back," he finally said. "When I saw you next, but we didn't play you guys again that year."

"And then you were gone," Paul said.

"And then I was gone." They were standing so close to each other, so still. Somebody was sure to notice any second. "Do you want it back now?"

Paul let the necklace drop back to Robbie's chest. He smoothed his hand over it, keeping it on Robbie for the space of a few heartbeats. "Nah. I like knowing you're wearing it." He slid his hand up until his finger brushed lightly against Robbie's neck and Robbie's body came down firmly on the side of fucking.

"What are you doing?" he whispered, aware of the other people around them.

Paul shook his head. Ghosting his thumb across Robbie's jaw line, he took a step back and shoved his hands deep into his pockets. He shook his head again. "I don't know what you do to me. I can't hardly think straight around you."

A snorted laugh forced its way out of Robbie's mouth. "No shit," he said.

Hurt flashed across Paul's face then he quickly realized what he had said, and he blushed. His fair skin turned bright pink, and Robbie could feel the heat coming off of it.

He wondered if Paul's ass would get all pink and hot with a few well-placed slaps.

Okay. That was officially enough of that. With a deep breath, he stepped back, turning to his locker to pull out his dress shirt. "We're going to be late for the bus," he said with a mental shake.

"Yeah," Paul answered. "How long is the flight to Chicago?"

"'Bout three and a half hours."

"Damn. Going to be a long night," Paul said. "Guess I'll just go get my stuff."

"It's probably already loaded," Robbie said slipping into his jacket.

"Oh, yeah," Paul said, brightening. "The big leagues." He ran his hand through his hair. "I still can't believe it, you know?"

Robbie looked around at the fancy dressing room, at the locker with his name on it, and the trophies and photos lining the walls. "Me neither."

He almost couldn't take the look on Paul's face, the awe and excitement in his bright blue eyes. The slate blue suit he wore fit him like a glove, emphasizing the spread of his shoulders and his narrow hips.

Fuck. Why couldn't he just be ugly?

"Let's go," Robbie said gruffly.

They walked in silence, Robbie cataloging the vast number of reasons he shouldn't start anything with Paul, starting with him being so deep in the closet he'd need a map to get out, and ending with the effect on the team.

His resolve held strong until Paul sat down next to him on the bus and slid his hand up Robbie's thigh, and Robbie didn't stop him.

God *damn* it, it was going to be a long night.

12

PAUL—THAT'S JUST WHO I AM THIS WEEK

Flying with the big boys was nothing like Paul had experienced before, even on that one flight where he'd been bumped up to business class.

For one thing, the Thunder had a private room with their own security screening and a nice spread of food. Paul grazed as he waited for the security screening to be finished. Looking out the window, he saw their equipment manager and his staff supervising the loading of the chartered jet.

He felt Robbie walk up next to him. "Those guys work hard," Robbie said in his ear.

"That's what I was just thinking. It feels weird to be just watching. I feel like I should be out there helping instead of inside eating tiny pastries." The vague guilt didn't stop him from putting another delicious morsel into his mouth.

Robbie moved in closer to him, ostensibly to get a better look out the window, but with the added bonus of pressing his body against Paul's.

They were almost the same height, Paul maybe an inch taller, but Robbie was beefier, his muscles more rounded and fuller than Paul's long, lean muscles. As good as he looked in a suit, he looked even more amazing naked. Naked, he was all strong dips and curves.

Heat rose in Paul's face at the thought of Robbie naked. He could see their faces reflected in the night-darkened glass. Their eyes were locked on each other, and Paul felt as if his desire was being broadcast for anyone to see.

How could they miss it? The electricity between them felt so strong it should be visible.

What the hell was he doing? He couldn't be with Robbie the way he wanted to. He shouldn't. All these years, he'd managed to deny himself. He'd been able to resist just about any guy. Now, after two days with Robbie, all his self-control was out the window. All he could think about was that one night they'd had together.

He'd been sure it hadn't meant anything special to Robbie. After all, it hadn't been his first time with a guy. But Robbie had kept the necklace, damn it. Kept it and was wearing it. Just knowing it was there under that freaking suit was driving Paul crazy. He wanted to rip Robbie's clothes off.

His brain was buzzing with the excitement of the game, lack of sleep, and the incredible feel of Robbie's hard thigh under his hand.

He'd kept his hand on Robbie's thigh the whole bus trip. At one point, he'd slid it up just a little further. Robbie had exhaled harshly through his nose, and Paul felt his erection pushing against his hand.

Giving up on pretending to be asleep, Robbie glared at Paul and adjusted himself so his erection no longer stretched down his thigh. But he didn't tell Paul to stop, and he didn't move away.

Paul had a feeling neither one of them knew what they were doing. Robbie studied Paul's face in the reflection.

Giving Paul a hearty bro-slap on his shoulder, Robbie flashed a big smile that felt a little forced. "C'mon, Dyson. Let's get you on that plane. Ready for your first big boy plane ride?"

We good? Robbie signed, hands held low.

Paul nodded, then punched him in the shoulder. "Yeah. You can show me how they buckle you into your booster seat, shorty."

The plane had plenty of room. All the seats were the nice

reclining kind Paul had only ever passed by on his way to the back of the plane.

Paul noticed some guys sitting next to each other, some guys sitting alone. They obviously had favorite seats, so Paul waited for everyone to sit before he looked for an empty spot. He took off his suit jacket and his tie as he waited. A lot of guys complained about having to dress up to go back and forth from the rink, but Paul liked the way he looked in his suit.

"Hey, rookie. You can go sit with the flight attendant," one of the guys joked. "Maybe you can help her out."

Robbie sat by himself in a window seat. The two seats across the aisle from him were also empty.

Paul hesitated, and when Robbie didn't say anything, he took one of the two seats across the aisle.

As the plane rumbled across the tarmac, the exhaustion of the past three days and the reality of how his life had changed caught up with him.

Unbuckling his belt and kicking off his shoes, he reclined the seat as soon as he was allowed. Tucking the complimentary blanket over himself and burrowing against the surprisingly comfortable pillow, he decided he could get used to traveling in style.

He was asleep almost before the thought crossed his mind.

The smell of steak and the growling of his stomach woke him up. The flight attendant wheeled a cart down the aisle trailing delicious scents in her wake.

Paul perked up, peeking over the top of the seat to see how close he was to getting some food.

A laugh from across the aisle got his attention. He turned to see Robbie watching him.

"Have a nice sleep?"

"Oh, yeah. How long was I out?"

"About two hours, I think. I fell asleep, too."

It was about one a.m. Seattle time. It felt like a strange time to be eating a second dinner, but Paul was starving.

"Want to watch a movie while we eat?" Robbie asked to Paul's surprise.

"Um, sure." He pressed the button to slide his seat upright again, then hesitated. "Do you want me to…" he motioned towards Robbie's row.

Robbie slid his laptop off the empty seat and gestured for Paul to come on over.

"So how do you like the travel so far?" Robbie asked as Paul sat.

"Beats flying coach on Delta, that's for sure. I could get used to it. Actually, I think I'm used to it already. It's worth having to wear a suit."

"Wait until you see the hotel."

A handsome woman in a blue suit with the airline logo embroidered discreetly on her lapel stopped next to them. "Hi, Robbie," she said, reaching across Paul to hand Robbie his dinner.

"Hey, Sarah." Robbie took the tray from her. "How're the girls?"

"They're awesome," Sarah said with a smile that crinkled the laugh lines around her gray eyes. "Maya is home from college already for winter break. Zoe gets in next week."

"You have two college-aged kids?" Paul blurted out. He slapped a hand over his mouth. "Sorry, ma'am," he said from behind his hand. "I didn't mean to be rude. I just meant you look too young for…not that I'm implying you were like a teen mom or anything…sorry, ma'am." He knew his face must be bright red.

Robbie laughed out loud.

Sarah leaned a hand on the back of his chair. "You must be Paul Dyson, the new defenseman."

"Yes, ma'am." Paul forced himself to make eye contact. Sarah was still smiling, so he figured she wasn't going to throw his meal out or anything.

"Well, it's lovely to meet you, Mr. Dyson."

"Oh, no," Paul groaned. "Please don't call me that. It always makes me feel like I'm in trouble. Nothing good ever follows 'Mr. Dyson.' It's always 'Mr. Dyson, the coach would like to see you in his office.' Or

'Mr. Dyson, see me after class to discuss your performance on this last test.' Never good, ma'am."

Sarah laughed kindly, patting Paul on the shoulder. "Okay, Paul. How about I won't call you Mr. Dyson, and you stop calling me ma'am. Makes me feel about a hundred years old."

Paul was shaking his head before she even finished speaking.

"He's just a little ole country boy from Alabama," Robbie explained putting on a fake Southern accent. "I don't think he's capable of stopping."

Paul leaned back as Sarah placed his meal on his tray. "I could call you Miss Sarah," he suggested.

With a wicked gleam in her eye, Sarah put a hand on her hip and gave Paul a solid look. "Maybe one day, honey, but not on the first date." Winking, she rolled her cart away.

Paul turned to Robbie wide-eyed. Robbie's laughter was barely smothered by the hands he had clamped over his mouth. He snorted at the look on Paul's face.

"Did she just...?" Paul asked.

Robbie nodded, face turning red with suppressed laughter.

Paul craned his neck to look down the aisle where Sarah was distributing meals and chatting with the other players. Shaking his head, he turned to his food. "Definitely not like college," he muttered.

Robbie laughed at him again, then turned on the television in front of him and flipped through the choices. "Rick and Morty or Game of Thrones?" he asked.

"Rick and Morty," Paul answered, pulling up the show on his screen as well.

They each watched with one earphone in so they could hear each other talk. It was nice, Paul realized. Like they were almost friends.

Paul kept his eyes down when Sarah came to collect the trays. "You okay, boys? You want any coffee or dessert?"

"No, thank you, Sarah," Robbie answered.

Sarah looked down at Paul. "And how about you, country boy? Looking for something sweet? Maybe a little spicy?"

Paul choked on an answer and blushed to the roots of his hair.

Robbie burst out laughing.

"Maybe a little of both?" she suggested, leaning a hip against his chair, and running a finger down his arm.

Paul looked helplessly from Sarah to Robbie and back. "I'm...I..." he stuttered. Normally he handled this kind of thing better, but he so hadn't expected it.

Paul heard some of the guys laughing from somewhere up the aisle. Sarah joined in, and now Paul really didn't know what to do.

"You harassing that poor woman, Dyson?" Jake yelled from his seat. "Are we gonna have to have another sexual harassment seminar?"

"No!" He held his hands up as if to prove he wasn't touching her at all.

Sarah shook her head and smiled sweetly at Paul. Her body language changed instantly from seductive to protective. She patted Paul on the head. "I can tell you're a good boy, honey. It's just a little fun with the rookie."

She turned toward the front of the plane and put her hands on her hips. "Okay, you animals have had your fun. You be nice to this boy now or no dessert for any of you."

"Yes, ma'am, Sarah, ma'am," Jake answered. "We won't pick on him too much more."

"We can still a little, right?" Lipe asked.

Sarah looked back at Paul considering. "Just a bit," she answered. "He's awfully cute when he blushes."

Paul wasn't sure he had stopped blushing by the time she was halfway down the aisle.

When he turned back, Robbie was looking at him with an amused smirk. "She's right, you know," he said.

"What?" Paul asked.

"You are cute when you blush." He nudged Paul's knee with his.

Paul blushed again and dropped his head in his hands. He wished he could control his face better. Sometimes being a blue-eyed blond sucked.

Robbie patted him on his back. "You want to go back to sleep?"

"No," Paul said with a glower towards the front of the plane. "I don't trust those guys not to draw dicks on my face when I'm asleep."

Robbie reached down to pull his laptop out of his bag. "I can't say that hasn't happened." He flipped open the computer. "You can stay here and help me with my notes." He plugged in a gaming headset complete with a microphone into the laptop.

"What notes?"

Paul listened, growing more impressed every second, as Robbie told him about the extensive notes he kept about each game.

Robbie kept his voice low as people around them slipped back into sleep. "So first, I have goals for each game, right? Like points or some kind of improvement in a skill. And I record how I did with that." He pressed a button and spoke into the microphone almost too low for Paul to hear.

Paul was surprised to see the words appearing on the screen almost as quickly as Robbie spoke, complete with punctuation. "Oh, cool. That helps you write?"

Robbie nodded. "Then I keep track of all kinds of things. What worked, what didn't. What I was feeling before, during, and after the game. What my routine was. And I keep notes on strengths and weaknesses of all the other players."

"Holy crap," Paul said. "That's amazing. I mean, I know writing isn't your favorite thing. This is a lot of work."

Robbie shrugged and opened up a new document. "They pay us a ridiculous amount of money to play this game. Least I can do is make sure I'm working for it."

Paul thought about the sixteen long years of hard work they'd put in to get this far; the grueling schedule of practice, workouts, travel, games, and public appearances he'd been handed; about how much bodily injury he'd already sustained and how short a pro sports career could be. As far as he was concerned, everybody on the team was working hard for their money. He kept the thought to himself though.

"What's your email?" Robbie asked him. "I have some notes on the Habs you should look at before the game tomorrow. We can have some ideas ready for Coach in the morning."

"Thanks. That would be great." Paul read over Robbie's shoulder as he spoke softly into the microphone. Robbie's notes were thorough and insightful and made Paul realize he was going to have to seriously up his game to keep up at this level.

The soft sound of Robbie's voice lulled into a half-sleep. He started when Robbie closed the lid of the laptop. "Sorry," he said.

"For what?"

"Falling asleep," he said, though even he wasn't sure why he was apologizing for that. "Guess I'll go back to my seat." He pushed up from the chair.

Robbie put a hand on his arm. "Stay."

Paul tried to read Robbie's expression in the dim nighttime lighting. "Yeah? You sure?"

Robbie nodded. *We need to talk*, he signed. *Later*. He pulled up the armrest between their seats.

Paul settled back down. "Okay." His heart beat hard in his chest. Being around Robbie like this made him feel like a teenager again.

Looking pointedly at Paul, Robbie covered himself with his blanket.

Paul followed suit and soon felt Robbie's hand reaching over to his leg. With almost imperceptible movements, Robbie paid him back in full for the bus ride. His wandering hand never went exactly where Paul wanted it to as he drove Paul to the edge of orgasm, never letting him tip over.

Robbie got Paul hard and panting, then pulled off until Paul's breathing settled down, only to do it over and over again.

Robbie was killing him. Not that Paul wanted to come in his pants, that might be hard to hide, but the longer it went on, the less concerned he got. He'd find a way to explain any visible mess.

Robbie finally laid his big warm palm right over Paul's rock-hard cock. A whine pushed past Paul's lips, and his fingers clenched on the arm rest. Robbie pressed down, forcing a gasp out of Paul, and then the pressure was gone as Robbie pulled his hand completely out from the under the blanket.

Paul sagged against the chair.

He heard Robbie's low chuckle. "Night, Paul," he said softly.

Paul's head thudded back against the seat as he nodded in response, not trusting his voice.

Robbie turned towards the window, curling up on his seat.

Paul banged his head softly against the seatback. He was so gay. And so, so screwed. Robbie was every temptation he'd ever fought all rolled up into one dark-eyed package.

Is it really so wrong? A small voice in his brain asked. Is it really wrong to be gay? Who is it hurting?

Me, he answered to himself. *It's killing me*.

Somehow, despite his internal struggle between what he was, what he wanted, and what he'd believed all his life, he fell asleep.

Paul woke up when the lights fluttered on. The pilot was announcing that they were twenty minutes away from Chicago and they should prepare for landing.

Paul was slumped against Robbie, his arm across Robbie's stomach.

"Oh, look. The kids are awake," Lipe said, looking over the seats in front of them, a cell phone held in his hand. "You two are adorable. I got some good pics." He waved his phone.

Oh god, Paul panicked. Did they know? What had he seen?

Robbie gave Lipe the finger without even opening his eyes. "Fuck off, Lipe. You were practically spooning with Sergei the last flight."

Sergei nodded. "It is true."

"You're comfy, dude," Lipe said to the goalie. "And warm, like a big personal heater."

Lipe turned back to inspect them again. "You talk in your sleep," he said to Paul.

Paul froze. He'd thought he had outgrown that. Heaven only knew what he had said.

"Oh, yeah?" Robbie asked. "What did he say?"

"Couldn't really tell," Lipe confessed. "Something about taking a shot. And he was sorry."

"Sorry to have to know you," Robbie answered.

"I'm just saying, whoever he rooms with is going to need earplugs."

Paul froze. "Rooms with?"

Robbie gave him an unreadable look. "Yeah. Rookies share rooms."

"Oh. Well. I'd better get ready," he said.

Robbie nodded.

Paul moved over to his seat, put on his shoes and tried to decide if it would be worse to room with Robbie or not to room with him.

He'd find out soon enough which it was going to be.

13

PAUL—DON'T MEAN TO ACT A LITTLE NERVOUS AROUND YOU

Another bus met them at the airport, right on the tarmac. Despite all the special treatment, it was still three-thirty in the morning before Paul was opening the door to the hotel room that he was indeed sharing with Robbie.

The hotel was the nicest one he had ever stayed in. He'd gotten an impression of wood, leather, and stately modern elegance as he'd dragged his half-asleep, half-aroused body through the lobby.

Floor to ceiling windows framed what Paul was sure was an amazing view of Lake Michigan, but he only had eyes for the bed. A warm hand between his shoulder blades pushed him gently further into the room.

"Out of the way. If I'm not in bed in thirty seconds, I'm going to fall asleep in the hallway."

Paul nodded in agreement. He sat down heavily on the edge of the bed furthest from the door and groaned. "Dang, that's nice." He barely had the strength to pull his jacket off before collapsing backward onto the plush mattress.

Robbie was methodically stripping next to the other bed. "Unless you've got another suit in there, you might want to take that one off."

"I don't hardly have any clothes," Paul admitted. "I haven't had any time to shop, and my stuff won't be in Seattle for a few more days."

"Now you know why I don't have any furniture. Who has time to shop? Now hang up that sexy suit. You've got to put it back on in," he checked the time, "six hours."

"I quit," Paul said, toeing his shoes off.

Robbie threw a pillow at him. "Strip, Dyson."

Paul put the pillow over his face and groaned again. "I really want to take that as an opening, but I am plumb tuckered out."

"Is that something contagious?" Robbie said with a laugh.

Paul gave him the finger without even moving the pillow off his face.

"Too tired to move even if I was Sergei?" Robbie asked.

Paul sat up. "Seriously, dude. *Dayum*." Paul said before he could censor himself.

Relief washed over him when he realized he didn't have to. He would never have to around Robbie. My God, Robbie had had his hand on Paul's dick a few hours earlier. A weight he hadn't noticed carrying dropped off him and he almost gasped with the feeling of freedom.

Robbie dug through his carry-on for his toothbrush wearing nothing but his white Y-front underwear and that damn necklace. Acting like what Paul had just said wasn't earth shaking. Like this was a normal conversation. For him, it probably was. He probably drooled over other guys with his friends all the time.

"How do you not stare?" Paul asked, curious, as he made no attempt to not stare at a mostly-naked Robbie. Robbie almost made the ugly as sin, K-Mart underwear look good, and Paul was probably going to get an erection every time he saw a Saint Sebastian medal from now on.

"Years of practice, my friend. As I'm sure you well know."

Yeah, Paul knew. Figuring out how to not cross the line between the expected locker room dick jokes and outright ogling took practice.

“I try not to be in the shower with him,” Robbie answered more seriously. “I’m sure I’ll get used to it eventually.” He paused and looked up at the ceiling as if imagining Sergei in the shower. Paul was right there with him. “Or not,” Robbie said.

“Is he your type?” Paul asked honestly curious. Did he have a type beyond Robbie?

“Not normally,” Robbie said walking into the bathroom. “But I wouldn’t say no.”

Paul stripped off the rest of his clothes, pulled out his toothbrush, and followed Robbie into the bathroom. Double sinks. Nice.

“It was worse when Bryce was still around,” Robbie said through a mouthful of toothpaste.

“Bryce Lowery? Dude, I had such a crush on him.” He ran his toothbrush under the stream of water, then squeezed out a neat strip of toothpaste.

Robbie reached over and shut off Paul’s water. “Yeah me, too. I had his poster in my room when I was a kid.”

“Did you know he was gay before he came out?”

Robbie spit toothpaste into the sink, and then shook his head. “No. But I’d always thought he might be. More so when we were on the same team. No pun intended.”

Robbie finished before Paul. By the time Paul came back into the room, Robbie was on his back under the covers, arms crossed behind his head and his eyes closed.

Heart beating a little faster than normal and mouth dry, Paul hesitated at the foot of Robbie’s bed. Were they going to continue anything from the plane? Paul was a bit more awake, and his body was starting to remember how good Robbie’s hand felt.

“Go to bed, Paul,” Robbie said without opening his eyes.

Disappointed and relieved at the same time, Paul did. After plugging in his phone, he slid into the bed. He sighed as his head hit the pillow. It really was a superlative mattress. He could definitely get used to this lifestyle. With the press of a button, he shut out all the remaining lights.

"I actually ran into Bryce in the bathroom of the bar when I was drunk and said something to him about him being gay," Robbie said into the darkness. "This was before I think he even knew."

"Oh, dang. Did you die?"

Paul heard the sheets rustle. The light of their cell phones was just enough for Paul to make out Robbie turning on his side to face him.

"I was mortified. In front of his ex-wife, no less."

"Well, you weren't wrong. What was it like in real life to meet him? Did it help your crush?" Paul wasn't sure he would have been able to speak to the man. Bryce Lowery was almost a legend to him.

"It made it worse. Because not only is he gorgeous and a hockey legend, he's one of the nicest guys you'll ever meet. Never says a bad word about anyone."

"I'm bummed I didn't get to play with him." He'd missed it by a few weeks. Lowery had retired after a bad knee injury right around Thanksgiving.

"You'll probably get to meet him. I got to spend Thanksgiving with him and his family and his boyfriend and his friends."

"Oh, man," Paul fought the urge to turn on the light. "Were you there at the hockey game? With the kiss cam and everything?" Bryce Lowery's outing himself with a kiss at an ECHL game had shocked a lot of people. Including Lowery's boyfriend, apparently. "How was it? I heard his boyfriend freaked out."

Robbie grunted in annoyance. "Freaked out is a little strong. And he was right to be mad. I know it sounds romantic in theory, but you don't out other people, man. It's not cool."

Hearing Robbie say that lessened a small worry Paul had been carrying around. Yes, Robbie had said in the garage that he wouldn't out Paul to the team, but now Paul believed he meant it.

"What's his boyfriend like?" Paul's question ended on a yawn. Across the room, Robbie yawned in response.

"Dakota?" he asked sleepily. "Younger, closer to our age. Quiet.

Serious." Robbie nestled deeper under the covers, his words coming slower. "He has this cool orchard farm thing out in Colorado."

Exhaustion returned to Paul's limbs, crowding out his low-level sexual frustration. "Sounds nice," he answered in a sleepy mumble.

Robbie's breathing grew heavier, and Paul felt himself slipping into sleep.

"Paul?"

Robbie's husky voice pulled Paul off the edge of sleep. He rolled on his side to face the other bed. Robbie's eyes glittered in the low light. "Yeah?"

Robbie grinned. "I like the way your ass looks in those boxers."

Paul groaned softly as arousal quickly shoved exhaustion out of the way. "I hate you. And, for the record, I hate your tighty-whities."

Robbie chuckled, rolling onto his back. "Good night."

"Night," Paul said softly. Why did whatever was building between them have to be so fucking easy? Why did it feel so good just to talk to Robbie? Paul hadn't been so comfortable around someone since — Paul's mind hesitated at the precipice of the thought, then jumped right over. The only other person he'd ever felt like this with had been Eubee.

Holy crap. Had he been in love with Eubee? Had Eubee been in love with him? Fuck. What crap timing for an early-morning revelation. He had to be on a bus to the stadium in a few short hours.

Tomorrow was going to suck.

14

ROBBIE—ASK ME WHAT THE HELL I'M LOOKING FOR

Paul looked like leftover death the next morning. Robbie barely managed to drag him out of bed in time to get dressed and on the bus.

He did find the time to push Paul up against the door for some hot and heavy making out that left them both hard and panting, nothing between them but underwear.

"You suck," Paul said as Robbie straight-armed him away. "What are you trying to do to me?"

"Fuck if I know." Robbie's laugh sounded a little choked. "What are you doing to me, is the real question."

"Believe me, I have no clue what I'm doing," Paul answered sincerely, hands slipping down Robbie's sides and settling on his hips.

With a moan, Robbie let himself collapse back against Paul. He attacked Paul's neck as he ground their cocks together almost painfully hard. With the high-pitched whimpers and little hitches of breath Paul made every time Robbie's teeth closed on his skin, it took all of Robbie's self-control not to give him the mother of all hickeys.

That would be impossible to explain.

A heavy pounding on the door made them both leap away from it. "Five minutes!" the assistant coach cried from the hallway.

"Fuuucccckk," Paul dragged out, hand to his chest. "I think I just had a g.d. heart attack."

Robbie wasn't in much better shape, bent over with his hands on his knees and breathing heavily. "You curse in the weirdest way," he panted. "You'll say fuck but not God-damn."

Paul pulled himself together and punched Robbie on the shoulder. "I don't take the Lord's name in vain, and neither should you, you heathen."

Laughing breathlessly, Robbie took a minute they didn't have to enjoy the sight of Paul's erection and tight ass. "Crime to cover that up," he said as Paul stepped carefully into his suit pants.

"Get dressed, Rhodes, or I'm telling the coach you were too hungover to get up."

"Oh, I can get it up just fine," he said, leaning against Paul's back to prove it to him.

Paul swatted him away, and they made the bus only a minute or so late.

The next hours were filled with workouts, getting to know the ice, and coaching sessions. Robbie was gratified to find he and the coach agreed on the strengths and weakness of the Blackhawk players.

He and Paul interacted no more and no less than any other of the guys. Everyone had someone they naturally gravitated to. Sergei and Lipe were thick as thieves most of the time. And given a choice, Jake ended up sitting next to his fellow first-line winger, Gabriel Jansson.

So he and Paul hanging out didn't raise any eyebrows. They kept it strictly platonic, except for the way Robbie could feel the energy between them whenever Paul was near. He knew without looking when Paul was behind him.

It made him want to bang his head against a wall. Rationally, he knew better than to get involved with Paul. There weren't just red flags; there were flashing neon warning signs with skulls and crossbones and 'here be dragons' printed along the edges.

The biggest problem was, obviously, Paul's internalized homophobia. Sure, it looked like he wasn't having any problems with it right now, but Robbie knew there was a huge difference in how guys reacted before and after a mind-blowing orgasm.

Guilt had a way of crashing down after the brain came back online.

Robbie couldn't really wrap his mind around the kind of religious homophobia Paul had grown up with. It made zero sense. Surely, Paul must have realized it was all bullshit by now. Maybe after they'd hung out a bit longer.

He should introduce Paul to Bryce and Dakota if he could. Paul probably hadn't met a whole lot of out gay people growing up in Alabama. That would help.

They'd deal with the whole sleeping with a teammate and how that could end in disaster later. After, you know, they'd actually slept together. So far, it had been a whole lot of teasing with no reward. Robbie had high hopes that would be changing during the traditional post-lunch nap. Paul had better not be planning on getting any actual sleep.

The team lunch dragged on, and by the end of it, Paul was almost asleep in his seat. Only Robbie's quick thinking saved Paul from picking up the tab for the whole team.

"You tuck him in all nice and cozy, now," Sergei said as Robbie pushed the button in the elevator. "He's a growing boy, and he needs his sleep."

"I'm fine," Paul said, leaning against the back of the elevator, arms crossed over his chest and eyes closed.

"Yeah, sure," Robbie said, leading Paul down the hallway by the arm.

Inside the room, he peeled off Paul's suit jacket and shirt before pushing him gently down onto the bed. “Did you sleep at all last night?” he asked, crouching down to pull Paul’s shoes off.

“Not much,” he confessed. “Too much on my mind.” He slid his pants off.

Robbie rested his hand on Paul’s shin. “Good or bad?” *Regrets*?

Paul shook his head. “I don’t know. Confusing. Some good, some bad.” The flirty edge that had been in his eyes the whole day was completely gone. Paul just seemed limp.

Robbie rubbed a hand up Paul’s thigh, trying to convey comfort rather than lust. “Why don’t you take a nap? I’ll make sure you get up on time.”

He stood up, and Paul reached out to grab his wrist. “Stay with me?”

It was what Robbie had been planning, but he’d pictured a more active scenario. “Sure,” he said. “Give me a second.” He undressed to his underwear and climbed into bed next to Paul.

Paul made a happy sound and rolled over into Robbie, burying his head in Robbie’s chest. Robbie didn’t know what was going on in Paul’s head, so he simply rubbed his hands up and down Robbie’s back.

“Why does this feel so good?” Paul asked quietly.

Robbie didn’t have to ask what he meant. They fit together perfectly. They shouldn’t. It should be awkward and new, but it wasn’t. Robbie didn’t trust it. Surely there would be a price to pay later. “I don’t know,” he answered truthfully.

Paul tilted his head up to look at Robbie.

This close, his eyes were a crystalline sky blue, and his eyelashes were a thick, sandy blonde fringe. With his pink cheeks and porcelain skin, the effect was surprisingly delicate.

“Kiss me?” Paul asked.

“You sure?” Robbie replied.

“Sure I want you to kiss me, or sure it’s a good idea?”

Robbie slid his hand under the back of Paul’s white undershirt. “Both.”

"I'm sure I want you to kiss me, and I think it might be a terrible idea."

"Me, too," Robbie said leaning in to kiss him anyway.

The kiss started soft and gentle, fitting for the sleepy vibe and the late afternoon sun slanting through the huge windows.

After a few closed-mouth kisses, Paul tightened his hold on Robbie and rolled them until Robbie lay blanketed over him. "More," he demanded. Robbie obliged, pushing into Paul's mouth.

Paul spread his legs, his knees coming up around Robbie's sides. Robbie rubbed his hips against Paul's thigh.

Paul moaned slightly and lifted his hips to meet Robbie's thrusts. His hands crept down to Robbie's ass as if Paul weren't sure it was allowed. Reaching down, Robbie wrapped Paul's hand firmly around his ass.

"Oh, fuck," Paul whispered. "That feels so good. Why does it feel so good?" he asked again.

"Because I have a great ass?" Robbie joked against Paul's mouth, attempting to lighten up a moment that felt poised on the edge of more than Robbie wanted to deal with.

"No," Paul said, sounding almost angry. His fingers bit into Robbie's cheeks, driving them tighter against each other. "Why does touching you feel so different, so much better than touching a girl?" He sounded pained as if he needed Robbie to have an answer.

Robbie pushed back until he was sitting between Paul's legs, his hands on Paul's knees. "I don't know. Because you're gay?"

Paul pulled Robbie back down to him with a groan. There was nothing soft or gentle about their kisses this time. They were wet and loud and punctuated by sharp inhales and hissed exhales as their erections rubbed over and against each other.

Paul's fingers toyed nervously with the waistband of Robbie's underwear.

Robbie suddenly knew Paul hadn't done anything with a guy since the night they'd shared two years ago. "Do it, c'mon, touch me."

Wide-eyed, Paul slid his hot hands down the back of Robbie's briefs.

"Fuck, yeah," Robbie said as Paul squeezed with both hands, his long fingers caressing the soft crease where leg met butt. Way more gently than he wanted to, he bit at the curve of Paul's neck and was rewarded with a shudder and the lurching of Paul's cock.

There careful exploration of each other's bodies was rudely interrupted by a deafening, shrill beep. Before Robbie could even ask what it was, a loud recorded voice announced that a fire emergency had been reported in the building and that everyone should proceed to the nearest fire exit and evacuate the building.

"Are you fucking kidding me?" Paul groaned, throwing his hands in the air. "Is the whole damn world trying to cock block me?"

Robbie jumped off the bed and threw Paul's shirt at him. "Get dressed. Try to look less like you've been, well, doing what we were doing."

"Damn it," Paul said, jumping into his pants while looking for his shoes at the same time. He grabbed their overcoats while Robbie grabbed their messenger bags. They might be outside for a while, and the Chicago weather in early December was no joke.

The shrieking continued until Robbie thought it would drive him mad. Out in the hallway, it was even worse with flashing lights and the rest of his teammates streaming out in various stages of undress.

"Think it's real?" he asked Jake. Luckily for him, he had on some cozy looking sweatpants and a sweatshirt under his overcoat.

"Could be. Hope not," he added.

"Me, too."

Jake pushed open the fire door, and they started down the stairs.

It turned out to be a false alarm, but by the time the hotel got everything sorted out and let guests back into the building, they were barely able to grab their stuff and get to the arena before the start of the game.

At least they won the game, even if going directly to the airport afterward, flying to Detroit and checking into another hotel left them too exhausted to do anything but collapse into bed at the end of the evening.

What the hell, Paul complained. He was young, in top shape, and horny as hell. You'd think he'd be able to stay awake long enough to get his hands on Robbie. But no.

They won the game against the Red Wings, too. That seemed like a good thing to Paul until they got back to the hotel, and Robbie dropped a bomb on him.

15

PAUL—YOU'RE MAKING IT SO EASY TO THROW MYSELF AWAY

"What do you mean we can't come?" Paul's head thudded back against the door Robbie had pushed him against the minute they were in the room.

He couldn't process what Robbie was saying. Seemed to him like they'd been well on their way to orgasm-city a second ago. Paul was more than ready. This was the first chance they'd had to do more than make out since the night before when they'd had a spectacular and unexpected win against the Red Wings.

"Look," Robbie said reasonably as if Paul could be anything approaching reasonable with Robbie's hand on his dick. The bastard was brushing his fingers over Paul's balls even as he explained why no one —no one in *this* room anyway—was going to get off.

"We won last night, right?"

"Yeah? And?"

"And the night before?"

"Yeah?"

"Well, we keep getting interrupted before we can, ah, finish. And it's making you all frustrated and on edge."

"Damn right, I am." Between the exhausting travel schedule, the constant presence of their teammates, and stupid fire alarms, they hadn't been able to do more than share a few quick, unsatisfying, groping sessions despite having a hotel room all to themselves.

Now they were finally in the room alone after escaping from the celebration down at the hotel bar. They had the day off tomorrow, and Paul's plan had been to get into bed and stay there as long as they could before someone inevitably came looking for them.

Privacy on the road was a rare commodity. And now they were going to waste it by *not* having sex?

Robbie leaned in, his breath ghosting over Paul's neck. He pressed his tongue against the pulse there, and Paul shivered. He didn't know why, but that weakened his knees every time. "Shit," he whispered.

"You were on fire out there. We were awesome together."

Grabbing a handful of his soft hair, Paul pulled Robbie's head up. "Yeah, we were." He flipped them, putting Robbie's back against the door and kissing the breath out of him until Robbie was whimpering and trying to push Paul off.

"Wait, wait," he said, hands flat on Paul's chest.

"What?" Paul asked with a pained sigh, rolling his forehead across Robbie's.

"I think," he said through deep breaths, "I think that all this sexual frustration is why we were so good."

Paul was sexually frustrated all right. Robbie looked half-wrecked. Eyes bright and unfocused, cheeks flushed, and lips swollen and pink. His jacket lay on the floor at their feet, his tie hung loosely around his neck, and his cock made a huge tent in his impeccably-tailored suit pants.

"But I haven't even gotten to touch your dick yet," he said, defeat in his voice. They'd gone further in a couple of hours back in Minnesota than they had in the four days since they'd started this thing.

Robbie pulled Paul's hand to him, pressing it against his cock. "You will. I promise. You can touch it right now. But you can't come, and you can't make me come."

Paul closed his eyes and took his hand back, pinching the bridge of his nose. He knew what Robbie was thinking now. "Until we lose, right?"

"Yeah," Robbie said.

"I'll throw the next game then," he said as Robbie grabbed him by the lapels of his jacket that he miraculously still wore.

"You won't," Robbie said smugly, pushing Paul's jacket down his arms.

"Fuck you."

"Not until we lose."

"Fucking superstitious hockey players," Paul cursed.

"Do you want to risk it?" Robbie asked. "How would you feel if I dropped to my knees right now and sucked your brains out through your dick, and then we lost?"

Paul knew then that he wasn't going to come tonight. "I hate you."

"We can do anything you want," Robbie said breathlessly. "Except that." There was an almost feral look in his eyes, and his hands were clenched at his sides.

"Oh, my God," Paul exclaimed. "You love this. You're getting off on not getting off."

Robbie's blush and the challenge in his eyes were all the answer Paul needed.

Paul shook his head. "I can't tell if that makes you a sadist, a masochist, or both," he said, impressed despite his frustration. He was beginning to see the appeal of Robbie's plan.

Robbie pushed himself off the door. Paul took a step back at the look in his eyes. "Now what would a nice boy such as you know about either of those things?"

"Enough." Granted, ninety-five percent of all of Paul's sexual knowledge was theoretical. But he had a feeling he was about to get some more hands-on experience.

Five minutes later, they were lying face to face on the bed, still mostly dressed. Screw the suits, tomorrow was a day off; they had time enough to get them dry-cleaned.

Paul had finally gotten his hand on Robbie's cock. He'd almost come when he'd carefully peeled back the sides of Robbie's fly and lowered his underwear carefully over the head. "We're getting you some decent underwear," he muttered in a desperate effort to distract himself from the velvet over steel feel of Robbie's cock against his palm.

He gave an experimental stroke, curving his fingers around the thick width and sliding slowly up from root to tip.

Robbie twitched, almost pulsing against his palm, and made the sexiest sound Paul had ever heard. He had to hear it again. He tightened his fingers, rubbing his thumb across the tip before sliding back down torturously slowly and almost too dry.

"Jesus," Robbie forced out between clenched teeth. "Stop. Stop." He pushed Paul's hand away and threw his arm across his eyes while he struggled to pull back from the brink.

Paul thought the way he looked then would be seared into his brain forever. Spread out on his back, white dress shirt completely unbuttoned and open, his pants unzipped and pushed down his thighs, Robbie was a long line of muscles and skin from the pulse throbbing at the base of his throat, to the hard cock twitching against the dark nest of curls Paul was dying to scratch his nails through.

He didn't think he would ever be over how visceral his reaction was to Robbie's body. In contrast to Paul's sinewy muscles, Robbie's curved under his skin in plush swells. Paul wanted to follow those curves with his hands and mouth, wanted to sink his teeth into Robbie's thick thighs.

If he was completely honest, the intensity of his desire terrified Paul. Deep in his brain, he worried that it couldn't be normal to physically want somebody this much. The things he wanted to do and have done to him went so far beyond what he'd been taught was natural.

"Okay," Robbie said, sending Paul's fear scattering back to the depth of his mind. "Okay." He sat up and pulled off his shirt, tossing it to the floor. Lifting his hips, he tugged his pants off as well, then sat up and turned to Paul.

Paul's mouth was dry as a desert, and his heart slammed against his chest as Robbie slowly unbuttoned his shirt. He gasped when Robbie slipped his thumb under the cuffs as he undid them, gently caressing the thin skin there.

Fuck.

Paul shrugged the shirt to the carpet, so keyed up that the feel of the cloth sliding over his skin raised goose bumps on his arms.

Keeping his eyes locked on Paul and watching for any sign of hesitation, Robbie tugged him up to stand between his legs. With a kiss to his bare stomach, he flicked his tongue against Paul's navel in a move that had Paul grasping onto his shoulders for support.

"Fuck," Paul said out loud this time. Naively, he'd thought that the only touch that mattered was a hand or a mouth directly on his dick. Robbie had turned his entire body into one big erogenous zone. He couldn't imagine anywhere Robbie could touch him that wouldn't feel amazing.

"This okay?" Robbie asked with a hand on his belt.

Paul nodded, not trusting his voice.

By the time Robbie tapped on his knee like he was a show horse to get him to step out of his pants, Paul was trembling from head to toe. There was a wide damp spot where his cock strained against the black cotton of his boxers. He couldn't remember ever being so hard.

Robbie's eyes zeroed in on the hard length, and he licked his lips.

When he reached for the elastic waistband, Paul stopped him with a hand on his wrist. "I can't. I won't be able to..." Just thinking about it had Paul trembling.

"Do you want to stop?" Robbie asked. "We absolutely can. I only want you to feel good. Do you feel good?"

Paul exhaled a shaky breath. "Way too fucking good."

"Do you want me to stop?" Robbie asked again.

He was torn between running away and asking Robbie to keep touching him forever. "Maybe you could just kiss me?"

"I would love that," Robbie said with a smile. Taking Paul by the hand, he tugged him down until he was on his back on the bed.

He crawled over Paul, trapping him in a cage of arms and legs, then leaned to press almost chaste kisses against Paul's lips. Connected only by their mouths, Paul's breathing smoothed out, and his heart stopped beating against his chest so hard.

That was good. Paul could handle that, as long as their bodies didn't touch.

Then Robbie shifted his weight onto one hand and flick his tongue across Paul's nipple.

"Oh, shit," Paul cried as the feeling went straight to his cock.

"No one ever done that to you before?" Robbie asked with a grin.

Paul held onto the arm Robbie had planted on the bed, loving the feel of the hard muscles under his hand. "There's a lot of things no one's ever done to me," he admitted. "Do it again."

Robbie did. Alternating sides and continuing his maddening kisses and nips at Paul's lips until he arched off the bed with a yell and had to clamp a hand over his dick to stop from coming.

Holy fucking shit.

Robbie fell sideways onto the bed, pressing the heel of his hand painfully against his cock. "We'd better win this fucking game," he said, voice rough.

Personally, Paul had never wanted to lose a game so badly in his life. Rolling silently out of bed, overwhelmed with feeling, he almost ran into the bathroom.

As he let the cold water sluice over his overheated body, he marveled again over how not coming with Robbie was a thousand times better than any orgasm he'd had with the few women he'd slept with.

This thing with Robbie was starting to feel like an addiction, like an obsession. And it wasn't just the sex. They'd spent almost every minute, waking and sleeping, together the last few days, and Paul still wanted more.

Shutting off the water, Paul dried off, then eying his dirty underwear with distaste, wrapped a towel around his waist and went out.

He pulled his last clean pair of underwear out of his suitcase and slipped them up under the towel. With a smile for Robbie, he sat on the other bed, facing him. "Shower's free," he said inanely. As if there was a line of people waiting to use it.

"You gonna sleep over there tonight?" Robbie asked.

Paul rubbed his palms across the cloud-soft duvet. "If you want me not to jinx us, I'd better."

He wasn't lying. If he slept next to Robbie, he'd probably end up humping him in his sleep; he was that frustrated. He just needed a little space, get his thoughts in order. He wished he had someone to talk to about what they were doing, but he couldn't think of one single person on the planet who could help.

Luckily, Robbie didn't call him on his excuse. He laughed sweetly. "I know what you mean. You're so freaking sexy; it's hard enough keeping my hands off you in public. I don't think I would last long with you in my bed." With a groan, he rolled gracefully out of bed. "I think I will take that shower. Want me to turn the light out?"

"Yeah, that would be nice. Thanks. Oh, and I guess we have to do some clothes shopping tomorrow."

"Or we could do the laundry," Robbie said dryly.

Paul scoffed. "We'll let the hotel do that. But I'm going to get you out of that horrible underwear one way or the other."

"I'll take them off right now if you want." Robbie hooked his fingers in the waistband. "Say the word."

Paul's brain might have been conflicted, but his body knew exactly what it wanted. His cock twitched at the promise of seeing Robbie completely naked. Paul stifled a moan. "The word is I hate you. Go away. You're a bad man, Rhodes."

Robbie laughed out loud, and then shut off the room light. "Night, Paul."

"Night, Robbie." Despite his expectation that the confusion, fear, and desire swirling in his brain would keep him awake all night, Paul fell asleep to the sound of the water running in the shower.

16

ROBBIE—I WANT TO SCREAM I LOVE YOU FROM THE TOP OF MY LUNGS

Robbie approached the giant Twelve Oaks shopping mall the way he imagined most people approach a trip to the dentist. Hockey players got used to the dentist real quick. Arms crossed, he frowned up at the marble and glass Mecca of consumerism.

Paul paid the Lyft driver and pushed Robbie forward with a hand in the middle of his back. "C'mon, Mr. Crankypants. It will be fun."

This close to Christmas, the mall was packed. People streamed around Paul and Robbie's bodies like water around a rock. The whole place was decorated with a tasteful ostentation that somehow implied Christmas without specifically identifying which light-and-poinsettia-filled winter holiday they were celebrating. Soothing instrumental versions of Christmas music floated across the parking lot.

It was the last place on earth Robbie wanted to spend one of his very rare days off. He almost begged off, but when he turned to Paul, he knew he wasn't going to.

Paul looked like a kid in a candy shop. Or a teen at a mall at Christmas.

Robbie sighed. Entering the mall somehow felt like he was betraying everything his parents had taught him. And that they would know the minute his foot touched the faux marble floor and sense a disturbance in the fair trade shopping force. "Okay, okay. I'll go. But you have to lead."

Immediately, the visual and audio assault on his senses overwhelmed Robbie. And the heat. It had to be fifty degrees warmer inside than out. He clawed his way out of his wool overcoat like it was suffocating him, almost elbowing a child in the face as he did.

Paul removed his coat with much more grace.

"How big is this place?" Robbie asked, staring at the high ceilings and store-lined hallways that seemed to stretch out to the horizon.

"Never been in a mall this big?" Paul asked as he navigated them through the crowd, threading his way through the people like he was on the ice.

"Never been in a mall, period."

Paul stopped walking. "Never been in a mall? Where do you get clothes from?"

Robbie shrugged. "Target? Thrift store? I don't know. I have some places online I shop when I need something new."

Paul shook his head as if he'd never heard of anything so strange in his life. "Did you grow up on a commune or something like that?"

Kind of, Robbie realized, but he wasn't getting into that right now.

"I grew up outside of Cleveland, thank you very much. I just didn't go to malls. Besides," he continued defensively, "it's not like we need a whole lot of clothes. I mean, we spend half our life either in hockey uniforms, workout clothes, or a suit."

Rationally, he knew Paul was only teasing him for what Paul took as a lack of opportunity, not an aversion to malls. But, still, he couldn't help feeling attacked. More than once in college he'd had to defend his unwillingness to give his money to corporations with what he felt were deplorable business practices.

Granted, it was easier to find fair trade coffee in Oberlin than in Northern Minnesota, but it wasn't that much more work if you knew where to look.

He wasn't some social justice warrior, despite what they'd called him. He just had a conscience, okay? He couldn't enjoy something he knew someone else had suffered to produce.

Paul ignored his prickly defensiveness and rolled his eyes. "No matter what you're wearing, you need underwear. And that's what we're here for. The whole team is tired of your K-Mart specials," Paul said firmly as if he had won an argument. He strode confidently into the crowd towards a destination only he knew.

"Like I'd shop at K-Mart," he called at Paul's back.

As Robbie kept an eye on Paul's blond hair bobbing above the crowd, Paul must have realized Robbie wasn't following him. He stopped, ran his hand through his hair and turned back to where Robbie still stood.

His eyes crinkled and he smiled wide as he caught Robbie's eye.

He looked so adorable and sexy with his sparkling eyes, wide, white smile and his biceps straining the sleeves of his Seattle Thunder branded T-shirt that Robbie couldn't resist smiling back.

Robbie noticed more than one head turn to see who Paul was looking at like that. He's with me, he wanted to say. He wanted to go up to Paul and plant a big wet one right on his mouth and see how the shoppers would react.

Unfortunately, knowing how Paul would react kept him from doing it. He suddenly had a lot more understanding of how Drew must have felt when they were dating. Robbie didn't hide his relationship from his teammates and friends, but as Paul had rightly pointed out, it wasn't like he was leading Pride parades in his uniform or anything.

"Come on," Paul said, coaxing Robbie forward with a curl of his fingers like he was teaching a baby to walk. "You can do it. One step at a time."

"Jerk," Robbie said with a grin as he closed the distance between them.

When he was close enough, Paul grabbed his arm and pulled him into a one-armed side hug. "It will be fun. And if you're really good,

I'll buy you an ice cream afterward. Okay, little buddy?" has asked, knuckling Robbie's head.

Robbie swatted his hand away and twisted out of the hug. "You'll buy me dinner. And maybe a movie."

"It's a date," Paul said, waggling his eyebrows.

It kind of was. Which made Robbie wonder. "Are you sure you'll be okay with that? With us hanging out like this in public?"

Paul's guilty look confirmed Robbie's suspicious. Paul wasn't as okay with it as he wanted to be.

"I think we'll be okay. No one knows us here," Paul said, the light in his eyes dimming.

Robbie felt like a jerk for bringing it up. Paul was so different in private, so enthusiastic, it was easy for Robbie to forget how new it all was to him. Closeted, Robbie reminded himself ruefully. What went on behind closed doors was one thing. In public, he was a straight boy.

Damn it. But it wasn't forever, Robbie told himself. Eventually, Paul would realize how ridiculous he was being, and that no one cared.

Except maybe the fans. And the press.

Fuck. Stupid. The whole homophobia thing was ridiculous. Robbie put the blame directly on people like Paul's father and the church leaders who were telling them how evil gay people were. Why couldn't they just live and let live?

"You okay?" Paul asked.

Fuck *them*, Robbie thought. Whoever they were. He wasn't going to let *them* ruin his first day out with Paul.

"I'm great," he said with a big smile. "And I'm at your mercy. Teach me your bourgeois ways."

"Ooh, big words. Sexy. Keep that up, and I might buy you popcorn, too."

Paul kept up a stream of talk as they walked through the mall.

Robbie half-listened, making what he hoped were appropriate responses but mostly enjoying the way Paul's southern accent rose and fell almost like a song as he spoke.

He knew Paul was a little self-conscious of it and tried to suppress it as much as could. But when he was excited or tired or stressed, the accent came out. He couldn't wait to hear Paul whispering dirty things in his ear with that soft drawl.

So far, Paul wasn't much of a talker in bed. Robbie would work on it. He counted the people checking Paul out as he imagined how Paul would sound saying some pretty specific things.

He'd counted six women, two teenaged girls, and five guys, and worked himself up into a bit of a state by the time Paul stopped in front of Nordstrom's.

"That okay?" he asked Robbie.

"Huh?" Robbie blinked at the store and tried to remember what Paul had been talking about.

Paul's eyes dragged down his body, stopping on the bulge in his jeans that was a little larger than normal. "Distracted?" he asked with the lift of an eyebrow. He crossed his arms over his chest, flexing as he did.

Oh, damn, he must have caught on to Robbie's mild obsession with his arms. Two could play at that game. Robbie stepped close enough to whisper in Paul's ear. "I was remembering how that accent sounded when you begged me to let you come."

Paul stepped back, mouth open in shock and admiration. "You are a right bastard, Robbie Rhodes." He stuck a hand in his jeans pocket, discreetly adjusting himself.

"Only until we lose," he promised.

"I'm gonna make you pay for that," Paul threatened.

Robbie couldn't wait.

17

ROBBIE—BUT I'M AFRAID SOMEONE ELSE WILL HEAR ME

Buying underwear at Nordstrom's was nothing like buying underwear at Target. There, Robbie's biggest problem was packages hung on the wrong hook, and he certainly never tried them on.

"You can't try on underwear," he hissed at Paul who was flipping through the tables of various types of briefs laid out like an underwear buffet. Robbie shuddered to think how much they cost.

"This is the kind I like," Paul said, holding up a dark green pair. "Tommy Johns." He read from the label. "They have a no wedgie guarantee. That sound nice, but I don't think they've ever been in a locker room. Ooh, a 'contour pouch that nestles the boys.' My boys like being nestled, that's for sure."

Robbie flipped the tag towards him to read the price. "What? Thirty-four dollars for one pair of underpants?"

A few heads turned towards them.

Paul moved so they stood side by side at the display. "You like the way they look on me?" he asked in a low voice, eyes on the table in front of them.

"Yeah. A lot."

"Well, I would like to see you in these, okay? Anyway," he said a little louder. "It's not like you can't afford them."

Robbie made a frustrated sound.

"What?" Paul asked, turning to face Robbie. "What is your problem with spending some of your extremely hard-earned money on something nice for yourself? It's not a Ferrari. It's underwear. Something you have to have anyway and something you wear every day."

"I know. It's just –" Robbie picked up the tag of another pair on the table that was even more expensive than the first pair. He flinched, but his hand lingered on the cloud-like material, betraying him. As usual, what his body wanted and what his conscience told him was right were at odds.

He slid his fingers deeper into the neatly stacked pile of briefs. They did feel awfully soft.

He searched for a way to explain his hesitancy without sounding like a douchebag or like he was judging Paul for the way he lived. Because he wasn't. Really. He didn't expect everyone to have the same standards.

Paul noticed Robbie fondling the underwear, and sensing potential capitulation, pressed his argument. "It's thirty-four dollars, dude." He held the briefs up by the waistband, waving them like a flag. "Say this pair lasts a year and you wear it once a week. That's less than a dollar a day for the ability to cradle your ass and the boys in some comfort and style. I think you can swing it. Hell, go crazy, get seven, one for each day of the week and it still wouldn't make a dent."

Robbie sighed. "It's not just the cost and the fact that it makes me feel kind of pretentious to buy fancy underwear. I worry that with every pair of these I buy, I'm consigning another eight-year-old Vietnamese kid to a short life of drudgery in a sweatshop."

Paul blinked at him. "You are ree-fucking-diculous. That's the first place your mind goes? For the record, you have no idea where these are made." He rolled his eyes. "Secondly, who do you think makes those Fruit of the Loom specials you've been wearing?"

"I know. I know, okay." Robbie rubbed his head. This is why he didn't shop. It was exhausting, with ethical pitfalls everywhere he looked. Sometimes he felt like he could grow his own cotton and weave his own clothing and still feel bad that he had used the wrong dye or something.

Sometimes a person just wanted some nice underwear. Was that a crime?

Paul twirled the shorts around his finger. "Maybe this will help. I refuse to look at or touch those tighty-whities anymore. You either –"

"Excuse me, gentlemen," a voice called from behind Robbie.

A salesman, Todd according to his name tag, smiled at them. "I couldn't help but overhear your conversation."

A good-looking thirty-something guy in a subdued but classy suit and a strong gay vibe, Todd's smile made it clear that he had overheard everything, even the sentence Paul had left unfinished.

Robbie hoped Paul didn't pick up on that. If Paul realized people were assuming they were a couple, their quasi-date would definitely be over.

"I think I can help," Todd said. "I'll be right back."

He came back with an armful of different cuts and colors of underwear. He also had a few pairs of what looked like pajama pants and some T-shirts.

"All of these brands are made within ethical guidelines. See?" He showed Robbie the tag.

The tiny words swam in front of Robbie's eyes. Shaking his head, he handed the briefs and the attached tag to Paul.

"'Independent, objective, non-profit team of global social compliance experts,'" Paul read out loud. "'Safe, lawful, humane, and ethical manufacturing.'"

That did make him feel a little better. "Thanks, Todd. I know it's kind of obnoxious."

Todd shook his head. "Not at all. It's a valid concern, and I'm here to address all your concerns. Would you like me to set up a dressing room for you?"

Robbie paused and put down the underpants he had been fondling, looking at it in a new, much less pleasant, light. Had somebody else tried this exact pair on? "You can try on underwear?"

"Yes," Todd said, lips tight as he fought a smile. "Over your current attire, of course."

"Of course," Robbie echoed.

"Take your time, look around some more," Todd told him. "I'll set up a dressing room, and then I'll be back."

"I think what you have is more than enough." More than enough. There was no way he was going to buy all that.

Todd didn't blink an eye when Paul followed him into the dressing room. He simple asked them if he could get them coffee, tea, or something else perhaps. The whole thing made Robbie uncomfortable.

"Really, no, thank you. I know you must be busy with Christmas stuff. I'll be fine." Being waited on like this was excruciating. He just wanted the nice man to go away now.

He shut the door with a sigh. Unsurprisingly, the dressing room was the biggest one he'd ever been in. He hated that there was a small part of him that didn't hate it.

Paul made himself comfortable on the small, padded bench along one side of the small room while Robbie kicked off his shoes and took off his jeans.

Paul wrinkled his nose.

"Yeah, I know you hate them. The whole world knows." He picked a random pair off the pile Todd had set up neatly on a table in the corner. "Some people like them, you know. Like, really like them. As in 'I have a folder of pictures of guys in white briefs on my computer' like them."

"Are you doing this for me?" Paul asked.

Something in his voice made Robbie pause with the new underwear halfway up his leg.

Paul looked a little shell-shocked, and a lot turned on. He liked that idea a lot apparently.

"Well, yeah." Hadn't the whole thing been Paul's idea? Robbie wasn't the one offended by his normal underwear.

"You hated the other ones. I mean..." He broke off, blushing. Now that he thought about it, it did seem like a pretty intimate thing to be doing for someone he had just started whatever it was they were doing.

He wasn't just buying a specific type of underwear because Paul said he wanted to see Robbie in them, he was trying them on in front of him. In front of a guy he'd only really known for four days.

Sure, he'd changed in front of Paul plenty of times already, but the locker room didn't count. Hell, his grandmother could walk into the locker room, and he'd probably keep changing.

"You're making me nervous now," he said to Paul, yanking the boxer briefs up all the way.

"Do you want me to leave?"

"No. You might as well just sit there and perv on me since it just hit me that's the whole reason we're here." His cock thickened at the thought. Even two pairs of underpants couldn't hide it.

"So, do I get to vote on what I like?" Paul asked, fingers wrapping and unwrapping around the ends of the bench.

"Yeah, sure." Robbie frowned. "This is stupid. I can't tell how these feel over my old ones."

"Try them on with nothing underneath," Paul said.

"I can't do that!"

Paul rolled his eyes. "If you don't like them, I promise I will buy them. They're my size, too."

"Fine," Robbie said grudgingly. He pushed both pairs off at the same time, feeling awkward standing there in a nothing but a T-shirt.

The whole thing felt kind of slutty. He liked it. In the mirror, he saw Paul behind him, staring at him with a mixture of desire and what almost looked like fear. He'd caught that look in Paul's eyes before. It was gone before he could analyze it.

Paul caught his eye in the mirror as he separated the briefs. His expression spelled trouble for Robbie. Good trouble.

With a grin, Paul reached out and ran his hand over Robbie's naked ass.

"Don't —" Robbie started to say but was cut off by Todd's voice calling from right outside the door.

"Everything okay in there, boys?"

Cut it out, Robbie signed

"Just great, Todd," Paul called out. "Y'all wouldn't happen to have any bottled water, would you?"

"You can't ask that," Robbie whispered, insulted on Todd's behalf. "He's not your servant."

"Of course," Todd replied. "Still or sparkling?"

"Still for me, please. Robbie?" Paul ran his hands around the front of Robbie's thighs, light dragging his palms across the soft hair.

Not helping, Robbie signed to Paul even as he answered the question. "Nothing, thank you." Robbie hoped his voice didn't sound too strangled. His dick had noticed how close Paul's fingers were to it.

It was hard to hear Todd's footsteps over the plush carpeting, but they both held their breath until it felt like he must be gone.

"Cut it out," Robbie said as Paul pulled him in closer.

"Don't want to." His hands caressed Robbie from knees to hips, scratching through his pubic curls, around the curve of his ass, and along the crease of his thighs.

Paul dug his fingers hard into the tops of Robbie's thighs. "You have the sexiest fucking legs." He leaned forward and pushed the T-shirt up so he could kiss the small of Robbie's back.

"Gargh," Robbie said less-than-intelligently, yanking himself out of Paul's grasp. "So not helping," he said, pointing to his rapidly growing cock.

"Oh, it's helping me." He reached down and swooped the silky dark-green boxers off the floor and threw them at Robbie. "Try these on now," he said voice low and eyes dark with lust.

God, Robbie felt like he'd been at least half-aroused forever. Watching Paul squirm on the hard bench only fueled the fire. Maybe Paul was right. Maybe he was a sadist and a masochist combined because he loved this game they were playing.

Turning to face Paul fully, Robbie made a show of bending down and slowly stepping into the expensive boxer briefs. He pulled them up just as slowly in a kind of reverse strip-tease.

The feel of the material against his skin distracted him from his evil plan. "Oh, my God," he sighed as the pants settled like a silken hug around his hips. The front pouch did, in fact, cradle his junk perfectly.

These were the best things he'd ever had against his skin.

Paul's expression was deservedly smug. "See?" He stood up and crowded into Robbie's space. "Just let me..." He stuck his hand down the front of Robbie's underwear and adjusted his package.

He pulled back far enough to get a look at his handiwork. "Fuck," he said reverently. "Turn around. Shii-it." He dragged the word out long and sweet.

"Hey, boys. I'm back. And I got some snacks, too. Just in case. You still doing okay?"

Paul opened the door, making sure Robbie wasn't visible. "Thanks, dude. And yeah, we're definitely taking those green ones. Can we get one pair in every color you have?"

Todd smiled and handed him two water bottles. "I brought one up for your friend, too, just in case he needed something to cool him off," he said, voice laden with innuendo.

"Thanks, Todd," Robbie called from behind the door.

They tried on a few different styles, the groping escalating rapidly until Robbie found himself completely naked and pushed up against a wall with a fully-clothed Paul plastered against him.

That was easily the sluttiest thing Robbie had ever done, and he'd never been so turned on in his life. He was so hard it hurt, and somehow the hurting turned him on more.

"Jesus, stop," Robbie panted, pushing Paul away as far as he could without unclenching his fingers from Paul's shirt. "I'm gonna come if you don't stop."

"Fuck. Me, too." Paul looked as wrecked as Robbie felt. "Is it just me, or does it make it hotter knowing we can't?"

"It's not just you." Robbie forced his fingers to let go of Paul's shirt.

"Now go sit down and don't move or Todd's going to get an eyeful of something I'm sure he'd pay money to see."

"I'll be good," Paul promised. On the bench, he sat on his hands to show how good he would be. It didn't last.

After a thorough hands-on inspection that left them both hard and panting, Paul declared the boxer briefs that extended a few inches down Robbie's thighs the winners.

Robbie ended up getting seven pairs of them, some matching T-shirts, and a pair of bamboo lounge pants that were so soft he wanted to live in them.

He blanched at the price as he signed the credit slip.

Paul noticed. "I think I know something that would make you feel better," he said as they wandered back into the main mall.

"What?" Robbie could practically feel his parents' withering glares if they ever found out he had spent a couple of hundred dollars on underwear and pajamas.

"Come here." Paul let them to a gigantic Christmas tree at the intersection of two corridors. It had to be ten feet tall.

As he got closer, Robbie could see index cards hanging from the branches. A sign read "Adopt a Family for Christmas." Several people were glancing through the cards, making sure to check out the ones near the top and the ones on the bottom as well as the more easily accessible ones near the middle of the tree.

"Pick a card, any card," Paul said. "It's something my church does every year. Families in need fill out these cards, and people can pick one or more and play Santa. It's one of my favorite things."

He reached through a couple of cards before picking two. "I like to get ones with the teenagers because I feel like they get overlooked. It's easier and more flashy to buy toys for the little ones, but I hate thinking of some kid who just wants a decent coat so he can be warm on his way to school getting shortchanged because he's not cute anymore."

He turned to hand one to Robbie but stopped at the look on Robbie's face. "Or not. I mean, you don't have to. I'm gonna, but if it's not your thing."

"I want to kiss you so badly right now," he said, keeping his voice low.

Paul blushed to the tops of his ears. "It's no big deal. Just thought you could spend the same amount here. Kind of balance the scales, ease your conscience."

Robbie gave in to his heart, and pulled Paul in for a hard hug. The bags and coats they carried made it awkward, but Robbie didn't care. From the way Paul hugged him back, he didn't care either.

"You're a good man," Robbie said when the hug ended. He turned to the tree and started looking for two families of his own. It wasn't much, but it felt good to think of making Christmas happier for a few people anyway.

"What about the people on the top?" he asked, tilting his head to look up the tree.

A young woman in an Adopt a Family T-shirt answered him. "We make sure they get rotated down. We do it a few times a day."

"That's great," Robbie said. She was someone who was making a difference. He bet she did more than play sports for a living.

After a few minutes of thoughtful perusal, he settled on a single mom with three kids, all in a STEM magnet school, and the family of a veteran who only asked for supplies for their service dog. They would get that and presents for the kids and the parents as well.

Tears pricked at Robbie's eyelids. Tears of gratitude for the amazing life he'd had, of sorrow for all the struggling families, and a little for how much Paul's thoughtfulness had touched him. He knew Robbie was struggling with the spending and he'd found a way to help Robbie and other people at the same time.

He was a good man. It was eons too early to be thinking like this, but he couldn't help but wonder if Paul could be someone worth facing the public for.

He was starting to think Drew had been right when he'd accused Robbie of not loving him enough.

Pushing those thoughts away, he gave Paul another quick hug. "Let's go shopping!"

18

PAUL—THIS NIGHT FEELS BRAND NEW

They lost to the Calgary Flames in their first home game after the trip. Jet-lag and exhaustion from their travels were part of it, but so was the fact that the Flames had been major dicks.

Despite historically racking up a low number of penalty minutes per game, the Thunder had given almost as good as they'd gotten tonight. Paul himself had ended up spending four minutes in the penalty box.

Two of them he'd served for Sergei after the usually unflappable goalie had been driven to slashing at the royal-dickwad of a forward who'd been screening him hard the whole game.

When the guy actually turned his back on the play to face Sergei, chirping major crap at him, Sergei had cracked. He took the jerk down with one quick swing of his stick. Paul had taken that penalty gladly. Luckily, the ref had ruled on the Flames' forward with the Avery rule, so there wasn't a power play to burn.

Paul had earned his second two-minutes. He was lucky it hadn't been a double-minor.

Both teams had been fighting hard for possession during a four-minute stretch with three line changes. Robbie picked the puck right from the Flames' right wing's stick and sent it sliding over to Paul's tape. Then the winger slammed Robbie so hard into the boards,he dropped to the ice like a fallen tree. His helmet popped off, rolling down the rink.

Paul's gloves were on the ice, and he was on that guy in a hot second. The few hits he got in before getting pulled off the guy were very satisfying.

After a quick concussion check, Robbie was back on the ice more on fire than he'd been before the hit. But, just to be on the safe side, Paul kept a hard eye on anyone who looked like they might be targeting Robbie.

Ultimately, they lost. Even though they'd won the three on the road, the mood in the locker room after the game was pretty low. Thank goodness they had two days off in a row next. Everyone needed some rest, a couple of massages, and time to regroup.

It was only December, and they had more than fifty games left to play in the regular season. Then, if they were lucky enough, there would be playoffs. Everything already hurt, and he was young. He couldn't imagine how older guys like Jake must feel.

Shitty players and bad calls aside, Paul had never been so happy to lose a game in his life. If he didn't get to come soon, he might just have a spontaneous orgasm the next time he rolled over in bed. He was ready to jump Robbie in the locker room.

The normal post-game ritual lasted forever with Paul second-guessing his behavior around the team the entire time. Was he being too obvious around Robbie? Was he being too standoffish? Or just being weird in general? Probably the last one.

He finally broke out of the stadium, heading for the parking lot. Robbie met him there, grabbing him around the neck and pulling him down in a move somewhere between hugging and wrestling. "Hey, dude."

Like that's all they were. Just bros hanging out. But Paul had seen the look in Robbie's eyes when he pulled on those soft green boxer briefs.

"Hey, look who got some grownup underwear," Jake had commented because of course he did. Nothing was sacred.

"Yeah, yeah," Robbie answered with an eye roll. "I got tired of hearing Dyson bitching about it."

Paul threw a rolled-up towel at him. "You try sharing a room with those things for five nights."

Robbie had glared at him, but then made a point of walking slowly across the room under the pretense of getting something off the snack table. Jerk.

"Did you walk or drive here?" Paul asked. They hadn't discussed what, if anything, was going to happen tonight, but Robbie's place was way closer than his. The last thing he wanted to do was drive across Seattle right now.

"I walked."

"Want a ride home?" That was a safe question, right? If anyone overheard, they wouldn't think anything. And he wasn't making any assumptions about what would happen when they got to Robbie's place. Except for the way he totally was.

"Yeah, sure." Robbie lowered his voice. "You're coming up, right?"

Paul grinned and matched Robbie's low tone. "Oh, I'm up. And there had better be coming."

Robbie elbowed him. "Just keep walking."

"Wait." Paul stopped Robbie with a hand on his chest. "What's the parking like at your place?"

"I have a covered spot in the lot. Why?"

"How mad would you be if I asked if I could use your spot?" Paul worried his bottom lip. "Or we could go to my apartment."

"What the hell are you driving?"

"Oh, you'll see." Twirling his keys around his finger, he waggled his eyebrows at Robbie.

Robbie shook his head. "Just show me."

The car was covered, but they could make out the shape of it under the tan canvas. Robbie raised his eyebrows but didn't say anything as he helped Paul carefully remove the cover.

He whistled low in appreciate. "Now that is a gorgeous car. I can see why you'd be concerned." He ran his hand appreciatively over the curves of the classic car. "What year is it?"

"Seventy-six."

"Nice." He trailed his fingers over up over the low roofline. "I love the color."

"Are you going to get in it, or just fondle it?"

"I'm getting." He opened the door and slowly lowered himself in.

Paul started the engine, and Robbie grinned at the sound. "Nice, right?" Paul asked.

"Yeah." He laughed, grabbing onto the dashboard as Paul peeled out of the spot much faster than he would have if he were alone.

"Seatbelt!" Robbie yelled, but he was still laughing as he pulled the belt around his shoulder. He looked helplessly for something to attach the clip to.

Stopping at the top of the exit ramp, Paul wedged his hand under Robbie's butt and dug the waist belt out from the crack in the seat. Robbie wiggling against his hand didn't make it any easier.

Robbie quickly figured out the belts and stretched his legs out as best he could. "Not very practical, is it?"

"Not even a little bit," Paul said with a big grin. He eased the Stingray onto the road. Too late to be going out, too early to be going in, the traffic was as light as it ever got.

Robbie looked up at the ceiling. "Is it a convertible?"

"T-top," Paul answered, tapping on the ceiling. Dang, he loved this car.

Robbie stared out the side window as they sedately cruised the side streets to his apartment. "Seems a shame to have to go slow."

"Tell me about it," Paul agreed. "I haven't taken her out in a while. Not since I drove her here from Bakersfield."

"Turn here," Robbie instructed, then realized what Paul said. "You drove this tiny car here? Where did you fit your stuff?"

Paul laughed. "Now you know why I don't have any clothes."

He looked around the cramped interior, then at Paul. He grinned. "Totally worth it."

"So worth it." Paul shifted into second as they approached

Robbie's driveway. "You want to take her up into the mountains tomorrow?"

Robbie grinned like a little kid on Christmas morning. "Hell, yeah."

"Then go move your granny-mobile so the Queen can have a nice, cozy spot. Safe from packs of marauding teenagers and pooping birds."

With a roll of his eyes, Robbie got out of the car.

It took a little patience, but they finally found a spot on the street for the Prius and got the Stingray settled to Paul's approval in the garage.

19

PAUL—IF I LOSE MYSELF TONIGHT

They didn't talk on their way up to the apartment. The way they bumped shoulders in the elevator and the press of Robbie's hand against Paul's lower back said everything Paul needed to know.

Robbie flicked on the light, giving Paul a good look at the apartment. Not that there was much to see. He wasn't there for the tour anyway.

He crowded Robbie deeper into the apartment, not giving him time to do more than drop his overcoat on the back of a kitchen chair as they passed by. Paul tossed his in the general direction of the table. He plastered himself to Robbie's back, herding him to the nearest convenient surface, hands working at loosening Robbie's tie as they walked.

"Eager?" Robbie asked with a laugh even as he yanked his belt off, sliding it through the loops and dropping it to the floor.

"Like you're not," Paul said, reaching down to palm Robbie's rapidly growing package.

Over Robbie's shoulder, Paul saw a piece of furniture he remembered well. "Oh, man, I can't believe you brought that ratty futon with you."

"It's a perfectly good piece of furniture," Robbie explained, shrugging out of his suit jacket. It followed the belt to the floor.

"Oh, it's a classic alright." Paul slid Robbie's tie through the collar of the shirt, nuzzling at his neck as he did.

Robbie grabbed his head to hold him in place and groaned. "Says someone driving a forty-year-old car." Letting go, he turned to face Paul, pushing his jacket off his shoulders.

Paul grabbed his wrists. "Hey, Queenie is a classic. Don't dis my car if you ever want to ride in her again."

Robbie kissed him with a swipe of his tongue across Paul's mouth and a nip to his bottom lip as he pulled away. "I'll apologize to her tomorrow, okay? Buy her a nice air freshener."

"Okay." Paul grabbed Robbie and pulled him in for a deep kiss, keeping them locked together as he walked Robbie backward to the futon.

Robbie went down with an *oof* when the back of his knees hit the edge of the futon.

Paul went down with him, straddling his lap, and wrapping his hands around Robbie's neck. He ran his fingers through Robbie's hair from the nape of his neck up to the top of his head. "Hey."

"Hey," Robbie answered. They were both grinning like fools.

"So, we lost."

"Yes, we did." Robbie started tugging Paul's shirt out from his pants.

"I really, really think we should have sex now. Just in case. Set a new, better, precedent." He leaned back far enough so that he could unbutton Robbie's shirt.

"Oh, you do?"

"Um hm." He really did. He didn't know where this forwardness was coming from, but he bet it had something to do with being teased to within an inch of sanity for the last five days.

Robbie reached his hands under Paul's shirt, sliding his fingers down the back of his pants. "You do know this, us, is a terrible idea for so many reasons?"

"I do. But we're doing it anyway, right?" Paul traced Robbie's jawline with his thumb, grinding his weight down on his legs as desire started to build higher inside him.

"Yeah," Robbie said a little breathlessly. "Yeah."

Paul spread his hand against the back of Robbie's head, pulling him close. Robbie opened to the first touch of Paul's lips against his. He moaned as Paul's tongue pushed into his mouth.

Robbie's hands tightened on Paul's hips, and he pulled Paul down against him, kissing him at the same time as if he were desperate to be inside Paul in any way he could: cock, breath, or tongue.

"You punched someone for me."

"Well, yeah." Paul frowned. "An asshole forward, more specifically." Paul shifted away just a hair. "Was that okay?"

He held his breath as Robbie seemingly pondered the question. Paul tried very hard not to rock against the hardness between his legs.

"It was kind of hot. Like I have my own personal enforcer."

"Just point the way, I'll take anyone down."

Robbie laughed. "My hero."

Robbie pulled Paul down to him, kissing him again in the way they'd perfected over the last few days. It was all hands and mouths and clothes coming off until they were both naked and breathless.

The knowledge that there would be no stopping this time overlay every touch, every kiss. Paul would have bet money that he wouldn't last five minutes naked with Robbie. He'd half-expected to go off as soon as Robbie's hand touched his dick. But maybe all the teasing they had done over the last few days had trained his body to hold back.

Not that Robbie's mouth didn't feel amazing. Robbie had a bit of an oral fixation and a biting kink. Which worked out great for Paul since he'd discovered that he liked being bitten.

They had to be careful not to leave any marks they might have to explain in the locker room. Everyone knew everyone's business a little too well. They knew who'd been on a date, who had a steady sex life, and who didn't.

Paul was stretched out on top of Robbie with Robbie's legs wrapped around him, Robbie's favorite position.

"I love feeling you on me," Robbie said, arching up to feel Paul's weight against him. "We should move this into the bedroom. Some lube would feel amazing right now." He thrust against Paul, demonstrating the sticky stop and slide of their cocks against each other.

Paul rolled off Robbie and held his hand out for him.

"So gallant," Robbie said with a grin, hopping up. He slapped Paul on the ass and hurried past him.

Paul took in the glorious sight in front of him. He loved the deep valley of Robbie's spine nestled between the strong muscles of his back. The two dimples at the top of Robbie's ass seemed perfectly made for Paul's fingertips.

The bed creaked as Robbie threw himself on it, rolling immediately to pull a half-crushed tube of lube out of the nightstand drawer with a triumphant *aha*!

"Come here," Robbie said, sitting on the edge of the bed and beckoning Paul over with the crook of his finger. He squeezed out some lube as Paul walked over to the bed.

When Paul got close enough, Robbie grabbed him by the hip and slid his slicked-up hand down Paul's very erect cock.

"Oh, holy fricken' crap," Paul moaned, thrusting into Robbie's fist. He braced himself on Robbie's shoulders as Robbie leaned in to nip at his stomach.

Robbie's hand felt amazing, and he closed his eyes at the sensation. Way too soon he felt the orgasm he'd been denied for too long building in his balls. "Stop. Shit, Robbie. Stop." He pushed weakly at Robbie's shoulder. "I'm gonna come."

Robbie stopped immediately. "Isn't that the goal?"

"I don't want it to be over so quickly."

Robbie grinned. "Oh, my sweet summer child. This is just round one. To take the edge off."

Oh. That was different.

Robbie laughed at the expression on Paul's face. "You thought we were one and done?" Robbie stroked Paul's cock hard from root to tip. "I have plans for you."

Paul couldn't speak, his cock throbbed against Robbie's palm. He wrenched himself free, groaning as he slipped quickly through Robbie's grasp. "Holy fuck."

He didn't want to come this way. If this whole thing between them went horribly wrong, or if Robbie was some kind of a test from God and Paul was failing, he wanted to fail big. He wanted it all. But how did he ask?

Paul bit his lip, all his assertiveness gone, embarrassed by himself, by his inexperience. He was such an idiot. Just say the words, Paul.

It wasn't like Robbie was going to be disgusted and throw him out. So what exactly did he want? To fuck Robbie? He felt his cheeks flaming pink even for thinking it.

He didn't even know if Robbie did it that way. Didn't some guys only like to be the 'pitcher?' And shouldn't he let Robbie...let him... fuck him? That would be something he couldn't take back. That was no turning back, one hundred percent gay.

He got a hot feeling in his stomach, nervous excitement, a mixture of yearning and fear, and his hole clenched at the thought.

"Paul, you look like you're going to throw up," Robbie said. With his clean hand, he tugged Paul down to sit next to him on the bed. "What's going on in your head?"

He had to say it. "I want to have sex with you."

Robbie looked down to Paul's cock, glistening with lube and still hard despite his mental crisis. "You are having sex with me."

"I mean real sex." He waited for Robbie to make fun of him, to tell him this was all 'real sex.'

It didn't happen. "Are you sure?" Robbie said. "I'm perfectly happy with this. And if I can get my mouth on you even better." He gently rubbed Paul's legs and wherever he could reach. It was comforting even as it kept Paul around and hyper-aware of his body.

"We don't have to."

"I want to. I really want to."

"Why?"

"Why?" Paul asked with a frown.

"Yeah, why?"

"Is there a wrong answer?" Paul asked jokingly.

"Yeah, actually, there is," Robbie said.

"Are you going to tell me what the wrong answer is?"

"Because you think you need to do it to be 'really gay' or someone is pressuring you, or you think you need to prove something to yourself or someone else."

Robbie pushed Paul down onto the bed and lay down on his side next to him. His hands roamed all over Paul's body, from his collarbones to behind his knees. Robbie's fingers caressed all the place he'd learned drove Paul crazy - the hollow of his throat, the pulse points at his wrist, and the inner crook of his elbow.

He leaned up and kissed Paul so passionately that all Paul could do was hang on to Robbie's shoulders and try to remember how to breathe.

Robbie pulled away slowly, smiling, and stroked his palm down Paul's cock.

"Fuck," Paul whimpered as Robbie's hand slipped lower.

"Yes, that is what we were discussing. Now tell me why you want me to ride that big cock of yours."

Paul blushed down to his nipples.

"There's that blush I love. But you do want to, right?" He bit Paul's earlobe.

That was another place on Paul's body that was apparently wired directly to his cock.

"You want to see what my face looks like when you slide into me?" Robbie's warm breath sent shivers down Paul's neck. "Want to hear the sounds you can pound out of me?"

"Sweet baby Jesus," Paul breathed. "I want it because the guys in the videos always make it look like it feels so fucking amazing."

Robbie flopped down onto the bed with a contented sigh. "Now that is an excellent reason. And it can totally feel fucking amazing."

"Do you like it?" Paul turned to face Robbie.

"I love it." His grinned

"Which, um, which way?" Paul couldn't make eye contact.

"Any way you want it, babe," he said salaciously.

Paul laughed.

Robbie ran his hands over Paul's chest. He seemed to know how much his touch calmed Paul. "But I really do want to ride you."

"Yeah? Really?"

"Yeah, you good with that?"

Paul could only nod.

"Okay. Breathe now."

Paul drew in a huge ragged inhale and let it out with an equally ragged laugh. "Show me what to do?"

"For tonight, you just lie there and look pretty."

And that was all he would let Paul do.

At first, Paul was relieved that he didn't have to worry about the mysterious preparation he'd heard was so important for pain-free anal sex.

He had done some research after all; whenever he'd had some privacy. And he hadn't known how he would react to it. For some reason, it seemed dirtier to stick his finger in someone's ass than to stick his dick in the same place.

It was like he could think of dick as something separate from himself. There was a certain detachment he'd always felt during sex. But his hands were part of him. He ate with them, held his stick with them. Would he be turned off? Maybe even grossed out? Would he have to talk himself through it?

By the time Robbie was up on his knees straddling Paul's legs, arm stretched behind him with two fingers buried in his own ass as deep as he could reach, Paul was begging Robbie to let him touch, to let him see.

Robbie's cock strained upward, bouncing with every thrust of his fingers. The look of concentration mixed with pleasure on Robbie's face, and the sighs and curses coming from his mouth were driving Paul crazy.

Robbie slapped Paul's hand away as he reached for Robbie's cock.

"Stop that. Try to touch me again, and I'll tie your hands to the headboard."

He laughed when Paul's cock jerked hard against his stomach at the words. Paul blushed pink, but gave Robbie a sheepish grin, not denying the effect the image Robbie was painting had on him.

"Oh, we are so going to do that. And very, very soon." He pulled his finger out from where he had been stretching himself. "But right now, I need you to hold on."

He placed Paul's hands on his hips while he rolled a condom over Paul's dick and lubed him up.

Paul's hands trembled. This was really happening. He was really going to do this.

Robbie kneeled up a little and reached behind himself to grab Paul and line him up. "Ready?" he asked?

No. Yes. I don't know. "Yes," Paul whispered. "Please."

Robbie kept his eyes locked on Paul's as he pressed down.

Oh, my fucking God, Paul thought as Robbie opened up for him. *Oh, my God.*

"Fuck, Paul," Robbie said, eyes fluttering shut. "You feel so fucking good."

Paul couldn't breathe. The hot, silken crush of Robbie's body forced all the air out of his lungs. He may have forgotten *how* to breathe. His hands slipped down, fingers scrabbling and grabbing at Robbie's strong thighs.

Oh, my fucking God. Holy fuck. Jesus Christ.

Now he knew why people always took the Lord's name in vain during sex. The feeling was that overwhelming. It was a religious experience.

Back in high school and then in the Major Juniors, it had been easy enough not to date. He hadn't felt any burning need to, so he became every girl's safe date. Parents loved him. He was a nice Christian boy who wouldn't take advantage of their daughters.

There had been girls he'd kissed in college; he'd gotten awkward blowjobs from girls that left him unsure of what he was supposed to do afterward.

And he'd had intercourse with women exactly twice.

Neither time had been terrible. He'd been able to do it and have an orgasm, but it hadn't seemed worth the trouble.

It certainly hadn't touched his soul and blown his mind.

Robbie slid down the last little bit with a groan. "Fuck, yeah."

Nothing had ever felt so good.

And then Robbie moved, and Paul lost the ability to think.

He leaned back, hands behind him, bracing himself on Paul's thighs. The muscles of his torso flexed with the sinuous roll of his hips.

Paul couldn't resist running his hands over every inch of Robbie's abs. Robbie moaned on every slow slide out and grunted when he slid himself back onto Paul's cock.

Paul lifted his head off the bed to see. Robbie's cock stood out from his body, red and hard. Paul had to touch it.

"Oh, yeah. Touch me," Robbie said, panting when Paul wrapped his hand around him.

It felt like Paul's soul was getting sucked out of his dick. With each drag up Robbie's walls tightened around him like Robbie was reluctant to let Paul leave.

A gorgeous red flush started to work its way from Robbie's cheeks and down his throat. He leaned forward on his knees, thrusting himself harder against Paul.

Paul felt his orgasm build in his entire body. Robbie's cursed steadily as he slammed himself down on Paul.

Paul wasn't going to last much longer. "Kiss me. Please," he begged, pulling at Robbie's shoulders.

Robbie folded down on top of Paul, sliding his arms underneath his shoulders and pressed their lips together. Neither one coordinated for anything so complicated as an actual kiss,

"Feels so good," Paul said with a moan, crushing Robbie against him. "So fucking tight around me."

"Jesus, Paul. Fuck, fuck. Come on. Fuck me. Show me how good you can take care of me." He slid his hips almost all the way up.

Only sheer force of will and five days' practice kept Paul from coming right that instant. With a growl, he planted his feet flat on the mattress and thrust up, slamming himself into Robbie over and over as fast as he could pump his hips.

The slap of his body against Robbie's was shockingly loud in the room.

"Fuck, yeah," Robbie cried. "Harder. Fuck."

Robbie buried his head in Paul's neck and cursed, loud grunts forced out of him every time Paul slammed home.

Paul drove into Robbie like he would die if he stopped. Each time his cock hit just the right spot, Robbie shouted and jerked. Paul felt their heartbeats pounding where they were joined.

Paul shoved his cock into Robbie and held him still against his body. Robbie trembled on top of him. "Touch yourself," he begged. "I have to come. God, please."

Robbie snaked a trembling hand between them. As he reached for his cock, Paul pulled out quickly and then slammed back in.

Robbie's hand clenched around his cock, and he arched up from Paul's body. Back bent, he yelled as he shot out pulse after pulse of hot come all over Paul's stomach, chest, and chin.

Watching Robbie's face contort with pleasure, feeling Robbie clamp down on his cock, dragged Paul over the edge, too.

White-hot ecstasy jolted up his spine and slammed into the base of his skull. His muscles locked up as he shot hard into the condom.

Robbie collapsed down to Paul, spent, as his orgasm trailed off. The change in position jolted another quick orgasm out of Paul. He groaned from deep in his soul and, closing his eyes, hugged Robbie as tightly against him as he could.

That was it. It was done. Paul could never go back. He could never un-know what it felt like to be inside another man.

20

PAUL—IT WILL BE BY YOUR SIDE

"So?" Robbie asked, rolling off of Paul. "Was it good? Was it everything porn promised you?"

Paul couldn't speak. He didn't trust his voice, and he could feel the tears trying to escape. So he signed. *Better. Best.*

Robbie took his hand and kissed each finger one by one. "I can't believe you learned sign language because of me."

"It wasn't just because of you," Paul objected.

"Yes, it was. Admit it."

Paul reached for the Saint Sebastian medallion resting on Robbie's chest. "Why did you keep this?"

"Touché." Robbie took the medallion back, flipping it from Saint Sebastian to Saint Christopher and back. "I kept it because it reminded me of you. I don't know why, but I felt we had a connection that night."

"Me, too," Paul admitted. "And I did learn how to sign because of you. I thought I could impress you if we ever met again."

"Well, it worked. But I'm more impressed with the way you fucked me just now."

Paul moaned in embarrassment. "You can't just say things like that out loud."

"If you can't talk about it, you shouldn't be doing it," Robbie said. "That's what my mother always told me. That, and you can never have enough lube."

Paul gasped. "She didn't! You didn't talk to your momma about that."

Robbie laughed out loud. "Oh, she did. And we did."

"I can't even imagine."

Robbie sat up with a groan and stretched. "God, that was amazing. Please tell me you'll want to do it again soon?"

"Tonight?" Sleep was already tugging at Paul's eyelids.

Robbie yawned. "Not unless you don't care if I'm awake for it. I had big plans."

"I guess you're all talk," Paul said through a matching yawn.

"Yep. A big, fat liar." Robbie disappeared into the bathroom. Paul heard him turn the water on and then off. A few minutes later, he came out with a warm washcloth.

He tossed it onto Paul's stomach. "I'm too tired for a shower, and I don't want to go deal with my hair. Did you want to shower?"

"Not if you don't mind."

"I don't." Robbie shoved Paul over and slid under the covers. "I can't stay awake another minute. Try not to snore too much." He took the washcloth from Paul and tossed it in the direction of the bathroom. "Night." He rolled onto his side, his back to Paul.

"Night." Paul stared at the ceiling, afraid to move. They hadn't shared a bed before. Rooms, yes. Beds, no. Not all night.

"I can hear you thinking," Robbie muttered. He reached behind himself, hand flailing until Paul grabbed it.

Robbie tugged Paul forward until he wrapped his arm around Robbie's waist. "Be the big spoon and go the fuck to sleep."

He must have fallen asleep at some point, because he woke up to Robbie's morning wood digging into his side and Robbie's mouth nipping at his shoulder.

They made out slowly, leisurely, in no hurry to get anywhere. Paul's stomach audibly rumbled.

"Hungry?" Robbie asked.

Paul rolled onto his back. "Yeah. And I have to pee."

"Me, too," Robbie confessed. "Want to shower and then go get some breakfast? There's a nice place down the block. I have zero food in the apartment."

"Sounds like a plan. Can I borrow some clothes? All I have is my suit."

"No problem."

They got out of bed.

Paul had been expecting a little bit of awkwardness at least from him. But being around Robbie didn't feel any different than it had. It was easy. It was always easy.

At least until Robbie called out from the bathroom. "Hey, who's U.B.?"

What? He couldn't have heard Robbie right. "Who? What did you just say?"

"U.B?" Robbie said, walking into the room with a towel wrapped around him. "You were talking in your sleep last night."

"Oh, no."

Robbie shrugged. "I'm getting used to it. Usually, it's just nonsense. But last night you apologized like six times to someone named U.B."

Paul considered making something up. He could tell Robbie that Eubee was his old math teacher or coach or something. But maybe Robbie was the perfect person to talk to about Eubee. He could help Paul figure out what he'd felt.

Paul grabbed Robbie by the towel as he passed by, pulling him down onto his lap like he wasn't six-feet-tall. "Still want to go for that ride after breakfast?" he asked, nuzzling Robbie's neck. He smelled so good. Fresh and clean, skin still warm from the shower.

"Hell, yeah." Robbie tilted his head so Paul could kiss his neck. "Or we could just stay here," he said, letting his towel fall open.

"That is a very tempting offer," Paul said, running his hands up and down Robbie's body. "But we're burning daylight as it is. And I need food."

Robbie slid off Paul's lap onto his knees. He pushed Paul's legs apart. "I don't think this will take too long."

It didn't. Paul didn't even have a chance to reciprocate because Robbie got himself off at the same time.

"Sorry," Robbie said, not sounding sorry at all. "The sounds you make when I blow you are so fucking hot. And the look on your face when you come? It's too much." He pushed himself up, standing naked between Paul's legs.

"I guess I can't be mad about that," Paul agreed, running his hands over Robbie's legs. He had it bad for those thick, hard muscles. They were so wide, he couldn't wrap both hands around them. "But I can blow you later?"

Robbie put a finger to his chin and pretend to think about it. "I think I can squeeze you in later." He smirked. "See what I did there? 'Squeeze you in?'"

"I saw." Paul slid his hands up to knead Robbie's firm ass cheeks. "Promise?"

With his index finger, Robbie drew an X over his heart. "Cross my heart."

"Okay then. Get dressed, and I'll buy you breakfast, and I'll tell you all about Eubee while we're driving."

"Who is he? Short version," Robbie asked as he got dressed.

"He was my best friend most of my life, and Queenie was his car before she was mine."

Robbie picked up on the past tense, and his eyebrows drew together in concern, but he didn't ask for more.

21

ROBBIE—YOU KISSED ME LIKE YOU MEANT IT

The day was surprisingly sunny and warm for Washington in December. They bundled up in sweatshirts, and Paul took the roof off of the Stingray so they could enjoy the sun.

Paul opened her up as they broke free of the traffic on the freeway.

"I've never been a car person, but I think I want to have sex with your car." Robbie caressed the dashboard, leaning his head back so he could watch the tops of the trees speed across the cloudless blue sky. With the top of the car open, they had to speak loudly to be heard over the roar of the wind.

"Sorry. She would never cheat on me."

"Sex in the car then?"

Paul glanced over to Robbie, not losing a beat as he guided the Stingray around the curve. "We barely fit in the car. I can't see that happening."

Robbie started to say something, and Paul cut him off. "Don't you even hint about having sex on top of my Queenie. First of all, she's a lady. Secondly, I'm not putting dents in her or ruining the paint job even for you."

"Can I look at a picture of her while I jerk off?"

"Sure thing."

He wanted to ask about Eubee and the car. Wanted to find out why Paul talked about him in the past tense. Had the friendship gone bad? Probably not, or Paul wouldn't have his car. So Eubee must be dead.

No one Robbie loved had ever died. Oh, he shouldn't have said that. He looked around for something wooden to knock on to stave off the bad luck. Unsurprisingly, there was no wood inside the car. He settled for thumping himself on the head.

Paul looked at him quizzically.

"Knocking on wood," he explained.

"Oh, okay. Why?"

"I was just thinking how I've never lost someone I've loved, and then I was afraid I'd jinxed it."

Paul nodded, jaw tight. He concentrated on driving harder than he'd been doing. "You've had a very charmed life, Robert Rhodes."

"I know." He'd thought he'd had a pretty average life. Sure, the learning disabilities made school tougher for him than for a lot of people, but his parents never let him forget how privileged he was by simply having the opportunity to go to school. Millions of kids didn't have that chance.

They drove for the better part of an hour in a not quite uncomfortable silence. The roar of the wind made conversation difficult anyway.

At one point Robbie reached across and rested his arm on the top of Paul's seat. The wind-blown strands of blond hair whipped at his fingers as he gently rubbed Paul's neck.

Paul tilted his head into the caress, so Robbie kept doing it as the road unrolled beneath their wheels.

Paul slowed down as they approached a turn-off. A few short turns brought them to a parking lot near the beach that was almost empty.

"This is amazing," Robbie said spinning in a slow circle to take in the three-sixty view. Sand shifted under his feet, and the cold wind blowing off the water tugged at his sweatshirt, but it only added to the feeling that they were the only two people around for hundreds of miles.

Robbie felt wild and free. Reaching for Paul's hand, Robbie pulled him against his front, and kissed him soft and sweet, a hand on the back of his neck. "Thanks for bringing me here. It's perfect."

They kissed for a while in the sun and fresh air. He dug his fingers under the layers of Paul's shirt and sweatshirt to feel the soft, warm skin under his fingertips.

Paul twisted away with a laugh. "Tickles." Keeping a hold of his hand, Paul led him over to the trunk of a fallen tree half buried in the sand and bleached white by the sun and salt water.

Where had it come from? Robbie wondered. Had it fallen from the cliffs above them? Drifted here from somewhere else?

They sat side by side on the trunk, watching the waves crashing along the shore, the sound rising and falling as the water fell onto the sand and was dragged back.

"Remember I told you I had messed around with a kid a long time ago, back at church camp?" Paul asked without preamble.

"Yeah. I think so."

"That was Eubee." Paul bent down and picked up a handful of the rocky sand.

"Tell me about him."

Paul did, picking out the larger rocks from the sand and throwing them into the waves as he did. Robbie listened, making the occasional sound to show he was listening and laughing in the right places.

Even though he'd figured it was coming, it was hard to watch Paul talk about Eubee's death. He was obviously struggling to hold in tears.

"Oh, Paul," he said when Paul told him he had gone right from the funeral to the hockey game. "That must have been so hard."

"It was." Tears dripped down Paul's cheeks.

Robbie pulled him in for a hug. "It's okay to cry. You loved him, and he died. You should be crying."

Paul choked on a sob, then let go of what felt like two years' worth of grief. He clutched onto Robbie as if he was the only thing keeping him upright.

Robbie held him tightly, one hand cradling the back of his head, the other wrapped around his back.

The sobs died down, and Paul stopped shaking. With a wet kiss to the side of Robbie's neck, Paul pulled way.

"Sorry," he said, wiping his eyes.

"Don't be."

It was obvious to Robbie that Paul had been in love with Eubee, and he'd put money on Eubee feeling the same way. And then the guy just enlisted while Paul was in Canada with the Juniors? It didn't make sense.

"Feeling better?" Robbie asked.

Paul nodded.

"Can I ask a question?"

Paul motioned for him to go ahead. He picked up some more pebbles, pouring them from hand to hand.

"I don't get it," Robbie said. "Eubee just up and joined the army? Just like that?" Something doesn't add up. "What happened? Why did he change his plans? Your plans?"

Paul tossed an entire handful of pebbles at the ocean. "Beats the ever-living fuck outta me. I never got a chance to ask him. After he was already in, he texted some bullshit about skills training and job placement, but he wouldn't talk to me on the phone or anything."

"Why not?"

"He knew I'd get the truth out of him. The boy never could lie to my face." Paul smiled wanly.

Robbie let a few more waves roll up and slide back down the beach before he spoke. "Why do *you* think he left?"

Paul pushed off the tree trunk with a sigh. Shoving his hands into his pockets, he strode down the beach, keeping close to the high water line. Robbie was right behind him.

"I think he got scared. I think he figured out what was going on between us before I did, and he couldn't, wouldn't, face it."

“That you guys were in love with each other?” Robbie asked softly.

Paul chuckled harshly. “Yeah.”

“When did you figure it out?”

“Chicago,” Paul admitted.

Robbie stopped walking. “Chicago? As in a few days ago, Chicago?”

Paul strode a few more steps away before realizing Robbie had stopped following. He turned, holding his hair back from the ever-present wind. “Yeah. As in four days ago.” He walked back to Robbie.

“How could you not know? You knew you were gay, right?”

“Yes. But I didn’t want to be. Gay was bad. What I felt for – what I had with Eubee was good. Therefore, it wasn’t gay. Everybody loved us together. Girls and old ladies down at the church smiled. Pops Franklin loved me as much as he loved Eubee.”

Paul headed back toward the tree, much more slowly, eyes distant. “If Eubee and I had been gay...” He held up a hand to forestall Robbie’s argument. “If they suspected that we were even fooling around, they would have hated us.”

Robbie didn’t even know where to start. So many questions bounced around his brain. “Was it really that bad? Were people that homophobic?”

Paul looked up at the sky and sighed. “It was...” he searched for the word. “Constant. Ubiquitous. Something that almost didn’t have to be said because you knew it like you knew your own name. Water is wet. White sauce is the best. God is good. And gays are perverts who want to destroy families, wreck the American way of life, and will end up in hell.”

“Damn,” Robbie whispered.

“Literally,” Paul agreed with a humorless laugh. “I heard of this one little girl, couldn’ta been more than twelve, thirteen. I was probably sixteen at the time. She just disappeared. Stopped coming to church. I heard her own momma call her an abomination while she was standing in the social hall sipping a glass of tea like it were nothing.”

He drew in an unsteady breath and shook his head, rubbing his face with one hand. "I heard from some kids at school they'd sent her away. Well, not so much sent as had her kidnapped from her own bed. They came in the middle of the night, took her to some kind of 'camp' for 'troubled teens.' So they could pray the gay away or some bullshit."

Robbie felt sick. "Fuck. I didn't know places like that were still around. People still do that?"

"Yeah, Rhodes. People still do that."

They'd reached the tree trunk they had been sitting on earlier. Paul dropped heavily back onto it.

Robbie sat down close to Paul but not touching him. He wasn't sure what Paul's reaction would be to the hug he desperately wanted to give.

He didn't expect Paul to reach out to him, wrap an arm around Robbie's waist and pull them together. Paul rested his head against Robbie's. "My dad threatened, veiled threats mostly, to send me someplace more than once."

"What kind of parent could do that?"

"One who cares for his son's immortal soul, Rhodes. And you can just keep your comments to yourself about that right now. One thing I know; my father loves me. If you saw how he was when my mom first got sick." Clenching his jaw, Paul cut that line of thought off, pressing the heel of his palm against his eyes.

"He's my biggest fan. Anything I ever needed for hockey, for anything. Anything he could give me. All I had to do was not be gay. Just one thing. And I couldn't do it."

Robbie didn't understand any of it. He hadn't gone to church ever, but he'd always kind of vaguely imagined it as a place you went to on Sunday and didn't think about the rest of the week.

Paul inhaled deeply. "So," he said, "all week you get faggot jokes, bullying, and all the good ole boys going on about 'them queers' and what they'd do if they found any homo messin' with their boys. And the nice southern ladies who allowed as it was fine and all for their pet gays – the hairdressers and interior designers, bless their hearts –

but goodness gracious that wasn't the same as letting them get married. Stars, no. And be around the children? Well, of course not."

Paul's accent was so thick now Robbie could practically see the women standing around all wide-eyed and clutching their pearls.

Paul reached down and grabbed another handful of damp pebbles. He stood, tossing it viciously at the choppy gray water. "And then—" He gathered more ammunition against the memories. "And then on Sunday, you hear that gays go to hell. And if you're a kid just starting to understand what the fuck gay even means..." He let the pebbles slip through his fingers and trickle to the sand. "And then you realize, oh no, no, that ain't me. That cain't be me."

He walked up to the edge of the water, head down, staring at the waves. Exactly like he'd been standing that day in the Stationstore parking lot.

Robbie hung back, unsure what to do, what Paul needed. When Paul raised his arm, wiping his eyes with his sleeve, Robbie couldn't stand there anymore.

He walked up to Paul, wrapping his arms around him from behind and hooked his chin over Paul's shoulder. "I'm sorry. I'm so sorry you had to go through that."

Paul covered Robbie's arms with his, lacing their fingers together. He sighed and laid his head back on Robbie's shoulder.

"So you and Eubee never, I don't know, talked about it? Acknowledged it in anyway?"

"Never. Not a word. Then he left me, and then he died."

"I'm sorry," Robbie said, tears pooling in his eyes. Sorry was such an inadequate word, incapable of saying all the things Robbie wanted to say. But words had never been his strong point. "That sucks."

Robbie searched for a good way to ask his next question. "Did he die in the war?"

Judging by the way Paul tensed in his arms that probably hadn't been a good way.

"Helicopter accident in Texas if you can believe it."

Robbie lifted his head in surprise. "You mean he was in the U.S., and he wouldn't call you?"

"Yeah." Paul tried to shrug.

Robbie grumbled something unflattering under his breath.

Paul turned in Robbie's arms. "Don't speak ill of the dead. It's not our place to judge him. He did what he felt he had to do. Whatever judgment he faced was between him and God."

Robbie frowned.

"It's almost impossible for you to understand, isn't it, Rhodes? How much you can hate what you are. You don't know what it's like to pray every day for years to be something other than what you are and have those prayers go unanswered."

"No, you're right. I don't. I'm sorry." He stopped again and squeezed Paul's hand. "I don't understand. But I don't have to. You tell me you felt that way, that Eubee felt that way, and God only knows how many other gay kids feel that way still, and I believe it. I don't have to understand; I only have to believe you when you say it's real. It makes me so sad."

"Yeah."

There was one thing Robbie needed to know, a question he had to ask that he really didn't want to ask. But if there was going to be anything between him and Paul, and he'd realized in the last week he wanted something with Paul, then he had to know one thing.

He loosened his hold on Paul, putting a little space between them. "Do you still feel that way? That being gay is wrong and that you're going to hell?"

Paul dropped his hands from Robbie's and took a step away. He shoved his hands deep into the pockets of his jeans. The wind whipped his hair against his face, and tugged at Robbie's longer hair, making it hard for him to see Paul's expression.

Paul kicked at the wet sand, and Robbie held his breath waiting for an answer. "Rationally, no."

Robbie exhaled.

"I know I'm not a bad person," he said, looking directly at Robbie. "And God, does it feel right, being with you. It feels so good it scares me."

Robbie gave him a tentative smile. "That's good, right?"

Paul shook his head. “No, I mean I’m really scared.”

“Why?” Robbie asked, frustration and despair in his voice. “Why should something that feels so good, and is so easy, be bad? I don’t get it?” There was so much about this he didn’t get.

“You’re going to think I’m a fuckin’ redneck backward idiot. I can see it in your eyes.” Paul looked so sad.

This was supposed to have been a good day. A fun drive into the country where he would learn about someone important to Paul, and they would trade stories of growing up. Get lunch someplace nice, and then back to one of their houses for a nap and then hopefully more sex.

He should let the whole subject go. Get the hell out of here, go back home and maybe get drunk and screw around.

But that was the issue, wasn’t it? He didn’t want to go any further with Paul if Paul was only going to hate them both for it.

“Just tell me,” Robbie said. “I won’t think you’re an idiot.”

Paul looked doubtful and a little scared. His hand trembled as he raked it through his hair.

“Hey,” Robbie said, walking to him. He wrapped his arms around Paul. “Hey. Whatever you say, I promise I won’t judge, okay? I’ll just listen. You feel what you feel.”

“Okay. But don’t look at me. I can’t talk about it.”

“You want me to turn around?”

“Yeah. Stand behind me again. I like that.”

Robbie did, wrapping his hands around Paul’s waist. “Feel good?”

“It always feels good when you touch me. That’s part of the problem.” He stopped as if waiting for Robbie to say something. When Robbie didn’t, he took a deep breath and plunged on.

The words came out haltingly at first, then gained speed as Robbie kept his promise and didn’t interrupt.

“How can something that feels so amazing, so intense, be good?” His fingers tightened over Robbie’s hand. “You’re like heroin or something. I can’t stop thinking about you. I see you all the time, and I still want more. You’re a walking, skating temptation. It’s like you were crafted by the Devil specifically for me. To tempt me.”

He took a huge breath when he stopped, his body tense in Robbie's arms.

22

ROBBIE—THE KISSES AND THE BRUISES

Robbie listened to the waves crashing on the shore and watched the quick-legged plovers chase the water back down to the sea, searching for the tell-tale sign of air bubbles rising from the freshly revealed sand.

He was so grateful he had promised not to say anything because he couldn't think of one single thing to say in reply to that. That kind of thinking was so beyond anything he knew.

Seagulls screeched loudly

"Say something," Paul said quietly.

Robbie kissed his neck. Paul tilted his head to the side, so Robbie did it again.

"You haven't run screaming yet, so that's good," Paul said.

"I don't know how to drive a stick-shift," Robbie said deadpan.

"So you're at my mercy then."

"More than you know."

"What do you mean?" Paul turned in his arms.

"I wanted to hate you when you got here."

"I know," Paul said.

"Nope. My turn to talk. You listen." He grabbed Paul's hand. "Can we talk and walk back to the car and drive some more? Maybe to someplace with coffee? I'm getting cold."

Paul nodded. Not talking.

"So I wanted you to be a jerk. But you weren't. And I couldn't stop thinking about you and about that night."

"That was the night after Eubee's funeral."

Robbie stopped walking again, almost jerking Paul off his feet. "What the fuck? You never said anything."

Paul frowned at him, a furrow appearing between his eyebrows. "Not something I wanted to talk about. I wanted to not think about it. And you helped me with that."

"Glad I could help."

Paul tugged him to get him walking again. They walked slowly towards the car. A golden retriever ran up to them, sniffing and leaning in for pets.

A couple heading in their direction called out for the dog, apologizing.

"It's okay," Paul said, as they got closer. "He's beautiful."

"Rover," the man called, slapping his leg for the dog to come over. "Come." He and the woman with him could have been on the cover of Seattle Hipster Weekly. With a small wave, the couple left, Rover running down the beach ahead of them.

"Rover?" Paul asked incredulously.

"Welcome to Seattle. Where even the dogs are ironic."

Paul laughed. A small laugh, but genuine. Robbie was glad to hear it.

"No wonder you punched me the next day. I wouldn't have even been able to skate."

Paul shook his head. "It was all I could do."

"I get that."

They reached the car.

"Do you want the roof open again?" Paul asked.

"Yes, please."

Robbie watched as Paul pulled the hard panels off and stowed them in the trunk.

There were so many things Robbie wanted to say or to ask. Did Paul believe in a literal devil? Did he actually think Robbie could be some sort of tool of the devil if he/it existed? Really?

Robbie sighed heavily.

"What?" Paul asked as if he'd been waiting for the questioning to start.

"I just need to hear you say one thing." This was it.

"What?" Paul's eyes narrowed.

"I need to you to say that yes, you are gay and that you want to be with me."

"Or?"

"Or we'll just have to be good friends. I'm not going to stop being your friend." He started to lean against the car, then stopped himself, leaning instead on the split rail fence separating the parking lot from the beach.

"It's ironic. When Drew, my last boyfriend, left me, one of the things he complained about was that I wasn't willing to be out for him. That he wasn't important enough."

"Do you need me to be out to the team?" Paul shook his head as he asked as if he couldn't even face the thought.

"No. Just to you and to me."

"We already know."

"I just need to hear you say it out loud."

"It's hard."

"I know. But if you don't, it's gonna suck."

"For you?"

"No! For you, dude." Robbie paced in a circle, trying to put into words something he'd been feeling lately. A niggling thing that had been growing in just the past week. "It's just... life deep in the closet sucks. I've seen those guys. They're angry all the time. It's frustrating."

Oh, great. Great word. Talk about frustrating. He needed the words to be there so he could help Paul, and he didn't have them.

But Paul did. He'd said them a few minutes ago. Robbie stopped pacing. "I'm scared, too," he said.

"Of what? What do you have to be scared of?" Paul leaned against the rear of the car.

"You."

"Me? I'm not going to punch you again or anything."

"I know that." He walked up to Paul and stood in front of him.

Paul reached for his hips, fingers slipping into the belt loops of his jeans.

"What about the paint?" Robbie asked with a grin, despite the seriousness of what he was trying to say.

"My car, my rules. Now, what are you scared of?"

"You're right," Robbie said. He reached out, sliding his hand behind Paul's neck, his fingers reaching inside the sweatshirt and his thumb caressing the short hairs on the back of Paul's neck. "We are really good together. I want to touch you all the time, too."

Paul shuddered.

"I think you're amazing. For a lot of reasons. And, not to put any pressure on you, but there is a lot at stake here. No matter how casual we try to keep it."

"It's not casual. I couldn't, never." It was Paul's turn to search for words. "You know how hard this is for me. I couldn't with anyone. Just you. I trust you."

"And I want to trust you."

Hurt, Paul tried to pull away, but Robbie kept his hand on his neck. "You don't have to tell anyone else. But I need to hear you tell me, out loud, that you are gay and you want to be with me. Every time we're together, I'm terrified that you're going to freak out. And then you'll never be able to look at me again, and not only will that suck for me–"

"It will fuck up the team," Paul filled in.

"Yeah. It could fuck up the team."

Tugging slowly at his belt loops, Paul reeled Robbie in to him until he could wrap his arms around him. He stared at Robbie for what felt like endless long seconds. The close scrutiny was unnerving.

Finally, Paul exhaled, breath warm against Robbie's face. "Can I kiss you?" he asked.

"Of course," Robbie replied automatically.

Paul kissed him like he was testing out a theory. Gentle at first, then with more pressure. Robbie opened his mouth at the touch of Paul's tongue. When he sucked on it, Paul made a pleased sound and wrapped his arms around Robbie, pulling him tightly.

He kept his hands in Paul's hair. Paul spread his legs to get Robbie even closer, sliding down the car a bit as he did. Robbie liked having the height advantage for once. He curled his fingers into Paul's curls and pulled his head back to take control of the kiss. If this was a test, he was going to make Paul understand what he'd be giving up.

He wrenched Paul's head to the side and bent down to kiss his way up Paul's jawline. He bit harder on Paul's earlobe than he normally did, knowing it wouldn't leave a mark.

There was no place on Paul's body could mark up without someone on the team seeing it. *Stupid showers*, Robbie thought as he dropped his mouth to the vein on Paul's neck. He bit as firmly as he dared, sucking the skin into his mouth.

Paul shuddered, and pressed Robbie's face against his neck, trapping him. "Harder," he whispered hoarsely.

Robbie shoved his hands and arms under Paul's sweaT-shirt. "I can't," he said, dragging his nails down Paul's back. "People will see." He was rewarded with a long, wavering moan.

Paul gripped onto Robbie's upper arms and flipped them so Robbie's back hit the car. "Someday I want them to see." He moved so he was straddling Robbie's thigh. Robbie clamped his hands on Paul's ass.

A school bus rumbled into the parking lot, and Paul smiled against Robbie's mouth. "Guess we should move this somewhere else." He pulled back but kept hold of Robbie's hand.

"For the record, I would like to state that yes, I am gay. I want to be with you."

"Yeah?"

"Yeah." Robbie's heart did a little lurch at that. He knew it wasn't going to be easy, but Paul would come to his senses eventually. He had to.

He pushed himself off the car, smiling at Paul. Paul took a quick step back, alarmed. He must have thought Robbie was going to kiss him.

Wearing rain boots and carrying small fishing nets, the little kids tumbled off the bus. The adults attempted to keep them corralled. A few of the kids noticed them and started nudging each other and pointing.

Please, let them not be hockey fans, Robbie thought.

One of the taller girls waved at them and yelled across the parking lot. "Hey! Nice car!"

"Thanks!" Paul yelled back.

"Seventy-seven?"

"So close!" Paul answered with a big smile. "Seventy-six."

"Sweet."

The chaperones called the kids over, and the girl gave them a wave goodbye.

"Wanna head home or drive some more?" Paul asked.

"Lunch, my place, and more sex?" Robbie asked hopefully.

"Lunch, my place, and more sex," Paul countered. "I need my own clothes."

"But I like the way you look in mine," Robbie said with a smile.

Paul shoved his hands deep into his pockets like he was trying to stop himself from touching Robbie. "Lunch, then sex at a location to be determined."

"Deal."

As tempting as the idea of food and sex was, they took the long way back to the city. During the season, they had so few days off to enjoy the gorgeous scenery. And besides, watching Paul's expert driving, and feeling the classic Corvette vibrating under them as it hugged the curves and crested the ridges of the mountains was sexy all by itself.

The radio faded to static, so Paul shut it off.

Robbie had his arm slung casually over the back of the seat, fingers occasionally running through Paul's hair.

“Thanks for not freaking out on me back there,” Paul said. It was the first thing he’d said since they’d gotten back in the car.

“I told you I wouldn’t.”

“But you don’t quite understand where I’m coming from.”

“Not really.”

“It’s so frustrating. I don’t have anyone to talk to about all the sides of me, you know? I get the feeling that talking about God in the gay world is a touchy subject. And I can’t talk to anybody in the church about what it means to be gay.”

“Why don’t you just find a gay-friendly church and go talk to someone there?”

Paul jerked his gaze over to Robbie, slowing down from an illegal eighty-miles-per-hour to a slightly less illegal seventy-five. “They have those?”

“Yeah. I know of least three back in Columbus. This one church, something congregational, they have a married lesbian couple as co-ministers. There’s got to be something like that in Seattle.”

“Yeah, huh.” Paul pushed the car a little faster.

“I think you should,” Robbie said. “Because I really, really like you. More than I wanted to. And I want to give us a good shot.”

“Me, too.” Paul rested his hand on Robbie’s leg.

“But as long as you hate yourself, we’re not going to work.” Robbie said as kindly as he could.

Paul looked away. “I know. I’m trying. Do you think I have to out myself to the team or anything?”

“No. I already said that. There’s no timeline for doing that.” Robbie sighed. “But I have to be honest. You know how it is. Everyone is up in everyone else’s business. If we’re together, eventually they’ll find out. And, thinking rationally here, we really should tell Coach before he finds out from someone else.”

“Yeah. Fuck.” Paul ran his fingers through his hair. “I fucking hate that they did this to me. I hate that something I love made me hate myself. How is that fair? In what world is that fucking fair?”

“Look I don’t know much about religion, but I thought the whole thing was that God made man in his image, right? And God is love, etc., etc. Why would he make you gay if he wasn't okay with it? And don't give me any of the mysterious ways cr- stuff."

"As a test?

"I don't know man. Occam's razor. The simplest solution is usually the best. Maybe he's just okay with it." Robbie tried not to say it, but it came out anyway. "Or maybe there is no God."

Paul didn't react as shocked as Robbie expected. "Maybe not," he shrugged. "But back to Occam's razor, I don't think that is the simplest answer for anything. If there is no God, why is there anything at all?"

"I don't know," Robbie admitted with a rueful laugh. "So much I don't know, I try not to think about these things."

"I've been thinking about them a lot lately," Paul said.

"Yeah. Me, too," Robbie admitted. "More so since you."

"Ditto," Paul gave him a white-toothed grin.

It felt good to talk to someone about these things. He had achieved the goal he'd been working for his whole life. Ten thousand kids would give their right arm to be in his place. And yet he couldn't help feeling a vague sense of dissatisfaction, and he couldn't put his finger on why.

"I think," he started, shaping his thoughts even as he spoke them. "I just figure, well, we're here, all of us. So let's make the best of it. Like, how can I make it a better world, an easier world, for someone?"

"What, like Gandhi or someone?"

"Not like that level. But, you know, volunteering. Doing something good. Like working for Doctors Without Borders."

"Hockey Players Without Boards," Paul joked.

"Life's hard. Like you said, I've had an easy life. I have had a lot of privilege. I'm a white guy, and if things keep up like this, I'm going to be a *rich* white guy. I feel like I should use my position, my privilege to do something to make a difference."

"I think that's admirable. But what are you going to do?"

"Beats the hell out of me."

"If only," Paul said.

Robbie's jaw dropped. He turned to Paul, shaking his head gently. "Was that a joke? Did you just make a joke about me being evil?"

"Don't molest the driver, Satan!" Paul said in mock alarm.

"I'm going to beat you."

"Promises, promises."

A sign on the road pointed to a scenic overlook half a mile ahead. "Pull over," Robbie said. "And I'll show you promises."

With a grin, Paul stepped on the accelerator, throwing Robbie against the back of the seat.

Robbie had expected the pull-off to be a sandy spot on the side of the road, but the overlook boasted a large paved parking lot with a walkway and freakin' binoculars, for God's sake. It was empty now, but he'd have to work quickly before another school bus showed up. He pointed to a spot furthest from the entrance. "Park there. And park with my door facing out."

"I'll have to park sideways," Paul pointed out.

"You worried about getting a parking ticket?"

"Kinda," Paul admitted.

Robbie patted his leg. "Don't worry. No one is going to notice how you're parked."

Paul maneuvered the car into position.

"Stay," Robbie said, pointing at Paul as he got out of the car.

"Bossy today," Paul joked.

He wasn't laughing when Robbie opened the driver's side door and tugged Paul's legs out of the car. "What if someone comes?" Paul whispered when Robbie dropped to his knees in the parking lot.

"That's the whole goal," Robbie answered, unbuttoning Paul's jeans since he was taking too long to get with the program.

Paul peered nervously out the window in the parking lot, craning his neck to look behind them. His dick didn't seem to share his concerns as it was growing hard under Robbie's hand.

"Focus," he said, lowering his mouth to Paul. "Who knows how much time we have before someone else wants to check out the scenery?"

"You are evil," Paul whispered, putting a hand on the back of Robbie's head to push him down. He slumped down as far as he could in the bucket seat.

Robbie loved giving head, and from the muffled sounds escaping the fist Paul had crammed into his mouth, Paul loved getting it. Really, who didn't?

He heard a car pull into the parking lot. A quick peek showed the sedan pulling into a spot much closer to the entrance. Apparently, Paul hadn't heard them, so, encouraged by the small thrust of Paul's hips, Robbie kept going.

The thump of the car doors closing echoed across the parking lot. That Paul heard. He tensed under Robbie's hand as they heard voices.

The car sheltered them, but they weren't hidden. It wouldn't take too long for someone to figure out what they were up to.

He pulled off Paul with a hard suck, replaced his mouth with his hand.

Paul grunted like he'd been punched. "Shit. Fuck," he panted, eyes tightly closed.

"Shh." Robbie rubbed the head of Paul's cock back and forth over his lips. "Do you want them to hear you?"

Paul whimpered through tightly clenched teeth and his hips jerked up hard.

Robbie filed that bit of information away for the spank bank and concentrated on driving Paul crazy. He held Paul's hips down with both hands, as he bobbed up and down. Paul was going to have teeth marks in his fist for sure.

He slid off with an obscene pop. Paul let out a garbled yell.

Shooting a glance through the window, Robbie saw the woman look over towards the car with a small frown. She said something to the man she was with, and he looked over as well.

"Uh oh," Robbie said, running a finger across the tip of Paul's dick. At the sexy broken whimper Paul gave, Robbie did it again. "Fuck that's sexy," he whispered. "But it looks like those nice people can hear you, baby."

Paul's cock jerked hard under Robbie's hand. Seemed like Paul had a bit of an exhibitionist streak. Sucked for him because this was a one-time thing.

"Better hurry," Robbie warned. "You've got about fifteen seconds before I have to stop."

Paul's hand flew to the back of Robbie's head, holding him in place as he fucked his face. Robbie couldn't complain, he'd kind of asked for it. He grabbed on to Paul's thighs, hoping the wind was covering the unmistakable moans and slurps of a fast and dirty blow job.

The clench of muscles under his hand and the sharp sting of his hair being pulled were the only warnings Robbie got before Paul came as quietly as he could. It wasn't that quiet.

Robbie pulled off more quickly than he would have liked.

"You boys okay over there?" the man from the other car called out.

Paul's laugh had a decidedly inappropriate edge to it, so Robbie smacked him on the leg.

"Yeah." With a wink at Paul, he cleared his throat and licked his lips. "We're good, Thanks." He pushed himself up and leaned his elbows on the doorframe, hoping the giant tent in his pants wasn't visible. "My friend just, uh, sprained his knee. And I was fixing him up."

The man didn't seem convinced, but what was he going to say? *'That sounded like a blow job to me'*?

His wife gave Robbie a look that said clear as day, *Really? That's the best you could come up with?*

Robbie smiled wide at her.

She shook her head and tugged her husband further away from the Stingray.

Inside the car, Paul shook with silent laughter, eyes bright.

Robbie nudged his knee against Paul's. "I really like your car."

"I really like you in my car," Paul answered with a grin as he zipped his pants back up. "Want to put the existential crises on hold for a while and get some lunch?"

"I think that's an excellent idea." Robbie waved at the couple before getting back in the car.

23

ROBBIE—THEY DON'T KNOW ABOUT US

Robbie shifted his shoulders, settling his suit jacket around his shoulders better. He was definitely over-dressed for what was basically a coffee shop in Columbus, Ohio, but his parents had picked the place, and he and Paul had to head right to the stadium after the meal.

He and Paul stuck out like sore thumbs in the small café that looked like a throwback to 1978, complete with macramé plant holders and posters for concerts from forty years ago on the walls.

The timing of the meal was terrible for them, but his mother had said she couldn't possibly get out of teaching her one o'clock class. Wouldn't get out more likely, Robbie thought irritably. Would it kill her to let a T.A. teach the class one day? The students would survive.

Spotting his parents and Georgia in a booth against the wall, Robbie assured the hostess he could find his way. Touching Paul lightly on the lower back, he pointed his chin to his parents.

"You sure you're up for this?" he asked quietly as they threaded their way through the mostly-empty tables. Three o'clock wasn't peak time at any restaurant.

"You couldn't pay me to miss it."

"You didn't have to pay. I did." Team members who met their

families when they played in their home states had to pay a 'fine.' All the money went to end of season bonuses for the staff, so Robbie didn't mind.

"Thank God, Georgia is here," he sighed. "I wasn't sure she could make it." Since meeting Paul, Robbie had become painfully aware of how many times he said 'thank God' without actually meaning it literally. He hadn't been able to find a suitable substitution, though. Thank heaven? Just as bad, and made him sound like his grandmother. What else was there? And he didn't even like to think about how he used 'Jesus Christ' solely as a curse.

Robbie introduced Paul to his family. "This is my mother, Jenny Massie. Mom, this is my friend Paul."

"Nice to meet you, ma'am," Paul said, dipping his chin at Paul's mother.

"My dad, Grant Rhodes."

Paul shook his hand firmly. "Nice to meet you, sir."

"This is my favorite person in the world, Georgia Blue."

Georgia stood up to give Robbie a big hug. He hugged her back hard. She was a tall, wide-shouldered woman and her hugs were worth their weight in gold.

"Very nice to meet you, ma'am," Paul said with a smile after they broke their hug.

"I didn't know you were bringing a friend, Rob," his mother said. "I would have gotten a table."

"I did tell you, Mom."

Jenny looked at her husband for confirmation. Grant shrugged.

"I think we can put a chair at the end of the table," Georgia said. "Why don't you two take the bench seat?

Paul and Robbie slid in as Georgia went to talk to the hostess. Robbie ended up against the wall.

Georgia came back with a chair and sat down in it. She looked at Paul, studying his face. "You look so familiar to me, but I just can't place it."

"Might be from my college hockey team?"

"No. That's not it. Dyson. Dyson. What's your whole name?"

"Paul Stonewall Dyson, Jr, ma'am."

Georgia snapped her fingers. "That's it. Is Stoney Dyson your dad?"

"Yes, ma'am, he is."

"You are the spitting image of him at your age." Georgia turned to Robbie. "I played football back in college with his dad."

"Really?" Paul said with surprise. "Roll Tide!"

"Roll Tide!" Georgia agreed.

"No offense, ma'am, but you look 'bout ten years younger than my dad does."

Georgia pointed at him. "You can stay. Robbie, keep this one around."

"Stoney?" Robbie asked Paul with the lift of an eyebrow. "Is that why your nickname is—"

"Don't you say it," Paul warned.

"Chip," Robbie finished with a laugh. "A chip off the old stone?"

Paul punched him hard in the arm.

Robbie's parents looked somewhere between amused and alarmed.

"I didn't know Stoney got married," Georgia said with a look meant only for Robbie. "Whatever happened to Skipper, do you know? Those two were thick as thieves back in the day."

Robbie had never heard Georgia's accent so clearly before.

"Sorry, I don't know, ma'am. Dad never mentioned him."

She shrugged. "It was a long time ago. And please, call me Georgia. How's your mother?"

Paul's face dropped. Under the table, Robbie put his hand on Paul's knee for comfort. "She, um, passed about a year and a half ago, Miss Georgia."

"Oh, I'm so sorry." Georgia looked flustered.

"So, I heard Gary's daughter is in Uganda with *Médecins Sans Frontières,*" Robbie's mother said, changing the subject. "That's Doctors Without Borders," she explained to Paul.

He nodded with a tight-lipped smile.

"Did you guys order yet?" Robbie asked.

"No, we were waiting for you."

Robbie kept his leg pressed against Paul's while they examined the menu and ordered. Considering they had a choice between three different sandwiches, two types of quiche, and a soup, it didn't take too long to decide.

They made small talk, mostly about what other people's children were doing, which apparently involved joining the Peace Corps, earning PhDs, and single-handedly saving the world. Sometimes all at once.

"Robbie's scored 25 points already this season," Paul said during a break in the conversation. "And he's got an average time on ice per game of about twenty-two and half minutes."

"So do you, idiot," Robbie said at the same time his father asked, "Is that a lot?"

"Yessir. Especially since we're the second line and we've only played thirty games this season. Lotsa guys don't rack up that many points in an entire season." Paul smiled at Robbie. "He makes me look good."

Robbie knew he was grinning like a fool, but he didn't care. Seeing Paul offended on his behalf warmed his heart.

He knew what Paul was doing, and it wouldn't make a difference. His parents would never be impressed with statistics of all things, but the fact that he was trying felt great.

"It's very good," Georgia added. "Congratulation, Robbie. I only had 23 points. I must have missed some."

"He had two assists last night," Paul told her.

Georgia pulled out her phone and tapped on the screen. "There. Up to date. How are you feeling about the game tonight?"

Robbie and Paul exchanged glances. "Pretty good," Robbie said, answering.

The server brought their food over, and they at as they talked about the Blue Jackets' strengths and weaknesses, who was on the injured reserve list, and who the coach might start.

Robbie was smugly satisfied to see his parents' eyes glazing over.

Normally, that was his situation. He squeezed Paul's leg again, more grateful for the support than he could say out loud.

"I think half their hits come from Jenner," Paul said. "I'll keep an eye out for him." He finished up the last crumb of the chips that came with the sandwich.

Robbie and Georgia murmured their agreement.

"I don't know why there has to be so much fighting in hockey," Jenny said. "I hate seeing it." She swirled the straw in her drink, ice cubes rattling against the sides of the glass.

"When do you watch hockey?" her husband asked.

"I try when Robbie's playing, though the game moves so quickly, it's so hard to tell who's who."

"It's just part of the game, Mom. No big deal."

"I always thought you should write a paper on it," Grant suggested. "Something on violence and the performance of masculinity in sports."

"Speaking of college," Jenny jumped in.

"Which we weren't," Robbie said, knowing he was fighting a losing battle. Georgia patted his hand in sympathy.

"Have you thought any more about finishing your degree with those online classes I showed you?"

Robbie held back a sigh. "I don't have time, Mom. I'm too busy. I barely have time to buy underwear." He didn't look directly at Paul as he said that, but out of the corner of his eye, he saw Paul smiling around his straw.

"Twenty-two minutes of work every few days and you're too busy?" Grant asked.

Paul's eyes widened. Robbie clamped a hand on his knee before he could say something.

Georgia came to the rescue, as she had so many times before. "That's just time he spends on the ice, Grant. I know we've had this discussion before. They have skill drills for everything, different workouts and post-workout care. Equipment has to be maintained and then the travel. How many miles did the Thunder travel last year?"

"I wasn't on the team, but from what I remember, they hit fifty thousand, but they made the playoffs," Robbie answered.

"And how many games?"

Paul answered that one. "Eight-two for the season. Forty-one home, forty-one on the road."

"Over how long?" Georgia asked.

Robbie was more than happy to let Paul and Georgia carry this conversation. He'd told all this to his parents before, but he got the feeling they thought he was exaggerating.

"In six and a half months. Twenty-eight weeks, ma'am. Miss Georgia."

"So about three games a week. For twenty-eight weeks with no breaks."

"Yes, ma'am," Paul answered with a grin. "Assuming we don't make the playoffs. Which I am not willing to do right now."

He and Robbie shared a fist bump.

"Well, we do have that bye week in the spring," Robbie interrupted. "So, we get one week off."

Georgia turned to Robbie's parents. "When I was in college we played thirteen games over thirteen weeks, seven of them at home. The NFL teams play sixteen regular season games over seventeen weeks."

"That's a big difference," Grant admitted it. "When you put it that way..."

"And the numbers don't reflect the pace of the season. How many back-to-backs do you have guys have this year?"

"Thirteen," Paul and Robbie said simultaneously.

"But who's counting, right?" Georgia said with a smile. "And how many of those require you to travel to or from Seattle between games?"

Robbie pulled up his schedule and conferred with Paul. "Do we count California or Vancouver? Because they're really close."

"It's travel, it counts."

"Five?" Robbie asked, looking at Paul.

"Sounds about right. So, not too bad."

Robbie shook his head. "Those back-to-backs when you're on the road are killer."

"I assume you mean playing two games on subsequent nights," Grant said. "What exactly does that entail, especially with the travel?"

"It means," Georgia explained, "you work a whole day – morning skate, couple of hours of workouts, go eat lunch with the team, go back to the hotel, catch a nap, and then show up in your lovely suit – looking good, by the way guys - at the rink by 5:30 to watch some tape, strategy planning, and last minute equipment adjustments. Game starts around 7:30."

She checked in with the boys to make sure she wasn't leaving anything out.

"Sometimes we eat and go to the bathroom, too," Paul added.

Robbie motioned for Georgia to continue. This was the most fun he'd had at a meal in ages. Between Georgia and Paul, he'd never felt so supported in front of his parents. It wasn't that they didn't love him, they just couldn't find it inside themselves to care about hockey. Which was his whole life. Robbie pushed that thought away for another day.

"So," Georgia continued, "they play the game, which takes about two, two and a half hours, skating an average of five miles a game, taking hits the whole time. Then there's the post-game interview, shower, change, and get on the bus to the plane. Then you fly through the night, landing just in time to check into the hotel, have a few hours' sleep, and then do it all again."

"Are you doing that today?" Jenny asked. "Did you play somewhere else last night?" She looked like she had realized for the first time that her son and his team had been bouncing around the country like madmen since October.

"No. We're lucky, we had a travel day yesterday, and we'll have one tomorrow."

"You've always worked so hard at your sports," Jenny said. "I love that."

"And school work," Paul said quietly.

Even Robbie was surprised to hear that. "How do you know?"

I pay attention, Paul signed. *I remember*. He painstakingly finger-spelled *dyslexia* and *dysgraphia*. "Right?"

"Right." Robbie was half a second from kissing Paul right in the middle of the restaurant.

"It's true. I'm sorry, Robbie." His mom reached across the table. "You have always worked very, very hard. And I know I, we, haven't said this enough, but we are extremely proud of you for your accomplishments. I'm sorry we make you feel like we weren't."

"Did we do that?" Grant asked, worry evident in his expression.

Robbie looked between Paul and Georgia. Paul nodded.

Robbie took a deep breath. "Yeah, kind of. I mean, I know it's not the Peace Corps—" He broke off as both Paul and Georgia kicked him under the table. "Ow! Okay, fine."

Robbie felt a tiny bit bad at the guilt on his parents' faces, but it felt good to finally say it.

"You're playing tonight?" Grant asked.

"Yeah." Robbie answered, gesturing at his suit. "I didn't get dressed up just to come to Sunshine's Café."

"Is it too late to get a ticket?" Grant asked.

"Really? You want to watch?"

"Of course."

"You'll be rooting against the home team," Paul warned them. "Are you sure you're ready for that?"

"Bring it on," Jenny said with a wave of her arm. "I can handle it."

"Okay then. I'll see if I can get two more tickets."

"Excellent."

There was more hugging than usual when Paul and Robbie had to leave. Even Paul got a hug from his mother, something Robbie had rarely seen.

While the other three were finishing up their goodbyes, Georgia tugged Robbie aside. "Is that the guy from that night? The one who spent the night and then punched you?"

"You remember that?"

She rolled her eyes at him. "How could I forget? You didn't tell me he was gorgeous and polite."

"Sorry?"

"By the way," she leaned in and whispered. "Have you met his dad yet?"

"No. And from what I've heard, I'm in no hurry. He a super religious homophobe."

They both looked over at Paul. "Oh, dear. Bless his heart. But it's funny, you know."

"What's funny?"

"Back in college, I would have put money on Stoney coming out and ending up with Skipper. Talk about two boys in love." She shook her head.

"Hey, quit lollygagging," Paul called. "We gotta go."

"Yeah, yeah." Robbie hugged Georgia and kissed her on the cheek.

Paul came over and did the same. "Lovely to meet you, Miss Georgia."

"Lovely to meet you. I hope we'll be seeing a lot more of you in the future."

"Unless they kick me off the team, I'm sure you will."

24

PAUL—GOOD TIMES THAT HAVEN'T HAPPENED YET

"I think you missed a spot," Robbie called from the couch. "Down by the bottom. I think we need more ornaments."

Paul frowned at the Christmas tree standing in his living room. It was looking a little bare. "No way am I going out to the store on Christmas Eve. Did you get a concussion to go with the twisted ankle?"

Robbie answered by throwing popcorn at him.

Paul picked up the fluffy kernel and examined it. "You know, we could go old school and use popcorn."

"For what?" Robbie threw some more popcorn at him.

"Stop wasting it," Paul said. "For decoration. Haven't you ever seen popcorn strings on a Christmas trees?"

"Maybe in a kids' book once? Do people still do that?"

"I don't know, but we are." Paul walked over to the kitchen and started digging through some drawers.

"What are you doing?" Robbie called from the living room. He was under strict orders not to put any weight on his ankle for the next few days if he wanted any chance of playing the next game. Luckily, through some miracle from the gods of scheduling, they had the next few days off.

"Looking for a needle and thread. I think there were some in the welcome kit the realtor left." *Aha*, he was right. He shoved another bag of popcorn into the microwave and went back to sit on the couch next to Robbie.

Both of their places were starting to look more like people lived in them rather than squatters with terrible eating habits. He'd talked Robbie into furniture shopping, and they'd spent one day wandering through some giant furniture warehouse on the edge of town.

Now they both had actual places to sit and eat in their apartments. Robbie had argued that the giant leather sectional with three recliners, built-in speakers, and a beer cooler in the ottoman was not only ridiculously overpriced, but designed to appeal to every male stereotype there was. The sales person had practically spit out the gum they'd been chewing when Robbie burst out with "I can't believe it's not decorated with penises."

Of course Paul had to buy it after that. He didn't hear Robbie complaining at all while they were hour three of video gaming.

They'd spent another day at Ikea. Also known as the Day from Hell. Robbie had almost had a toddler-level breakdown in the checkout line. After a whispered but vehement argument, Paul had ordered Robbie to the cafeteria to eat something while he checked out for both of them.

The soccer moms on either side of them thought it was the most adorable thing ever. Paul was sure he saw a few taking pictures with their phones.

Christmas Eve was proving much calmer. They'd begged off from visiting their families. Robbie's injury provided a convenient excuse.

He lifted Robbie's legs up and slid under them. He threaded two needles and handed one to Robbie.

"What do I do with this?" Robbie asked.

"You stick it through a nice fluffy kernel. Like this." Paul demonstrated, or tried to. The first few kernels broke.

Robbie tried, and most of his went flying to the carpet.

Paul managed to get three on in a row, so he held his needle up in triumph. The kernels slid off the thread.

"I feel like this would work better if we weren't using popcorn with butter and salt." He moved to wipe his hands on the brand-new houndstooth blanket Sissy had sent him for Christmas.

"Oh, no you don't," Paul said, lunging forward and capturing Robbie's fingers.

"Well, what am I supposed to do?" Robbie asked.

Paul proceeded to lick the grease off Robbie's hand, which led to the blanket and the popcorn both falling to the floor, and Robbie's shirt getting thrown over the back of the couch.

Paul's phone rang, and he automatically looked at it.

"Ignore it," Robbie said. The way he slid his hand down Paul's pants made a very convincing argument.

"Oh, crap," Paul said, pushing himself up, "what time is it?"

"I don't know. About eleven?"

"Crap." Paul rolled off the couch. "Put your shirt on. It's probably my Dad."

He scrambled for the phone. Yeah, it was. And Facetime, too. Turning away from the couch, Paul answered it.

"Chip!" he sister Sissy screamed. "I miss you!"

"I miss you, too, boo." Sissy was six years younger than Paul, and he'd always doted on her. In return, she adored him. He wouldn't have survived his mother's death without her.

They talked for a while. Paul careful not to get Robbie in the frame, and Robbie keeping silent in the background.

It felt good to talk to his father about hockey. His dad had always been his biggest supporter, something he had taken for granted before meeting Robbie's parents.

They'd been better lately, texting before and after games, asking questions about hockey, and listening when Robbie answered them. The best had been after a game that had, as far as Paul could tell, blind officials.

There had been four voice mails from his mother waiting for Robbie after the game. The first one started out tentatively, asking for clarification on why the ref hadn't called the one penalty on the guy who had high-sticked Robbie. By the last one she was ranting and calling for the refs to be 'disbarred or whatever it is that happens to bad referees.'

Tears had been streaming down Robbie's face by that point. He'd been extra sweet to Paul that night. He kept telling Paul thank you for what he'd done until they were past talking.

Talking stats and standings and strategy with his father was something Paul had been doing his whole life. He settled down into one of the recliners and let his father talk. Sissy chimed in every now and then. She was his second biggest fan.

"So where are you going to church tonight?" Stoney asked, catching Paul by surprise with the change of topic.

"Oh. Um, nowhere, sir. I haven't had time to find any place yet. I've only been here a little over a month, and I've been a little busy."

"No need to get snappy, I just don't like you being alone on Christmas."

To Paul's surprise, his father didn't sound upset.

"I won't be alone," he reassured Stoney. "Some of the guys are coming over for dinner tonight."

"Oh, that's nice. Who?" Stoney kept up on Paul's teammates, too.

"Well, uh, Robbie. Rhodes."

"Your defensive partner, right? How is he after that fall? It looked like it could be bad. Media is saying it's just a sprain, but I know how the PR people like to downplay things."

"No, it's just a sprain." He looked over to see what Robbie was up to. He'd put his shirt back on and was half-asleep on the couch. It would be weird not to acknowledge his presence, right? If nothing were going on between them, he would have introduced Robbie over the phone. Thank goodness he was asleep enough for that not to be an issue.

"As a matter of fact," he swung the phone so Robbie was visible in the background, hunkered down under the blanket, ACE-bandaged-wrapped foot propped up a pillow. "I'm keeping an eye on him."

"Oh, you got the blanket," Sissy said from over Stoney's shoulder. "It looks awesome."

"Roll Tide," Robbie mumbled from the couch without opening his eyes.

Sissy laughed. "You been teaching him? Made him watch any games?"

"Nah. I been fixin' to, but the timing never works out."

"So who else is coming?"

"Some of the younger guys, Sergei Progov, the goalie, maybe some of the staff."

"It sounds like a nice night. I'll let you get to it. Try to catch a service on the internet if you can, okay? It's important."

"Yessir, I will." Paul thought of something that would ease his father's fear and maybe hold off the questioning for a little longer. "The league has a ministry, did you know that?"

"No, I did not. But I'm glad to hear it."

"They come 'round 'bout every two weeks, so I've only seen them once. But they seem like a nice buncha people."

"I am very glad to hear that. And do some of your other teammates take advantage of it, too?"

"A few," Paul hedged. In truth, he'd only heard about the ministry. He hadn't talked to anyone involved in it yet. It didn't seem to be a high priority for anyone around him.

They chatted for a little longer, with Paul promising to send his sister some team swag she could show off to her friends. "Now don't about selling it on eBay or something, you hear me?"

"Cross my heart, Chipper. Merry Christmas." Her smiled made Paul homesick for the first time in a while.

"Merry Christmas, Sissy. You oughta plan a trip, get yourself out here. I'll show you around. Introduce you to the guys."

Sissy clapped her hands. "Oh, I would love that so much. Can I go, Daddy?"

"Can't see why not. Maybe we'll both make a trip out. Catch a game." Stoney smiled.

Since that night back in Minnesota, he'd played it completely straight in public. He'd pushed all his feelings down as hard as he could, concentrating on hockey and getting the family through the last few months of his mother's life.

He and Stoney had grown closer, and he missed his family. He'd be able to play it cool around Robbie for a couple of days.

"I'd like that very much," Paul said sincerely.

"That sounded like it went well," Robbie said after Paul hung up. He pushed himself up the couch so he could lay his head in Paul's lap.

Paul combed his fingers through Robbie's hair, enjoying the feel and the way it made Robbie practically purr. "It did. Did you hear the part about them coming out for a visit?"

"I did. You ready for that?"

"I think so. Think you can keep your hands off me for a couple of days?" Paul tried to make a joke of it, but Robbie's silence spoke volumes.

Paul knew Robbie hated the need for secrecy around their relationship. Because of Paul, Robbie couldn't even tell their teammates or his family.

He wished for the hundredth time that he could tell everyone – hell, anyone – about him and Robbie.

"Guess I'll get some practice tonight."

"I'm sorry," Paul said, heart heavy. "I'm sorry I make you live like this."

Robbie opened his eyes and turned onto his back to look in Paul's eyes. "I know. I know you are." He reached up to touch Paul's face. "It's okay."

They both heard the *for now* he left unsaid. "Now kiss me, and then take me to the bedroom and do unspeakable things to me so I can make it through dinner." Robbie's tone was light, but his eyes didn't hold their usual sparkle.

Trying for the same tone, Paul bent down to kiss him. "How come I have to do all the work?"

"I'm injured. You promised the doc you'd take good care of me. They were going to get me a nurse to stay at my place. But you wouldn't let them. I think the least you should do is get some sort of hot nurse's costume and wear it."

Paul swatted him. "The painkillers have gone to your head." He tugged Robbie up onto his lap. "Come here. I'll do unspeakable things right here. Then you can nap, and I'll finish the tree."

"Is that the recommended treatment, Nurse Dyson?" Robbie fluttered his eyelashes.

"Doctor's orders," Paul said solemnly, sliding his hand down Robbie's pants. "First step, a thorough physical."

They both ended up falling asleep, and it was a bit of scramble to get everything ready. They had just finished laying out the glasses when the doorbell rang.

"I got it," Paul called.

"No kidding," Robbie said, waving his crutch.

Paul pulled the door open and stopped dead at the sight of Bryce Lowery, arms full of Christmas presents. Another guy who had to be his boyfriend stood behind him carrying bags stuffed with food.

"Holy crap," Paul said.

25

PAUL—THIS IS WHERE THEY KNOW MY NAME

"Hi, are you Paul Dyson?" Bryce asked. "Jake said this was your place, and that you and Robbie would be here."

Paul's brain wasn't up to processing words yet. Robbie wasn't kidding, Bryce was even better looking in real life. He wore dark blue jeans and an off-white fisherman's sweater that looked like it had been handmade by an actual fisherman's wife in Ireland. He looked like a catalog ad.

"Can we come in? I know we weren't invited." Bryce smiled sheepishly. "But we do come bearing gifts." He held his arms out.

"And food," added the guy behind him.

Paul searched his memory for the guy's name. Chicago? Boston? No, those were bands.

"Who is it?" Robbie called from the couch. "Never mind, even if it's polite burglars let them in. You're letting all the warm air out."

"Suck it up, Rookie. It's about sixty degrees out," Bryce called from the door.

"Bryce? Is that you? Holy shit. Did you bring that younger and much-better looking boyfriend of yours?"

Paul turned to see Robbie struggling to get up from the couch. "Sit!" he said, pointing at Robbie.

Bryce laughed.

"Oh, man, I am so sorry. I just didn't expect you. Please come in." Paul stepped back from the door.

Bryce shifted his packages to one arm and held out a hand to Paul. "Bryce Lowery. Nice to meet you."

Paul shook it enthusiastically. "Yeah. I mean, I know who you are. Nice to meet you, sir."

"Dakota," the other man said, offering his hand to Paul.

"Yes! That's it!" Paul said, slapping his forehead.

"Yeah. I know," Dakota said with a laugh. He lifted the bags he was carrying. "Mind if I drop these in the kitchen?"

"No. Please. Please come in." He stepped away from the door to let them in.

"What, are you Santa Claus now?" Robbie asked. "Who are all those presents for?"

"The whole team," Bryce answered, placing them under the tree. "Plus special ones for Nikki and Jake and you."

"Me? Why me?" Robbie looked stunned.

Bryce stood up and shrugged. "You ate Thanksgiving dinner with my mother. That makes you family now. Sorry. You're stuck with us."

Robbie's eyes grew bright, and he couldn't seem to find anything to say. Paul gave Robbie's shoulder a friendly pat as he followed Dakota into the kitchen. It was all he could do to let Robbie know how much the Lowery family's gesture meant to him.

Paul watched in awe as Dakota unpacked more food than Paul's kitchen had ever seen.

"You didn't have to bring so much," Paul said, examining a tube of some cheese he didn't recognize.

"Yeah, right," Dakota said. "I know how you guys are. None of you can cook, and none of you have time to shop for groceries. I don't feel like spending Christmas Eve eating bean dip and Doritos." He gave a knowing look at the cans of beans sitting on the counter.

"Dang. Called out in my own kitchen, on Christmas Eve no less."

The next hour or so was happy chaos as more people showed up than Paul had been expecting.

Jake surprised him by showing up with a woman who turned out to be Bryce's ex-wife Nikki. He'd invited Jake, of course, but he'd assumed the older captain would have friends or family to spend the evening with.

"Here you go, Dyson," he said, shoving a case of beer into Paul's arms. "Since you can't come to the party because you're babysitting the Rookie here, we brought the party to you."

Nikki had another armload of presents that she added to the growing pile under the tree. Paul had no idea why there were presents. He and Robbie hadn't even gotten each other anything. That bothered Paul, but he couldn't think of anything to get Robbie. Besides, they were together pretty much twenty-four seven. It was hard to surprise someone like that.

Sergei came in with a case of mixed wine and hard liquor. "I wasn't sure what you would need," he explained, handing Paul the case.

"So he brought it all." A guy about Paul's age came in behind Sergei. Paul didn't recognize him, so he assumed he was Sergei's friend. They were an odd pair. The new guy was tiny and slender, very blonde, and, not that Paul could be sure, but he seemed pretty gay. Maybe it was the tight red jeans.

"Guess I'll introduce myself," the guy said, "since some people have *no manners*." He pitched that last part loud enough for Sergei to hear over the general chatter of the room.

"Alex Stanton," He held out his hand. "Figure skating coach for a few of your teammates. We haven't met." He eyed Paul from top to bottom. "*That* I would have remembered."

Paul blushed. Yeah, definitely gay. "Well, um, I'm Paul Dyson. Defense. Please come on in and welcome to my home."

"Thank you very kindly," Alex replied with a smile. "A southern boy with manners. Lovely. Now, where's the bar?"

Lipe and a couple of the guys Paul didn't know very well arrived not long after, already halfway drunk, and the party was on.

Between what Dakota had cooked and the random items everyone else bought, there was plenty to eat. And lordy was there alcohol.

None of the guys on the team drank much usually, but it was Christmas Eve, they had the next four days off, and even better, Jake had given them a special Captain's Dispensation. "Just don't do anything stupider than usual. Off-the-ice injuries can get you in big trouble, and I'm not bailing anybody out of jail."

Three hours later, Lipe and the guys had gone, leaving what Paul realized were four couples. Well, two that he knew off.

Everyone knew about Bryce and Dakota, of course. But no one knew about him and Robbie. He had no proof that there was anything between Jake and Nikki, but he would have put money on it. And he was definitely getting some vibes between Sergei and Alex. That surprised him the most because he'd never heard of Sergei being with anyone, male or female.

Paul had seen all three of those pairs make their way up to the solarium at one point or another. He was jealous that he couldn't get any alone time with Robbie.

They weren't dancing with a lampshade on your head drunk, but none of them were feeling any pain. Even Robbie, which was proving a problem for Paul.

Robbie kept forgetting he wasn't supposed to put any weight on his foot, and kept trying to get out of the recliner he'd been sitting in all evening.

It had taken Jake threatening to tell the coach to bench him to get him to sit down. "Do I have to get Dyson here to sit on you to keep you in that chair?" Jake asked.

Paul wasn't sure Dakota's coughing fit after that was completely coincidental. He narrowed his eyes at Bryce's farmer who only blinked back at him with a suspiciously innocent expression. Figured it would take the gay guy to pick up on him and Robbie. Took one to know one, he guessed. That sounded like a problem for future, sober Paul.

Paul pointed a finger at Dakota, then walked a little unsteadily to the bar for another cocktail for him and one for Robbie. He had to admit to being a little starstruck. He'd only been on the team a month, and here he was with Bryce Lowery and Jake Donovan in his living room. Insane.

Alex had taken over mixing cocktails, despite not drinking any himself. "Habit," he admitted. "Too many calories. Figure skating is worse than ballet with the anorexia. You can never be too thin. Makes it easier for someone to pick you up."

The whole room laughed at that. "Sheet," Paul drawled. "You ain't bigger than a minute. I could pick you up one-handed."

Alex raised his eyebrows. "I'd love to see you try it, country boy."

Sergei got to Alex first. Without a word, he scooped Alex up with an arm around his hips. With a quiet *yup*, he kind of bent down, got his hand under Alex's butt, and lifted him up to shoulder height.

Eyes wide and laughing, Alex braced one hand on Sergei's head.

"Damn, Serge, you're a monster," Robbie called into the slightly-stunned silence.

Alex patted Sergei on the head. "You can put me down now, Sergei Ivanovich."

Sergei lowered Alex gently with a smile. To Paul's eye, the little guy looked a tad flustered. His cheeks were pink, and he wasn't making eye contact as he walked over to the part of the kitchen counter set up as a bar.

Paul looked over at Robbie, who met his eyes with raised eyebrows and a tiny smirk. So it wasn't just Paul who'd picked up on it.

Paul handed Robbie his drink. He had no idea what Alex was mixing, but it went down awfully smooth. "Sit next to me," Robbie said. He grabbed the waistband of Paul's pants and dragged him down to the couch.

Paul ended up next to Dakota and Bryce, who subtly moved over to make room on the couch. Dakota ended up in one of the recliner seats.

"Oh, this is nice," he said, pressing the button to make the seat recline and the footrest come up. "We need to get one of these," he told Bryce.

Robbie might have been drunker than Paul realized. It was hard to judge because he wasn't walking around much. His eyes were looking a little glassy.

Definitely drunk, Paul realized as he felt Robbie's hand slipping behind his back. He fought the urge to leap up from the couch.

"How'd you manage to sneak out of spending Christmas with the family?" Nikki asked as Jake handed her a plate of food, then sat down on the floor next to her.

"I think Thanksgiving was enough excitement for all of us," Bryce said.

"You got that right," Robbie said loudly. "That was crazy." Swinging his feet up over Paul's legs, he turned and narrowed his eyes at Bryce. "For the record, what you did was half romantic and half a dick move. Maybe 25/75."

26

PAUL—STOP PLAYING THOSE EYES

Paul froze, he couldn't believe Robbie had brought up Bryce's outing of himself and Dakota on the kiss cam. He braced for Bryce's anger.

Luckily, Bryce just laughed and dragged Dakota in for a hug. "Believe me. I know that. I knew that about one minute after I did it. And only because it took me that long to find Dakota."

"The way you went over that railing was awesome, Dakota" Jake laughed. "And then that picture of you guys kissing was all over the internet in like ten seconds."

Paul knew the big outing had happened at Thanksgiving, only a month earlier. Everyone seemed pretty comfortable with it, including Bryce's ex-wife. It couldn't possibly be that easy, could it? Though if he remembered correctly, Bryce and Miss Nikki had been divorced for a while already.

So what was it with Bryce and Dakota? Love at first sight? Was that even real? He felt the weight of Robbie's legs and thought about how they'd basically been living together since his first day. What did that mean?

"How has the big coming out been so far?" Robbie asked.

"Robbie!" Paul was shocked. "That is a very personal question."

But he might as well have been talking to a fence post for all the attention Robbie paid him.

Now that it was out there, Paul was kind of interested in the answer. Judging by how Sergei's ears perked up, and the way Alex not-quite-aimlessly headed over to lean against Sergei's chair, he wasn't the only one with a vested interest in the answer.

Bryce shrugged, looking embarrassed. "I kind of took the coward's way out, retiring right then. Not like I was risking anything."

"No!" Robbie said vehemently, leaning across Paul to poke Bryce in the arm. He wrapped an arm around Paul's neck for stability. "There's no right time or place or way to come out or be out." He stopped and thought. "Definitely some wrong ones, though."

"Now you sound like Dakota," Bryce said smiling.

Robbie collapsed against the back of the sectional, legs still hooked over Paul's. "Do you think I should come out?"

Jake caught Paul's eye and looked deliberately from Paul to Robbie. Fuck. Busted. Paul took a big sip of his drink to hide his blush and avoid further eye contact.

"Do you think everyone should? Like, do we have an obligation or something?" Robbie stared at his drink like it held the answers to the universe or maybe he had no recollection how he came to be holding it.

Paul took the glass from him and set it on the table.

Bryce exhaled loudly. "I don't know, Robbie. It's not like I'm an expert on any of this. I'm still figuring it out. I had enough money for the rest of my life, and my family behind me, and still it was tough. I mean, it took me until I was thirty-something even to acknowledge that I was..."

"Gay," Nikki supplied from the floor.

"Yeah. Gay. I'm sorry," he apologized.

Nikki waved his apology off with her glass. "I need another drink," she said, pushing up. "Bartender?"

Alex popped up. "Right away, madam."

"I could use another one, too," Robbie called, leaning his head over the back of the couch.

"No, he couldn't," Paul yelled, reaching over to slap Robbie on the back of the head. "You've had enough."

"Party pooper," Robbie said, crossing his arms over his chest.

Paul laughed. "You're ridiculous."

"What about the league?" Sergei asked, startling everyone. "How do you think they would react? It was different for you since you are retired. I think an active player would be different, no?"

"I think they're waiting for it," Bryce answered. "I know for a fact they are. You know John Meilen, the media guy?"

The four players nodded.

"When he found out, he was mostly disappointed because I ruined their big plans. They have this whole campaign in place for the first one to come out. Gay-friendly reporters and newspapers lined up. He's gay, too, by the way. Married."

"The fans?" Paul asked, drawn into the conversation. That was one of his biggest fears, getting attacked by some random person.

He knew for a cold, hard fact that if he were to announce that he was gay to the public, hell, if he were to announce it to the people that were supposed to love him, people would hate him. They would spit on the ground he walked on. Shit, strangers who didn't even know him from Adam would be hating on him and telling him he would burn in hell.

Just the thought of it made him a little nauseous. But Bryce had done it. And Dakota and Robbie. And probably Alex. They were good people. In Bryce's case, his professional idol. They were way braver than he could ever be.

"I don't know," Bryce admitted. "They're just people. Judging from the comments I see on Twitter, some will hate it; some will love it – because you know we have gay fans – most won't care as long as you don't suck."

Robbie snorted and raised his eyebrows, breaking the heavy mood.

Bryce blushed bright red.

"Get your mind out of the gutter," Nikki told him, tossing a crouton at him.

"I can't. I'm a growing boy. My mind is permanently in the gutter. Hey." That last part was directed at Bryce. "How do you know what people are saying about you on Twitter and shit?"

Paul smacked him on the leg. "Language. There is a lady present."

"Thank you," Alex said from the bar where he was doing something with the leftovers. "Grab some of those for me, darlin'," he said to Nikki, indicating a stack of shot glasses. Plucking an unmarked bottle of clear liquid out of the ice bucket, he rejoined the group.

Gracefully, he sank to the floor in front of Sergei's chair. He placed a plate of pickles on the floor and took the shot glasses from Nikki.

"Sergei Ivanovich has graciously supplied us with this nectar of the gods, straight from the bosom of Mother Russia, which I realize is a mixed metaphor but just roll with it. It would be unbearably rude not to drink it. As it is only to be drunk in the company of family and dear friends, a rule I made up just now, I think this is the perfect time."

He filled shot glasses and passed them around the room until everyone had one. "Some of you are family, some of you are dear friends, some of you are both, and some of us hope to be one or the other."

He lifted his glass in a toast, and the others mirrored him. "To our host, the newest member of the Thunder and the one with the most adorable accent, Mr. Paul Dyson. Thank you for inviting us to your home. To Paul!"

"To Paul," everyone echoed and drank. Alex and Sergei exhaled deeply and drank.

He passed around the plate of pickles. Robbie looked at Paul. He shrugged. He had no idea what was going on, but if Alex wanted him to eat a pickle, he'd eat a pickle. No skin off his back.

Jake caught his eye as he passed the plate to Bryce, and stood up. "Dyson, I gotta talk to you before I have too many shots."

"Do you have to have too many shots?" Nikki asked with a grin.

"I don't have to, but I find myself wanting to. Is that okay?" Jake smiled down at her.

"It's not my head and stomach. You knock yourself out."

He pointed at Alex. "Wait for me, I'll be right back."

"Yes sir, your Captainness." Alex held his hand out for Robbie. "In the meantime, let's see if we can't get you up to the social media speed of your average fourteen-year-old. Following what the great unwashed say about you is one of the purest forms of self-flagellation there is. If you're into that sort of thing."

He kept his voice light, but bitterness lay close underneath it. There was a story there, Paul was sure.

Paul moved Robbie's legs off him and followed Jake upstairs to the solarium. His head was spinning trying to figure out what Jake wanted to discuss. It couldn't be anything good, or he would have said it in the room.

27

PAUL—MY HEART IS YOURS TO FILL OR BURST

Jake walked to look out the windows. The view was arresting. Paul would never get tired of looking out over the bay. At night, the lights of downtown Seattle sparkled on the water. All the additional Christmas lights only made it more magical.

"Nice view," Jake said.

"Thanks. I love it."

"Look, Dyson. Paul." Jake ran his hands through his brown hair. It was long enough that he could hold it back off his face. "I know we don't know each other very well yet, but you gotta trust that I care about the welfare of the team and each of my players."

"I do, sir." Paul had a sinking he feeling he knew exactly what Jake thought he knew.

"I should be talking to you and Rhodes, but I have a feeling he'll be lucky to remember anything that happened tonight. Not the best time for a serious conversation. He's what, twenty-one? Probably just learned how to drink."

"Yessir." Paul clasped his hands together tightly, ready for whatever Jake wanted him to do. Jake was Team Captain. He was the leader of the team. Would they kick him off the team? Could they? Would they trade him?

Jake looked at Paul and sighed. "Oh, for Chrissake kid, you look like you're gonna pass out." He led Paul over to one of the window seats. "Sit down. I'm not going to bite your head off."

Paul sat.

"I'm too old, tired, and drunk to beat around the bush. Whatever is going on with you and Rhodes, you gotta tell the coach."

Paul had been ready for Jake to ask him if anything was going on with him and Robbie. His mind had been racing between lying and letting it all out. But Jake acted like he already knew.

Jake shook his head. "I'm not blind, son. Look, I just got through this with that idiot Lowery and his farmer. I saw that smitten look enough times on his ugly mug that I would recognize it a million miles away. Robbie looks at you like Bryce looked at Dakota when he thought we weren't looking."

He dropped heavily down onto the seat next to Paul. "Don't even get me started on Sergei and his twink. That's gonna be fun."

"I'm sorry," Paul said, not sure what he was apologizing for.

"Sorry for what? I've seen enough to know that we love who we love. Can't do a damn thing about it. Love is totally irrational." Jake stared out the window, fingernail scratching a flake of loose paint.

Paul had a feeling he was talking to himself as much as to Paul. "I'm not…I mean…we're…it's new. It might not be anything…" Paul trailed off.

Jake laughed. "Yeah? How many nights you guys spend apart in the last say two weeks?"

Paul didn't answer.

Jake laughed again. "That's what I thought. Whatever it is, you have to tell Coach. He needs to know. You can't blindside him with this when you have your first lover's quarrel."

Paul dropped his head into his hands with a groan. "I know. You know how much I worry about that?"

"And you should," Jake said, not unkindly.

“I’m not out. Like at all,” Paul said into his hands. “My father would kill me. I can’t be out.”

Jake rubbed Paul’s back reassuringly. “You don’t know that. It might not be so bad.”

Paul sat up and grabbed Jake’s hand. “No, sir. I’m being as serious as a heart attack. We’re Southern Baptist. My father and all his friends believe gays are tearing the fabric of society apart and all of them will, and should, burn in hell.”

“Jesus,” Jake whispered with a shake of his head.

Paul laughed at his choice of expletives. “I’ll tell Coach, I swear on my life. But you can’t tell anybody else. This can’t get out.”

“Man, you have some serious shit to work through, don’t you?”

Paul barked a laugh. “Yessir, you could say that.”

Laughter floated up the stairs. He heard Bryce laugh and say something loud. There was another burst of laughter from the room.

“I don’t think they’re waiting for us,” Paul said.

Jake paced the short distance across the room. “You know we have people you can talk to. Therapists, counselors. This is a tough, tough job we have. People on the outside only see the money and the perks. They don’t see what the lifestyle can do to people. I’ve seen it all, Paul. Drugs, cheating, alcoholism, suicide. It’s tough.”

Paul thought about how exhausted he always seemed to be and how he’d been going full-throttle since he’d hit Seattle. “I didn’t know it would be like this in the show, sir.”

“No one ever does.” Jake clasped Paul’s arm reassuringly. “You know the team has people you can talk to. About anything. Lots of us need someone to keep our secrets.”

“Thank you, sir. I’ll keep that in mind.” He did have to find someone. Maybe he’d look for the kind of church Robbie had talked about. “And I will tell the coach. As soon as I can.”

“Good man. Talk to Robbie about it. Make sure you guys are on the same page. I can promise me and the coach won’t breathe a word of it. But if you don’t want anyone on the team to figure it out, you two had better work on your poker faces. I expect to see little cartoon hearts flying around your head every time one of you idiots looks at each other."

Paul laughed. "Are we that bad?"

Jake huffed a laugh. "Yeah, dude. You're that bad."

"I really like him."

"No shit," Jake said wryly. "He's a good guy. You could do worse. So could he."

"Thank you."

Jake clapped him on the shoulder. "Come on; let's get back down there before they drink all the vodka. Personally, I feel the need for about six more shots."

Paul smiled and followed behind Jake. He couldn't resist asking. "So, about you and Nikki..."

Jake stopped so fast that Paul slammed into his back. "That obvious, or did you just take a stab in the dark?"

"Pretty obvious, to me anyway, sir."

"Stop calling me that. Jeez." Jake ran his fingers through his hair again, scratching at his neatly trimmed beard. "Well, like I said, we all got something. Come on."

They came down to a very different room. Sergei and Alex were gone. Dakota had his coat on and was holding Bryce's jacket. Bryce and Nikki were having an animated whispered conversation in the kitchen.

Robbie slept on the couch, oblivious to it all.

"How long were we up there?" Paul asked Jake.

He shrugged and crept up to Dakota. "Hey. Should I ask?"

Dakota's expression was clouded with worry and the effects of the alcohol. "Bryce let it slip that we're planning on getting married in February. During the Thunder bye week."

"Oh, damn," Jake said. "That's fast."

Dakota's smile held no humor. "And he told her we're doing it because we need to be married if we're going to foster some kids."

"Oh, for fuck's sake," Jake said, gaze flying to Nikki.

"Yes," Dakota agreed. "We were going to tell everyone, obviously, just not like this." He waved his hand across the detritus of the party.

"I'd better take her home."

"Good plan."

The goodbyes were more perfunctory than the hellos had been. Paul promised to make sure to deliver the gifts to the team. Dakota and Bryce hugged him. Paul took a minute to fanboy over being hugged by Bryce Lowery. It was a superlative hug.

"I know Robbie is going to forget," Dakota said. "But you two are invited to come visit us anytime it fits your schedule. Okay? We can argue over which state has the best peaches. It's Colorado, by the way."

"It's a deal. Thank you so much. It was nice to get to meet you both."

Jake patted him on his back, and Nikki hugged him. "Sorry for ruining your party," she said.

"I don't think you could ruin anything, Miss Nikki."

Nikki laughed. "You are just the cutest thing. No wonder Robbie's so smitten."

Told you, Jake mouthed from behind Nikki's back. "C'mon, let's get you home."

Paul shut the door behind them. He looked around at the mess and Robbie asleep on the couch and decided to deal with it all tomorrow.

He walked over and shook Robbie awake. "Hey. Wake up."

Robbie looked around, bleary-eyed. "Where'd everybody go?"

"Home. It's late, and we're all drunk." He hauled Robbie up to a seated position. "Let's go to bed."

Robbie grinned and reached for Paul. "That sounds like a great idea." He leaned back down, hauling Paul with him, and kissed the daylights out of him.

Paul pulled back. "You taste like pickles."

"I'll taste your pickle," Robbie retorted.

Paul laughed at him. "That is mighty cheesy, even for you."

"Okay, how about, help me get to the bedroom, and I'll blow you. Or I could do it right here."

Paul pushed himself off Robbie and stood up. "Bedroom," he said, holding out a hand. "Where did your crutch end up?"

Robbie looked around. "I have no freaking idea."

"Never mind, hold onto me and I'll get you there." Paul draped Robbie's arm over his shoulder. "Keep your weight off that foot," he reminded him.

"Yessir," Robbie said.

They got ready for bed. Paul found the crutch in the bathroom. He sighed heavily when he dropped down in the bed next to Robbie.

Robbie immediately rolled into his side, hissing slightly at the pain in his ankle. He hadn't wanted to take the painkillers with all the alcohol. "That was some night, huh?"

"You don't even know the half of it, you drunk. You slept through it."

Robbie pushed himself up with one hand. "Really?"

"Really. I'll tell you all about it in the morning."

"Okay." He rested his head back down on Paul's chest. He slid his hand up Paul's shirt, caressing gently and making patterns on his skin. "It's Christmas in the morning."

"Um hm."

"I didn't get you anything."

Paul kissed the top of Robbie's head. "That's okay; I didn't get you anything either."

Robbie pushed Paul's shirt up to his armpits. "Take this off. As a matter of fact, just get naked."

"Bossy," Paul said, but he managed to get his T-shirt and boxers off. Robbie stripped his off as well.

"That's much better," Robbie said, running his hands all over Paul, and sliding their bodies against each other.

Paul didn't think he'd ever be over how amazing it felt to touch Robbie, to feel the hard muscles under his skin.

Paul rolled onto his side to kiss Robbie better. There was something different about their kisses tonight; something deep and gentle. He felt like he could kiss Robbie forever.

Tears pricked behind his eyelids as he thought about how amazing the night had been.

How accepting everyone had been. Jake's kindness and concern. Bryce and Dakota's easy offer of friendship, and Sergei's calm, quiet presence. Even Alex had been funny and easy to hang out with.

And they all liked him just the way he was. Gay, straight, bi, it didn't matter. They didn't care. They didn't judge him for it.

He wouldn't have had any of it if it wasn't for the man in his arms right now. He crushed Robbie hard against himself as it hit him how much he cared about Robbie, how important he was.

Robbie pulled away. His brow furrowed and he reached out with his thumb to wipe a tear away from the corner of Paul's eye. "You okay?"

Paul nodded.

"Yeah?"

"Yeah."

Robbie cradled Paul's face with both hands and placed soft, sweet kisses on his lips.

Paul felt a tear trickle down his cheekbone.

"You sure you're okay? Is my kissing so bad that I make you cry?"

Paul's laugh sounded a little too close to a sob for his liking. He felt like his heart was going to explode. "No. It's that good," he admitted. "It makes me feel..." he took a deep breath. "It feels like..." He hesitated, unable to get the words out. What if he were wrong? What if it was just him?

He would die. Right here right now in this bed they'd bought together, he would die.

"It feels like?" Robbie prompted, hands still on Paul's face.

Paul shook his head. He couldn't say it.

Robbie scooted back, putting enough distance between them that he could use his hands. *It feels like I love you?* he signed.

Paul could only nod, every blink of his eyelids sending another tear slipping down.

Robbie smiled. That's because I do.

I love you, too, Paul signed back, grateful they didn't need to speak. What he felt was too big for words.

Robbie's eyes burned into his. *Then show me. Make love to me.*

So Paul did.

It was the best Christmas of his life.

28

PAUL—POPPIN' CHAMPAGNE, LIVING MY LIFE

New Year's Eve didn't suck either.

They'd played the Sharks early, and the crowd had been pumped up. Paul loved that home game energy. When the unmistakable opening notes of Thunderstruck blared out of the speakers, building and building to a crescendo, and the deep voice of the announcer yelled for everyone to bring the thunder, the stadium floors shook with the reverberation of thousands of people stomping their feet in unison and the ceiling rang with the sound of thousands of fans screaming THUNDER!

Paul would never forget the feeling of skating out to that as long as he lived.

They'd won their game that evening by a respectable two goals, mainly by not giving the Sharks a chance to score. Most of the action had been around the Sharks' defensive ice. They could barely move the puck through the neutral zone without the Thunder taking ownership.

Of the twenty shots on goal they had gotten, Sergei had blocked all but two of them. And one of those was a lucky rebound off the Sharks' center's skate.

In addition, Paul and Robbie had gotten tapped to jump in with the penalty kill line. They'd kept the Sharks from even getting a shot on goal during the power play. Paul and Robbie passed the puck between themselves and around the Sharks' offensive like they were playing a game of monkey in the middle.

After the game, the media analyzed the crap out of the increased skill and speed of the Thunder defense while the team gathered at the Pucker Up, their main hangout in town.

Close to the arena and public transportation, the Puck was an institution. A sports bar that had hit the jackpot when the Thunder had moved into the neighborhood with the redevelopment of the Key Arena.

Yeah, it was a pretty good New Year's Eve.

It would have been perfect if that one guy would stop touching Robbie.

Paul knew Robbie was out to the team, but he hadn't realized it was an open secret with the local fans, as well. How open was the question? He should find out what, if anything, the world was saying about Robbie.

Paul grit his teeth and smiled as he watched the guy touch Robbie's arm again. Of course, the stupid guy was freaking gorgeous, with freckled light-brown skin and a riot of copper-colored corkscrew curls. How was that fair?

Robbie's laugh rose above the general bar chatter, and Paul forced himself not to look in his direction. What the hell could be so funny anyway?

Why didn't Robbie tell the guy to buzz off and come sit at the table with Paul and the rest of the team?

Paul poured himself another beer. It was probably for the best that Robbie stayed out of his arm's reach. Since the end of the game, Paul had been counting the minutes until he could get Robbie naked. Robbie on the ice, playing like he was possessed, was the sexiest thing Paul had ever seen.

Since Christmas Eve and the whole exchange of I love yous, it had gotten significantly harder to hide their relationship. Most of the time they tried not to make too much eye contact.

Jake was making eyes at him, so he plastered on a smile and put his arm around the woman in the short red dress who had been hovering around his chair for the last few minutes.

"Hey, darlin'," he said, laying on the Alabama thick as molasses. "Did you see the game?" He raised his voice as the eighties cover band in the back made it hard to hear anything.

"I did. You were great. I was glad Coach Williams tried you and Rhodes on the penalty kill. I was hoping he would." She tapped a manicured fingernail against her martini glass full of something pink. "'Course, the Sharks weren't playing their best tonight. Holiday games are hard."

"Yeah, they are," Paul said trying to keep the note of surprise out of his voice. Out of the corner of his eye, he could see Jake silently laughing at him.

He pulled his arm off the woman's hips, and really, his momma would have had a few choice words for him for being rude. "Paul Dyson, ma'am," he said, holding out his hand. "Nice to meet you."

She shook his hand firmly. "Sarah Lipe, nice to officially meet you."

Paul had a sinking feeling in his stomach. "Lipe? That can't be a coincidence."

"Sister," she said with a grin. "Little sister."

Paul groaned as the rest of the table burst into laughter. He kicked Jake under the table. "You couldn't say something?"

"Could have," Jake said. "Didn't. More fun this way."

Paul craned his neck, searching the bar for Lipe. Luckily, he was on the other side of the room, hovering over a tiny redhead who barely came up to his nipples.

Sarah patted him reassuringly on the shoulder. "Don't worry, Danny's not my keeper, much as he'd like to think he is."

Paul sprung out of his chair. "Please, sit down. I can't believe I was so rude. My baby sister would tan my hide. She's small, but mean."

"Thank you," Sarah said, sliding into the chair. "These stupid shoes are killing me."

"Can I get you another drink?" Paul asked.

"I wouldn't say no to a cosmopolitan."

"You got it." He gathered up the empty pitchers. "I'll get this round, too. Though you bastards don't deserve it. No offense to you lovely ladies," he said to the girlfriends, wives, and fans hanging out in their rather large group.

It just so happened that his path to the bar passed by the high table where Robbie and the douche were standing. He smiled and bumped shoulders with Robbie. "Hey, loser, come join the rest of us. I'm buying, and it's almost countdown time." He couldn't kiss Robbie at midnight, but he at least wanted him there. Paul's jaw clenched at the idea of douche guy kissing Robbie.

"Hi. I'm Sam," the guy said to Paul, flashing a charming grin. "Big fan."

"Nice to meet you, Sam. I'd shake hands, but…" Paul motioned to the glass and pitchers he was carrying.

"I really should," Robbie said to the guy.

Did Paul detect a bit of apology in his tone? Robbie should be apologizing to Paul for ditching him.

Robbie wasn't done being Mister Congeniality. "You can come with us if you want," he offered. "Meet some of the other guys."

Paul stepped on Robbie's foot. Yeah, he knew it was childish, but he didn't give a crap.

"Thanks for the offer, but I should get back to my friends. They probably think I skipped out."

Robbie took one of the pitchers. "Sorry, Sam. It was great talking to you."

"Maybe we can do it again, some time?" He pushed his curls back from his face and gave Robbie a grin.

Good Lord, Paul thought. Could this guy sound any more desperate? Paul stood there waiting to see what Robbie would say.

"I don't have a lot of free time," Robbie said. "But if you see me around, come say hi."

Sam nodded and spoke deliberately at Paul. "Yeah. I'll do that."

Paul was going to punch him. Instead, he settled on pasting on a smile and elbowing Robbie in the side. "Come on, Rhodes. Make yourself useful."

With a wave and a Happy New Year to Sam, Robbie left. They pushed their way through the heavier than normal crowd.

"He seemed nice," Paul said deadpan.

"He was. I've seen him around a few times before. How about that woman you had your arm around? She nice?"

Paul snorted. "She's great. And Lipe's little sister," he admitted.

Robbie burst out laughing, and Paul couldn't help laughing along with him.

"Did you know his first name is Danny?"

Robbie shook his head as he pushed his way to the bar, using his bulk and smile to clear the way. "I don't think so."

"Hey, guys," Isaac the bartender said. "You're just in time. I've got a case of champagne on ice for you."

"Oh, sweet," Robbie said. "Forget the beer then, hand over the bubbly."

Isaac called for a barback, and the kid eventually got four buckets of champagne bottles set up. "You need any help carrying those?"

"Nah, we're good," Robbie said, scooping up two of the buckets. Paul grabbed the other two and followed him back to the table where they were met with happy cheers.

"Now it's a party," someone said, grabbing one of the bottles.

The barback showed with a tray full of champagne glasses. "You forgot these."

At first, Paul and Robbie squeezed themselves into opposite ends of the gathering. But as the crowd shifted and people changed spots, they ended up leaning against the sill of the big front window, pressed together hip to hip.

Robbie leaned into him, and some of the tension left Paul's shoulders. This sucked. Hiding sucked. It had been easier when it was just his theoretical gayness he was hiding. He was so jealous of the way Robbie got to be so open. If Paul hadn't existed, Robbie could have brought that Sam person over to the table, and maybe even kissed him at midnight without anyone batting an eye.

As it worked out, neither of them kissed anyone at midnight, though Robbie did reach behind Paul's back and squeezed his hand. Then he leaned over and said right into Paul's ear. "At least you didn't punch me this year."

Of course, Paul punched him.

There was much champagne drunk, and many kisses and hugs exchanged. Paul wouldn't have wanted to be anyplace else. Well, maybe one other place, he amended, watching Robbie's eyes sparkle as he laughed, his cheeks pink from the champagne.

As soon as it was possible to leave without getting too many comments, Robbie said his goodbyes.

Robbie's apartment was a short walk away from the bar, so they were headed there.

Paul could only make himself wait a couple of minutes, rather than the ten they had agreed on. Every part of him screamed to be with Robbie now.

As Jake hugged Paul goodbye, he whispered in his ear. "I thought you were going to punch that guy who was hitting on Robbie. Talk to the coach soon, or I'll have to."

"I promise," Paul said.

Outside, Paul zipped his jacket up against the cold drizzle that couldn't decide if it wanted to turn into a full-fledged shower or not.

He hadn't made it a block before he saw Robbie waiting for him under the awning of a jewelry store.

He smiled as Robbie snagged him by the scarf and pulled him into the shadowed doorway.

"Happy New Year," Robbie said, wrapping his arms around Paul for the kiss they hadn't gotten to do at midnight.

"Happy New Year," Paul answered after the rather long kiss ended. "Ready to move this party inside?"

"Beyond ready."

They walked next to each other, arms brushing as they headed to Robbie's place.

"We have to talk to coach Williams," Robbie said, breaking the silence.

Paul's sigh was a plume of white in the chilly air. "Yeah, I reckon we should."

Robbie hip checked Paul. "Are you going to be okay? Saying something out loud is a big step."

"I might freak out. But I'll try to save it for when I'm alone. That good enough for you?"

"That's good enough." Robbie crowded as close to Paul as he could. "I know it's hard for you."

"You're worth it," Paul said seriously. "We're worth it."

The smile Robbie turned on Paul was worth it.

"I just hope the guys can keep their mouths shut," Paul said with a scowl.

"We don't have to tell the whole team," Robbie reminded him. "Just the coach."

Paul sighed and leaned his head briefly against Robbie's shoulders. "I want to. I need someplace besides our apartment where I can relax."

He pulled away from Robbie, pacing and waving his hands as he ranted a little too loudly for a public street. "I hate feeling like I'm constantly looking over my own shoulder and second-guessing everything I say to you. Am I standing too close to him? Was that a normal friendly smile or something else? Did I hug him too long? It's fucking exhausting."

"You don't have to tell me, man. But you might want to keep it down a little." Robbie nodded at the couple holding each other up as they walked past the boys.

Paul yelled in frustration, head tilted to the sky. "God, I hate this."

Robbie didn't answer. He didn't have to.

Paul's shoulders heaved with the force of his exhale. "So. Yes. I do want to tell the team. I just don't want them to be dicks about it."

Robbie laughed and put his arm around Paul's shoulders. "Oh, I one hundred percent guarantee they will be. Total dicks."

29

ROBBIE—THE PART WHERE THE END STARTS

They walked into the team lounge to a chorus of catcalls, whistles, and some clapping. Robbie noticed a few turned backs and some blank stares, but they were vastly outnumbered by the jokers.

Which was great. Private humiliation was how jocks showed love.

The talk with the coach had gone better than Robbie had expected. He and Paul had tried to figure out all the possible repercussions but eventually gave up in the wee hours of the night.

Coach Williams hadn't seemed surprised in the least at the confession. They sat awkwardly in chairs across from him, a large wooden desk between them. Jake leaned against a four-drawer metal filing cabinet with his arms crossed and studied them.

"The league's not stupid, boys," the coach said finally. "We've known this was inevitable, and there's been a lot of discussion with managers and owners about how to handle it. What rules and regulations, if any, to put in place. How to handle the media. Changing room, shower issues and all that."

"What have they decided?" Robbie asked, exchanging glances with Paul.

The coach shook his head. “Nothing. Can’t agree on a damn thing. I think half of them don’t have the sense God gave a goose. Especially that shower bullshit.” He waved a hand at Robbie. “You came here with a boyfriend, for chrissakes. Anyone on the team give you shit about showering?”

“No, sir.”

“Any harassment on the ice from other teams?”

“No more than the normal chirping. Nothing I can’t handle.”

The coach nodded. “Good, good. Well, I’m not gonna say I ain’t worried about you boys having a falling out and messing up my team. You’re young, dumb, and, well, you know what else.”

He leaned forward over the desk. “You fuck up my team, and I will trade one of you to Winnipeg and the other to the Panthers. Got it.”

“Yessir,” they said in unison. Robbie wanted to clutch Paul’s hand, but that seemed like a terrible idea.

Coach leaned back in his chair. “So are we telling the team or not? How hush-hush is this? Rhodes, I know your love life is an open secret, but still, nothing official, nothing confirmed. I haven’t even gotten any direct questions from the press. Dyson?”

Paul blushed, but kept eye contact. Now Robbie did squeeze his hand. “I want to tell the team, sir. I don’t like keeping secrets from them. It’s not a good way to build trust.”

Coach nodded as if he were impressed with Paul’s decision.

Paul’s eyes darted to Robbie’s, so Robbie gave his hand another squeeze.

“But, if you don’t mind, I would much appreciate it if we could keep it just to the team. My family, they wouldn’t understand. I’m not ready for that.”

“And the staff?”

Paul blanched.

Robbie understood. The more people that knew, the greater the chance of someone talking to someone they shouldn’t be. Robbie did a quick calculation of everyone he knew worked for the Thunder and came up with about fifty people. He knew there were people he was forgetting, too.

"Can that be on a need-to-know basis?" Robbie asked.

"Absolutely."

"I think I should talk to the guys without you around," Jake said, standing upright. "Give them a chance to speak freely."

"I agree," the coach said. "Why don't you boys come a little later tonight?"

"Yessir," Paul said.

"No problem," Robbie agreed.

They sat in awkward silence as the coach turned back to his computer.

Go? Paul signed

Robbie shrugged.

The coach looked up at them. "You waiting for me to marry you? I'm a coach, not the captain of a ship. Get the hell out of my office."

Paul and Robbie rushed out without a word.

Once the catcalls had died down, Lipe walked up to them, gave them an unreadable look, and pushed past them to the wall of corkboards, whiteboards, and smart boards on the wall. He reached into a cabinet and pulled out a piece of poster board. Sticking it to the whiteboard with some hockey puck magnets, Lipe turned back to the room. "Okay, who was in the pool?"

On the poster was a grid. Written across the top were dates and places such as New Year's Eve, Chicago, Dec. 26th, and game dates.

There were only three entries down the side: The Big D, Rhodes, and mutual.

"You assholes," Robbie said laughing in spite of himself. Paul turned about a hundred shade of red.

"Who voted no?" Lipe asked.

A couple of the guys raised their hands. "You're all losers," he said, pointing at them. "Get your heads out of your asses next time. That was a sucker's bet."

"Now to figure out who gets what, we're gonna need some information right from the source." He waved Paul and Robbie up to the board. "Ok. Give us the deets. First hookup, date, place? Who made the first move?" he asked Robbie. "You or Big D? You've got the experience, but he's got that smooth southern style."

Someone in the back of the room with a surprisingly good voice started singing "Black Velvet."

"Fuck you, Lipe. I'm not telling you anything."

"Fine. Big D?" He raised his eyebrows expectantly.

Paul bit his lip and looked at Robbie. Robbie kept his face as blank as he could.

With a wink, Paul turned back to Lipe. "Chicago."

"Told you!" someone said.

"And..." he pretended to be concentrating. "I'm gonna go with me."

"Damn," Sven Robertson, another defenseman, whistled. "That was your second game with the team. You're a fast mover, D."

"There you have it, boys. Straight," he snorted, "straight as it can be from the horse's mouth. Sergei, you called it on the nose. Very nice. You get the big pot. The rest of you who got it half right will get something."

Robbie walked to the front of the room, heart in his throat. He knew better than to think it would be smooth sailing from here on in; he'd been a gay jock for too long. So he wanted to get some things out while everyone was still making an effort to play nice.

"Guys, guys. I need to say something."

The room quieted, and all eyes were on Robbie. He swallowed, trying to get some moisture back into his suddenly dry mouth. "Thanks for being so awesome. I know this is weird. So, seriously, if this is a problem for anyone, talk to me. Or Jake or someone."

He glanced over at Paul, to see if it were okay if he spoke for both of them. Paul nodded and motioned for him to keep going.

This next part was for those guys who were hiding behind blank faces or avoiding making eye contact with him or Paul. "I know you guys got our backs, but I can't stress how important it is for Paul that this doesn't go any further than us. It will be a disaster if this gets out. But you guys needed to know."

"Plus you suck at hiding it, Rhodes." Sven clasped his hand under his chin and fluttered his eyelids. "Oh Paul, I just love the way you handle a stick."

Robbie threw a dry-erase marker at him.

"Seriously, though," Jake said from the back of the room. The team settled down. Everyone liked and respected Jake. He was a great captain, and his words carried a lot of weight.

"If I find that someone has leaked anything to the press, or talked to your buddies on other teams, there will be serious repercussions. This is for Rhodes and Dyson to share with who they want when they want. Got it?"

There were nods and general murmurs of agreement.

"Great. Now let's get started. We got a game to win tonight."

Paul's sister called seven days later.

They were hanging at Paul's house on an off day. Over the last week, they had fallen into a routine of sorts. Home game days, they spent at Robbie's because it was closer to the arena. Off days they gravitated to Paul's because it was a nicer place to hang out.

He had that awesome couch and video game set up, great views, and a parking spot for the Stingray, which they took out every chance they could. Today was rainy and cold so they'd opted for video games and Chinese food with movies and sex on the menu for later.

"Hey, Sissy, what's up?" Paul said, putting her on speaker and not taking his eyes off the screen.

"You're Tumblr famous!" She sounded more excited than Robbie felt that accomplishment warranted.

"Is that good? Damn it," Paul cursed as his virtual Sidney Crosby missed a shot.

"It's adorable. There's fan art and everything. Hold on; I'll send you some. You guys are starting to pop up everywhere."

Robbie nudged Paul with his foot. *Does she know I'm here?* he signed when Paul looked his way.

Paul shook his head no. "Wait."

Should I keep quiet? Robbie asked just as Sissy's text came through.

Pausing the game, Paul picked up his phone. "Oh, fuck me," he said with heartfelt sincerity.

"What?" Robbie leaned forward to see what Paul was looking at.

It was a lovingly-detailed drawing of him and Paul locked in a passionate embrace. Full on mouth to mouth kissing with both of them in their Thunder jerseys. The tags under it were #RhoDy, #Hockey #Thunderstruck. "Holy shit."

"Who was that?" Sissy demanded. "Is it that cutie pie, Robbie? Is he there? Did you show him the picture?"

What should I say? Paul mouthed silently.

Up to you, Robbie replied. This wasn't a call he could make. Paul had to decide how much to tell his sister.

"Yeah, it's Rhodes," Paul admitted. "We're playing video games."

"Oh, my stars!" she squealed. "Take a selfie and let me post it! I'll get like a thousand new followers!"

"Not in a million years. Besides, aren't you too old for Tumblr?" Paul did something with the phone Robbie couldn't see.

"Well, where else am I supposed to be getting my porn from without Daddy finding out?"

"Cecilia Jean Dyson!"

Robbie laughed out loud at the look of shock on Paul's face.

"Is he shocked, Robbie?" Sissy's voice came through loud and clear.

"He's clutching his pearls like a proper Southern lady," Robbie told her, laughing.

"It's not funny, Sissy Jean. You know Dad can find out everything you do." He held the phone out to Robbie.

He'd searched for the #RhoDy tag on the Tumblr site. There were way too many posts with not only that tag but his and Paul's full names and the team name. It would be so easy to track.

"Don't be ridiculous," Sissy said. "I'm way better than you ever were at keeping things away from him. Plus I doubt Daddy even knows Tumblr exists."

"I bet someone in the media department knows," Robbie answered seriously.

"Fuck," Paul said again. He jumped up from the couch, running his fingers through his hair.

"Chip, what's going on? I thought you would think it was funny. It's just some little girls having fun, letting their imaginations run wild. Right?"

Paul stopped pacing and looked at Robbie. "No. Yeah. It's just, you know, I didn't expect it. It's uh," he dropped his eyes to a spot on the carpet, "hard to see yourself like that, you know?"

The tiny spark of hope that Robbie had let himself have that maybe Paul would start to open up to someone started to die.

"Uh huh." Sissy didn't sound convinced. "So you guys aren't a thing? You do seem to spend an awful lot of time together. I see the interviews with you and him, joking and laughing. You like him. I can tell. Sisters know."

"Sissy! There's nothing going on. We're just friends. I'm not gay, for heaven's sake."

Even though he was braced for it, the words hit Robbie like a blow. He couldn't stay here right now. Moving quickly, he jumped up and started looking for where he'd left his sneakers.

"Uh, hold on, Sissy. Give me a minute." Paul hit the hold button on the phone. "Where are you going?"

"Home. My place." Robbie found his sneakers behind the couch and yanked them on.

"Don't go. I'll get rid of her." Paul reached for Robbie's arm.

Robbie brushed him off with an irritable shake. "Just talk to her. Tell her whatever you have to. I'm going to go home and call John. See how much trouble we're in."

"Robbie," Paul said, a world of meaning packed into that one word. "Are you mad at me? You know I gotta..."

He looked lost, worse than lost. He looked abandoned. "I know you gotta." Robbie sighed, trying to find someplace to put his anger. Paul had to do things in his own time. "I'm not mad. It's just kinda hard, okay? To hear you say it right out like that." He shoved his arms into his jacket.

"I'm sorry. Don't go."

Robbie could tell he was sorry. He looked miserable. This was hurting him more than it was hurting Robbie. "I'm not mad," Robbie repeated. "I just don't want to have to listen to you lie in our, I mean your, own damn house!" Despite his inner battle for control, his voice rose at the end.

"I know. I'm sorry." Paul said. *Sorry* he signed. *Sorry*.

"I know." Taking a deep breath, Robbie took a step towards Paul.

Paul recoiled as if he were scared of Robbie. "Jesus Christ, Paul." Robbie reached for him and pulled him into a hug. "I'm not leaving. I'm just going to take a walk, clear my head, okay? I'll probably get a cup of coffee and do some looking into this. I'll be back. I promise."

"Promise?" Paul sounded very young.

"Promise. I'll bring you back a maple bar, okay?"

"Okay."

Robbie kissed him, and Paul clung to his arms when he tried to pull away. "What are we gonna do?" he asked.

Robbie shook his head. "I don't know, Paul. But this," he pointed at the phone, "sucks."

As he reached for the door, he heard Sissy's voice calling from the phone. She sounded pissed. "Paul Stonewall Dyson, Junior you get your ass back to this phone right this minute. And next time, double check if you've actually put a call on hold before you go running your mouth."

Paul turned pale and snatched the phone up.

Robbie heard Sissy tell him he was dumber than a bag of hammers before the door shut behind him.

30

PAUL—CHOOSING MY CONFESSIONS

"Oh, shit, Sissy. Um, I..." How much had she heard? What was she thinking? What did she know? Oh, shit. Oh, shit. Tears filled his eyes. He couldn't bear it if she hated him.

He couldn't catch his breath. "It's not...I mean..."

"Paul," she said sharply. "Stop. Just stop. I can hear you panicking clear across the country. You're panting like a hound dog in the sun" Her voice was calm, soothing, and more serious than he'd ever heard her sound. "Just breathe. Can you do that?"

He forced himself to take a deep breath in, then another. Blood pounded in his temples, making him dizzy and he dropped down to the sofa.

"Oh, God, Sissy." He tried to get his breathing under control before he passed out. "Say something. Do you hate me?"

The silence stretched until he thought he was going to puke.

"Oh, big brother," she finally said. "I could never hate you. Not in a million years."

Paul let out the breath he had been holding. "Thank you," he whispered.

"So, just to be clear, is something going on between you and this boy?" Her tone brooked no equivocating.

"Yes." He was still whispering as if that would somehow lessen the impact of his words.

"And is he a nice boy?"

"He's a good man, Sissy. Really good." His leg shook nervously as he debated how much to tell her. "But he's...I think he's an atheist." It was the first time he'd said that out loud, too. What a day for confessions.

To his vast surprise, Sissy laughed. "Honey, I think at this moment that is the least of your problems. You're okay with being in love with a man, but him bein' a nonbeliever is a problem?"

"I'm not...It's not that." Paul sank back into the sofa cushions. "I don't know." Was it a problem? With everything going on, Paul hadn't even thought about that aspect of their relationship. He was just so used to everyone around him being Christian, in the back of his mind he kept forgetting Robbie wasn't.

"Well?" Sissy asked sharply. "Is it gonna be a problem?"

Was it? Paul searched his heart as best as he could. "No. I don't think so. It's not like he makes fun of me, or tells me not to believe what I believe. He kind of just lets me be who I am, you know?"

"I do know. And that is good to hear. Do you love him?"

"I've only known him for a little over a month," Paul hedged.

"Don't matter. Not what I asked. Do you love him?"

Paul scrubbed his face with the hand not holding the phone. "Yeah. I think I do."

"And do you love me?" she asked as if that was a real question that needed answering.

"'Course I do! What kind of a dumbass question is that?"

"I'm not a believer. Not anymore. Not for a long time." It was her turn to whisper as if that would soften the blow.

"What?" Paul sat up ramrod straight on the couch. "Since when?"

"Since Jasper died and the pastor told me that he wouldn't be in heaven with me 'cause he was just a dog." Jasper had died twelve years ago, and Sissy sounded as angry as if it had happened yesterday.

"Aw, Sissy. You can't let something stupid like that make you stop believing. Maybe the pastor was wrong." The reflexive need to comfort his sister made the words come out automatically.

"Yeah, Paulie, maybe he was. And then when little Rachel Bloomfield died when she was only eight, remember that?"

"Of course." Sissy's best friend at school had been hit by a car at a street crossing. After she died, the city had finally put up the stop light people had been asking them to put in for years.

"Same pastor told me that I wouldn't see her in heaven either, on account of she was Jewish. I decided right then and there, that if they weren't going to heaven, then neither was I, because it sounded like heaven sucked."

"Sissy, don't say that." Paul needed to believe that he would see his mother again in heaven. "I don't think God would..."

"Would what? Send a child to hell for being born into a Jewish family? Not let dogs into heaven?" she challenged.

"Jeez Louise, I don't know, Sissy! Maybe that pastor was just wrong. Maybe he don't know what the hell he's talking about." Paul never thought he'd hear those words come out of his mouth.

"Exactly. So either God is kind of a douche—"

"Cecilia Jean!" What had happened to his sweet baby sister? Maybe he didn't know her as well as he thought he did.

She ignored his outrage. "—or his minions are just fallible humans who are making it up as much as the next person. Either way, I'm not interested."

Paul had to walk around. He couldn't sit still with this. He paced the room, phone to his head. "Okay. Let me think." He'd been brought up to respect authority. To be an obedient, good son, and not to question his betters.

God was the top of the pyramid. The Word of God was not up for debate.

But there did seem to be a lot more to consider than he had let himself realize.

What if that pastor had been wrong about Sissy's dog and little Rachel? If they were wrong about that, and Paul found himself hoping they were if only for Sissy's sake, then they could be wrong about other doctrines. Like that one that said all gay people were damned.

"Sissy?"

"Yeah?"

He loved the way she drew the word out to two syllables. *Yeah-uh?* Suddenly he missed home something fierce, missed the South in general. He wanted waitresses to bring him sweet tea without asking. He wanted long summer nights at the river and tailgate parties in some farmer's field.

Most of all, he wanted back that childhood certainty of knowing for sure what was right and what was wrong, even if he were on the wrong side.

Sometimes being an adult felt like trying to navigate a swamp, never really sure if it were solid ground or quicksand up ahead.

"You still there?" his sister asked.

"I'm still here. Tell me right out, do you think all gay people go to hell?"

"No, I do not. Are you telling me you're gay?"

"Damn, Sissy, you know I am. I just told you I was in love with Robbie!"

"Don't you yell at me, Paul Stonewall. I am trying to help you here, but if that's the attitude you want to have, I might as well hang up right now!"

Paul could see her clear as day in his mind's eye, scowling at him with her hands on her hips, and it made him smile despite everything.

"Okay, Sparky, calm down. I'm sorry. You're right. It's just a lot, you know?" He opened the fridge, not really looking for anything. All he saw was beer and leftovers.

The freezer held some healthy frozen meals from the nutritionist, but he wasn't hungry. Just restless.

He checked the clock. Eleven a.m.? Maybe not beer then. They did have a game tomorrow. He'd make coffee. It would give him something to do with his hands.

"I don't know what to do."

"About what?"

"About Robbie."

"What do you mean, exactly?"

Paul sighed deeply and then gave voice to his biggest fear. "If I don't come out, be with him in public, eventually he's gonna leave me."

"Oh, honey," she said. "Bless your heart."

"I don't hear you saying not to worry about it." He tried to smile.

"I ain't gonna say that. I think you should pray on it."

"What?" He set the coffee pot down on the counter with a thud. "I thought you said you didn't believe in God anymore."

"I don't. But you do. So talk to him. Remember what that poem Momma always read to us said? 'Be at peace with God, whatever you conceive him to be.'"

Of course, he remembered. "My favorite part was always 'You are a child of the universe.' I love how that sounds. I loved thinking I was a child of the universe." He smiled thinking of it. He missed his momma in so many ways. He wondered if she would have liked Robbie. If he could have told her about him.

"You've always believed, Paul. Since you were a baby. Heck, you're the only thing that kept me going to church as long as I did. It made you so happy. I kept searching for that feeling, but I could never get it."

"I'm sorry."

"You got nothing to be sorry for. That faith, it's in you. It's a shining part of you separate from any dogma. Don't go throwing the baby out with the bath water. Pray on it."

"Well, look at you all wise."

"That's me. So, do you feel better telling me about your flaming gayness?" She laughed.

"Sissy!" She was something. "So you really don't care? You don't hate me, don't think it's weird?"

Somehow he could hear her shrug. "I always had my suspicions. I mean, you and Eubee..." she trailed off.

Paul busied himself making the coffee. He only had a regular old

Mr. Coffee coffee pot, so it wasn't anything that required a great deal of concentration. Still, he gave it all his attention. "Yeah, me and Eubee."

"He was a great guy," she said.

"He was."

"So, tell me all about Robbie," Sissy said brightly.

He loved his sister so much. Why hadn't he talked to her before? "I love you, Sissy."

"I know," she preened. "Now tell me all about your hot boyfriend before he gets back with your dessert."

They talked for almost an hour. It was the longest he'd talked to his sister in probably two years, and Paul vowed to make it a regular occurrence. By unspoken agreement, neither one of them mentioned their father.

Paul was just saying goodbye when Robbie came back with a slightly greasy paper bag in his hand and a concerned expression on his face. "We have a problem," he said as soon as he was in the door.

"Sissy says hi," Paul told him, waving the phone.

Robbie pulled off his sweatshirt and tossed it onto the couch. "You're still talking to her?"

Paul nodded.

"Everything cool?" He looked worried that Paul might have been getting yelled at or preached at the entire time he had been gone.

"Everything's great," Paul said, smiling.

"Then tell her I say hi back and hope I can meet her soon."

Paul did, ending with a promise to call her once a week at minimum.

"What kind of problem do we have?" Paul asked as he took the bag from Robbie.

"I did some searching around with what your sister showed us. There's a lot more out there that I didn't know." He handed Paul his phone, pointing out the different things for him to look at.

He scrolled through Tumblr blogs and Twitter threads. Message boards and Reddit threads. There was a lot of discussion about Robbie's sexuality and whether he and Paul were a couple. There wasn't a lot in one place, no obvious mentions of them. But taken all together, it showed that they weren't as under the radar as Paul wished they were.

Reactions seemed to be mixed.

Over on Reddit, a lot of younger hockey players seemed to be excited about the prospect, some didn't see the big deal about it, and some people called them cowards for not coming out in public.

Some people were disgusted, but only a small minority went completely homophobic.

Over on Tumblr, the girls thought they were as adorable as a box of puppies.

Over the next week or so, things only got worse as far as Paul was concerned. It seemed like everywhere he looked, there were more people speculating on his and Robbie's relationship.

"They're mostly teenaged girls on Tumblr," Robbie pointed out with a hint of exasperation in his voice. He was obviously hitting the end of his patience for Paul's freak outs. "What are the chances of your father being on Tumblr, and would he even care? It's not like you are making these people draw these things."

Paul pressed his thumb hard against the bridge of his nose and squinted his eyes against an imaginary headache as he scrolled obsessively through the website. His head didn't actually hurt, but he felt like it should.

"Oh, he would totally blame me. He would say that I must have been doing something to put the idea in people's minds. And there are video clips of us here, too!" He couldn't believe people had the free time to break their interviews down into two-second clips, caption them, and then assemble the clips into an internet-ready post.

He frowned at the screen as a long text post showed up under #RhoDy tag. Gun to his head, he would admit to thinking the name was cute. In his head, he pronounced it Rho-Dee. Was it Rho-Die? Whatever. Secretly he loved the posts about them, and had made his own Tumblr blog to keep them all in one place.

"Oh, holy moly!" he exclaimed as he read the post.

Robbie snorted. He thought it was hilarious when Paul used what he considered grandma phrases. He liked things that made Paul 'clutch his pearls' as he put it.

"What?"

"People are writing porn about us!" Paul handed Robbie his phone. He watched as Robbie scrolled through the post.

"That's so hot," Robbie said, handing the phone back. "And surprisingly well-written."

"This is so weird." Of all the things Paul had expected to deal with as a result of his getting called up, fan fiction hadn't been one of them.

He was getting the hang of navigating Tumblr now, so he followed a few links until he came to the original source, HockeyFanfiction.com. "Holy crap!" This was getting out of hand.

With a sinking heart, he realized there was no way to stop people from thinking he and Robbie were together. Eventually someone was going to point it out to his father.

The worst thing about it was that it was one hundred percent true.

"It's just a matter of time, isn't it?"

"I think so." Robbie poked at his phone with a frown. "Wait, I think I just saw something. Oh. Here. Look at this."

He turned the phone so Paul could see what he was looking at. It was an Instagram post with a picture of him and Robbie holding hands behind their backs in the window of the Pucker Up on New Year's Eve.

They weren't tagged by name, but the original poster had asked if anyone knew who these 'darling' men were. The poster said they were sure that was the Thunder corner of the bar and they assumed it was two of the players.

Someone was bound to identify them sooner rather than later.

"I think we have to talk to the PR people," Robbie said.

"Me, too." Paul slammed his coffee cup on the counter. "Damn it. I just want to play hockey. Is that such a sin? Why does this shit even matter?"

Robbie could only shrug.

31

PAUL—I'M IN LOVE WITH MY OWN SIN

The PR guys were nowhere near as concerned as they should be, Paul felt.

"It's nothing," Frank said. Or maybe it was Fred. Paul hadn't tried that hard to tell the brothers apart. "We don't respond to rumors of any kind about players. We advise you to do the same."

"Has anyone from the press contacted you directly about anything?" maybe-Fred asked.

"No. Nothing directly." Paul was grateful for that.

"The fan stuff is a non-issue. You should see how much Crosby/Malkin stuff there is out there." Frank, it was definitely Frank, said.

"You've read it?" Robbie asked.

Both brothers nodded. "I like to send it to Crosby's publicist, give her suggestions on how to use it."

Everyone but Paul laughed. He was glad this was a big joke to them.

"Don't sweat it," Frank said, with a friendly hand on Paul's shoulders. "In a way, it helps obscure the fact that you guys are actually together. It's like a smoke screen."

"My father isn't going to feel that way," Paul muttered.

Fred shook his head. "Most people don't even know this kind of stuff is out there. I wouldn't worry about it."

Easy for him to say. He hadn't seen fan art of him getting boned by Robbie. Something that hadn't happened yet. Paul wasn't sure how he felt about that situation.

Paul tried to put it out of his mind, but the knowledge that people were thinking about – *writing about!* – him and Robbie having sex pricked him like a burr under his saddle. It made him second-guess every action, especially in public.

Now, whenever they were in Seattle, instead of both of them sleeping at whichever place was more convenient, he and Robbie spent nights apart more often than not. His car was way too identifiable; the last thing he needed floating around were pictures of him pulling out of Robbie's apartment building in the wee hours of the morning.

Their relationship was starting to crack under the strain. Paul sensed Robbie was near the end of his patience, and he expected Robbie to dump him any minute.

Except, maybe not.

After the game last night, they'd both gone back to Paul's house. Robbie had talked him into it with a very persuasive make-out session in Paul's car. Every time Paul argued with his dick, he lost.

By the time Paul woke up, Robbie was gone.

A fist squeezed Paul's heart. Had he left? Gone home? "Robbie?" he called, as he got out of bed. No answer.

Paul swung between telling himself Robbie just couldn't hear him, and convincing himself that Robbie had split like an embarrassed one-night stand. Quickly, he pulled on a pair of sweatpants and the first T-shirt his hand found in the drawer.

"Robbie?" He crept out of the bedroom as if by moving softly enough, he could keep bad things from happening.

"Upstairs," Robbie called.

Paul exhaled sharply. Thank god. Robbie had already made coffee, so Paul grabbed a cup before walking up the stairs like he was walking to his execution.

What were the chances Robbie wasn't going to want to talk about last night? Close to zero, he reckoned.

His first view of Robbie stopped him in his tracks.

Robbie sat in one of the window seats in the solarium, head leaning against the window and his legs bent in front of him.

He cradled his coffee cup in both hands as he watched the ferries and boats move across Elliott Bay. The sunlight reflecting off the choppy waters glittered like spilled diamonds and highlighted the strands of copper in Robbie's auburn hair.

The expression on his face was as soft as the old flannel sleep pants and BSU T-shirt he wore. He didn't look upset at all. He looked content and so beautiful it made Paul's heart hurt.

That feeling in his heart that he couldn't get enough of Robbie, that if he pulled away from Paul like he should, Paul would feel empty, that had to be love, right?

Paul was almost certain it was. And, against all logic, Robbie claimed to love Paul. Bless his heart.

Robbie deserved someone different. Someone confident, with fewer issues.

Trying to shake off his melancholy, Paul closed his eyes, took a deep breath, and walked over to Robbie.

"Hey," Robbie said with his gorgeous smile. He reached for Paul, wrapping his arm around Paul's hips and reeling him in. "Morning." He tilted his face up for a kiss.

"Morning," Paul said, leaning down to give Robbie what he wanted. Robbie's hand on his cheek turned his would-be peck into a sweet lingering kiss.

Robbie's hand slid up to the back of Paul's head, fingers carding through his hair. With a deep sigh, all the tension left Paul's body.

"There we go," Robbie said. "That's what I was looking for. You've been all keyed up for days."

"I'm sorry. And I'm sorry about last night."

"Don't worry about it," Robbie said, keeping his warm hand on Paul as he straightened up.

"If you say it happens to everyone, I'm going to beat you."

Robbie dropped one leg to the floor and patted the space between his legs on the bench. "Sit with me. Check out the view. It's a beautiful day, and we have nowhere to be for a couple of hours."

It was a tight fit with two big guys, but Paul managed to squeeze between Robbie's legs, his back against Robbie's chest.

Paul leaned his head onto Robbie's shoulder and sighed as Robbie wrapped his arms around him.

"So, I found this old BSU T-shirt in your drawer. Looks like I'm not the only one who keeps things." He kissed Paul's temple.

"It's very soft," Paul said. "Seemed a shame to get rid of it."

"Um-hm." With long, smooth strokes, Robbie caressed Paul everywhere he could reach; down the outside of his legs, up his inner thighs and up to his chest. Nudging Paul's head with his chin, Robbie kissed and nipped at Paul's neck.

His hands left trails of goosebumps in their wake, and Paul shivered at the feel of Robbie's lips on his skin. Though he avoided touching Paul's dick directly, it seemed much more interested than it had been in a more direct approach last night.

Paul squirmed as Robbie bit a little harder than he had been doing. "I don't think you're enjoying the view," he said, smiling.

Robbie hooked his chin over Paul's shoulder and looked along the length of his body. "I like the view a lot."

"Kiss me more," Paul demanded, reaching back for Robbie's head.

"Bossy," Robbie said with faux annoyance, but he went back to driving Paul crazy with his lips, tongue, and teeth. He sucked gently on the thin skin under Paul's chin, then giving it a sharp nip, pulled off.

"Fuck," Paul whispered with a small shudder.

Robbie pulled Paul more tightly against him. Paul felt Robbie's cock grow firmer.

"When this season's over," Robbie growled softly into his ear. "I'm going to leave so many marks all over you; you won't be able to leave the house." He punctuated his words with a press of his hand over Paul's definitely interested dick.

Paul groaned and arched against Robbie.

"I'm crazy about you, you know," he said, sliding his hands under Paul's sweatpants. His hands traced the same path they had been, down the outside of his legs, then across and up the inner thigh. But now there was the bite of Robbie's fingernails dragging up the tender skin, and his fingers caressed Paul's balls and trailed lightly up his cock.

Paul gripped Robbie's legs. He knew the strength in those wide thighs, and he loved being trapped between them.

"You have terrible taste in men, then," Paul said breathlessly.

Robbie pushed Paul's T-shirt up with both hands. "Off?" he asked.

Paul leaned forward to pull his shirt off. Behind him, he felt Robbie doing the same thing.

The feel of skin on skin when he leaned back against Robbie was glorious.

He closed his eyes to better focus on all the places Robbie was touching him. They were both hard and breathing heavily, but there was no sense of urgency to their movements.

The sun fell on his chest and face like a second caress. When he opened his eyes, he could see people walking on the sidewalk below them.

He knew the privacy tint prevented them from seeing in, but he let himself imagine they could. That they could look up and see how beautiful they were together; see Paul brazenly letting another man touch him in front of God and the whole world.

If only. Robbie deserved someone who could do that for him. Well, maybe not this exactly, but someone who would at least hold hands with him in public, kiss him in broad daylight, and introduce him to his family.

Paul was never going to be that person.

Beneath his sweatpants, Robbie pumped his fist gently up and down Paul's cock, coaxing it to harden further.

Paul gave a quiet exhalation with every down stroke. "God, that feels so good."

"You feel good," Robbie said.

"Harder," Paul begged, suddenly filled with a need for that crazy urgency Robbie could stir in him. "Make me feel good. Make me stop thinking."

Robbie wrenched Paul's head around, kissing him hard, taking possession of his mouth. They were both panting when Robbie pulled away.

He slid one hand up Paul's neck, tilting his chin to the ceiling as his fingers closed gently but firmly over Paul's throat. With the other hand, he reached for Paul's cock, stroking him hard and fast until Paul whined desperately, pulse beating against Robbie's fingertips, breath reedy as it strained to get past Robbie's grip.

"Downstairs. Bedroom." Robbie growled. "I need you to fuck me."

"Yes," Paul gasped as Robbie released him. "God. Yes. Please."

With all the curtains drawn, the bedroom was a dim cave compared to the windowed solarium. By the time Paul's eyes had adjusted, he was flat on his back with Robbie straddling him, a heavy weight across his thighs. His ass cradled Paul's dick, the heat of him branding Paul's skin.

Paul fumbled for the lube and condoms. They hadn't done this very often. Paul found the sensation of being inside Robbie almost frightening in its intensity. Many times, he'd wondered if he would survive Robbie fucking him. One day, he promised himself. One day.

"I want to feel you, all of you," Robbie said, flipping the condom over and over. "You know we're both clean."

He did. They'd been tested for everything under the sun before the start of the season. On top of that, Paul had been basically a virgin before being with Robbie.

Robbie rocked against Paul, and Paul's eyes rolled at the thought of slipping bare into that silken heat. His fingertips bit into Robbie's legs. "Oh, yes, please. Please." Those seemed to be the only words his brain could form. Yes. Please. Whatever the question, the answer was *yes, please.*

Robbie gasped as he slid a lube-slicked finger into himself. Rocking back onto his hand, he moaned softly.

Paul wanted to do that for him, but he couldn't move, pinned to the bed by Robbie's weight and the knowledge of what they were about to do. Again.

"You like me like this?" Robbie asked. "Riding you?"

Yes, please. Paul nodded, already beyond words.

Paul watched silently as Robbie prepped himself, the little grunts and moans and the obscene squelching sound making his dick jerk against the air. He gripped Robbie's thighs, trying to keep his hips from thrusting.

"Please," he groaned. "Robbie. Please."

"Yeah. Okay. Okay." Robbie squirted some lube into his hand, then tossed the lube onto the floor. Reaching behind him, he flailed for Paul's cock.

Paul shouted as his fingers wrapped around it, slicking him up rough and quickly. "Careful. God, I'm so close." It was embarrassing how quickly Robbie could reduce him to a quivering pile of need.

Robbie didn't laugh at him, though. He bent forward, bracing himself with a hand on Paul's chest as he quickly jerked himself until his breath caught with a hitch.

"Fuck me, please. Please," Paul chanted shamelessly, face flaming as the words burned like hellfire on his lips. "Fuck me. Fuck me."

Biting his bottom lip, Robbie grabbed Paul's cock and held it as he positioned himself. Staring into Paul's eyes, he slid down Paul inch by halting inch.

"Oh, my god," he groaned as Paul filled him. "You're so fucking big. Holy fuck, it feels so good like this. So, so good."

Paul screwed his eyes shut, needing every ounce of concentration to keep from coming as soon as Robbie took all of him. Every muscle in his body drew tight as a bowstring.

"I have to move," Robbie said, voice drawn. Without waiting for a response, he pushed himself slowly up onto his knees. He hovered there, with Paul barely inside him, before sliding down as slowly. "Oh, my fucking god," he moaned.

Paul's breathing was strangled. He knew it would feel different with no barrier between them, but this was almost too much to bear. Blood throbbed in his temples, and his heart pounded in his chest.

He yanked Robbie down as he thrust up, trying to get closer than humanly possible. Robbie yelled. He leaned back, hands resting on Paul's thighs as he thrust his hips faster and faster, chanting *oh God oh God* with every down stroke.

"Harder," he begged. "Harder."

Paul groaned. He was so close, but he hung on the edge. He needed something, something more. With a growl, he pulled Robbie down to him and rolled them until he lay on top of Robbie.

"Oh, fuck, yeah," Robbie yelled as Paul thrust deep into him." "Fuck me, fuck me harder. God." He clamped his legs to Paul's side, knees up by Paul's shoulders, hands gripping the bed covering so tightly his knuckles turned white.

Paul struggled to his knees, dragging Robbie up his thighs as he did.

He slammed into Robbie over and over, drawing ragged, high-pitched gasps from Robbie with each thrust.

His balls pulled painfully tight against his body and his orgasm barreled towards him like a freight train. "I'm gonna come," he warned Robbie with a gasp. "Gonna—" His words cut off as his muscles clenched and he came harder than ever. He convulsed with each pulse that Robbie's body yanked out of him.

Distantly, he registered Robbie's yell as he came, too, back arching off the bed as he shot up his chest, white streaks spraying wildly as his cock jerked.

Paul collapsed like a puppet with cut strings as his muscles turned to mush. He landed heavily on top of Robbie, trapping his still jerking cock between them.

Robbie's high-pitched moans filled his ears, and Robbie's fingernails dug into the skin of Paul's back.

Robbie hissed as Paul slid out of him. With a deep groan, Paul rolled onto his back next to Robbie.

"Holy shit," Robbie said reverently. He clapped a hand dramatically against his heart. "I thought I was gonna have a stroke."

Paul laughed weakly, body not fully under his control.

"No, seriously," Robbie laughed, grabbing for Paul's hand and pulling it onto his chest. "Feel. Feel what you did to me."

His heart was pounding hard, matching the rhythm Paul felt in his own chest.

The shrill squall of music blasting from crappy phone speakers made Paul jump. He rolled onto his side, reaching for the phone.

"Let it go to voicemail," Robbie said. "It's too early."

"It's after eleven," Paul said chuckling.

"And my day off," Robbie whined, rolling onto his side and pressing his sticky, sweaty body against Paul's back.

"Oh, gross," Paul said, reaching back in a futile attempt to push Robbie off. Robbie just laughed and wrapped himself around Paul like a baby monkey.

Squinting at the phone, Paul could make out an unfamiliar number with a very familiar area code. Huntsville, Alabama. Wondering briefly who it could be, Paul answered the phone.

"Hello?"

"Paul," said the last person he'd ever expected to be on the phone.

Paul bolted upright.

"Hey," Robbie bitched. "Who is it? If it's one of the guys, tell them we're dead."

Heart in his throat, Paul hit Robbie harder than he meant to in order to make him shut up.

"What the hell?" Robbie sat up, rubbing his arm and trying to see who Paul was talking to.

"Is there someone with you, Paul?" Pastor Ruebens asked. *Pastor Ruebens! Fuck.* "Am I interrupting something?"

32

ROBBIE—I KNOW THAT I'M RIGHT, 'CAUSE I HEAR IT IN THE NIGHT

"No, sir, Pastor Ruebens. I was just resting up." Glaring at Robbie, he stressed the word pastor. *Shut up,* he signed at the same time.

Oh, fuck no. Robbie wasn't going to let Paul talk to those brainwashing bastards alone.

Put him on speaker, Robbie signed.

No way, Paul mouthed.

They argued silently while the pastor presumably told Paul how many ways he was going to hell.

Finally, Robbie threatened to start saying very inappropriate things very loudly if Paul didn't put the fucking phone on speaker.

Glaring daggers at Robbie, Paul grudgingly gave in.

"I'm sorry, Pastor Ruebens, my phone cut out for a second. Can you repeat that?"

The instant the guy opened his mouth, Robbie hated him. He sounded condescending, sanctimonious, and officious. Oh, hey, look at him with the big words. All that studying must have paid off. His reading teachers would be so proud.

"Well, son, the Church is concerned about you and the state of your soul. Some of our younger parishioners have brought several disturbing things to our attention."

Oh, fuck. Fuck, fuckity, fuck.

All the blood rushed from Paul's face, and Robbie was convinced he was going to puke. He shoved the bedroom trashcan between Paul's feet, then went into the bathroom.

Even as a natural-born atheist, he felt weird listening to this pastor guy talk while he could feel Paul's come sliding down his thigh. Paul must be dying.

So much for the afterglow.

He shut the door, so he wouldn't be heard and cleaned up quickly, cursing the pastor and organized religion in general for taking such an amazing thing and making it dirty and wrong.

To his surprise, tears sprang to his eyes and his throat tightened. Damn it. He'd gone from cloud nine to this.

He wanted to punch someone. Preferably 'Pastor Ruebens.' Asshole.

Robbie rubbed his tears away and splashed some water on his face.

He came out of the bathroom with a glass of water and warm washrag just in time to hear Paul insisting to Pastor Douchebag that he wasn't gay.

Funny, considering his dick had been in Robbie's ass not ten minutes ago. That seemed pretty gay.

For some reason, Paul still had the guy on speaker phone.

"What about the other young man you've been seen with?" the windbag asked. "Robert Rhodes? There are some fairly long-standing and credible rumors concerning his sexuality."

Robbie tossed Paul the washrag, set the glass down on the nightstand, and flipped the guy on the phone the bird.

How? What? Paul signed barely coherently.

Say yes and fuck off, Robbie replied.

Paul frowned and shook his head. "You would have to ask him that yourself, sir." Paul wiped himself down quickly, then picked up his sweatpants off the floor and slid them on.

Without looking back at Robbie, he picked up the phone and walked away. Robbie didn't hear Pastor Douchebag anymore, so Paul must have taken him off speaker. Paul shut the bedroom door behind him as he left.

Good, now Robbie could slam the dresser drawers as loudly as he wanted as he dug through them trying to find some of the many jeans and a T-shirt he knew he'd left here.

Oh, great, he thought as his hand landed on the pair of green boxer briefs Paul had made him buy in Detroit. Gritting his teeth, Robbie pulled them slowly out of the drawer.

Clenching them in his fist, he dropped heavily to the end of the bed. Maybe he was the dick now. After all, did he really expect Paul to out himself so soon to the very same people who had been telling him he was evil his whole life?

No. That was too much to expect.

Still naked and sticky, Robbie dropped his head to his hands and tried to pull himself together. A shower, he decided. Then another cup of coffee, and he would talk to Paul. Help him deal with whatever this phone call was doing to him.

After all, they loved each other. They could work through this. And eventually, when Paul was ready, they'd come out as a couple.

To everyone? a little voice in Robbie's head asked. *Publicly*? *On the cover of Sports Illustrated?* The voice sounded a lot like the ghost of his ex-boyfriend, Drew.

Shut up, brain-ghost Drew. We'll cross that bridge when we get to it.

Twenty minutes later, showered and dressed in jeans and a long-sleeve T-shirt, he felt much more under control. Taking a deep breath, he pushed the door open and went to find Paul.

He found him pacing the kitchen, hair wild from running his fingers through it. He was still on the damn phone. When he looked up, Robbie could see tear tracks on his face.

Goddamn it. So much for Robbie's Zen.

Paul stopped, covered his mouth with his hand, inhaled deeply and dropped his hand. "Is this an official admonition then?" His voice wavered.

Everything in Robbie wanted to go to Paul and pull him into his arms. He took a step forward, and Paul looked at him with alarm. Robbie's eyes widened as Paul actually took a step back.

You've got to be kidding me, he thought. Robbie shoved his hands deep into his pockets before he could sign something cruel.

Ignoring Paul as much as he could, Robbie made himself a second cup of coffee and grabbed a banana.

Paul looked at him in alarm as he stomped out of the kitchen, only exhaling when Robbie headed for the stairs to the sunroom instead of storming out the front door. Like he would do that to Paul. He wasn't going to leave him alone and traumatized. Despite whatever bullshit Ruebens was pouring into Paul's ear, gay didn't equal evil. He was a human being, for fuck's sake.

Ugh. Robbie threw himself on the same window seat he'd been sitting on earlier in the morning. It felt like a hundred years ago.

Paul's hand gently shaking him brought Robbie back to consciousness.

Paul's hair was wet, and he smelled like the ridiculously expensive body wash he used. Robbie teased him mercilessly about it, and liked to replace it with Axe Body Wash when Paul wasn't looking. Truthfully, it made Paul smell edible, and his skin as silky soft as the copy on the bottle promised.

"You showered?" Robbie asked inanely.

"Yeah."

Paul still looked drawn. The shower hadn't done anything to make his eyes any less red-rimmed from crying, and he was still pale.

Robbie scooted over so Paul could sit next to him. When Paul didn't move, Robbie patted the seat next to him. "Sit, before you fall down. I'll move, so I don't get my gay cooties all over you." Fuck. He hadn't meant to say that.

"Don't be like that," Paul said flatly. He dropped down on the seat.

"So. That sounded fun," Robbie said. "Are you in trouble?"

Paul nodded. He pulled his legs up onto the window seat,

wrapping his arms around them and resting his head on his knees.

Robbie wanted desperately to put his arm around Paul, but he was half afraid it would scare him away.

"Yeah," Paul said, voice muffled. "He said it wasn't an 'official' admonition, but it was near as good as."

"What the hell is an admonition? Where do these guys get off telling you what to do with your life, anyway? They don't own you."

Paul sighed and picked at a loose thread on his jeans. "An admonition is the first step in church discipline. Where they talk to you and try to get you back in line with church teachings. Bring you back to the truth."

Leaning back so Paul couldn't see him, Robbie rolled his eyes. "What's the last step? They kick you out?"

Paul nodded, rubbing his face against his knees.

"So, they kick you out of the church, so what? Find another one. Or stop going altogether?" As far as Robbie could tell, the only thing Paul got from those people was a never-ending pile of crap.

"I knew you wouldn't understand. You can't. You've never been a believer. You're not even a member of a church. Any church. You don't know what it's like." Paul sniffed and wiped his hand across his nose.

"So, tell me. Please." Now he did touch Paul, grabbing his knee and squeezing.

"It, the Church, was my whole life growing up. I've known these people my whole life. I spent every Sunday with them: choir practice, youth group, service trips. Every holiday, every milestone in my life was spent there."

"When my momma—" Paul's voice cracked. "When my momma got sick, and then when she, when she died..." He shook his head, not even bothering to wipe away the tears running slowly down his cheek.

"I wouldn'ta made it one day without those ladies. I wasn't even living at home. I was on campus, and they made me stay in school. They fed me and cleaned my clothes and prayed with me and got me through the roughest time of my life."

What the hell was he supposed to say to that? He wrapped his arm around Paul's shoulder. Paul turned to him, fisted his hand in Robbie's T-shirt and sobbed like his heart was breaking.

Robbie knew his was.

There was just so much he still didn't understand. When Paul finished sobbing, he pulled away with a humorless laugh, wiping futilely at his eyes and nose.

Robbie pulled his shirt off and handed it to him. "Might as well use this. It's already a disaster."

Paul's eyes widened, but he took the shirt and looked studiously down at the floor.

Robbie's jaw ached from how hard he was clenching it. Fuck it. He had to know. "So, all these nice church ladies. If they knew you were gay, they would just turn their backs on you? There wouldn't be any help for Gay Paul?"

"I don't know," Paul whispered. "I can't even...I mean...I'm still me. They love me. They're trying to help. They're worried. I mean, it's not the life any parent wants for their child, is it?"

"What? What the—" Robbie took a deep breath. "What kind of life are you talking about?"

Paul stood up. Robbie followed him with his eyes as he paced the length of the narrow but long room. "Most parents want their kids to fall in love, settle down, have a family, right? Be happy."

"I guess," Robbie said. "But how does being gay mean you can't have any of that?"

Paul shoved his hands into his pockets, walking and talking quickly as if he could outrun the trail of bullshit he was laying. "Well, two guys or two women can't have kids naturally." Paul laughed nervously. "I mean, like don't get me wrong. Obviously I, I liked—" his voice dropped to a hoarse whisper, "like it, what we did."

"Fucked?" Robbie wasn't giving him any wiggle room.

Paul blushed, then paled so quickly Robbie worried that he was going to pass out again. "Yeah," he said, surprising Robbie by looking him right in the eye. "I liked it when we fucked."

Past tense, Robbie noticed a little hysterically.

"But you have to admit, the whole thing is kind of unnatural, Paul continued. "Sex is supposed to be for procreation. And what we did? Not how God intended."

Robbie's head spun. Now he was afraid he was going to pass out. He dropped down on the window seat and gulped down the dregs of his ice-cold coffee while he tried to wrap his head around what he was hearing.

Where to even begin unpicking how many things were wrong with that?

"So, according to you," he asked, "infertile couples shouldn't have sex, then? Or older women past menopause? They're just supposed to be celibate?"

Paul's brow furrowed. "Well, no, I guess they can still have sex. Just normal sex."

A pulse started beating in Robbie's temples. He was going to have to end this conversation very soon before he said something he couldn't take back. "Normal sex? Name one thing gay couples do that heterosexuals don't."

Robbie didn't give him any time to answer. "And don't tell me anal sex. Straight people like anal, too. Straight guys like to get pegged by their girlfriends. Women give blowjobs, handjobs. Same as you."

He couldn't sit still anymore. He had to move. Jumping up from the window seat, it was his turn to pace the room.

Paul watched him in silence until Robbie whirled on him, pointing a shaking finger at him. "Why is it that all you people can focus on is the sex? Why is that always, *always* the focus? Being gay isn't about sex acts, for Chri— for fuck's sake. If that's all you think this—" he waved his hands between them, "is, maybe we should...maybe."

Paul gaped at him.

Robbie stepped right up into his face. "You—" His voice broke, and he stopped, coughed and started again, more quietly but no less intense. "You said you loved me. Not more than two hours ago in this very place, you said you loved me."

"Robbie." Paul sounded anguished.

Robbie turned away from him, staring at the ceiling and blinking back tears. "You say it in your sleep, you know? All the time. You tell me you love me. You tell your *father* you love me in your sleep."

"I do," Paul said. "I do love you. But it's not the same, right? Not like with a man and woman. Is it? Can it be? Pastor Ruebens said—"

"Don't even finish that sentence. I could give two shits what Pastor Douchebag has to say."

Paul got quiet. So quiet Robbie was afraid he'd finally overstepped. He was just about to apologize, but Paul spoke first.

"What if I just think I'm in love with you?" Paul spoke to the floor, not lifting his head up even an inch. Robbie could hardly hear him.

"Maybe I just love you like a really good friend? And I, I let you...I got confused? I felt like this, almost, not as much, not quite, with Eubee."

"That's because you were in love with him, too, you idiot!" Robbie's head would explode if he had to hear one second more of this.

"But Eubee and I, we never did nothing. Not really." Paul sounded like he was pleading with Robbie to understand, to assure him that he was right. Their love was purely platonic.

"You don't need to fuck someone to be in love with them! God!" That was it. Robbie was done. For now or forever, he had no idea. That depended almost entirely on Paul.

"I can't deal with this right now. I can't stand here and listen to any more of this bullshit. I thought you were starting to see how wrong they were. But I guess not."

Closing his eyes, he turned away from Paul and practically jogged down the stairs.

"What if they're right, Robbie?" Paul cried at his retreating back. "What if they're right?"

Robbie stopped. "You need to talk to someone else. You need to get your head on straight. You are setting yourself up for a long, lonely, sad life. And I don't want to have to watch you kill yourself one piece at a time."

He ran down the stairs, grabbing nothing but his cell phone, the closest T-shirt he could find, and his jacket as he left.

33

ROBBIE—IT'S THE VERY MOMENT THAT I WISH THAT I COULD TAKE BACK

The sun lancing off the water stabbed Robbie's eyes as he ran into the street. Why couldn't it be cloudy and gray like it was supposed to be? The bright blue sky, not anything at all like the color of Paul's eyes, bordered on offensive.

Now what was he supposed to do?

His stomach growled, reminding him that regardless of how upset he was, he needed to eat more than coffee and a banana if he was going to make it through the day.

He jogged slowly down the waterfront towards the water taxi. He'd stop in at Marination Ma Kai and get a loco moco. That was practically breakfast, right? It had fried eggs, that made it breakfast.

What day was it? He often lost track during the season. All he knew was that it wasn't a game day. He should hit the gym, work out and check in with the PT doc since his shoulder was aching a little bit more than he was happy with.

What he really wanted to do was go home, close the curtains, and wallow like a teenaged girl. He was allowed, right? For at least one day?

Despite the bite in the air, he picked a table outside. Sometimes it felt like he went weeks without feeling the sun on his skin. He ordered, pushed up the sleeves of his sweatshirt, and turned his face to the sun with a sigh.

The waitress brought him his third cup of coffee because he wanted more coffee and his stomach lining was not the boss of him.

As he stared blankly at the Seattle skyline, he felt that familiar feeling of being looked at. Sure enough, out of the corner of his eyes, he saw a few kids sneaking glances in his direction, trying to figure out if he was who they thought he was.

He knew how it would go. Eventually, one of the kids would be persuaded to go up to him and ask. He was pretty generic looking, so he didn't get recognized very often. When it happened, he felt a combination of weird and extremely flattered. Sergei always got recognized. But that's what happened when you were a giant with a Russian accent and a killer smile.

One of the kids stumbled forward, and with a glare back at his friends, walked nervously towards Robbie's table. Robbie smiled at him when he got close. "Hey."

"Uh, hi." The kid glanced back over his shoulder at his friends, and then back to Robbie. "My, uh, friends wanted to know if you're Robbie Rhodes, from the Thunder. Number 22?"

"That's me," Robbie said with a smile. "You guys watch hockey?"

"We play hockey!" The kid's smile was adorable. He was maybe twelve or thirteen, still small and young enough to not feel like he had to hide his excitement under a veneer of coolness.

Robbie loved this part of being recognized. It was so odd to be on the receiving end of fanning, but he remembered how happy it made him when his hockey idols took the time to speak with him. It was the very least he could do.

"Oh, yeah? What's your name?"

"James," said the kid, blushing.

"Nice to meet you, James." He looked around the kid and smiled at his three friends. "Why don't you tell them to come over?"

Waving wildly, James called his friends over.

The waitress brought Robbie his breakfast, and he convinced the kids to sit down and tell him about themselves.

They were great kids, animated, intelligent and wild about hockey. The way they peppered him with questions, interrupting each other loudly, and arguing among themselves over what strategy the Thunder should use for some upcoming games, made Robbie laugh in spite of everything.

It hurt when they talked about him and Paul as a team, but he grit his teeth and agreed that they made great partners.

"You guys are going to go to the All-Stars next year," James said with authority.

"Sucks about the Olympics, dude," one of the older boys said, referring to the League's decision not to take the seventeen-day break it would need in order for players to participate in the games.

"I think it was a good decision," Robbie said, shoveling the last of his sandwich into his mouth. James stared at him, eyes a little glazed, and Robbie's gaydar gave a little ding.

Uh-oh, was James a baby gay hockey player? Robbie knew that feeling well.

The other kid's well-thought out argument in favor of the break was interrupted by two women calling for them across the patio.

James waved them over. "It's my mom," he told Robbie. "She'll want to say hi, too."

Paul had had better luck beating some manners into Robbie than his parents had so he stood up as the two women approached the table.

"Mom, it was him!" James said.

A pleasant-looking woman in her mid-thirties, James' mother rested a hand on his shoulder and smiled at him. "We figured that when you guys didn't come back." She looked up at Robbie. "Thank you so much for talking with them. I hope they weren't too annoying."

"Not at all. They're great. They know a lot about hockey."

The kids preened under the compliment. James' eyes practically sparkled.

The other woman, who looked like an older version of the first one, smiled at Robbie the way more than one female fan had and held out her hand. "Veronica River. Aunt to half of these boys. Janey's younger sister."

Robbie caught James' eye roll out of the corner of his eye and bit back a smile. "Robbie Rhodes, nice to meet you, ma'am."

Veronica held his hand slightly longer than necessary and undressed him with her eyes. She wasn't exactly subtle, and one of the older boys snorted, then looked down studiously at the ground.

"James is right," she said. "You are the cutest of the Thunder players."

Robbie forced a smile.

"Aunt Ronnie!" James yelled, turning eight different shades of red.

"Gross!" One of the other boys yelled. "Don't flirt with him, Aunt Ronnie. You're so old!"

Robbie tried to cover his laugh with a cough. By the look Ronnie shot him, he wasn't completely successful.

Janey grabbed her sister's arm above the elbow and squeezed hard. "We've got to go. It was nice meeting you."

James gave his mom a pleading look. She looked down at him, and up at Robbie, doubt clear in her expression. James grabbed her shirt and pulled her down to whisper in her ear.

"I gotta do it, Mom. I gotta know," he said just loud enough for Robbie to hear.

Janey didn't look thrilled, but she nodded. "Okay, baby. But I'm going to wait right there." She pointed to a spot on the railing about ten feet away. "Ronnie, can you load the boys into the van? We'll be there in a minute."

Veronica herded the other three boys away with a wink to Robbie, and Janey gave Robbie and James some privacy.

James's face was still red, and he stared intently at his sneakers.

"What's up?" Robbie asked.

"Never mind," James said. "It's stupid."

Robbie sat back down, so he wasn't looming over the kid. "I bet it's not. Whatever it is, I promise not to laugh or anything, okay?"

"Yeah?" James risked a glance up. His eyes met Robbie's and then flicked back down.

"Yeah." What in the world could be bothering the kid that much, he wondered?

James took a deep sigh, his thin shoulders rising and falling. "Some, some people, say...they said, that you...you were gay."

Robbie could practically feel the heat coming off James' face. Shit. He should have known that's what the kid was going to ask about. What was he supposed to say now? Well, technically, it wasn't a question. "And?" he asked gently. "What about it?"

James looked up at him, face set in determination. "Are you? Gay?"

Robbie almost laughed. He'd never expected the first fan ever to ask him directly to be a twelve-year-old kid. He'd wondered what he would say when it happened. Now he knew. He would lie like a little chickenshit.

"No," he said. "I'm not."

"Oh." James' voice was small. "Okay. Sorry."

Damn it; the kid sounded near tears.

"Well, um. I gotta go." He tore out of there before Robbie could say anything, running right past his mother.

She spared Robbie a look he couldn't read, and then took off after her son.

Fuck. Just. Fuck.

This is it, a voice whispered in his head. This is where you decide what kind of man you're going to be.

He stood there, paralyzed for what felt like an eternity.

Fuck it. Fuck the haters. It was his life, and he had to live it out loud. Enough talking the talk, it was time to man up and walk the walk if he wanted to be able to look at himself in the mirror ever again.

He tossed a couple of twenties on the table and ran through the restaurant. Hitting the parking lot, he quickly scanned the cars, looking for James and his mom. A flash of blonde hair caught his eye, and he cut through the rows of cars towards them.

"James," he called out when he got close enough. "Wait."

Janey turned at the sound of his voice, her hand tight on James' shoulder. He couldn't blame her for glaring at him.

"Hold on," Robbie said. "Can I talk to you for a second?" Janey's eyes narrowed at him. "And you, too, of course, ma'am."

She looked back at the van, then nodded. She led them a few feet away from the other people.

James wouldn't make eye contact with Robbie, so Robbie squatted down to be closer to his eye level. "Hey, James. I'm sorry. I lied. I am gay."

Janey gasped softly. James looked up, red-rimmed eyes narrowing suspiciously. "Really?"

Robbie laughed. "Really. Trust me. I'm not saying it just to make you feel better."

"Why are you saying it?" Janey asked softly.

Robbie straightened back up. "To make me feel better."

She smiled at him. "Good."

James was all smiles now. "I won't tell anybody. I promise. I just wanted to know 'cause..." he blushed and looked away.

"Yeah, I get it. I felt the same way about Bryce."

"Oh, my God," James said, eyes wide. "Did you see what he did?"

"I was there, at the game," Robbie admitted.

"Was it awesome?"

"It was epic." Robbie shared a grin with him.

"Thank you," Janey said sincerely. "I know that wasn't easy. But it meant the world to him. And don't worry, we won't tell anyone."

Robbie shook his head. "I know you won't. But I'm going to tell everyone. Just give me a little while to figure out what I have to do." He spoke directly to Janey now, James almost forgotten between them.

"Really?" Janey asked. "You're going to do it?"

Robbie's stomach lurched. Maybe he shouldn't have had that third cup of coffee. "Yes?" he said tentatively.

James squeaked, and Robbie looked at him. He looked like he'd gotten everything he'd ever wanted for every Christmas of his life. His eyes shone, and his hands were clasped together tightly in front of his chest.

"Yes," Robbie said definitely. "I'm going to do it. I'm going to come out in a press conference." Holy shit.

Janey squeaked and threw her arms around him. "I'm so proud of you!"

It felt so motherly, Robbie almost cried. He hugged her back. "So, would you want to be there when I do? At the press conference I imagine they'll want to do? If there is one? Would you be there?" Damn, his words wouldn't come out right.

James clapped once, then clasped his hands together.

"We'd love to," Janey said. "Just let us know."

"Okay."

They quickly exchanged contact info, James staring at him with stars in his eyes the entire time. Robbie promised to get in touch as soon as he had anything to say.

"Just keep it to yourself a little longer," he told James. "But if you have any questions about hockey or about anything, you email me, okay?"

James could only nod.

"Thank you," Janey said pushing James gently towards the van.

"Thank *you*," Robbie said sincerely. "For giving me a kick in the ass...I mean butt. Shit."

Janey laughed. "It's okay. Good luck. You call me if you need anything, okay?"

"Yes, ma'am." He watched as they drove out of the parking lot, then headed for the water taxi with a thousand thoughts twirling around in his head. Looked like he had a lot of phone calls to make.

The hardest one would be the one to Paul. If it wasn't already dead, this would be the final nail in the coffin of their relationship for sure.

34

PAUL—THEN YOU'LL SEE MY HEART IN THE SADDEST STATE IT'S EVER BEEN

The first thing he'd done was turn his phone off. He didn't want to hear what anybody had to say to him about anything. Then he'd stripped the bed, shoving the dirty sheets into the washing machine. Emotionally wiped out, he crashed onto the bare mattress, and pulled the comforter over him.

He drifted in and out of sleep most of the day. When he was awake, Paul measured time passing by watching the shadows on his bedroom walls shrink away towards noon, then lengthen throughout the afternoon, and finally disappear as the short winter day came to an end.

Finally, the room was full dark, and Paul was starving. He'd moved past his initial shock, and now he was angry. Angry at Pastor Ruebens, at his father, at Robbie. At everyone in the whole damn world who felt they had a stake in who he was and what he did with his life.

He just wanted to live and be happy. Was that so much to ask? He was a good person. He didn't lie, cheat, or steal. He was polite and kind. He was a damn good hockey player and loyal friend. Why wasn't that enough?

Hauling himself out of bed, he stumbled to the bathroom. His stomach was growling, but he needed a shower more than he needed food.

Before he got under the hot water, he turned his phone back on. He listened to it bing its electronic brain out, and almost vibrate off the counter as the phone calls, texts, and notifications he'd been avoiding all day caught up with him.

While he waited for his dinner to heat up, he scrolled through the missed phone calls. There were plenty from his father, of course. One more from Pastor Ruebens. He deleted all those voicemails without listening to him.

Sissy had texted a couple of time. He'd read those later when he felt more like dealing with it.

To his surprise, Robbie had texted a few times over the day.

Don't forget to eat

I'm done at the gym, just thought you'd want to know

How are you feeling? Are you okay?

I'm going to stop bothering you now. I'll see you tomorrow.

And a last one, two hours after that one.

About tomorrow. Can we pretend everything is okay? I don't want to deal with shit from the guys.

Paul stared at the phone. Where they okay? What did okay even look like? They hadn't officially broken up, had they? Paul didn't have a lot of experience, but that seemed like the kind of thing you had to talk about. So, what were they?

His fingers hovered over the keyboard. *I'm eating. Business as usual tomorrow*. He hit send.

Biting his lip, he debated saying more. He might as well. It wasn't as if they could avoid each other. He typed and retyped his message a couple of times before sending it.

I'm sorry. I just need some time to think.

Me too Robbie sent back almost immediately.

They did okay the next day, he thought. At least no one said anything to him. He caught Sergei giving them searching looks, but he never asked anything.

On the ice, they were as good as ever, maybe better as they were laser-focused on the game. They joked around less, keeping their communication strictly about strategy.

Paul always knew where Robbie was and, more importantly, where he was going to be. During the second period, a miracle occurred, and Paul just knew the ice between him and the Blue Jackets' goal was going to be empty in two seconds.

Leaving his position, he took off down the ice as quickly as he could. Just as he passed the Blue Jackets' last defenseman in the neutral zone, he looked to his left right in time to catch the puck as it banked off the boards to land almost gently in the curve of his stick.

"Go!" he heard Robbie yell over the roar of the crowd.

His vision narrowed until all he could see was the goalie and the net. Skating full out, just short of the net he faked a shot, pirouetted, and then shot behind his back, sending the puck into wide open glove-side of the net.

With a whoop, Paul allowed himself a knee-sliding fist-pumping skate of victory. Robbie was the first one in the congratulatory hug pile.

So far, so good.

Rooming together for the next road game was as awkward as Paul expected it to be. There wasn't a way for them to room separately without drawing way too much attention to themselves.

They'd been moving around each other silently, only saying the bare minimum, until Paul came out of the bathroom, and Robbie said, "We have to talk."

Robbie sat cross-legged on his bed in a pair of shorts and nothing else.

To Paul's eye, he looked a little skinnier than he had been a few months ago. Paul knew he was staring, but he couldn't help it. He'd missed the freedom to look at Robbie's body. Definitely missed touching it. Robbie was still wearing Paul's necklace. That had to be a good sign, right?

"I think we do, too," Paul said, sitting on his bed and facing Robbie.

Robbie didn't say anything, but he fiddled with the necklace, rubbing it between his fingers almost unconsciously while he stared at Paul.

"I'll start," Paul said.

Robbie nodded and looked like he was bracing himself against whatever it was Paul was going to say.

"I don't know how to say this without sounding stupid, so I'm just going to say it." He took a deep breath. "Are you breaking up with me?"

Robbie jerked back, blinking as if he wasn't sure he'd heard correctly. "What?"

"Are we broken up?" It was a question Paul never envisioned himself asking. You'd think you would know.

"I...," Robbie took a deep breath. "I think that's up to you. But there's something you need to know, first."

Paul listened, his heart breaking with every word, as Robbie told him about his decision to come out publicly. There would be a press conference next week, after the All-Star weekend.

It wasn't fair, dammit! Robbie was just so far ahead of him here; he would never catch up. He could never be the out and proud boyfriend Robbie needed, that he deserved.

But he couldn't let Robbie's schedule dictate his own, any more than he could let Pastor Ruebens or his father dictate his life anymore.

"This is how I can make a difference," Robbie was saying. "This is my Doctors Without Borders. If you could have seen that kid's face when I told him I wasn't gay. I felt like I'd kicked a puppy. Hard. I could practically see his dreams crumbling." Robbie clutched his heart like he was in actual pain. His eyes pleaded for Paul to understand.

"Don't hate me," he begged.

"I could never, ever hate you," Paul said. "I'm proud of you."

"Yeah?" He sounded surprised. "Really?"

"Really." And he was. He was so proud of Robbie for being so brave.

"I'm kind of nervous." Robbie pulled the necklace up to his mouth, tapping it against his teeth. He pulled it back out again. "I'm scared."

Giving in to the urge he'd been fighting since he'd come out of the bathroom, Paul went over and sat down next to Robbie. He wrapped an arm around him and pulled him in for a side hug.

Robbie went willingly, resting his head on Paul's shoulder.

"It's going to be great," Paul said. "You're going to be amazing. And you'll make life so much easier for so many little kids, and not so little kids. Maybe even for someone like me."

"After I do this," Robbie said, "we won't be able to fly under the radar anymore. Even if we do breakup, if you hang out with me so much, people are going to make assumptions."

"I know."

"So?" Robbie lifted his head but didn't pull out from under Paul's arm.

"I don't know. How many days do we have?"

"Five."

"Okay. I guess we'll find out in five days."

Robbie sighed and rested his head back on Paul's shoulder. He felt so good there; Paul wanted to cry. He turned his head, burying his nose in Robbie's hair. He'd missed the scent of him, missed everything.

Robbie raised his head again, looking directly into Paul's eyes. "Can I kiss you?" he asked, and Paul heard the echo of their first night together in what felt like another lifetime.

Slipping his finger under the chain of the necklace, Paul pulled Robbie close and kissed him softly, barely a whisper of pressure against Robbie's lips. He pulled away, then leaned in for a second, longer kiss.

Robbie grabbed his arm.

Paul broke the kiss. "I do love you," he said.

"I know. I love you, too. But." He hesitated, searching for the words. "But I have to be able to love myself first. And, lately, I haven't really even liked myself. Do you know what I mean?"

Paul's laugh sounded a little hysterical even to him. "Yeah. I think I do."

Robbie laughed bitterly. "I thought love was all we needed?"

"That's what the songs say."

"The songs are wrong then." Robbie sagged back on the bed, the necklace sliding through Paul's fingers. Robbie lifted it off his chest, holding it out. "Do you—"

"No." Paul cut him off. "Keep it. Please."

Robbie nodded. "I'm tired," he said, though it was barely ten p.m. They'd had a travel day and had arrived at the hotel at a reasonable hour.

"Me, too," Paul said. It wasn't a lie; he felt like he could sleep for a week. He got up and went over to his bed. Sliding under the covers, he turned off the light. "Good night."

"Night."

What else was there to say?

The next morning, Robbie got a call from Georgia that changed everything.

As soon as Robbie finished relaying Georgia's information, Paul was on the phone with his father.

He didn't respond as his father got out everything he'd been dying to say over the past week that Paul had been ignoring his calls and text. Paul let it wash over him in a rush of words and bullshit.

"Are you done?" he asked when Stoney's tirade petered out.

"That's all you have to say to me?" Stoney asked, irate.

"No. I just wanted to make sure you were finished yelling at me. Are you?"

"Yelling at you? Son, I am only—"

"So that's a no then?"

"What has gotten into you? I knew that Rhodes boy was a bad influence."

Paul rolled his eyes. "We need to talk. In person. Can you come out here? Bring Sissy, too, if she can come."

Stoney sputtered and blustered until Paul interrupted him again. "It's about Skippy."

Dead silence, except for Stoney's heavy breathing. "Dad?"

"Where did you hear that name?" he asked quietly.

"Just come to Seattle. I don't want to do this over the phone. I'll buy you both tickets."

"Fine. I'll have your sister call you to make plans." He cut the call.

"Is he coming out?" Robbie asked.

Paul nodded.

"That talk is...going be interesting."

Paul barked a laugh. "That's one word for it."

35

PAUL—I DON'T WANT TO HURT YOU, BUT I NEED TO BREATHE

Once again, Paul found himself in Queenie and headed north out of the city. He was in the same car and traveling the same roads he had traveled with Robbie months ago, but this time he was with his father. This trip promised to be not nearly as much fun as the first one.

The mountain roads they'd taken were closed for the season now. He planned to take the highway out of town and cut over to the coast as soon as he could.

The only way he was going to be able to have this talk with his father was if he didn't have to make eye contact. Driving helped with that. Also, driving prevented his father from simply walking away when he didn't want to hear what Paul had to say.

Stoney was trapped. He had to listen, but they could avoid all the awkward eye contact. And if Stoney was going to lose his shit, at least no one else would hear him.

Driving the Stingray also made Paul feel like he had a part of Eubee with him.

God, poor Eubee. Paul wished with all his heart he could talk to

Eubee one more time. That they could laugh and cry together and finally say all the things that had gone unsaid and unrecognized because they had been children.

He hadn't even been able to say goodbye.

Would it have made a difference if he and Eubee had known and labeled what they were to each other? Or would it have ended in tragedy anyway?

Paul blinked back the tears and spared a quick glance at Stoney who looked as tense and uncomfortable as you could in the front seat of a Corvette.

Maybe it wouldn't have made a difference, but Paul was angry that the choice had been taken from them before they'd known it existed.

They were forty-five minutes out of the city, and Stoney had yet to say anything. He'd gone quiet when he'd seen the Stingray and realized they would be driving in her. *He looks like he's seen a ghost*, Paul thought.

"This Eubee's car?" he'd asked as if mint-condition, forest-green seventy-six Stingrays were thick on the ground and he couldn't be sure this was the one he was thinking of.

"Pops Franklin left it to me, remember?" Paul asked, knowing full well his father remembered.

Stoney nodded. "I didn't know you still had her, that's all." He reached out but let his hand drop before touching the curved edges of the car. Shoving his hands into his pants pockets, he looked away.

Paul couldn't remember seeing his father look unsure about anything before. Stoney had always been the ultimate authority on everything, one step below God and on equal footing (in Paul's eyes) with the pastors of the church. Stoney was older, wiser, and his father. His word was law. Paul hadn't questioned it.

Now he was starting to realize that his father was just a man trying to figure out his way in the world, trying to find a way to make the pain and hard times mean something, to make the suffering have been worth it somehow.

Human, and like Paul, and like Pastor Ruebens, and Robbie and everyone else, answerable only to himself and God in the end. *Whatever we conceive Him to be.* Paul wondered what his mother had conceived God to be at the end when He took her from her husband and children.

Whatever it had been, she'd been at peace with it. That much Paul knew for sure.

He reached around his father and opened the passenger's door. "Come on, Dad. Let's go for a ride."

It was just the two of them. Sissy had tests she couldn't miss. She was going to fly out later and meet them right before Robbie's press conference. Assuming Paul's father hadn't disowned him and flown home and out of Paul's life forever.

Contemplating that possibility made Paul nauseous, but the weight that lifted from his shoulders at finally getting everything out in the open more than compensated.

If only he could figure out how to start the conversation. The silence stretched awkwardly, painfully. Stoney coughed, Paul hoped it was an opening, but his father kept staring out the window.

"Dad," Paul said, clearing his throat. "I need to talk to you."

"That's what you said, that's why I'm here."

Paul did have to give him credit for that. Stoney had to know what this conversation was about. He had to know the skeletons Paul was going to dig up, and the confessions he was going to make. And yet he had still come out. Had flown across the entire country to be with Paul and talk with him semi-face-to-face.

It said something about his father, Paul realized, that he had done it. And it said something about their relationship that Paul hadn't questioned that Stoney would do it; that when Paul called his father and said I need you, please come, he would come.

Damn it. Maybe Paul needed to rethink his plan. If every damn thought was going to make him teary-eyed, maybe he ought not to be driving seventy miles an hour.

He took the nearest exit and headed west. No idea where he was going, but he didn't care. He had a strong need to see the water.

"Paul," his father said. "Just say what you need to say, Son, before you end up dragging us all the way up to Alaska. I don't think Queenie is going to do so good in the snow, and I didn't bring my winter coat."

Paul bark a short laugh. Had his dad made a joke? Okay. Stoney had done so much, reached out so far; the least Paul could do was meet him halfway.

"Um. Okay. I'll just say it. I'm gay."

Stoney sighed. He reached out and rubbed his hand along the dashboard. "I know, Paul. I've always known."

Okay. Okay. He hadn't expected that. He'd expected anything from yelling to denial, and he'd prepared several responses to those. This quiet admission pulled the rug out from under his feet and left him struggling with his thoughts.

He felt himself reaching for the sign language he used with Robbie, searching for another way to express himself other than with the words rolling and tumbling all over themselves in his brain.

Fuck it. The time for crafting clever arguments or comebacks was over. He had to speak from his heart.

"If you know, why did you let them tell me that it was wrong to be gay? That I was wrong? Evil? Going to hell?" *Why did you let them hurt me? You were supposed to protect me?*

"Oh, Paulie. I was trying to protect you. That's my job. I'm your father, and I love you. I'm supposed to protect you, body and soul." He sounded so sad.

Paul vaguely remembered saying something like that to Robbie, that his father and his church had done what they had done out of love. He still had serious doubts about Pastor Ruebens' motivation, but he believed his father completely.

He'd done what he'd done with the best of intentions. But Paul knew where that path could lead.

"I know you were. But I think it damaged me. It hurt me in deep-down ways that are going to take a long time to fix."

Without realizing it, Paul had driven them to the same beach he had visited with Robbie. It was a cold and gray day. The wind whipped the water into choppy whitecaps, the spray leaving a slick of ice on the rocks.

He parked the car but left it running. It was safer than driving when he felt like this.

"Protect me from what, Dad? From people who would hate me and hurt me? That didn't work. You know what it's like being thirteen, fourteen years old, finally understanding what gay even meant, and having this horrifying revelation that it's you? That when the preacher is up there talking about evildoers and fornicators burning in hell, they are talking about *you*?" Paul's voice broke.

Stoney shook his head. *No.*

"No. And what kind of ..." He shook his head, lips pressed tight. "You had me hating something before I even knew what it was. You had me condemned before I'd even had my first kiss."

He couldn't stay in the car anymore. He'd rather freeze to death than suffocate. When he opened the door, the wind yanked it, pulling it wide.

Stoney got out the other door. His thin windbreaker did nothing to keep the cold at bay, and he wrapped his arms around himself.

"Paul. Paul. Stop," he called as Paul paced the parking lot. "Listen. Just because you're, you're how you are, it doesn't mean you're going to hell."

Paul stopped, curious where his father was going with that line of thought. He was pretty sure he knew. Since the call with Pastor Ruebens he'd done a lot of research on what different churches had to say about homosexuality, what science had to say, what darn near everyone in the world had to say about it.

What he'd realized was it didn't make one lick of difference what anybody but him had to say about it. It was his life, and he had to live it in a way that felt true to him.

Stoney stood next to him, the wind making his jacket flap like a flag. "I know you can't help being gay, Chip, but you don't have to give into those urges. God understands. Try to live a normal life, and you'll be safe."

Safe. Was that the goal? Get through life safely? Unhurt? If that was the goal, Paul had missed it years ago. "But would I be happy?"

Stoney looked away. "Happiness is beside the point. God put us here to test us, to see what we are made of."

Paul threw his hands up. He was so tired of that way of thinking. "Is that really what you think? That life should be some sort of ordeal? If you survive long enough and pass this test, you might get a reward at the end?"

"Or fail and go to hell," Stoney said. His words were hard, but the sorrow in his eyes that had been there since he'd gotten to Seattle was still there.

"What if," Paul said, "what if we just don't believe that?"

"Not believe in God?" Stoney looked scandalized.

Paul watched two seagulls lift themselves heavily into the air, wings beating as they hung almost motionless over the earth as they faced into the wind.

It felt like the perfect metaphor for this conversation. Paul could beat his wings against Stoney's beliefs all day and never get anywhere. But he owed them both his absolute best try. His father hadn't given up on him yet, and he wasn't going to give up on Stoney.

"Not believe in a God that condemns his own creations for something they can't control. Who would create people full of love and then tell them they can't ever have love, and the love they feel is wrong. I can't believe in a God who would be so deliberately cruel. I won't."

"But what if you're wrong?" Stoney said. Something in his voice told Paul his father had been searching for the answer to that question for a long time. "What if you're going to go to hell?"

"Then I'll be in good company, won't I? Including your *friend* Skippy," he snapped.

That got a reaction out of Stoney. He staggered a step backward, reaching to the car for support. "What do you know about Skippy?"

A gust that felt like it came straight from the Arctic Circle whipped across the parking lot. "Get back in the car, Dad. No point freezing to death."

The inside of the car was warm and quiet. Paul turned the heater on full blast, aiming the vents at his fingers. "Do you want to drive more or stay here?"

"Drive. If you don't mind."

36

PAUL—AT THE END OF IT ALL YOU'RE STILL MY BEST FRIEND

Paul put the car into reverse and pulled out of the beach parking lot. "I love driving this car."

Stoney drummed his fingers against the door handle and then shifted in the seat until he could look at Paul. "So what do you know about Skippy?"

His voice was so flat; Paul couldn't get a read on his mood. Might as well lay it all out there. "I know he was your friend. I know he moved to San Francisco, and I know he probably died of AIDS a few years after."

Paul concentrated on merging back onto the highway more than was strictly necessary.

"How do you even know about him?" Stoney asked. "I know I never talked about him."

"Robbie's friend Georgia knew you and Skippy. She played with you at college before she went pro. Said you'd know her as George Simpson."

When Stoney didn't answer, Paul shot him a look.

Stoney looked like he got hit with a two by four. "What? She? What are you talking about?"

"Georgia is a transsexual, no, transgender." Robbie had corrected him on that several times. She's now Georgia, and she lives with Robbie's parents. They have some kind of boarding house. She recognized me. Well, you, technically. She thought I looked just like you. And well, the name."

"Simpson is a woman now? What?"

"I know it's weird, Dad, but can we talk about that another time? It's really not the main issue."

Stoney's leg was jittering so hard, Paul felt it through the floor. His father looked out the side window, watching the trees fly by. With a sigh, he turned back to Paul. "Skippy was my Eubee. He was my best friend from high school and through college."

"And?"

"And I loved him."

Wow. Based on what Georgia had said at lunch the day they'd met, Paul had suspected that, but he'd never expected Stoney to say it flat out.

"What happened?"

Stoney scratched his fingertips across the dashboard. "I've never told anybody about this. No one. Ever. No one knew, not for sure. We were so careful."

Holy crap.

"After college, when we knew neither of us was going pro, he asked me to move to California, to San Francisco with him. As, as, a couple."

"Wow. I don't know what to say."

Stoney rubbed his face.

"Are you gay?" Paul pulled into the right lane and slowed down as he waited for the answer.

Stoney groaned.

"Nobody here but us chickens," Paul said with a strained laugh.

"And God."

"And God. But God already knows."

Stoney laughed, surprised. "Then yes. I think so. I am gay. Wow."

"It's hard to say out loud, isn't it?"

Stoney nodded. "Almost as hard as telling you kids your mom wasn't going to survive that last bout with cancer."

Paul reached over and grabbed his father's hand tightly. Stoney covered Paul's hand with his, squeezing back.

"Robbie made me say it to him," Paul said. "Now I know why he needed to hear me say it. Saying it makes it real."

"I loved your mother you know."

"I know," Paul said automatically, but he'd be lying if he said he hadn't wondered about it.

"Please, never think I didn't. Barbara was an amazing woman who deserved more than I gave her. I took her from her family. Did you know that? You have grandparents and aunts and uncles you don't even know."

That was news to Paul. He'd assumed his mother was an only child. Wow.

"But Skippy, Nathan, was my first love. I loved him like I've never loved anyone else."

"So why didn't you go with him? I know it was a different time, but people did it, lived together. Why couldn't you? Was it the church, your family?"

"No, I didn't get saved until after he was gone."

Holy shit. Another thing Paul had never known. Everything he had ever thought about his dad had crumbled. He felt like he was sitting next to a stranger.

Stoney hadn't lied to him, not directly, but he'd left so much out, he might as well have.

"Then why?"

"I was scared. Terrified. I saw the pictures and films of what it was like out there." He looked out the window like he could see it even now. "I didn't want to live like that. I didn't want to die."

"You don't die from being gay."

"You did back then."

Paul started to object, but Stoney cut him off. "You don't get it. You can't get it because you don't know, because no one ever showed you. Pull over."

"What?" Paul looked to his dad and back to the road.

Stoney pointed to the truck stop looming over the highway. "Pull over. I want to show you something, and you can't be driving."

Paul took the exit ramp, and Stoney surprised him again by directing him to the parking lot of a Denny's.

"I'm hungry. I don't think I've eaten since you called me," he explained. "Is that okay with you?"

"Yeah. Fine. I love Denny's," he said inanely. In a million years he never pictured his dad wanting to talk about any of this in a public place.

By unspoken agreement, they picked a booth near a window where Paul could keep an eye on the car. The waiter, a smiling young man with the dark hair and dark eyes Paul was starting to associate with a Native American background, handed them their menus.

They both ordered coffee and Paul looked through the menu while his dad got lost looking for something on his phone.

Paul was dying to know what his father was going to show him, but he kept his impatience in check. Nothing had gone the way he'd expected this morning, and he felt a little like he had slipped sideways into a parallel world.

This Denny's looked like every other Denny's he'd ever been in, but he'd never been in this exact store, never seen that exact view out the window. His father looked almost the same as Paul remembered, but he had no idea how this man across from him would react to anything. He didn't know this version of his father.

It was unsettling, terrifying, but it also held the promise of something Paul never thought he would have – an honest relationship with his dad, where they could both be authentically themselves and know that they were loved unconditionally.

Paul held the menu up to hide his face and wiped his eyes with the napkin. If he had any tears left after today, he'd be surprised.

"You gentlemen ready to order?" the waiter asked cheerfully.

"Grand Slam with biscuits and gravy on the side, please. Over easy eggs," Stoney said. "And some more coffee."

"Dang, you are hungry," Paul laughed. "I'll have the same thing but with scrambled eggs."

"You got it. And I'll bring you some more coffee."

Stoney watched the guy leave. When he seemed satisfied the waiter was out of earshot, he handed the phone to Paul.

The browser was open to the AmFar website. Paul had never heard of the organization, but he realized quickly it was an AIDs/HIV research organization.

"AIDs?" he asked Stoney, puzzled.

"Take a look at the numbers. Remember, I graduated high school in 1984. College in 1988. You were born in 1993."

"That I know," Paul said absently as he scrolled through the timeline. He stomach dropped with every year that he saw.

1982, the first year on the chart, showed sixty-two cases of a mysterious 'gay cancer.' 1983, the very next year, there were 771 reported cases and 618 deaths. The numbers grew exponentially, horrifically. And this was just cases and deaths in the United States.

By 1984, the year Stoney graduated high school, there had been nearly 2000 deaths, most of them in the San Francisco area, almost all of them gay men.

1988, four short years later, and over sixty-thousand people had died from AIDS, and virtually all cases of HIV infection lead to full-blown AIDS and death.

"Oh, my, God," Paul said, covering his mouth with his hand. "I didn't know."

He was afraid to look, but he had to know. By the year he was born, over two hundred thousand people in the U.S. had died of AIDS. In 1995, the New York Times reported that AIDS was the leading cause of death among all Americans ages 25-44.

"Holy shit. How did I not this? No wonder you were terrified."

Stoney took the phone back from Paul. "It was horrific. And the numbers don't even do it justice. It was everywhere. The gay plague, people called it. God's judgment on sinners. And the photographs. God, the pictures. If you'd seen what those poor men looked like. What Nathan must have looked like."

Stoney covered his face with his hand.

Paul looked away to give his father a small bit of privacy for his old grief.

"I - I didn't see any pictures," Paul said softly.

"I couldn't find any," Stoney said, voice rough. He cleared his throat and took a sip of his coffee.

He looked older than Paul had ever seen him, but softer, more real.

"It's gone. Erased like it never happened. None of you kids, gay or straight," he said with a small smile, "knows about it. But we remember. Men my age and older, we remember. We were there."

"I'm sorry," Paul said, absently, thinking of Robbie. Paul wondered if Robbie knew. He probably did, Paul realized. He probably knew all about gay history, something Paul had just this second realized was a thing.

Paul felt himself shift from thinking of himself as a guy who just happened to be gay to realizing he was a gay man. Whether he wanted to be or not, he was part of a group with a shared history and a story that bound them all together despite all other differences.

No wonder Robbie had been so incensed by the idea of an essential part of his identity being distilled down to a single sex act. It was dehumanizing.

"Looking at you and Eubee," his father was saying, oblivious to Paul's worldview being realigned, "It almost killed me. It was like looking into a mirror. I loved you both so much, and all I could see was you both dead, ravaged."

"Eubee died anyway, Dad. He left me, and he died, and I never got to tell him I loved him."

"I'm sorry, Paul. Truly. If I could go back in time," his father said.

The waiter brought their food and set it down in front of them. Paul didn't think he'd be able to eat a bite.

"Why are you sorry? You didn't make him join the army. You didn't make him skip out without even talking to me." Paul stabbed viciously at his gravy-covered biscuits. Or what passed for gravy on the wrong side of the country.

"No," Stoney said slowly, "I didn't. But I didn't dissuade him either. When he came to me, I encouraged him. Told him some time apart might benefit both of you."

"Oh, Daddy," Paul said softly, near tears again.

Stoney reached across the table for Paul's hand. "Can you forgive me?"

Why did there have to be so much pain around something so basic and simple as love just because they were two men?

Being with Robbie had been so easy. He felt something important tickling his brain, something almost making sense.

"Paul," his father said.

"Ssh," he said, shocking them both. "Just...I need to..." He closed his eyes and gripped his father's hand. He reached out with his other hand, and Stoney took that.

Please, help me out here, Paul asked silently, talking to God like he hadn't done since he was a child, not concerned with getting the words exactly right. *What am I missing? I know there's something. Why does it have to hurt so much? Why is there so much pain and fear around who I love?"*

The answer popped into his head immediately. *Because people make it that way. It doesn't have to be that way. It's not supposed to be.*

It was easy with Robbie. All of it. It had been so normal—easy and free. Except when he fucked it up. When he let his fear take over. When he let the judgment of other people get between them.

He opened his eyes. "There's nothing to forgive. I know why you did what you did. But it's going to be different for me. I know it."

"How do you know? I don't see a lot of happy endings for gay men."

"How hard have you looked?" he asked.

Stoney looked surprised. "You're right. I haven't looked at all. And I haven't done anything but make it harder, have I?"

"I'll tell you some happy endings." As Paul ate, he told Stoney about Dakota and Bryce, about their upcoming wedding and the kids they planned to foster. About John from PR and his husband and how they were raising John's kids from his previous marriage.

He trailed off when his father didn't answer. To his surprise, Stoney was crying. In public. He'd covered his mouth with his hand, but the tears were slipping down his cheeks.

"Daddy," Paul said alarmed. "What's wrong?"

Stoney shook his head, unable or unwilling to say.

Paul slid out of his bench and went and sat next to Stoney. He wrapped his arm around his father's shoulders, offering him whatever comfort he could in a way he'd never done before.

An older woman at a table across from them looked alarmed but didn't say anything. The waiter approached, carrying a full coffee pot, but reversed course when Paul shook his head slightly.

The few other customers seemed oblivious to the drama. Stoney probably wasn't the first person to cry in a Denny's.

"He didn't have to die," Stoney said finally.

"Skippy?"

"Yes. Him. Any of them. If people hadn't...if they could have left us alone and let us live in peace, Nathan wouldn't have moved to California, and we could have had a life, just a normal life in Alabama."

"I know. Being gay didn't kill him. Ignorance and stigma and judgment did."

Stoney wiped his eyes, waved the waiter over for more coffee. "Go eat your food," he said to Paul, elbowing him gently in the ribs. "It's going to get cold."

With a smile, Paul did. He wasn't sure what had happened, but something major had shifted.

The waiter refilled their coffee, and with a quick look at both of them, placed a pile of clean napkins on the table.

"Pretty heavy conversation for a Denny's," Stoney said with a weak smile.

"I'm sure there's been worse."

"So where did you get all this insight from?" Stoney asked. "How did you get so wise, so young?"

"I prayed on it," Paul said, digging into his cold and definitely inferior biscuits.

"I thought you didn't believe in that anymore."

Paul sighed. "I'm gay, Dad, not an atheist. I'm exactly who I was, except now I'm more at peace. I have to be me. Trying not to be something I'm not has already cost me too much." He knew the chances of anything working out long-term with he and Eubee had been slim even if they had been able to talk about their relationship. They had both been too damaged in the same way.

He'd needed someone like Robbie, someone whose way of viewing the world was so different from his that they forced him to re-evaluate everything he thought he knew.

"So tell me about you and Robbie," Stoney said.

"Really? We don't have to. It's okay. I don't need to flaunt it," he said for lack of a better word.

"I'm your father. Telling me about someone so important to you isn't flaunting anything."

"Okay." Where to start? What was the most important thing? "You know what hell would be for me, Dad?"

Stoney shook his head.

"Watching Robbie fall in love with someone else."

"But you're not with him now?"

Paul hadn't realized his father even knew that much about his relationship. "It's complicated," he self with a self-deprecating smile. "But if we do break up, it will be my fault. I let my fear come between us. And that sucks because I love him. But you know what?"

"What?"

"I'd still be happier without him, and more at peace with who I am, then I ever was before. I can't go back. I can't fight for conditional love from you, from the church, from your version of God. And especially not from myself."

Stoney leaned back, stretching an arm along the back of the bench seat. Paul met his father's gaze evenly as Stoney studied him. "I can't speak for the Church. They aren't likely to change their teachings anytime soon."

"I know. I'm done with letting other people tell me how to think."

Stoney nodded. "I definitely can't speak for God, but I think you can work that out with God – whatever you conceive Him to be – for yourself."

"You remember that?" Paul asked, stunned.

"Your mother's favorite poem."

"Mine, too," Paul said.

"You know my favorite part?" Stoney asked.

Paul shook his head.

"'*You are a child of the universe*,' Stoney quoted. "'*No less than the trees and the stars*.'"

"*You have a right to be here*," Paul finished, smiling through the tears that once again threatened to fall.

"You do," Stoney said. "And speaking for myself, I promise you, and your sister, that I never want you to feel like my love is conditional again. Okay?"

Paul nodded, sniffling. He wiped his eyes with one of the clean napkins. "I think this is the most I've ever cried at a Denny's."

Stoney looked around and shrugged. "There are worse places. Now how 'bout you finish up and you take me for a nice long ride in that gorgeous car. You can tell me all about Robbie and what you plan to do to tighten up those holes in your defense before the game against the Kings next week."

Paul squawked in mock outrage, before launching into a thorough analysis of the Thunder's strengths and how they were going to destroy the Kings that lasted until they were back in his apartment.

37

ROBBIE—WE GOT OUR OWN FRESH SET OF RULES

Robbie's parents stared around the Thunder players' lounge in awe. It had been gratifying for Robbie to give them the grand tour of extensive facilities. They seemed completely impressed by the size and professionalism of the whole organization.

Robbie wanted to laugh. What had they expected from the NHL? Something like Pee Wee hockey locker rooms but with bigger men?

"This is outstanding," Grant had said, taking in the high-tech viewing room, the fully outfitted gyms, and the PT rooms with the hot and cold tubs, massage tables and medical equipment. The equipment room looked like a high-priced sporting goods store. His mother's eyes bugged out a little when he pointed out that some of the skates cost up to a thousand dollars a pair.

Robbie introduced them to the teammates that were there to support him as he took the leap and became the first person to come out as an active pro hockey player. Almost every player was there. Sergei had even made the trip back from the All-Stars earlier than he'd planned so he could be there.

He and Georgia and his parents were off to the side of the Thunder pressroom, waiting for the press conference to start.

It had been decided that it would be Robbie, Coach Williams, and the press spokesman at the table. At the last minute, Bryce had surprised the heck out of him by asking if he could be there as well.

"Of course," Robbie had responded. "That would be amazing."

Bryce was working the room, chatting with reporters and looking like a model in his perfectly tailored suit. He was getting a feel for the room, smoothing out any potential trouble spots and trying to minimize surprise questions. Watching him work, Robbie realized there was a lot more to being in the league than just playing hockey.

It should be fine. The media team had been thrilled to put their plan into place, reaching out to LGBT-friendly news outlets and reporters. Robbie saw representatives from Out and the Advocate, and local affiliates of most of the major networks.

It wasn't a surprise announcement. The media department had sent out press packets and spoken to every individual in the room. Still, Robbie felt mildly nauseous. There was no doubt his life was going to change after this.

Like it or not, he was going to be the gay face of pro-sports. He would be judged on everything he did from here on in as not just a player, or as a man, but as a gay player, a gay man.

Potentially, every misstep or mistake he made risked being attributed to his sexuality, every success achieved in spite of it as if being gay was a handicap he had to overcome heroically.

It was infuriating.

Unlike Bryce, Robbie wore the Thunder team jersey. The League wanted it to be one-hundred percent clear that Robbie had the full support of his team and his teammates. Looking out at a sea of blue and white jerseys did calm Robbie's nerves a little bit. No matter what happened, his guys had his back.

Any objections or issues they had with him would be handled in private.

The one person he didn't see was Paul. He hadn't expected him to be there, but he'd hoped.

"He's still not here?" his mother asked.

Robbie shook his head.

“You and he were dating, but now you’re not, correct?”

“Yes.” That wasn’t exactly true. He and Paul hadn’t talked much over the break. He knew Paul’s father and sister were flying in, and Paul was planning on having a long talk with his dad. But there was a huge gulf between Paul coming out to his father and Robbie coming out to the world on the six o’clock news.

Neither one of them knew if they’d be able to bridge that gap.

“Oh, that’s too bad. We like him,” his mother said. Robbie knew that. Paul had bonded with his mother over the phone. When she found out he loved to read, she’d starting sending him book recommendations, and they often had long text conversations about the books he read.

“I love him,” Robbie said simply. “And I know he loves me.”

His father rested a hand on his shoulder in sympathy. “I’m proud of you for what you’re doing.”

“I have to be out. I can’t hide who I am anymore. And he can’t be out, not without losing everything important to him. I mean, he barely accepts who he is,” Robbie said, trying to keep the bitterness out of his voice.

“Give him time,” Grant said. “He’ll come around.”

“I know. But apparently, twenty-four years of being told you’ll go to hell isn’t something you get over that quickly.”

Truthfully, Paul had made enormous strides in a short time. But this was a lot to ask of someone newly out. It’s not like any of the players Robbie knew for a fact were gay had asked to join Robbie at the microphone.

“It’s really not,” Paul said from behind them. “But people can surprise you.”

Holy shit. Robbie spun around so quickly he got dizzy.

Paul stood there, more gorgeous than ever, in his Thunder jersey.

“You came,” Robbie said.

“I had to come. Did you really think I wouldn’t?” His smile dropped.

“I’m sorry. I should have known.”

Paul shook his head. “No. I haven’t given you a lot of reason to trust me with this.”

“But you’re here!” Robbie said, more relieved than he thought he would be. Doing this without Paul in the audience would have been hell. If he didn’t get to wrap his arms around Paul in twenty seconds, he might die.

“Not just me,” Paul said, excusing himself to get by Robbie’s parents. He pointed into the audience. “Look.”

Robbie saw a man who could only be Paul’s father taking a seat at the back of the room.

Georgia was right. He did look exactly like Robbie imagined Paul would in twenty years. A pretty young woman with Paul’s blonde hair and peaches and cream coloring sat down next to him.

“Sissy?” Robbie asked.

“Yep. She’s dying to meet you. Like, crazy dying. I had to bribe her with driving the Stingray to not burst back here like an insane person.”

“And they’re okay with you being here? With you supporting me?” He couldn’t believe it. Having Paul here was a surprise. He hadn’t even considered that Paul Senior would make an appearance.

“I guess he didn’t disown you, then?”

“Not even close. We have a lot to talk about. A lot.” Paul turned to Georgia. “He’s really curious about you,” he said with a smile.

“I’ll bet.”

Paul looked out into the audience. Sissy caught his eyes, and Robbie saw her break into a huge smile and give him two thumbs up.

Paul’s dad turned to see where Sissy was looking, and Robbie found himself staring directly at him. Stoney held his gaze, looking long and hard as if he were evaluating Robbie from a distance.

Finally, he smiled slightly and nodded as if in approval. He searched for Paul and gave him a nod as well.

“Well, I guess you’d better go take a seat, too,” Robbie said, though he wasn’t ready to let Paul get that far away from him.

“Actually,” Paul said, taking a deep breath. “I was wondering if there was room at the table for one more?”

Jenny inhaled sharply, and Robbie's mouth fell open. "You want to be up there with me? Right next to me in public when I come out?"

Paul nodded.

"You know what people are going to think? And you're okay with that?"

"Well, I reckoned I would just tell them right out, so they don't have to guess."

"Oh, my!" Georgia said from somewhere behind Paul.

"How much time do I have?" Robbie asked the room in general.

"About ten minutes," Grant replied. "More like seven."

"I'll be right back." Grabbing Paul by the jersey, he dragged him over to the first door he could see.

It turned out to be a small closet stocked with supplies for the lounge kitchen.

"This is the exact opposite of what we're supposed to be doing," Paul said, laughing and breathless as Robbie shoved him into the closet and shut the door.

"Shut up," Robbie said. Hand still clenched in Paul's jersey, he crowded him up against the metal shelving in the almost pitch black room. "Are you sure? One hundred percent sure?"

Paul reached for Robbie, grabbing him by the hips and pulling him flush against him. "One hundred percent."

Robbie gasped as Paul slid his hands up under his shirt. "Don't do this for me."

"I'm doing it for me," Paul said. "I promise. I don't know how I'll live if I don't."

Robbie had to kiss him. Slamming their mouths together. Paul kissed back like the only oxygen he could get would be from Robbie's lungs.

"Oh, my God," Robbie said as Paul grabbed his ass and dragged him tight against him. They were both hard almost instantly. The four days they had been apart and on shaky ground had felt like an eternity.

Paul whimpered and straddled Robbie's leg, rutting shamelessly against Robbie. "Fuck, I love your thighs," he said. "Goddamn."

Robbie grabbed Paul by the hair and tugged hard, yanking his head back so he could reach Paul's' neck.

“Oh, fuck.” Paul’s strangled yell was loud in the small room, and they both froze.

“Shit,” Robbie said, releasing Paul and taking a step back. His cock throbbed painfully against his pants. Robbie pressed his palm hard against it. “We can’t go out like this.”

Someone pounded on the door. “Rhodes, Dyson, get the fuck out of there right now.” It was Jake, and he didn’t sound happy. “I’m opening the fucking door; you’d better be fucking dressed.”

“Nice vocabulary, Cap’n,” Paul said smugly as Jake yanked the door open.

Jake looked at both of them and scoffed in disgust. “Jesus, go out like that, and you won’t even have to say anything. A fucking nun would know what you two were up to.”

“Sorry,” Paul said.

“And I thought we agreed no screwing around in the arena.”

“Sorry,” Robbie said. “He surprised me.”

“Yeah. I hear it’s your coming out day, too. Congrats, Dyson. Now go makes yourselves presentable and I’ll buy you a few minutes. Jesus Christ,” he muttered as he stormed off. “Goddamn kids can’t keep it in their goddamn pants for two fricken minutes.”

Paul and Robbie snorted and ran to the bathroom to pull themselves together.

There was a murmur from the crowd as Robbie walked up to the table. It grew exponentially as Paul followed right behind him. Bryce’s eyes widened in surprise as he saw Paul, and he stood up. Checking the microphone in front of him to make sure it was off, he pulled Paul in for a hug.

“You doing this?” he whispered.

“Apparently,” Paul answered nervously.

Bryce hugged him again, then turned and enveloped Robbie in his strong embrace, too.

“You are a champion hugger, Lowery,” Robbie said with a small laugh even as he clung to the support of Bryce’s strong arms.

"I am so incredibly proud of you two. So proud." His eyes were suspiciously bright. "You know whatever you need, whatever you want, Dakota and I are behind you, one hundred percent."

Robbie blinked back tears of his own. Now was not the time. "I know, man. Thanks."

"You want me to stay up here, now that you have Paul?"

Robbie looked at Paul. Paul nodded, a little desperately.

"Please," Robbie said.

Bryce motioned for someone to bring up another chair, and the murmurs from the audience got louder.

Finally, they were all seated. "Ready to do this?" the press guy said, hand on the microphone.

Robbie squinted into the lights that seemed brighter than usual and nodded. He squeezed Paul's knee under the table. "Ready as we'll ever be."

He flicked the microphone on. Robbie leaned into it. "Hi. I'm Robbie. Hi."

The audience laughed, breaking the tension.

"I guess you all know why we're here." Robbie struggled with what to say after that. The words on the paper the PR guy had placed in front of him swam in the bright lights and tension. He was going to sound like a moron. Maybe he could get away with standing up, saying *I'm gay, I like dick, particularly this guy's*, and running out of the room.

Probably not.

The silence stretched until one reporter finally took pity on him. "So, Robbie, your team released a statement saying that you're coming out today. That you're gay and you wanted everyone to know it."

A little of the tension leaked out of the room. "Yes. Ah yes. That is true. I'm gay. That's what I wanted to say." Jesus. Why couldn't he speak like a normal person?

Paul squeezed his hand and smiled. Robbie saw all the eyes in the room track over to him.

"Hey, y'all," Paul said, laying it on thick. "I know y'all weren't expecting me here today. I know Rhodes wasn't. Hell, I wasn't really expecting me to be here."

"So why are you?" someone called.

"Well, I couldn't rightly let my boyfriend be out here all by himself, now could I?"

Not surprisingly, a bunch of people started speaking at the same time. One voice rang out over the rest. "Did you say boyfriend?" ask a woman Robbie didn't recognize.

"Yes, ma'am. I did. Just to be perfectly clear, I, Paul Dyson, current Thunder defenseman and formerly Huntsville Charger, *go Chargers!,* am gay, and I am dating – and I am truly sorry to admit this – a former Bemidji Beaver. I hope the fine state of Alabama will find it in their hearts to forgive me. He can't help being a Beaver. He was born that way."

A sharp wolf-whistle rang out from the sea of baby blue jerseys, followed by some rowdy howls and clapping. *U-A-H*, someone chanted *U-A-H*!

Robbie leaned in close to Paul. "You're amazing."

"I know," he said with a grin, leaning in.

"Kiss him!" Lipe bellowed from the floor. Robbie would recognize that voice anywhere.

"Bite me, Lipe," Paul yelled back.

Next to Robbie, the press guy dropped his head into his hands.

38

PAUL—HAND OVER THE FUTURE

Eventually, Bryce, Jake, and Coach Williams managed to get the press conference back on track. Mostly by kicking out the rest of the team.

When the conference ended, Paul and Robbie introduced their families to each other and to the coach. They got bullied into dragging everyone down to the Puck for celebratory drinks and food. Robbie was deeply grateful for his teammates, and he proved it by picking up the tab.

Paul knew things wouldn't always go this smoothly, there was bound to be a backlash, but for one night, he was going to enjoy being completely out and proud for the first time.

Both his and Robbie's phones blew up with texts and calls all night. Only one got Robbie's attention. It was a short one from his ex-boyfriend Drew. Paul read it over his shoulder.

Glad you finally found someone worth it he wrote.

Thank you, Robbie responded. *I'm sorry I didn't understand*

Don't sweat it, Drew replied. *Just be happy.*

I am.

Good.

There was a moment of awkwardness at the end of the night, as they tried to figure out logistics. Paul didn't care about his father's sensibilities one bit. If he thought Paul was going to spend the night without Robbie, he was crazy.

And, well, if he thought they were going to spend the night screwing each other's brains out, he was completely right.

They finally ended up having Grant drive Stoney and Sissy back to Paul's place in the Prius.

"This is your car?" Stoney said in surprise.

Paul snorted and Robbie elbowed him in the stomach.

"They get excellent gas mileage," Grant said seriously.

Paul's body shook with silent laughter.

Robbie ignored him. "You sure you're all okay with this?" Things had been a little stiff between Georgia and Stoney. Not bad, but awkward. It was going to be tight quarters in the car.

"We're fine," his mother said. "We'll drop them off and then head over to our hotel. We'll call you boys in the morning and make plans."

"Game day," Stoney said, as if Paul and Robbie might forget.

"I'll see if I can get tickets," Robbie offered.

"Great. That's great." Paul was done with company. He kissed his father and sister good night, and shook hands with Robbie's parents and Georgia.

Paul and Robbie waved as they drove away, collapsing against the wall of the bar as soon as their families were out of site.

"Holy moly, I didn't think they'd ever leave," Paul said with a sigh. "Jeez. Take a hint."

"Seriously. Can we please go home now?"

"Oh, yes."

They barely made it in the door before Paul had Robbie pressed up against the wall. "Talk tomorrow, right?"

Robbie nodded and pulled Paul against him, picking up where they'd left off in the closet. In between kissing and groping, they managed to kick their shoes off, and get their pants unbuckled.

Robbie dropped to his knees in front of Paul. Paul groaned as Robbie's breath blew over his cock. He reached for the hem of his jersey but Robbie stopped him. "Keep it on. I think it's hot," he said with a wicked grin.

"Only if keep yours on, too."

"Deal," he said, and then took Paul's cock into his mouth down to the root.

Paul had plans. There were things he wanted to do, but there was no way he could hold up under the onslaught of Robbie's mouth. He grabbed onto Robbie's head, burying his fingers in his hair.

Robbie pulled off slowly, obscenely. Wiping his mouth with the back of his hand, he looked up at Paul. "Do it. Come on. Fuck my mouth."

Paul didn't have to be asked twice. Bracing his shoulders against the wall, he thrust his cock down Robbie's throat. Moaning, panting, and cursing, he slammed in. The wet gagging noises had him slowing down and pulling back, but Robbie's fingernails dug into his ass, shoving him forward.

It didn't take more than a handful of thrusts before he was coming straight down Robbie's throat, bent down over him, hands dug into Robbie's shoulder for balance.

Struggling for breath, he almost slid down the wall, but Robbie's hand on his chest stopped him. Hand tangled in his shirt, Robbie dragged Paul over to the futon.

"You just want me to keep the shirt on so you can manhandle me with it," Paul groaned as his butt hit the futon. The years hadn't been kind to the old mattress. It was harder than it had been two years ago.

"I want you to keep the shirt on so I can fuck you in it."

They'd done everything but that. He didn't know why. Having

Robbie's cock in him shouldn't be any different than Robbie's fingers or, *sweet Jesus*, his tongue. But it was. Maybe it just seemed too real, too intense. Like as long as he was the one getting fucked, he could still maintain some plausible deniability.

But he didn't want that anymore. He'd claimed Robbie on national television. Now he needed Robbie to claim him here, to make it real. He needed Robbie to know how he felt about him, how much he loved him.

"Yeah, I'm sure." He reached out for Robbie's cock that was right at eye level, and stroked it. Robbie was as hard as a rock, and Paul wanted to taste it so badly, his mouth watered at the thought. But he wanted it in him more. "C'mon, fuck me."

Robbie was on him in a second, hand flailing to the floor to reach the lube they'd learned to keep stashed under the futon. "Yeah. Yeah, okay." He kissed all the oxygen out of Paul's lungs, kissed him and rubbed against him until Paul was dizzy with it, and begging for Robbie to fuck him.

Robbie sat up between Paul's legs, just as breathless as he. "God, Paul. Fuck. So good, so gorgeous." He fumbled the lube, fumbled the cap, and squeezed way too much out onto his hands. He slicked his hand up between Paul's ass cheeks, fingers dragging across his opening.

Paul whined deep in his throat and shifted his legs wider. "C'mon, Robbie. Do it."

Robbie wrapped his other hand almost too tightly around Paul's still-sensitive cock and slid one lubed finger into him.

Fuck that felt good. He cursed and pushed up into Robbie's fist, then slammed back down onto his finger, pushing it deeper. "Oh God, so good.

Robbie's brows drew together as he watched Paul's reaction to his every move. By the time they'd worked up to three fingers, Paul had his hands wrapped around his own thighs, holding himself open and his cock was at full strength again.

Robbie couldn't seem to stop rubbing his iron rod of a cock Paul's hip.

"Jesus Christ, Robbie. For the love of God, fuck me already." He grabbed at Robbie's hip, trying to pull him closer.

"Okay, okay, okay." Robbie's hand trembled as he grabbed himself and pushed into Paul for the first time.

Oh, it was so much thicker and harder and better than his fingers. So much better. Paul's mouth dropped open and he panted for breath as Robbie forced himself slowly but inexorably against the resistance in Paul's body.

Paul rolled and rocked his hips, pushing himself onto Robbie's cock. "Oh, fuck, yes, yes, yes," he chanted as the feeling went on forever until Robbie was flush against him.

Robbie braced himself over Paul with a hand on either side of his body. Paul was almost bent in half, legs wrapped around Robbie's waist.

He was right to be afraid of this. Afraid of the intimacy. He wondered how women do it so easily. How they let someone in over and over. He could never be that brave. He couldn't imagine ever letting anyone besides Robbie being in him. Couldn't imagine ever wanting to let Robbie leave.

Robbie's arms tremble. He looked like he couldn't believe this was actually happening. "Paul," he says, voice strangled. "So perfect. You're so perfect."

"Move, please. Please," was all Paul could say in return.

So Robbie moved. He pulled out, then slid back in so slowly and so perfectly, Paul's eyes rolled back in his head. Robbie fucked him as deeply and as perfectly as Paul knew he would. Time lost all meaning. It was just him and Robbie and the way they felt.

Whenever Paul had pictured this, and he'd pictured it many, many times, he'd imagined all kinds of filth falling from Robbie's gorgeous mouth. Imagined he would be moaning and groaning. But they were both so quiet. There was just their breathing and the slap of skin on skin.

Paul focused all his attention on Robbie. On the way it felt to have Robbie all around him, inside and out. He wanted it to last forever but they were both getting close to the edge.

Robbie's thrusts grew harder and more erratic. He pulled up onto his knees, pushing Paul's thighs back and lifting his hips up off the bed. He slammed against Paul's prostate over and over.

Paul moaned non-stop. He couldn't help it; it felt so fucking good. His cock ached, but he couldn't do anything but clench the sheets and curse.

"Paul. Fuck, Paul." Robbie's grip slipped up to Paul's calves as he drove into him again and again. "Gonna come. God." He thrust one more time and stilled.

Robbie pulsed inside of him, over and over, and Paul wanted to cry with how good it felt.

Still grunting out his orgasm, Robbie dropped one of Paul's legs and wrapped his hand around Paul's cock, pumping hard. "Come on, Paul. Come with me. I want to see it. Come on, come on," he begged.

And Paul was just gone. "Robbie. Robbie," he keened. "Jesus." His cock jerked, shooting all over his chest and up to his chin.

They shudder and twitched together until Robbie's arms gave out and he dropped down to his elbows, chest heaving against Paul's, foreheads pressed together.

When their breathing finally slowed down, Robbie pushed up with a groan and pulled his now-disgusting jersey over his head and threw it on the floor. Then he helped Paul get his off.

"That was incredible," Robbie said. "Are you okay? Was it okay for you?"

Paul was too tired to laugh. He'd just had two orgasm almost back to back. "Yeah," he said. "It was okay. We should probably do it a million more times, just to be sure."

"Maybe not tonight," Robbie said.

"Maybe not." Paul stretched luxuriously. "But fuck I feel good."

Robbie slapped him with an open hand on his stomach, the sound loud in the room. "Okay, princess. Get up. Shower, then bed."

Paul's eyes were already closed. "No. I'm good here." He groaned as Robbie pushed him off the futon. "You suck," he said as he hit the floor with a thud. "That's boyfriend abuse."

Robbie rolled off the futon and landed on top of him. He bit Paul hard on the shoulder. "I'll show you boyfriend abuse."

"Tomorrow," Paul said. "After the game."

"Deal."

They picked themselves up and made their way to the bathroom. Settling for a quick wipe down instead of a shower, they stumbled to bed.

Robbie pulled Paul into him, cradling Paul's head on his chest. "Thank you for doing that today."

"Letting you fuck me? If you're nice, I'll let you do it a lot more often."

"Shut up. I mean it."

"I know." Paul kissed Robbie's chest. "But I was serious. I didn't do it only for you. I did it for myself. I told my father—and I meant it—I told him that I was happier being out to myself and without you, than I had ever been when I was hiding who I was."

"I can't tell if that's a compliment or not."

"You know what I mean."

"I do. You're going to have to tell me everything you and your dad said. I am just blown away. I never expected any of this."

"I'll tell you all about it tomorrow. It was incredible. He was incredible." Paul wrapped his arm around Robbie. "I know it's not going to be easy all the time, but I don't have a single regret. I love you, and I want everyone to know. If I can help even one kid like me. I can make them see that they don't have to pick parts of themselves to hide, then it's worth it, right? Worth all the crap I know we're going to get?"

"Absolutely. You were so brave today. So much braver than I was. Think of all those kids like you in some church or somewhere, who've been told their whole lives that they're bad and wrong. Now they have you, not me. Not some atheist kid with college professor parents, but someone raised just like them, saying they're not. That they're okay the way they are. It's incredible."

Paul thought about how different his life might have been if he'd had someone to look up to. Someone to help him figure it all out. It might have been different, might have even been better. But then he might not have ended up here with this man and he couldn't imagine any better place to be.

"You're stuck with me, you know."

"Am I?" Robbie asked, his fingers drawing lazy circles on Paul's back.

"Yeah. I'm pretty sure I stuck tighter'n a tick to you."

"Oh, yeah, Forest Gump? Do you reckon?" He smiled.

"I'm serious as a heart attack," Paul said with a straight face. "I done tolt you fifty-leven times that I love your sorry ass. Now you know I'm fixin' to stay with you until you kick me out."

Robbie bust out laughing, and Paul couldn't help but laugh, too.

"I reckon I like the sound of that, too," Robbie said, when they had stopped laughing. "I think I'll keep you."

"Hmm," Paul answered, half-asleep. "That's good, because I got plans for you."

"Bring it on, country boy," Robbie said. "Bring it on."

PREVIEW OF CITY BOY

HOT OFF THE ICE #1

Chapter One
BRYCE

Inside the Pucker Up, the unofficial bar of the Seattle Thunder, Bryce Lowery, the six-foot-five, two-hundred-and-twenty pound team captain, hid in the bathroom from a tiny blonde woman in four-inch heels.

The bathroom wasn't very big; two stalls, two sinks, and an out-of-order urinal, so Bryce occupied most of the room. The door slammed open, and Bryce jumped.

Robbie, the Thunder's rookie defenseman, came in, the sounds of laughter and music from the bar wafting through the open door along with him. "Hey. So this is where you went. People were looking for you. Jess in particular."

Bryce sighed before he could stop himself.

Robbie laughed. "She who you're hiding from?"

"I'm not hiding," Bryce said.

"If you say so," Robbie replied, closing the door of the stall behind him.

Bryce tried to psych himself up to leave the bathroom. He stood awkwardly as Robbie came out and washed his hands.

"Want me to go out with you for moral support?" Robbie asked.

Bryce crossed his arms over his chest, testing the limits of the material of his black T-shirt. "Is she still out there?" he asked.

"Yeah, those women are relentless, man." His voice was loud in the confined space, and his eyes were glassy and sleepy from too much alcohol drunk too quickly. "I told my boyfriend that he's lucky I'm not into that."

"Boyfriend?"

Robbie gave him a look. "Yeah? Drew, that guy who is always with me? Who did you think he was?"

"I haven't been around much," Bryce said defensively. He and Robbie hadn't spent much time together, even though Bryce was team captain.

A serious knee injury during a game had benched him right at the start of the season, and it was the kid's first year with the pros. Just looking at him, all young and shiny and barely twenty-one, made Bryce feel old. He could swear the rookies were getting younger every year.

At thirty-four, Bryce was thirteen years older than Robbie. Bryce had been a kid when he'd left his family behind him in Chicago and moved to Quebec to play Major Junior Hockey in Canada. Fourteen years old and already on his own. He'd felt like a grown up.

When Bryce had been learning to play hockey at a whole new level, Robbie had been learning to walk.

God, Bryce felt old. "Is he, Drew, here tonight?"

Robbie grimaced. "No. He went back home for a while. He's trying to decide if he, quote, wants to be part of this life or not, unquote."

"Well, I guess at least you know he's not just sticking around for the money and cheating on you behind your back," Bryce said. It happened all the time.

The door banged against the wall as a striking brunette woman in tailored trousers and a deep red sweater strode in. "You can't hide in here forever, Lowery. There's a cake with your name on it. Literally." She smirked at her own joke.

"Nikki, this is the men's room!"

She scoffed. "Like I've never seen a dick before." She caught Robbie looking at her with a big smile. She tilted her chin at him. "Hey, Rookie."

"You're Nikki." He sounded starstruck.

"The one and only." She held out her hand for a shake.

Bryce hobbled over to his ex-wife who was still somehow, miraculously, his best friend. "Hey, Nikki." He kissed her on the cheek. "Did you just get here?"

She hugged him tightly. "Yeah. When I didn't see you in the crowd, I knew I'd find you hiding somewhere."

"I'm not hiding," he muttered not needing to see Nikki's face to know she didn't believe him.

"Right," she said. "So what are you boys talking about?"

"Robbie was just saying his boyfriend is still deciding if he wants to move here or not." He stressed the word boyfriend a tiny bit.

Nikki looked sympathetic. She dropped a hand on Robbie's shoulder. "It's a tough call, Rookie. Being a hockey player's partner is hard. You guys are on the road a lot, and there is a lot of temptation. But at least you know he isn't into you just for the money."

"That's what he said." Robbie pointed at Bryce.

"Don't be fooled by the pretty face; he's actually smart about a lot of things."

"Does that happen a lot?"

"Every day," Nikki said. "Half the women in the bar and a some of the guys would marry a player right now for their share."

"That's cold, Nik," Bryce said. "Not everybody is so mercenary."

Nikki squeezed Bryce's rock-solid bicep. "True, some of them are in it for other reasons."

Bryce let it drop. Though he'd gotten over Nikki leaving him years ago, it was still hard for him to understand how he had let her down.

God knows he'd tried. He'd planned on being married forever. Nikki called him a hopeless romantic. She'd also told him she could never be what he was looking for, and they both deserved someone who could give them exactly what they needed.

Seven years later, Bryce still hadn't found it. Hadn't even come close.

"So Drew left?" Nikki asked.

"You knew Drew was his boyfriend?" Nikki's lack of surprise surprised Bryce. Did everyone know but him? Did nobody care?

Nikki didn't bother asking him, just gave him the little head shake she often directed at him. He felt like he constantly disappointed her in some way he couldn't place. He hated that feeling.

"I thought we could make it work," Robbie said. "It could be the start of something huge for us, you know?"

Bryce felt for the kid. Despite constantly being surrounded by teammates and fans, this could be a lonely life without knowing someone special was waiting at home for you.

"Oh, I know," Nikki echoed, giving Robbie a sad smile. "Let me give you my number. Tell your guy he can call me if he wants some real talk about what he might be getting into."

"Really?" He smiled at her, wide-eyed.

"Really. But don't get your hopes up. If we talk, I'm going to give him the whole gory truth: good, bad, and horrific."

The excitement in his eyes dimmed. In a way, it made Bryce feel better. It showed that the kid had at least some idea what he was asking of his boyfriend.

Robbie stared at himself in the mirror and fixed his hair. Bryce had envied that hair from the first second he'd seen it. A deep reddish-brown, he kept it long on top, and razor-short at the back and sides.

"You know," Robbie said, looking at Bryce's reflection, "I always thought you'd come out after you guys split up. I mean, I get why you didn't. Different times and all that."

What? "Who? Come out of what?" Bryce felt like he had missed some part of the conversation somewhere.

Nikki put her hand on Bryce's shoulder and gave him that damn look again.

Robbie caught Bryce's eye in the mirror and gave him a shy drunken smile. "I had the biggest crush on you." He blushed and turned away. "It just would have been cool, having a role model and all, you know? But I get it. You gotta be careful in this gig. Maybe when you retire. Have you decided what you're going to do yet?"

Bryce didn't want to discuss retirement with a kid just starting his first season, nor did he want to think about tonight. He'd take his time off and decide later. For now, he was still on the team roster. He was still going forward with his new contract negotiations as if he had years more ice time in his future.

Thinking about it made him tired and made his body ache with the memory of twenty years of abuse.

Bryce did some quick math. "You would have been, what, fourteen when Nikki and I split up?"

Robbie's eyes drifted to the ceiling as he tried to remember. "Yeah. About. Had a poster of you and everything."

"You knew you were gay at fourteen?" Bryce couldn't remember even caring about anything but hockey at fourteen. Possibly the Teenaged Mutant Ninja Turtles.

"I just kind of always knew. I didn't admit it until I met Drew in college, though."

"What do your parents think about it?" Bryce couldn't imagine talking to his mother about his sex life under any circumstances.

Every few months, she asked obliquely if he'd met anybody. He sidestepped the question, figuring she didn't want to know about his ever more infrequent one-night stands or first dates that went nowhere.

If there ever were someone important, he'd tell her, although it looked like that was never going to happen.

God, not only was he getting old, he was getting maudlin. Hiding in the bathroom from women wasn't helping.

"They were cool with it," Robbie said, answering the question Bryce had almost forgotten he'd asked. "My mother loves Drew. I think she's more upset than I am that we might break up. But they still, you know, worry about me being in sports and all. If I'm out will it hurt my career, etcetera."

"I can understand that," Bryce said, trying to imagine it. Bad enough his marriage and divorce had been splashed all over hockey and celebrity magazines. At least he hadn't had people telling him he was going to hell on top of it.

Robbie turned to Nikki, expression serious. "Do you think I'll be okay if I'm out? I mean, the team knows, and the coach. But the fans? Should I get a beard girlfriend? Keep the ladies off my back? Maybe one of the women from the NWHL. Think Drew would appreciate that?" He laughed humorlessly. "Would it be okay?"

"I don't know," Bryce admitted. "I mean, someone's going to come out eventually, right? Given the way the world is going."

Robbie shrugged. "You'd think. God knows I'm not the only one in the league. I'm not even the only one on the team. And Seattle seems like a safe place to be out."

Grasping Robbie with both hands, Nikki turned him towards the door. "Okay, Rookie. Back to the party. And I think it's time you switched to water."

"I'm not gay," Bryce blurted out.

Robbie exchanged glances with Nikki who kept her expression carefully neutral. "Oh, man. I'm sorry. I didn't mean-" He blushed to the roots of his hair.

Nikki put her arm around Bryce's waist. She was tall for a woman, almost five foot ten, but she looked small next to him. "Come on, big guy, let's go meet your adoring fans. The Rookie and I will keep those tiny, scary women away from you."

Bryce rolled his eyes at her. "I think I would know if I were gay."

"You'd think." She kissed him on the cheek. "Let's get out of here."

Bryce checked his hair in the mirror and then adjusted the brace covering his leg from mid-thigh to below the knee. "Come on," he said over his shoulder. "I have cake to eat."

ABOUT THE AUTHOR

After time spent raising children, earning several college degrees, and traveling the world with the U.S. State Department, she is returning to her first love - writing.

A dreamer and an idealist, Amy writes about people finding connection in a world that can seem lonely and magic in a world than can seem all too mundane. She invites readers into her characters' lives and worlds when they are their most vulnerable, their most human, living with the same hopes and fears we all have. Avid traveler who has lived in big cities and small towns in four different continents, Amy has found that time and distance are no barriers to love. She invites her readers to reach out and share how her characters have touched their lives or how the found families they have gathered around them have shaped their worlds.

Born on Long Island, NY, Amy has lived in Los Angeles, London, and Bangkok. She currently lives in a town that looks suspiciously like Red Deer, Colorado.

VISIT MY BLOG
LIKE MY FACEBOOK PAGE
FOLLOW ME ON TWITTER
SEE INTO MY BRAIN AT PINTEREST

GET THE FREE STORY

SIGN UP FOR MY NEWSLETTER
AND GET
A FREE SUBSCRIBERS' ONLY STORY

ALSO BY A.E. WASP

HOT OFF THE ICE

CITY BOY

COUNTRY BOY

VETERANS AFFAIRS

INCOMING

CHRISTMAS OUTING

PAPER HEARTS

PAPER ROSES

BRONZE STAR

SOULBONDED SERIES

(*Paranormal Romance*)

BURIED DESIRE

SHATTERED DESTINY

CRADLE TO GRAVE MYSTERY

SPIRIT OF THE RODEO

Printed in Great Britain
by Amazon